A PORTRAIT I

NICOLE JARVIS

Enter a sumptuous world of art and magic in seventeenth-century Florence as Artemisia Gentileschi fights to make her mark as a painter and exact her revenge.

When Artemisia Gentileschi arrives in Florence seeking a haven for her art, she faces instant opposition from the powerful Accademia, self-proclaimed guardians of the healing and necrotic magics that protect the city from plague and curses. As artists create their masterpieces, they add layer upon layer of magics drawn from their very life essence into the paint or marble, draining their power but producing works that will heal hundreds and inspire generations. The all-male Accademia jealously guards its power over art, and has no place for an ambitious young woman arriving from Rome under a cloud of scandal.

Alone and fighting for every commission, Artemisia begins winning allies among luminaries such as Galileo and Michelangelo the Younger, as well as the wealthy and powerful Cristina de' Medici. But when the shadow of her harrowing rape trial in Rome sways her thoughts to vengeance, and an incendiary preacher turns his ire from Galileo to Florence's art world, Artemisia must choose between revenge and her dream of creating a legacy that will span the generations.

9781803362342 | 2 May 2023 | Paperback & E-book
$16.95 / CA$22.95 / £9.99 | 480pp

PRESS & PUBLICITY

US Press and Publicity: Katharine Carroll
katharine.carroll@titanemail.com

UK Press and Publicity: Lydia Gittins
lydia.gittins@titanemail.com

Also by Nicole Jarvis and available from Titan Books

The Lights of Prague

A PORTRAIT IN SHADOW

NICOLE JARVIS

TITAN BOOKS

A Portrait In Shadow
Print edition ISBN: 9781803362342
E-book edition ISBN: 9781803363356

Published by Titan Books
A division of Titan Publishing Group Ltd
144 Southwark Street, London SE1 0UP
www.titanbooks.com

First edition: May 2023
10 9 8 7 6 5 4 3 2 1

A CIP catalogue record for this title is available from the British Library.

Printed and bound by LSC in the United States.

To all who are driven to create

"Quel, che l'anima e 'l corpo mi travaglia,
è la temenza ch'a morir mi mena,
che 'l foco mio non sia foco di paglia."

"This thought burdens soul and body
And makes me dread my death:
Might my fire be only sparks and straw?"

—GASPARA STAMPA (1523–1554)
Translated by Nicole Jarvis

PART I

JUNE 19, 1614–SEPTEMBER 18, 1615

I

Artemisia Gentileschi held her chalk so tightly it threatened to snap under the pressure.

The husband of her subject hovered over Artemisia's shoulder while she sketched. She could feel his warm breath on the back of her neck when he leaned in to examine her work. A piece of red chalk crumbled beneath her thumb, smearing against the paper below.

The work promised to be one of her best designs yet. The Fenzetti had requested a sketched proposal for a painting of Europa and the bull, and she'd jumped to accept. She was still building her client base in Florence, and it was a subject she wanted to paint. The dark muscles of the bull contrasting with the vicious whites of its lustful eyes. Europa, hunched over its back and clinging for her life, staring down at the ocean washing over her knees. There was a sickly terror in every line, the threat obvious even to those who did not know the terrible end of the myth.

When they had arrived today, they had given the design a cursory glance before Signore Fenzetti requested that Europa's face be altered to represent his wife. Reluctantly, Artemisia had pulled out cheap gray paper and her red chalk to make some sketches. She worked as well as she could with the pompous fool of a husband nattering by her head. Her ear was still learning the Tuscan dialect, making his chatter even more grating.

"We'll also need you to include a certain necklace, a family heirloom. Wife, you know the one."

"The pearls," Signora Fenzetti said, heeding Artemisia's earlier warnings and speaking without moving her mouth.

She sat on the stool against the wall of Artemisia's small studio. Her face was round and pale, with wrinkles creasing the skin by her eyes and mouth. The early summer heat had dampened the small curls around her forehead. The rest of her silver-streaked hair was braided elaborately on top of her head, and her red gown tumbled to the floor like spilled blood. The Europa of the myth was a young woman, but portrait drawing always required the ability to imagine one's subject as they might be in their most gracious daydreams, rather than how they were.

"They'll make all the difference in the final painting. They're expensive, so we didn't want to bring them out until we'd met you."

"Were you worried I was going to rob you?" Artemisia asked, sketching in the aquiline curve of the woman's nose.

"It's these streets. You're not in the best part of town."

That, at least, was accurate. The Fenzetti likely lived in the heart of Florence, along with most of the gentry. Artemisia, for affordability, lived across the river in Oltrarno, on a small side street off the Piazza Santo Spirito. Without central Florence's broad, modern architecture dominating the narrow streets, her area was more crowded and unpredictable. She was not the only artist in the neighborhood, though the most popular painters would have more expensive studios across the city. Still, Artemisia had come to Florence with little, and this space was hers.

Signore Fenzetti had attempted to convince her to come to

them so that he and his wife wouldn't have to cross the bridge to meet her, but Artemisia had refused. She would not let Fenzetti believe he could control her entirely. She was an artist, one of the blessed and powerful—not a servant.

Signore Fenzetti leaned forward to peer at her sketch, and she tilted her shoulder to make it more difficult for him to see. "Is that how you plan to make her face look?" he asked.

"This is a sketch. I'm getting a feeling for your wife's features. I'll block it on the canvas before the first painting session so you can approve the design."

"Yes, but does it need to be so shadowed? You can barely see her."

"You saw how I paint," she reminded him. He had been coy about even requesting the sketch until she had shown him a half-dozen paintings to prove she truly was an artist.

"I don't understand this new style of painting as though everyone is sitting in a dark room," he said. "Where's the light? Where's the clarity? That's what art really is. Like San Raffaello. It's healing magic—it should be pure and light."

"The modern style is more realistic, signore," Artemisia said, with a loose rein on her patience. "I want to show things how they are. When's the last time you were in a room that was perfectly lit?" She gestured to the dramatic lighting of the studio around them. Away from the jagged edge of the sunlight coming through the window, there were corners of dusty darkness. "This is where art is going, and it's my strength. I used to stare at Caravaggio's work every Mass in Santa Mar—"

"Caravaggio?" the man scoffed. "That crazy painter who was killed in a drunken brawl a few years ago?"

Artemisia pursed her lips and took a moment to add a textured swirl to the sketch's hair. "Artists die young," she said, quoting her father. It was a phrase he'd used in all situations; whether he was happy or sad, celebrating or mourning, the refrain remained the same. He'd said it when they learned of Caravaggio's death—her father had once been imprisoned with the man, and had respected his art, if not his personality. Caravaggio was a notorious bastard.

The phrase was not a simple platitude: art was a manifestation of the artist's soul, and to drain one was to drain the other. The magics that flowed through the brush onto the canvas carried a piece of the artist's essence, infusing the art with their very life. The ability to heal had a price, and artists who were not careful found an early grave.

"My friend Belladonna visited Rome a few years ago, and she said his paintings look dirty," Signora Fenzetti commented, but closed her mouth when Artemisia frowned at her.

"Life is dirty. You've seen my art," Artemisia said. "I'll make some small adjustments for your preferences, but my style is my style. You chose me. Let me do what I do best."

Signore Fenzetti huffed but didn't push back.

Artemisia rarely included representations of her clients in her paintings at all. Her art was her passion, her legacy, and following the vain whims of an aristocratic patron was against everything she strained to be. But she needed money to keep painting at all. And keep a roof over her head.

A small voice in her head with the gruff cadence of her father reminded her that if she'd married as he'd wanted, she wouldn't need to worry about supporting her lifestyle on her own. She pushed the thought away, locking it back with all the other itching, nagging regrets from her time before Florence.

Better to be beholden to a patron for one painting than tied to a husband for the rest of her life.

"Should this work be tied to one of you, or open for all? That will impact my approach from the beginning. I imbue my magics from the first brushstroke, and that energy must remain consistent for the months of work."

If the art was meant to heal one person only, she could layer in their hair or blood at any stage of the painting, but the magics she pressed through her brush had to be deliberate from the start. Without the personal targeting, the painting would lose power every time a stranger passed the canvas.

An exchange of material was a contract of trust on both ends. The artist had to trust the client would pay them for their drained life force. The client had to trust that the magics the artist was weaving into the canvas were for good, rather than ill. It was only a matter of intent that separated healing from necrotic magics.

Fenzetti huffed. "We're not paying to heal everyone who walks through our house. It should be tied to only the two of us."

"That's not possible. It can be tied to one person, or none at all. You'll need to pick."

"Fine. Then you'll need my wife's hair. It's, ah, for fertility," Signore Fenzetti said.

And they had chosen the rape of Europa? Fenzetti had likely seen a depiction of the myth in the house of some man he respected and not thought twice about the story. The painting didn't need the symbolism in the design to work, no matter what superstition said. It only took the artist's will—and their life force. Still, there was normally some thought behind it. Perhaps thinking was not Signore Fenzetti's strength.

"The painting will take me a year to complete, at least," she told them. "Art is a long process, both by necessity and design. Fresco artists work far more quickly than those of us who use oils, but longer timeframes collect more magics. I'll target all of the magics toward making her womb catch, if that's your only concern. With luck on your side, she'll be with child soon after I deliver the painting."

"Luck? I'm done relying on just luck. We have been married for more than ten years, and I've yet to get an heir. This painting needs to…fix her."

On the stool, Signora Fenzetti flushed. She kept her eyes on the point across the room Artemisia had told her to stare at, but her hands twisted on her lap.

Artemisia hummed. "You're sure *she's* the one who needs fixed? Art can't change something that isn't broken. Making an heir does take two."

"No seed has taken root, but that doesn't mean the problem is with the tree," Signore Fenzetti snapped.

"Gregorio," Signora Fenzetti exclaimed, mouth dropping open. She lost her pose, turning to look at them. "This conversation is inappropriate. She's a lady."

"I'm no lady," Artemisia demurred.

"She has to understand if she's going to fix you," Signore Fenzetti argued. He gestured at Artemisia without looking at her. "Besides, we know it's not too delicate for *her* ears."

Artemisia's charcoal stilled mid-stroke. "Pardon me?"

Signore Fenzetti turned back to her. His chest was puffed, defending his bruised ego like a bird distracting a predator away from its nest. "You didn't think that we would do our research on you before we hired you? We asked around about you, heard about that disgusting business back in Rome."

It was as though Artemisia's veins filled with river water, thin and cold and rushing. She'd only been in Florence for three months, and her past was already haunting her. Would this shadow follow her everywhere?

"We weren't going to mention it," Signora Fenzetti said, giving up any pretense of modeling for her. She gave her husband a meaningful look, though he didn't seem to notice. Artemisia had the feeling that this man ignored most of what his wife said. "We just wanted to be sure you were really an artist. There are too many cons in this country. The reports said that despite the drama, you were as good as you claimed."

"Of course," Artemisia said faintly. She wasn't sure they would hear her. Her lips were numb. Her whole body was numb.

"Besides, all good artists have a whiff of scandal about them. It's part of the charm." She gave Artemisia a simple, earnest smile.

Charm. As though what had happened to Artemisia was a game she had played for their amusement.

She closed her eyes for a moment, reaching up to tightly grasp the amulet at her throat, and then said, "Get out."

"What? You haven't finished the sketch yet! We've barely been here a half-hour," Signore Fenzetti blustered.

"You can come back when you can keep your opinions to yourselves," she said, putting down the paper and standing up.

"I told you we should have gone with Paolo Lamberti," Signora Fenzetti said.

"A painting from the new woman artist… It would have been interesting," her husband said. He snatched up the original pen-and-ink design and began rolling it up briskly. "Ah well. He can finish this."

"Wait," Artemisia said, holding up a hand. "You can't take that."

"We commissioned it," he said, tucking it tightly under his arm. "These first sketches are a test, which you've clearly failed. The temper on you." He shook his head. "A full painting is an ambitious task. You should be proud we're impressed enough with your design to keep it."

"My design is flawless," Artemisia told him, hands trembling. "Who is this Paolo Lamberti?"

"He's from the Accademia delle Arti della Magica. He'll do the design justice."

"How could he? It's not his art. That's *my* design."

"Which we paid for," he said. He reached into his purse and then held out three giuli, eyebrows raised.

"This was not what we agreed to," Artemisia said, though she did not refuse the money. It was a pittance beside what she would have made for the full painting, but she could not spurn it.

As she took the coins, she dragged the tips of her fingers against the man's hand. Around her neck, her amulet pulsed. Signore Fenzetti winced and stepped backward. She bared her teeth at him in a vicious smile and closed her fist around the payment.

"You'll regret this," she said. "When every man of importance in Florence has an Artemisia Gentileschi painting in his gallery, you'll regret this day."

Signore Fenzetti shook out his hand and ushered his wife toward the door. Artemisia bit her tongue. Her face burned and a sting behind her eyes threatened to rip away the last of her dignity.

"One more thing," Signore Fenzetti said, pausing at the threshold. "You should find a husband sooner rather than later. With a better manager, perhaps issues like this could be avoided."

With that, her temper finally erupted. "Out!" Artemisia shouted.

The Fenzetti left. She slammed the door behind them and pressed her forehead against the wood. Through it, she could hear Signore Fenzetti loudly complaining about the fickle nature of women before their footsteps finally retreated down the stairs. She let out a shaky breath and then swore quietly.

Her hand ached from holding the chalk even for that short time. She flexed it, and then dug her nails into her palm.

Once she put away her supplies, Artemisia locked up her studio and left. If she had to sit still in her quiet studio, her nerves would boil over. Her work could distract her, but painting required energy, focus, and passion in order to transfer its magics, and right now all she could muster was bitterness. There would be no healing from her hands today.

Her design. Her *design*. And those stronzi were handing it to a stranger, just because he had the Accademia backing him.

The Accademia delle Arti della Magica—The Academy of the Art of Magics—was the heart of Florence's artistic community. The Accademia collected the best artists in the city for classes, ceremonies, and legislation. Standing apart from and above the guilds of simple craftsmen, the Accademia studied the most hallowed work: art. Members of the Accademia combined the exploration of magics with the perfection of technical artistic mastery.

Still, what *man* could take her design and do it justice? What man could capture Europa's feelings about being taken into the ocean on the bull's back, her rape or death imminent?

She needed commissions if she was going to be able to afford her rent and food—and her paints and canvas. Some days, she felt the latter were more vital than the former. She was not simply an artist for the money. With her youth and circumstances, there was certainly other, more reliable work to be found.

But she was no one without her art.

Even so, it was often thankless work. When she was not busy
with the few paintings she was being paid for, mostly for foreign
buyers unaware of her recent infamy, she spent her time on her
designs to impress potential new patrons. Her commissions from
abroad were not an infinite resource—she needed local patrons,
people who would see and support her regularly. Even though
she didn't infuse her sketches with magics, they were a drain on
her mind, her eyes, and her hands. She was flinging her energy
into a void that pulled everything away and left her with no trace.
Art did not love her back, and certainly neither did the attached
politics. Her smiles were worth nothing, and one harsh word had
destroyed the chance of a well-paying commission.

Her art was good enough. She was talented. There were
untapped wells inside her waiting for the right commission to
show themselves.

If she could not find more patrons, that would not matter.

Though she had not been in the city long, Artemisia had quickly
learned the shortest path to the river. In Rome, the Tiber had been
her constant companion. In comparison, the Arno was unfamiliar,
at least thirty meters narrower than the slow, vast water she knew
back home. Still, the sound and stink were the same in any city,
and were a comfort when nothing else felt familiar.

Ponte Vecchio, the city's central bridge, was crowded chaos.
The early summer heat had drawn people from their homes
like fish to bait. She crossed it without considering any of the
stalls of food and trinkets, ignoring the calls of vendors and
the arguments of shoppers. Someone collided with her in the
walkway and exclaimed in surprised pain. Artemisia grabbed
her amulet, ducked her head, and pressed forward. Quick, angry

words followed her, but the dialect was too thick and unfamiliar to understand.

Florence had more than double the population of Rome, all centered around the river. The crowds made Artemisia's pulse race, tripping and stumbling inside her ribcage. Too many eyes were on her in the press of people.

Judging. Whispering. Watching for any sign of weakness. Wanting to hurt her, to twist and torment her until she broke under their hands.

She turned right off the bridge, following an arched walkway along the water. She was moving too quickly, bumping into people as she fought free of the crushing crowd. The archway only lasted a few dozen yards before opening into a broad sidewalk along the water. The crowds thinned immediately, and Artemisia slowed.

She slumped against the barrier by the river. The stone was cool and firm. No matter how heavily she leaned on it, it stood steady. She took a deep, deliberate breath. The air, like all city air, was heavy with the scents of humanity, but there was a breeze over the Arno that brought a hint of freshness.

She could not be so sensitive and stubborn unless she wanted to lose all her clients. If she did not choose her compromises, they would choose her. Art would never be solely about her passion. She needed patrons to buy her work. That meant diplomacy. So, the rumors had followed her. She had known they would. She still had to press forward.

Her internal scolding did not work. Panic continued to churn inside her. She could not make her past feel small, no matter how she tried to smother it.

Was there a way to succeed single, alone, and penniless, with her reputation haunting her every step? Her talent was her only advantage, and none would see it if she were turned away at the door. She had no validation in Florence, and the Accademia would not look twice at a female artist.

After all her fighting, she could still lose everything.

The buildings back on the Oltrarno side of the river sat flush against the water, their façades soft shades of yellow, white, pink, and tan. The narrow buildings crowded together and peered over the river's shallow water like tourists over a bin of cheap jewelry.

The river trudged along far below, as though fighting against the silt beneath it to move forward.

After Artemisia returned to her studio, she clenched her teeth and set to work again. Even without commissions, there were things to do. Beyond its ability to heal, painting was a craft—one that needed constant practice to hone, and much work beyond putting a brush to canvas. She pulled out her sketchpad to design potential new painting layouts, trying to push the tension of the morning behind her.

The page was still blank when there was a hard knock on the door.

Her landlord stood outside, his face ruddy beneath an unkempt gray beard. Valerio Gori was an older man, but rather than becoming frail, his bulk had settled over time. It had taken much convincing for him to allow her to have her studio in his building. He was traditional, and the idea of an unmarried female artist living under his roof had made him uncomfortable. After she'd shown him her work and assured him that she would cause no trouble, he had reluctantly relented.

"Your clients left quickly," he commented. He lived in the apartment on the ground floor and kept a griffon's eye on the comings and goings through the front door. For the first week, Artemisia had found it comforting. Now, she felt scrutinized.

"They did," Artemisia said, not moving to let him inside the studio.

"I let you rent this place because you assured me that you had money coming. I'm beginning to doubt that."

"I paid my rent."

"For this month," Gori said. "And you were late."

She had lost her old patrons even before she had left Rome, along with most of the friends and family who could have made new connections. She had been certain her talent would speak for itself, and she would find a new audience more quickly in Florence. She had been wrong. "I'll have the money next month, too."

"It's bad for my business to have an unmarried woman living here. People will talk," he said.

"I'm an artist. My eccentricities are charming."

"Is that what people tell you?" he grumbled. "Stop scaring off your clients. Artistic fits of passion have no place here if you want to keep this roof over your head."

She swallowed a snarl, and its claws and teeth shredded her throat on the way down. "Of course, signore."

He examined her like a farmer considering if a sheep were ready for slaughter.

"I should get back to work," she said.

"You should," he said, as though it were his idea, and clomped back down the stairs. Her hands shook as she closed the door behind him.

That night, she paced her studio, running her hands through her curls and tugging at the ends.

Gori was searching for an excuse to evict her and fill the studio with a married couple with a steady income. He had no sympathy for her plight.

What would she do if she failed to support herself in Florence? She would not return to Rome, and she did not want to marry. But was death preferable to those options? If she were forced out of this studio, already small and barely affordable, she would end up on the streets.

She had survived terrible things in Rome, things she had thought would be unbearable, but homelessness in a foreign city could finally end her.

Nothing she did was enough.

If she did not act quickly, the world would not remember Artemisia Gentileschi. Her career was slipping from her reach.

She refused to die without leaving a legacy. The patrons of the world could ignore her all they wished, her fellow artists could condemn her—but her art had a power of its own. Power most artists were too afraid to use.

There was a piece she had tried before but had been too raw to complete. Magics took passion, but also restraint. One had to hold onto an emotion for years to fully weave it into art. A flood did not water a season's crop; it drowned it. Too much or not enough could ruin the magics. Perhaps now she had the distance needed. This would be a true test of her power.

She had tools with which to fight, even abandoned on her own. She could get her vengeance and make the world remember her with one painting.

Artemisia had nothing left to fear.

The night outside her studio window was quiet except for the early summer winds dancing over the city. The bells had stopped tolling, allowing the citizens to sleep during the darkest hours.

There were three mirrors in her studio and drapes she could pull over her windows when she needed to see beneath her clothing. She set one mirror against an easel so she could look into it to begin her sketch. She had to find the perfect design for this piece. Nothing less than transcendence would give her the power she would need. She needed to take the time to get it perfect now—she would start infusing the magics when she put oil to canvas, so could not afford to change her plan then.

She watched her face contort, and then freeze in place. Her charcoal moved quickly, trying to capture the emotion before it faded to rigor.

Effort. Determination. Disgust. Mercilessness.

With the candle flickering beside her, her face seemed demonic in the reflection. The shadows were dynamic, like one of her own paintings brought to life.

Her charcoal cracked as she colored in half her face in solid black.

2

When she opened her door to find a messenger boy waiting outside, Artemisia sighed. Once, she had looked forward to the appearance of letters. Most of her commissions had been established by mail. Since her move to Florence, though, it had been a humiliating experience of handing over her dwindling money for a flowery rejection from uninterested patrons.

She gave the boy a coin and closed the door behind him. She leaned against the wooden frame, rubbing her eyes with charcoal-stained hands. After the Fenzetti had left her without a commission in her queue, Artemisia had fallen deeply into the sketch of her new idea, working late into the night. It had created a fire in her belly that burned bright when the world was dark and still, but just the drafting, wrought with emotion even without the need to weave magics into the sketch, was exhausting. When she put brush to canvas, the energy would be harder to find. If she went through with it, this piece would drain her more than anything she had ever done. And yet, as she sketched, she felt a closed door finally start to open before her. It was still only a thought for now, an option, but it gave her a sense of purpose she had lacked for months.

Still, her hands were clumsy with exhaustion as she flipped over the letter.

The scarlet wax seal displayed a crest with a crowned shield, featuring six balls in flight. It was a familiar symbol, one found both in Florence and Rome on the cities' most important buildings.

Carefully, not breathing, she broke the wax and unfurled the letter. She clumsily mouthed along with the Tuscan dialect once, and then twice. By the time she understood the message, she could barely believe what it said.

Perhaps she had a chance in Florence after all.

Though Artemisia lived across the river from most of Florence's landmark buildings, such as the famous Duomo, she was only a three-minute walk from the sprawling Palazzo Pitti. The vast palace stood like a barricade to the west, so solid and imposing it might have been another city wall. Unlike its predecessor, the towering Palazzo Vecchio on the other side of the river, the Palazzo Pitti was a heavy, low building with a uniform, rustic stone façade. It seemed to stretch endlessly in either direction.

Artemisia stopped in front of the heavy man standing guard at the entrance, bathed in the golden light of dusk. He wore the Medici livery poorly. He was too large, too strong, to carry the embroidered velvet with any grace. A bear in a jester's costume. She stayed a few steps back. She'd spent too much time with hulking brutes who used their authority to manhandle people to put herself in easy arm's reach.

He looked her over. She expected him to turn up his nose at her dress. Though it was the best one she owned, it was only a sturdy, practical wool instead of the velvets and silks that this building's usual visitors likely wore, and would betray her as out of place. However, he simply said, "Invitation?"

She held out the scroll, which he studied carefully. Artemisia wondered if her thumb rubbing over the signatures at the bottom so often since its arrival had faded them. In the last week, she had checked the date and time on the letter often, fearful she might have misread it and lost her chance. After the guard checked the seal, he stepped aside to let her through the door.

As soon as Artemisia stepped inside, the Palazzo Pitti transformed from an impenetrable wall into a breathtaking masterpiece. The ceilings arched high overhead, ending in ornate, pastel frescoes framed by intricate gilding. Everything was decorated with gold and rich, dark wood. Even the simplest walls were accented with filigree and carvings in relief near the ceiling. The Medici's six-ball crest hung on the wall to the left of the entrance.

The Medici family had purchased the palace from its original owner—the eponymous Pitti—and transformed it into their own, filling its empty halls with the most powerful art in Florence. As the most influential family in the region for the last several generations, they had the money to make their home rival even the biggest churches. Over the years, the Medici's economic grip on Florence had grown into a political one, and their influence had spread like roots throughout Europe, including putting one descendant in the Vatican as Pope and another in France as Queen.

Artemisia had been searching for a client powerful enough to launch her career in Florence, and was now in the home of the most powerful family in Europe.

Another liveried servant cleared his throat, pulling her attention from a closer examination of the walls. He bowed and gestured for her to follow him. They skirted a massive inner gallery hall filled with marble statues, both free-standing and tucked into alcoves. Though the influence of artwork not tied to a specific client would spill out to reach everyone in the area, there were patches of rubbed white on their bases where passersby had attempted to draw upon the energy inside directly. Either the statues were long-since run dry, or the Medici were unusually generous.

The next hall was filled with paintings, and her eyes caught on a piece featured in the center of the room on a pedestal. A soft hand had painted a delicate Virgin and Child. Though framed with black shadows, this was no Caravaggio. It was gentle and clean, with skin so supple that she thought it might have been by Titian if not for Mary's slenderness.

"That is gorgeous," Artemisia blurted. She paused on the threshold of the hall, though her approach was blocked by a velvet rope. This answered the question of the statues—she was sure there was not a drop of magic to be found in that gallery. Here, there were likely still paintings with magics inside. They were displayed just out of reach of their guests, reminding them of the Medici's power without sacrificing the well of magic. "Who is the painter?"

The servant glanced back at the piece which had caught her attention. "San Raffaello," he said, and the breath caught in her throat at the mention of the saint. "This way, signorina."

He led her up a grand stairwell and down a hallway. From a window, she could see a vast garden behind the palace, lit in rich golds by the setting sun. It was so manicured that she might have thought the window a painting if the lush smell had not drifted in.

Voices came from the door at the end of the hall, quiet murmuring punctured by laughter. The servant opened the door for her, and then left her to fend for herself. Unsurprisingly, this room was as decadent as the rest. Tall bookshelves lining the walls, each stacked with ornately bound texts all the way to the ceiling, which boasted an intricate fresco of the Roman gods at ease.

The other guests were packed around the room in small clusters, talking to each other over glasses of wine. It was a more diverse crowd than she had expected—there were as many practical trousers as there were velvet doublets.

Artemisia scanned the dense crowd, looking for an entrance. Her father's approach to making contacts had been to get uproariously drunk and make friends with every person in the room. Though he had a vile temper, he was never without a crowd of companions, all of whom saw Orazio Gentileschi as a bosom buddy. Many Romans had used the Gentileschi's small flat as a meeting space, flitting in and out as if they'd paid rent. Some had been friendly, others had pursued Artemisia with unwelcome drunken advances, and all were fickle—few had stood by the Gentileschi family during the trial.

In a room like this, Orazio would have either found the man who looked like the most fun—or the wealthiest. Growing up, Artemisia had always been comfortable in crowds... until the day they had turned against her. Now, she felt as surrounded and overwhelmed as she did on the local market's busiest days. There were so many people here, so many strangers. She didn't recognize anyone, but that didn't mean no one would recognize her. As the Fenzetti had demonstrated, the gossip from Rome was seeping through the city walls.

"Artemisia!"

She jumped, but her shoulders slumped with relief when she recognized the older man approaching her. "Signore da Empoli," she said. "It's good to see you."

"Call me Jacopo, Artemisia. You're no longer a little girl. You've truly grown!" he said, kissing her on both cheeks. Once the pleasantry was finished, Artemisia stepped back so she had room to breathe. She'd left her amulet at home so she would not risk revealing it to the Medici, but she felt exposed without it. "I'm glad you could make it. I've been keeping an eye on the door all night!"

"I presume you are the one to thank for this gracious invitation," Artemisia said. She had sent Jacopo a letter when she arrived in Florence to request introductions to any patrons he thought would appreciate her work—especially someone from the Medici family. He, like all the other old family friends she had tried, had never responded, and she had assumed he had used the letter for scrap paper.

"I told the Grand Duchess they would regret not inviting you!" he said. "Your work rivaled your father's even years ago, and you've only grown. If they claim to be patrons of the arts, they can't allow Artemisia Gentileschi to roam their city without having her to one of their dinners! I told them all about you, and Madama Cristina had an invitation drafted immediately." Catching her expression, his smile faltered. "Not *all* about you, of course. I imagine you're looking for less talk of all that here."

"Indeed," Artemisia said faintly.

"I thought Aurelio might have put in a word for you, too. He comes through Florence often enough."

Aurelio Lomi was her father's half-brother, a fellow artist. He was successful in his own right and had supported both Artemisia and her father in their careers. He had always had an easier smile than her father. Even when he had clashed with Orazio's strong personality, he had been kind to Artemisia. When Artemisia had refused to marry before arriving in Florence, her connection to her uncle had dried like a well in summer. All letters requesting aid or advice had gone unanswered.

"I haven't seen him," she said. "How often do you dine with the Medici? Are there always so many people?"

"Usually more! You know the Florentines—plenty will slip in halfway through the meal, kissing cheeks and pretending not to know the time."

"Who are they? Are they all other artists?" She'd known the scene in Florence was competitive, but nothing like this. Was everyone here tonight vying to have the Grand Duke as their patron? It was little wonder so few patrons had answered her letters.

"Heavens, no," Jacopo laughed. "We'd be in real trouble then. No, the Medici have diverse interests. There are some other artists here too, of course. A few other painters, some sculptors. Most of the Accademia has some tie with the Medici." Jacopo was a member of the Accademia, just like the man the Fenzetti had given her design to. The organization was key to most artists' success in Florence. "The duchess Madama Cristina is currently favoring a weaver from the north who is said to be able to create tapestries so perfect they could be mistaken for paintings. Said, I suppose, by people with poor taste in paintings." Though the duchess's son, the Grand Duke of Tuscany, ruled the region, the older woman was renowned as both politician and patron.

Artemisia had met a handful of weavers in Rome, but they were rarer than painters. Their medium took more space, and though large teams worked on mundane tapestries, magical weavers were forced to work alone. Magics gained power from consistency and dedication, pooling in a piece of art over the months or years it took to complete. It was a delicate balance to maintain steady energy and passion for so long and would have been impossible with a partner.

"The rest are from a range of fields. Politicians, to be sure.

Leaders from the local guilds who are either looking for Medici favor or have control over something the Medici want. They invite philosophers regularly. I think the duchess likes to hear them argue, to be honest. And don't forget the other patrons in Florence. Wealthy people attract each other like drunks. They're always interested in someone who can get them more of what they already have."

Artemisia rolled her eyes. "Fun company."

"Don't be so cynical," Jacopo said, smiling. "Patrons are what make an artist's world turn, when the Church is being stingy. Your father told me that you're doing well. What pieces have you been working on?"

She was not surprised to hear her father had exaggerated her successes to his old friend. Artemisia's fall from grace was shameful enough without admitting he had written off responsibility for her when she had refused to marry or join a convent.

"Is this her?" The woman who interrupted them was dressed in full mourning, wearing a black gown and a widow's cap over her hair. In contrast to the severe cloth, her face was unexpectedly plain. Her chin was small, and her eyes were the warm brown of the earth by the Arno.

"It is," Jacopo said. "Artemisia Gentileschi, meet the Grand Duchess Cristina de' Medici."

Artemisia's breath caught. "Your Grace," she said, and curtsied a beat too late.

"You may call me Madama Cristina. You're our guest here. I'm so pleased you could come," the duchess said. "As soon as Signore da Empoli told me a story about the young painter in Rome who could paint so beautifully that her father's own friends couldn't determine which pieces had been done by her and which by him, I knew I had to meet you."

"You flatter me," Artemisia said. A flush warmed her cheeks.

"You're younger than I expected, and so beautiful. How old are you?"

"Twenty-one, signora."

"So much time ahead of you, and already the stories of your talent are spreading! I'm pleased you've come to Florence. All the best artists do." Artemisia smiled, though that was no longer as true as it had been during the era of San Sandro. Art had moved to Rome, closer to the heart of the Church, and Florence was on the decline. "Your father, he must have been disappointed not to have sons. It worked in your favor."

"I do have brothers," Artemisia said. "None of them showed any artistic talent."

"My goodness," Madama Cristina said. "He chose you over them? Your art must truly be special. You must show me your work sometime."

Artemisia smiled at her, finally recovering her wits. "I would love to. It would be an honor to create a painting for the house of Medici."

"We shall have to arrange it. But why don't you have any wine yet?" She lifted a hand, and a liveried servant bearing a heavy silver tray appeared. She took a crystal goblet and handed it to Artemisia. "We take care of our guests."

"Thank you, signore," Artemisia said, accepting the wine. It was rich and sweet, framed by notes of cherry and oak.

An attendant rang a bell by the door. "Thank you, everyone, for joining the esteemed Grand Duke and his family tonight," he called. "Dinner will be served shortly. Let us proceed to the dining room."

As one, the mob ebbed into the adjoining room.

"Perfect timing," Madama Cristina said, giving Artemisia a

quick smile. "I heard some academics complaining of their empty stomachs when they thought I could not hear. I was worried they might start upon the wall furnishings."

Each setting at the long wooden table was marked with a small slip of paper bearing the name of a guest. Jacopo helped Artemisia find her place but was swept further along the table before he found his own. He was near the far end, by the Grand Duke's family. Artemisia sighed and took her seat alone.

Though there was no food set out yet, the table was nearly its own form of art. Large floral arrangements accented with fresh fruit or pheasant feathers decorated the surface every few feet. The silverware was polished to a shine and was heavy in Artemisia's hand. She examined a fork closely. There was an intricate engraving on the handle of a griffon in flight.

"Is there something so interesting on the cutlery," asked an amused voice beside her, "or are you simply imagining the food that will adorn it?"

Artemisia turned to the man who had taken the seat beside her. He was close to her age, youthful and vibrant compared to the table's elder guests. His dark hair was pushed away from a sharp and angular face. The embroidered cloth of his tunic could have come from one of the Medici's elaborate wall tapestries.

"Are you so blind to the beauty around you that you didn't even notice when it's in front of you?" she challenged.

"I've been here before," he said with a shrug. His accent was smooth and cultured, slipping through the syllables like water down a stream. He gave her a considering glance, and then added, "And I've seen silverware before, as well."

Before Artemisia could retort that she'd *seen* silverware before, the servants arrived with the first course. The broad dishes they set in the center of the table were covered with an assortment of fresh crostini, spiraling by color across the platter: black olives mixed with bright green herbs; lush pieces of fresh fig piled on pale goat cheese; green capers and a dark smear of liver. Another set of servants came by to refill everyone's wine, leaving pitchers on the table for easy access. The delicate glasses were wide and nearly as flat as the plates, making them difficult to drink from.

Artemisia plucked two of each crostino off the platter and moved them to her plate. She had only had some bread as her lunch, and the wine threatened to untether her head. Her mouth watered at the promise of a rich meal—she had lived so long on crumbs that she forgot how it felt to be satisfied.

"All that fuss about the forks and you can't even use them for the first course," the man beside her said. His voice was solemn, but his eyes were bright.

He was right—everyone else at the table was crunching into the crostini using their fingers. "I'm sure I'll get the chance," she said, and took a bite of the liver crostino in as defiant a manner as she could. The salty musk of the liver tasted how velvet felt, and the burst of a caper between her teeth gave the mouthful a sharp echo. The complexity cut through the heaviness of the red wine, and she took another bite quickly.

"I don't believe I've seen you here before," the man continued.

"My obsession with the silverware didn't give me away?"

"That was my attempt at asking for an introduction," he said. "I'm Francesco Maria Maringhi."

"Artemisia Gentileschi."

He glanced down at her unadorned hands. "Is your father an associate of the Medici?"

"No," she said. "He lives in Rome. I'm here at the Grand Duchess's invitation. I'm a painter."

Unfazed by her coolness, Maringhi's expression brightened. It wasn't until she had his full interest that she realized how idly he had been speaking. It was like being engrossed in a puppet show, only for the puppeteer to step from behind the curtain. "That's unexpected," he said. "I don't believe I've ever heard of a female painter."

"You have now." She turned back to her plate, and he stopped attempting to draw her into conversation. Instead, he turned to the old man on his other side and began talking briskly about a shipment of stone from Pisa that had gotten stuck in a riverbank thanks to the low water levels in the Arno.

Artemisia glanced to her left, but the woman next to her was fully engaged with the man beside her. From the way she touched his arm, she was likely a wife or a mistress.

Artemisia ate another crostino. The figs were sweet and fresh, but the taste was dampened by her unease, like a cloud covering the sun.

Another course of antipasti arrived—fresh oysters in their half-shells were scattered with lemon slices on new platters. Artemisia took one, almost reverent. They were far from the sea in Florence, and transporting so many oysters for a dinner party must have been expensive. On the coasts, oysters were as common as bread, but they were a luxury here—Artemisia hadn't had one since she'd arrived in Florence.

Inflamed voices drew her attention before she could eat. In her youth, raised voices had been natural. Her father's friends were passionate, aggressive men, and had enjoyed arguing more than agreeing. Now, her spine tensed.

Across the table, a middle-aged man was drawing attention. His clothes were as luxurious as those around him, yet his graying beard was untamed, as though he hadn't given it a second thought before coming to dinner at the Palazzo Pitti. He was in a heated discussion with the men seated beside him while those around them watched with interest.

"Yes, we know how you feel. Your letter has been making the rounds," commented the man on his right.

"There's no need to read my private letters when I've published several books on the topic. I've made no secret of my astronomical inquiries. I am, in fact, the court mathematician. It is my job to try to understand the universe, and my duty to share those findings with the world."

"You truly believe that you and your telescopes can tell us more about the world than we can learn from the Bible?" demanded the man on his left. He had a florid face and thin, white hair.

The man in the center shrugged. "I've heard it said: the Bible is a book about how one goes to Heaven—not how Heaven goes. You must admit that as a teaching tool, the Bible is ineffective. God gave us our intellect in order for us to *use* it, to understand this universe he created. If the Bible was trying to teach people astronomy, you would think it wouldn't have skipped over the subject so completely."

"Perhaps the problem is with your *interpretation*," the other man said. The crowd rippled with hissed whispers. It was a damning comment. Since the Reformation troubles in the north, the Church had become even more determined for Catholics to leave the understanding of the Bible to the Vatican.

"Or perhaps it lies with yours. You!" The man pointed at Artemisia, obviously noticing her interest. "You're a simple girl, yes?"

Artemisia felt her face flush with the awareness of many eyes on her now. Her hands shook in her lap. She took a steeling breath and raised her eyebrows. "That's not how I would describe myself." Her Roman accent seemed harsh to her own ears, her consonants loud and blunt.

He waved away her defense. "I meant that you're not a scholar of astronomy or mathematics. Is that fair to say?"

"Yes," she admitted.

"If you saw evidence with your own eyes of something where someone had once told you there would be nothing, would you believe that you too had seen nothing?"

"No, not if I had seen something," Artemisia said.

"Even if the someone who had told you that there would be nothing was very respected? Perhaps even someone you personally idolized?"

"No," Artemisia said, voice growing cold. "I trust my own eyes, and my own experience. I don't allow others to shape what I believe."

The florid man interrupted. "This is distracting from the point. You're trying to contradict the Scripture."

"If your faith in the Scripture can be shaken by learning more about our universe, then your faith is weak indeed," the man said. "I'm uncovering secrets God left for us. There's nothing for me to discover that He did not create. Wouldn't you agree?"

The man floundered. "Well... Of course, I..."

There were chuckles from those around the table who were sympathetic to this scholar, and scowls from those on the opposing side.

"We're all simply attempting to appreciate God's work," the man continued. "It's unfortunate for you that you do not have the capacity to grasp its grandeur."

An impromptu round of applause came from the scholar's supporters, drawing the attention of the rest of the table. From their expressions, arguments were a common occurrence at Medici dinners. The loser of the debate, now so flushed he was nearly purple, spluttered for a moment before letting himself be pulled into another conversation with his seatmate.

Seeing the debate was over, those around them went back to their own conversations. The scholar leaned forward to speak to Artemisia more quietly, eyes still bright with triumph. "I hope you were not alarmed by my including you in our discussion," he said. "Sometimes it helps to have a voice of innocence, rather than indulging the biases of both sides."

She waved a hand. Now that everyone's attention was gone, she felt lighter. "I was raised with artists. I like my conversation with a bit of antiestablishment sentiment. Propriety is for people with nothing of importance to talk about."

"Artists, hm?" he asked. "I see you followed in their footsteps."

She raised her eyebrows, and he nodded to her hands. She realized now that there was still a streak of yellow paint on the underside of her right hand, where she had rested it against her palette in thought. She covered it with her left.

Beside her, Maringhi huffed quietly, a small, amused sound that told her he'd been following the conversation closely.

She didn't give him the benefit of her glance. Instead, she focused on the older man across the table. "I did."

"I like artists," he said. "They're innovators. They try to find the truth in the world and reflect it on canvas. Anatomy, geography—did you know that San Sandro's *Primavera* shows five hundred species of plants? But it doesn't look like a botanical study. It's beautiful."

"You've seen it?" Artemisia asked. San Sandro Botticelli had at least one painting in Rome, but it was woven with such powerful magics it was still reserved for the Pope and his cardinals a century after the artist's death. The Vatican was a treasure chest of the world's most powerful art, holy work for holy men, and it kept the religious leaders alive far longer than the average man. *Primavera* was one of San Sandro's works commissioned by the Medici, hidden away from the public eye.

He nodded. "It's here in the palace." He glanced down the table, as though making sure the Grand Duke was out of earshot. "It was a fertility commission, you know. All the magic is gone now, so they see no harm in showing it off to certain visitors. They like to brag that it was the magics that made a certain son born the year after its completion reach the success he found." He raised his eyebrows and put a finger to the side of his nose. "Pope Leo the Fourth."

"If a painting could make someone the pope, artists would be living in palaces," Maringhi commented, lazily plucking another oyster from the platter in front of them.

"I doubt it. Holding the power to extend someone's life hasn't even achieved that," Artemisia pointed out. "But it doesn't matter. Even San Raffaelo could not have painted a child into the papacy. Our magics can bring health, not success. There's only so much that we can control."

"But it's a good story, isn't it? San Sandro certainly never bothered to deny it," the scholar said.

"He should have. He was a saint. He was good enough not to need the lies. He should have been honest. I had a client last week half-convinced I was trying to scam him," Artemisia said. "There's so much false information out there, clients either expect more than we can promise, or assume it's all a swindle."

"From what I've seen, most artists like a bit of mystery to their craft," the scholar pointed out.

"Liars like to have something to mask their actions," Artemisia said. "I don't think the truth should be hidden in the shadows for anyone's benefit."

"Well said. I never had the chance to introduce myself," he said. "I'm Galileo Galilei."

"Artemisia Gentileschi." She hesitated, the lilting rhythm of his name stirring something in her memory. "I've heard of you. My father didn't pay attention to news outside our circle, but some of his friends did. I'm sorry—I don't remember any details."

"I prefer it that way. Rumors have not always been kind to me."

"I understand that. We shall have to decide our own impressions, then."

The next course arrived. Steaming bowls of pappardelle topped with meat sauce replaced the trays of oysters. Before she could reach forward, Maringhi set a portion on her plate before serving himself. When she looked over at him, surprised, he just inclined his head before returning to his conversation.

Artemisia took a bite and nearly moaned. The meat was hare, dark and strong, and had been roasted with herbs into a tender sauce. She wished she had been given an idea of how many courses the Medici would be serving—she could have happily filled her stomach with the pappardelle.

In the end, they served three more courses: a refreshing salad with croutons and peaches, a full roast peacock with its plume intact, and, for dessert, trays of morzelletti. The small cookies were topped with marzipan, an expensive almond paste. The wine continued to pour freely, and Artemisia's head grew light and her limbs heavy.

She was here. *Florence.* In the Medici's fortress, surrounded by the city's elite. If someone had told her two years ago that she would find her way out of Rome, defy her father's instructions to marry, and still end up *here*, she would have lambasted them for tormenting her with dreams that would never be.

She was torn between triumph and brooding when someone coughed beside her. The rest of the table was starting to peel away, leaving to continue drinking in another room or heading out for the night, but Maringhi was still seated beside her.

"I'm sorry," he said quietly. "I feel as though I unintentionally offended you several times tonight. That wasn't my goal."

"You opened by mocking me about the silverware," Artemisia reminded him.

"Well," he said with a crooked grin, "some of it *was* intentional teasing. You seemed so solemn."

Artemisia blinked. It had been a long time since she had been invited into a joke, rather than suffering as the target.

When she couldn't summon an answer, he simply nodded. "As I said, my apologies. I hope you have a pleasant night." He finished the last of his wine and left the table.

Artemisia looked after him. Though he'd had as much wine as anyone else, he walked with smooth confidence. She shook her head and drained her own drink.

Jacopo found Artemisia before she could leave and insisted on introducing her to a variety of local patrons and other artists. Their names and faces—all male, all older than her—became a blur within minutes. She leaned on Jacopo's arm to keep her balance.

Artemisia caught Madama Cristina's eye across the room. She was standing with her son, who was recognizable even at a distance. To her surprise, the Grand Duke Cosimo II was close to her age. She had heard that he had taken over his father's role at only nineteen, but he had always seemed larger than life. Following his mother's example, he was a great patron of the arts, and everyone in Rome spoke of him and his influence in hushed tones.

At a whispered word from his mother, he looked at Artemisia and raised his glass.

By the time Artemisia stumbled up the stairs back to her small studio after the dinner at the Medici palace, it was well after midnight. It was fortunate that she lived so close to the Palazzo Pitti—she did not have the spare funds for a coach, and only a fool would trek across the city alone so late. The opulence of the palace had been like the sun, beautiful but blinding. In her drab flat, Artemisia blinked to clear the stain of gilding from her eyes.

With the exhilaration and wine leaving her giddy, she expected to have trouble falling asleep in the small cot at the back corner of her studio. Her sheets were cheap and scratchy, and all she wanted was to crow her success to the roof. This was the beginning. Florence. The Medici. One of the richest patrons in the city already wanted to see her work. Her dreams were spread before her. She needed to decide her next steps as soon as the giddiness loosened its hold on her. She felt as drunk on the unexpected cessation of her melancholy as she was on the wine.

Her thoughts, however, slipped through her mind like salt through a sieve, tumbling faster and faster around her until they were a heady blur.

She drifted into sleep, light and triumphant.

Fear built, sickly slow.
Her heart was a caged rabbit in her chest.
Her limbs were weak. Helpless.

Her lungs absorbed her shallow gasps as though they would never be full, but her screams were unanswered. There would be no aid.

Then.

Eyes. Everywhere. Grasping eyes. Unpitying eyes. Judgement and intrigue and disgust.

There was nowhere to hide. Nowhere to run.

Artemisia woke with a gasp, kicking aside the tangled sheets of her cot until she was free. She scrambled to her feet and pushed the stifling curtain aside. Her studio was dark and silent. The cold floor nipped cruelly at her bare feet.

She was panting, her breath trapped deep in her lungs.

When she went to the window, the street below was just as still and quiet. The moon was a faint sliver in the air, and the stars were bright and cold.

Since the attack in Rome, her emotions had been so large and unwieldy. Her joy came in bright, blinding flashes that only made the darkness feel more complete when it returned. How could she cling to those heady moments of hope when this was what waited under the surface?

This was why she had started to stray from the healing magics. One dinner at the Palazzo Pitti did not mean she was free. Until she cleansed it, the past would haunt her.

Hands shaking, she lit a candle. The flame wavered in her grip. Wrapping a robe around her gown, she sat in the stool in the center of her studio with her sketchpad.

There was work to do.

3

S ummer melted heavy over the city. Artemisia was accustomed to long summers—the streets baked the residents of Rome, just out of reach of an ocean breeze—but the heat never grew less claustrophobic.

She spent the next two weeks in her studio, working with a quill instead of a paintbrush, though her skills were weak with the former. She drafted a dozen letters to the potential patrons she had met at the Medici party. She had a long list of politicians, businessmen, and clergymen who now knew her face, and would hopefully be convinced to hire her. She even sent a note to the intriguing mathematician, Galileo. Though he was unlikely to commission an artist, she was desperate for any kind face. Her writing was stilted and uncultured, especially in the Tuscan dialect, and she feared they would all toss her letters aside.

After many long days and longer nights, she got a response—another letter with the familiar Medici seal. Even after a night at their palace, their seal made her heart leap. It seemed Madama Cristina's request to see Artemisia's work had not been polite conversation after all.

A day later, Artemisia was back at the Palazzo Pitti. The grand palace was even more impressive in the sunlight. The night's shadows hid its true size; it was like seeing a mountain during a clouded day, only to see it again later and realize that you had been at the foot of majesty.

The servant who greeted her led her to a library on the third floor, tucked away from the rest of the house. While the grand staircases and sculpture garden were designed to intimidate and impress, the top floor was more quietly luxurious. It was astounding for Artemisia to remember that a family lived here, sleeping in these rooms and dining in these halls. Despite the servants, despite the gilded edges, the Medici were as human as she was.

The library, though seemingly simpler, was rich with craftsmanship. On closer inspection, the cabinets were decorated with intricate inlaid wood. Set in place like a puzzle, wooden pieces in different shades combined to form beautiful Tuscan landscapes and lush still-life images. Between two bookshelves, a panel with an ornate inlay lute caught her eye—it looked as though one could brush the narrow, pale strings and hear a thrum of music, though it was flush against the wall.

The Grand Duchess was seated behind a desk, still wearing the same mourning black as she had at the dinner party. It had been two years since the previous Grand Duke had passed away, but Madama Cristina would wear black until she followed him. Customs were stricter for the members of the duchy than others, and the Grand Duchess had no need to remarry.

Artemisia curtsied when the servant announced her formally.

"This library is beautiful," Artemisia said.

"Is it not? I use it as my study. The light here is the best in the house, and with my eyes candlelight simply will no longer suffice. I apologize for not meeting you somewhere more formal. I had work to finish and thought this would give us a chance to speak." There were papers scattered over the desk, and the quill at her side had been freshly dipped. Artemisia hadn't expected to find the Grand Duchess genuinely busy. From what she knew, most nobles worked only as idle distraction.

"I am not the Grand Duchess only by title, you know," Madama Cristina said, catching her gaze. "I would not permit my son to humor me. My husband's death did not take away my authority any more than Cosimo's marriage did. As long as I am the Grand Duchess, I shall continue to assist in managing the Medici estate. Which brings me to why I've asked you here today. I searched for more information about you after you left the dinner." Artemisia's back stiffened. "Of course I did my research. My son is a dilettante, but I am the main collector in the Medici household still, and I have a reputation to maintain. That's why I took time before contacting you again. It takes time for letters to come from Rome. I have many friends there. I found that the name 'Artemisia Gentileschi' causes ripples wherever it lands."

Her words felt as though they came down a long tunnel. They echoed and bounced, distant and close at once. "Is that so?" Her hands clenched into her skirts, though it made them cramp painfully. She had known she could not trust this. Success would not fall into her open palms.

"My question is this—do you anticipate those ripples to grow in Florence?"

"No," Artemisia insisted. "I only want to make my art."

"But there *was* a scandal in Rome."

"Yes."

"Is it also true that you refused to be married?"

The interrogation terrified her, but it was not yet a rejection. "It is, but I'm no normal young woman," Artemisia said, the words tripping from her mouth. "I'm a painter. I've learned how to protect myself. I don't need a husband. I can take care of myself, Madama Cristina."

"I'm certain you can," the older woman said, shrugging. "Having a husband smooths many ruffled feathers. Even if men see that you are uncowed in their company, they can at least comfort themselves by assuming you are subservient in your home life. Widows are some of the most powerful people in these lands, and it's not because they once had a husband. Unfortunately, it is still only widows who are able to make their own paths. Though I'm sure you could manage yourself, my only question is whether your independence here will damage your reputation further."

"What does it matter, Your Grace? I'm not looking to make an advantageous marriage," Artemisia said. "After what happened, it seems unlikely either way. I'm looking to create art. Artists are never known for having sterling reputations. I want all of Florence to know my name as an artist, not as a woman." That approach was a gambit. Madama Cristina was known for being pious, but she had hired men with far worse reputations than Artemisia's most vicious rumors.

Madama Cristina just inclined her head. "You have what I asked for?"

Artemisia pulled the cloth bag from her shoulder and withdrew the contents. One benefit of painting on canvas was its portability. Once removed from its frame, a canvas could be rolled and carried. She avoided traveling with any pieces imbued with magic, or any of her commissions, as it was too easy for even oils to flake or crack. However, she had painted enough practice paintings that she had taken more than an hour that morning to select the one she would show the Grand Duchess.

First, she unrolled a large canvas, standing so that the bottom edge would not brush the floor. She glanced over the top to be sure she had unrolled it right side up. She had debated whether to start the display with something more traditional, but she didn't want to be known as a mimic. She wanted to show the talent that made her stand out as a creator, not only as a curiosity.

The painting was a historical scene. The top half showed sumptuous scarlet drapes, velvet and soft. The bottom half was covered with white sheets, pristine in color but profane in their rumpled state. In the center was the star of the painting—a sprawling, naked Cleopatra. The pale body and luxurious fabric took up the viewer's gaze, luring them in until they noticed the small detail wrapped around her wrist in the foreground; an asp, preparing to strike its fatal bite.

It was a lush, intimate piece. Artemisia's Cleopatra wasn't dainty, like so many others. There were curves, and rolls of fat at the creases of the queen's arms and neck. This was a true woman, inviting and real. She wasn't casually draped in cloth or coyly covering a breast with one hand. An arm stretched behind her head, leaving her body on display.

The choice had been deliberate. Artemisia Gentileschi would not shy away from painting the nude female figure. Painting women would not remain the realm of men. Artemisia knew her own body, and she could paint plump, pale flesh as good as any Titian.

She wished she had chosen a smaller painting. With it held above her head to stay off the ground, the plain back of the canvas blocked her view of the woman's reaction.

Could Madama Cristina see the art, or would she only see a reminder of the body that lay under Artemisia's clothes?

The Grand Duchess was silent for a long while. Artemisia's arms began to burn from holding the pose. Finally, Madama Cristina said, "And the sketches?"

Artemisia rolled the canvas again quickly, and then handed a collection of her best sketches and designs across the desk.

The Grand Duchess examined them carefully, pausing over each page to examine the chalk and ink lines. There were a variety of subjects on display: still life, anatomy sketches, and the staging of full paintings. Finally, when she turned over the last paper, Madama Cristina looked up at Artemisia. "You know that the Medici consider ourselves great patrons of the arts, yes?"

"Yes, Your Grace," Artemisia said, her pulse fluttering in her neck. "Everyone knows of your generosity. The Medici have made Florence what it is today."

The Grand Duchess waved away the flattery. She must have heard it every day since her marriage. "Most collectors cannot take risks on unknown artists. They cannot suffer the lost investment if they are disappointed."

Artemisia winced. It was a story she'd heard many times before.

"However," Madama Cristina continued, "*we* are able to take risks. We do not need to only commission those artists everyone has heard about. We can be the first. And I want to take a chance on the young woman who arrived from Rome with stories of surpassing her father's art by the time she was eighteen."

"Thank you so much," Artemisia said, fighting against a well of relieved tears. Perhaps her battle was not yet lost. "I will make sure it's my best piece yet."

"I'm sure you will."

"Do you want the painting imbued with magics? I'm a strong healer."

"We'll put that to the test. I need powerful healing. I have the most terrible insomnia," Madama Cristina told her. "I lie down and stare at the ceiling until dawn."

"I'm sorry," Artemisia murmured.

It was rare for a client to request a painting for a specific ailment, though it was possible as long as the painting was tied to them specifically. Even the quickest painters needed months to finish their work, and few illnesses reliably lasted so long. No client would be happy to spend hundreds of scudi on a painting that did not do anything. Only chronic complaints—infertility, aging joints—were commonly targeted specifically. Only one of the Medici would spend their money on a painting exclusively for insomnia. With so much other art in their galleries, the family's overall health was secured for decades. Unless there was an accident, like the carriage crash which had killed Madama Cristina's husband, everyone in the Medici household was sure to reach one hundred. Artemisia had met such wealthy men in Rome, hunched and wrinkled with age but hobbling forward on the crutch of their personal art collections.

Madama Cristina brushed away the sympathy with a wave of her hand. "I had the late Grand Duke commission a piece from Signore Caravaggio. It was a beautiful depiction of Bacchus. He was a youthful, indolent boy, sipping wine and eating grapes, just on the edge of an indulgent afternoon nap. The magics imbued in that painting left me sleeping easy for three years. Since then, other artists have tried to give me their magics, but none have worked as well. Would you be willing to try the same?"

"Caravaggio is one of the greatest painters of the last century," Artemisia said humbly, but then smiled. "I would love to show you what I can do."

The sunlight streaming through her studio windows was pale and crisp, bringing a hint of the summer heat to come that afternoon. Everything seemed new early in the morning before the chaotic trade and bustle of the city began in earnest.

In the light of day—with Madama Cristina's advance hidden in her room—the ferocious, hopeless energy that had driven her during the weeks before her meeting seemed reckless. Perhaps her fears were for naught, and she could leave her desperate, half-formed flirtation with other, darker magics behind. She had a plan, and rashness would not help.

Artemisia normally spent her mornings sketching, finding ways to pull the shadows from her nightmares and cleanse them in the daylight. Today, her plans had been rearranged by a request from Galileo Galilei. They had exchanged several enjoyable letters since the party. He was an interesting, eager correspondent and did not seem to mind her inelegance in writing. He had questions about her work as a female artist, and she was fascinated by his experiments.

According to Jacopo, Galileo's theories—which Jacopo had been sure were too complex for Artemisia and had skipped over in his letters—were revolutionary, and potentially heretical. As the Grand Duke's former tutor and current court mathematician, he was undeniably brilliant, but over the last few years, he had been met with heated backlash from the Church.

His interest in the natural world had led to today's request— he wanted to observe her painting process to solve some mystery or another of the universe. Galileo was a respected member of Florentine society, and an interesting potential friend, even if he was not likely to commission anything with his own wallet.

Artemisia pulled the loose rag stopper from her bottle of walnut oil and tipped it to dribble a line across the small piles of pigment she'd ground for the palette. The oil mixed with the bone black powder at the twirl of her brush. Once she had created a black glaze, she pulled a section of the darkened oil over to mix with her vermilion pigment, made from crushed cinnabar gathered on the distant shores of the Red Sea.

Her palette, a flat dark square of wood with a hole through which to hook her thumb, was the most important part of her work. With the long life of oil, the palette became a library for colors once mixed. Though they dried over time, they could be reactivated with another drop of oil. Once Artemisia mixed a color, she could continue to pull and blend and reuse it until the painting was complete.

Blending her colors allowed no room for distraction. By the time the knock came, she had to blink away her focus.

"Thank you for agreeing to see me," Galileo Galilei said, nodding to her in greeting. He wore a practical wool tunic, and his beard was more riotous than ever.

Artemisia welcomed him and stepped aside to let him into her studio. He held aloft a round of cloth-wrapped cheese, and said, "If you have not eaten yet, I wanted to bring something to apologize for setting such an early meeting."

"I always say yes to food." In addition to the advance from Madama Cristina when her sketch had been approved, she had been given a small stipend of five scudi a month, but it wasn't enough to indulge in more than bread and wine. She needed the money to buy supplies good enough to sit in the Medici halls. It was fortunate she was not in the school of art that required gilding the canvas in gold foil, but rich pigments were still expensive.

She showed him to a rickety table pushed against the wall. Her studio was poorly designed for guests. Hosting potential patrons was part of any artist's work, but she needed patrons first to fund a nicer working space. It was a clumsy space, and visitors felt invasive. She kept her cot in a back corner, hidden carefully by drapes during the day.

He looked around, frowning. "You do not have a studio assistant? Or are they out just now?"

"It's only me," Artemisia said, gesturing for him to sit at one of the two stools. Assistants cost money, and she had none to spare.

He stayed standing. "And you don't have a chaperone?"

"I don't," she said, alarm searing through her like wildfire. Had she been a fool to invite him into her studio alone? How well did she know him after only a few letters?

"I do not wish to damage your reputation. You must be careful."

The tension drained, leaving her light with relief. "Galileo," she admonished, "you knew that I was a single woman when you asked to meet me. I assumed you were not tied to propriety."

"I'm worried only about your safety."

"If you're so worried," Artemisia said, and lifted the heavy amulet from where it was tucked under the neckline of her gown. "This is what keeps me safe." She clicked open the locket to reveal the miniature painted inside. The small canvas depicted a still life of a lily, the symbol of the city of Florence. Though Artemisia mostly worked with larger canvases, the small painting was intricately detailed. The stamen at the center of the delicate flower had been brushed into place with a single hair.

"You are very talented," Galileo said, examining the painting.

"It has magics woven into it," Artemisia said. "No one can touch me when I'm wearing it. Not unless they want their skin to feel like it's being flayed. I'm better protected here than most wives are with their husbands. There's no need to fear for my reputation."

A similar piece had been the first painting Artemisia completed in the studio. Until it had been finished, she had kept a chair against the door, and the jagged edge of a wooden frame by her cot.

"How does that magic work?" Galileo asked. "I've never heard of anything like it."

"It drains more quickly than a larger piece—far more quickly. Most patrons prefer to put their money into something that lasts, though I've made miniatures occasionally for those who could afford the regular need for replenishment. I've heard they're something of a fashion in Milan."

"I've seen art as jewelry. But magics can only heal, not protect."

"It's not protecting me, in that sense. As the artist, I'm simply exempt from its effects. Everyone but me is vulnerable to its power if they get too close to it."

"It's necrotic power," Galileo mused.

"It will only hurt those trying to hurt me," Artemisia said coolly.

"Don't let a blood drake sleep on your hearth," Galileo quoted. *Unless you want it to make a home*, the common aphorism finished.

She did not glance at the sketchbook tucked into the corner where she had been planning her new project. In the design stage, there were no dark magics infused yet, but she did not trust the astronomer's sharp eyes. In comparison to what *that* work would do, the amulet was a mosquito bite, a harmless annoyance. The crime of a pickpocket rather than that of a murderer. "I do what I have to do. You were the one so very concerned with my safety. I did not think you, of all people, would be so close-minded. These are only minor magics."

He nodded. "I do not condemn some experimentation, of course. It's impressive. Unusual. That's precisely what I'm curious about—the unexplored. It's what's always called to me. There's a science to magic. I just need to find out what it is." He gestured to the amulet. "Were you taught how to do this?"

Artemisia shook her head. "I wanted to guard myself, and this seemed the most subtle approach," she said. "It was the logical next step of my work."

"You'd be surprised how long those logical next steps often take to occur to someone," Galileo said. "May I...?" He lifted a hand.

Artemisia stilled, her pulse fluttering. But she knew her magic—knew her power—so she nodded. She raised her arm and took a steadying breath.

Galileo reached for her, brow furrowed in concentration as though he were listening to a far-off strand of music. The moment he met the resistance near her skin, he paused, testing the air. Then, he pushed closer slowly. By the time he was just a breath from her sleeve, his hand was shaking.

"You should stop there," Artemisia warned.

He pulled back without hesitation. "Of course. You didn't create the painting planning on wasting its reservoir with testing." Like all paintings, the magics would drain over time as its well of power was tapped, and with its small size, the well was minute. She had needed to make three in Florence already when their magics had faded—a new one sat in progress on an easel nearby.

"It's not that," she said. "I don't want to harm you for the sake of an experiment." She smirked and inclined her head. "Though if you stare at the sun as a hobby, perhaps you're accustomed to that."

"It's more painful than the approach?" he asked, shaking his hand absently. "That's powerful."

"So I understand your concern, but people will learn that I can stand on my own. The risk to my reputation is worth the freedom of having a studio," Artemisia said. She unwrapped the wheel of cheese he'd brought. It was pale and fresh, and her stomach rumbled. She broke off a piece to taste, and the bright tang was enrapturing. She had missed breaking her fast before midday.

"Signorina, these are stunning," Galileo commented. He had gotten distracted by a stack of discarded canvases on the table near her easel, examining them like a cook through a basket of rare truffles. He pulled one free and held it up to the light.

The painting depicted Santa Caterina, staring out at the viewer with a solemn expression. In her hand was a palm frond, the symbol of a martyr. A broken shard of a spiked execution wheel jutted beside her. The saint had confronted Emperor Maxentius for persecuting Christians and had been sentenced to death for her impertinence. The first execution method, a brutal scourging, had left her whole body covered in weeping, bloody wounds, but she had survived. The second method, imprisonment without food, lasted for twelve days before the emperor gave up. The third method, the most brutal yet, was to break her under the execution wheel, but the torture device—now called the Catherine wheel—shattered at her touch. Finally, she was beheaded, and it was milk, rather than blood, that poured from the wounds.

In the painting, she bore Artemisia's face.

"Impressive," he said softly, before finally putting it down and picking up the next one.

"Oh, don't look at that one," Artemisia said, putting down her knife and stepping toward him. "It's only a practice. I'm planning on painting over it."

"Why?" he asked, holding the canvas to the light. It was a painting featuring Judith, standing at the center of the frame with a sword over her plump shoulder. In front of her was her maidservant, Abra, turned away from the viewer. On her hip was a basket containing a graying, decapitated head. Judith was one of the Bible's most famous women. When the Assyrian general Holofernes prepared to destroy her home, the widow used her beauty to convince the lustful man to invite her into his tent. After she induced him to drink so much that he lost consciousness, she carved his head from his body and sent his army fleeing. "It's not bad. The fabric seems as though you could brush your hand against it."

"It's *tepid*," Artemisia said. "And the magics didn't stick." She had been too distraught, too wretched, to hold any emotion for long enough to weave it into a canvas. It was the failed ancestor of the new project she had begun. Fortunately, Galileo seemed unable to detect the type of magics she had tried to create with it. "It's from years ago. It couldn't... It didn't work."

"It's quiet," Galileo agreed. "But not bad."

"Just put it away," Artemisia said. "I'll show you what I can actually do."

He set down the canvas and walked back to her. "Judith never is quite bloody enough, is she?" he mused. "Not that most clients want a blood-drenched maiden, but if we're considering physics, that's how she would look."

"I don't mind blood-drenched maidens," Artemisia said. She offered the knife aloft with a hunk of cheese on the blade. He plucked it with deft fingers and took a bite. "Women are more accustomed to blood than men would think."

"Cutting off a head is nasty business. The blood would spray," he said. "It would arc through the air, not just dribble from the neck as some paint it." He waved a hand. "I'll lecture you about it some other time. We'll eat first."

After they split the cheese and an apple Artemisia had on her windowsill, she sat at her stool to work while Galileo watched from a few paces behind. She took a deep breath. Her ribs pressed against the coarse fabric of her shift. She could feel his eyes heavy on her back. It was the tense, hunted feeling of a rabbit in the field being stalked by a fox without being able to see it.

Artemisia rolled her shoulders back and lifted her chin. She was not prey, and this was no field. This was her domain.

She picked up the palette she had prepared earlier and dipped her brush in the black glaze. When the brush pressed against the canvas, Artemisia gathered the energy inside her chest and focused on the paint. Dark and thick, like a moonless night. Peaceful, like a locked bedchamber.

The first brushstroke mattered as much as the last. Artemisia had to paint with intent in every movement to imbue the canvas with the magics Madama Cristina had requested, no matter how long the process took. Like a weaver, she steadily unspooled a piece of her heart through her brush as she worked. Even as she drained her energy, the craft was soothing and quiet, taking her mind to a place beyond her body. Time slipped away as she blacked in the shadows in the canvas. There was only the paint and the magics.

By the time Artemisia came back to herself, the sun was streaming brightly through the windows, there was a bead of sweat at her hairline, and her hands ached. She wiped her brow and turned to Galileo, who tucked his notebook back into his pocket.

He smiled at her. "Excellent timing. I must leave for Mass. Thank you for letting me observe."

She shrugged. "I can't imagine that was very interesting for you."

"On the contrary," he said, "you've proven my hypothesis. Women paint in the same way as men, and, in this case, just as well. From seeing the effects of your painting in that amulet, the magics might even be stronger. Would that everyone who doubted you could see you work. You were completely in the painter's trance. I walked around the studio, and you didn't even notice."

A chill ran down Artemisia's spine at her unknown vulnerability. She reached up to grasp her amulet, feeling the metal edges bite into her skin.

Galileo's expression was solemn when she met his eyes again. "I wouldn't hurt you, signorina."

Artemisia shook her head and made herself focus. "You said you had a hypothesis? You'd wondered before about female artists?"

"You're the only female artist I've met, but I have hypotheses about just about everything in this world," he said. "Art is a particular interest of mine. I've learned so much about the stars in the heavens, and still know so little about the functioning of the magics I see in front of my eyes every day. I can tell you why the tides wash in and out. I can tell you how fast a cannonball will fall when dropped off the tower in Pisa. Energy moves in so many ways. There has to be a way to track how it's transferred from your heart and stored in a canvas."

"It's just…magic," Artemisia admitted.

"Everything can be explained. There's math at the heart of the world. We just have to figure out what it looks like. We lost so much history during the Grave Age. The amount of art destroyed was incalculable, and the surviving artists were hidden. We're creating a new base of knowledge with barely two centuries of data. But there must be an answer," Galileo said, opening his notebook and flipping to a page to show her a scrawling mess of numbers. "San Leonardo was the same, searching for the science, hunting out the facts behind the human form. It's all connected. That's why they have me teaching mathematics courses to members at the Accademia. I've asked them to open the classes to aspiring members as well, but the board wants some exclusivity. I'm no artist, so I have no true say, of course. You've gone to the open classes, yes?"

The Accademia invited all young creators from the three sacred arts—painting, sculpture, and tapestry—to come for lectures and workshops, elevating the work of all art in Florence while keeping an eye on potential new members. New members were selected during their monthly meetings, where prospective artists brought work for critique from the current members.

Every member in the Accademia's history was male.

"I have," Artemisia said. The instructor had asked if she was lost, and the whispers had grown louder through the course of the workshop. Artemisia was talented. She *knew* she was talented. And yet, being in a room with so many hostile eyes...

She'd stayed for the workshop, and then had gone home determined not to return. They would not accept her.

"Have you been to one of the monthly meetings to show your work?"

"No," she admitted.

"You should, and go to as many workshops as you can."

"I appreciate the advice," she lied, "but I'd rather not."

"Signorina, you need the Accademia at your back to succeed in Florence. They control every aspect of art here. They will improve your craft and give you the connections you need."

"I prefer to work alone."

"Don't we all? But even I have to give attention to the men who load the dice."

Artemisia stared at the paint glistening on her canvas. The painter the Fenzetti had hired to actualize her design had been a member of the Accademia. That standing had set him over Artemisia. She needed aid. The single commission from Madama Cristina would not assure her career. Few patrons would take the same risk as the Medici. She could feel the nipping hounds of poverty at her heels. Someday she would not be able to sustain her life on bread alone.

But to subject herself to the judgement of a crowd, or worse, the control of another mentor? The thought was nauseating.

"They'll be going to see an autopsy next week. Join them. Your anatomy is good, but you won't always be commissioned to draw women. You can learn from the best here."

"I can try," she finally said. "Tell me—why did you come to see me today, signore? You have friends at the Accademia. As you said, they're the heart of the work here. There are dozens of artists you could observe."

"And I've done so often. Science relies on accumulating a vast knowledge, and I never ignore an opportunity to learn. Some of the artists in the Accademia are innovators, but not many," Galileo said. "There are only a handful of artists in a generation who do anything *new*. I wouldn't miss the chance to meet one of them. The world needs more revolutionaries."

4

As Artemisia made her way toward the heart of Florence, the vast, rust-colored dome of the Santa Maria del Fiore cathedral rose to greet her, casting its own shadow over the city. It was strange to live somewhere so centered around one landmark. In Rome, there had been dozens, each more iconic than the last. Most were ancient tan stone inside and out, with all original decoration scrubbed away during the Grave Age.

Here, the city pulsed around the enormous Duomo. Despite its size, the church's colors were delicate, rusts and green, and broad expanses of white. No matter the weather, Santa Maria del Fiore looked like spring. It was a testament to the power of art, standing proud.

The church had been the wellspring where art had swept back into the world after the long Grave Age.

Even centuries after necrotic magics first created the worst plague in history, waves of the pestilence continued to sweep over the world. Big cities were normally struck the hardest, but in 1415, the disease had been stopped in its tracks when the Lord told San Donatello to create art for the city. Though artists at the time were in hiding from a world that reviled their powers, San Donatello stepped forward to carve a masterful sculpture of San Giovanni the Evangelist. The citizens of Florence made daily pilgrimages to the church for the healing power of the stoic marble figure. With the constant drain, the statue had only held onto its magics for four months, but that had been long enough to save Florence—and make San Donatello a legend. With that statue, he had become the only artist to successfully protect an entire city from the plague.

He hadn't survived to see it. With the life force he'd worked into the statue, he'd died only days after its reveal. His canonization had been swift and unanimous.

After that, no one could continue to deny the value of artists, and Donatello had been the first saint canonized since the early times.

At the base of the church, there was a worn patch along the multi-colored marble wall where for the last century and a half, passersby had dragged their hands along the walls, hoping to feel some dreg of the power inside.

The biggest hospital in the city, Ospedale Santa Maria Nuova, sat only a block away from the soaring Duomo. Though Florence sprawled out to the outer walls and spilled over, most of the city's important landmarks were located within easy walking distance. To visit each of Rome's seven hills, one could walk several hours and still not reach the Vatican.

The hospital, a long, two-story building, must have been able to hold hundreds of patients. It was pleasingly symmetrical, a long row of identical arches forming the portico below a line of small windows. It was late afternoon, and the sun painted the streets golden.

A dozen people were gathered below the portico near the main entrance, clustered together so the doctors, nurses, and visitors could get past. Even if Artemisia had not been told where the class from the Accademia was meeting, the charcoal sticks in everyone's hands would have given it away. Most were standing idly and chatting, but a handful were sketching the building or the passersby.

Artemisia joined the back of the group just in time. She had paced in her studio for too long over the last week trying to find the confidence to join the class. After Galileo had left, she had talked herself in and out of it a dozen times. The idea frightened her to her bones, and she loathed its necessity. He had been right. She needed more patrons, and Madama Cristina was proving to be the exception rather than a pattern—most Florentine nobility were following the Fenzetti's caution and suspicion. Art was an expensive contract of trust, and Artemisia needed the Accademia to help her to gain a foothold. Otherwise, she would drown before anyone could see her skill.

She simply needed to become the first female member of the Accademia delle Arti della Magica.

The man at the front of the group, dressed in heavy black robes that designated him as a senior member of the Accademia, looked up when the bells above the Duomo rang out. "And that's time," he said, straightening up and turning to look at the small group. He had the firm, slender build of someone who pursued activity for leisure, if a decade past his prime. His hair was midnight black, and silver flecked his trim beard. "I am Paolo Lamberti, if we have not met." The name sounded familiar, though the face was not. "I see some new faces, and some old. Macato, at some point you should consider leaving art and becoming a doctor, if you're so fascinated by the insides of people."

There was murmured laughter, and someone jostled a young man near the front.

"There are some who do not understand the Accademia's partnership with the hospital. For your artistic technique, how can you truly know what something looks like unless you know it both inside and out? You can stare at passersby every day, and you still might paint their faces wrong until you've seen the way the cheek and jaw connect from the inside. Secondly, the purpose of art is to heal. Why do healing magics matter if there are doctors—or vice versa? Anyone?"

The man he had teased, Macato, clearly knew the answer, but restrained himself to let Lamberti finish his speech. "Art is glacial, in terms of time," Lamberti said. "The art patrons of this city visit doctors less often than other citizens. Our work creates long-lasting health, a positive energy that enhances their daily life, healing aches as they appear and treating chronic illnesses. Even saints like San Sandro took time to create their masterpieces, and could only heal a finite number of people. Doctors are here for the broken bone you want set now, not in a few months or years. Doctors work in the moment. We need to respect the work that doctors do, just as they respect our powers. There is still so much we do not know—where does artistic ability come from? Is magic a fifth humor, or just an excess of blood? What force allows the transfer to life from one to another? The more we learn, the more we'll understand. These are vital skills you'll need to be accepted into membership with the Accademia. And if that's not enough to convince you, remind yourselves that San Leonardo studied here in 1507. No artist can go wrong following *his* footsteps. Tradition is the heart of the Accademia. Now, anyone who's late can find their own body to dissect. Everyone here, follow me."

He swept into the building, and the ragtag group of artists followed. Though Artemisia was the only woman, the group was still a diverse collection. There was a boy as young as thirteen near the front, nearly tripping on the teacher's robes. In the back, close to Artemisia, was a man near her father's age. Was he an established member expanding his knowledge, new to art, or simply still fighting to gain a place in the Accademia due to a lack of politics or skill?

It was rare for people to find their artistic talents later in life. Art was a compulsion as much as it was a gift. For a painter's heart, the need to create was difficult to suppress, and the magics poured out in uncontrolled ways if not properly trained.

Perhaps he was one of the pitiful men who believed that he *should* be an artist, and that if he tried for long enough, the magics would simply find him. There were artists without power, of course. Those men painted or sculpted for the aesthetic alone, finding joy in the craft. But none of them would ever become members of the Accademia delle Arti della Magica.

No matter her struggles, no matter the skepticism she faced, at least Artemisia could take pride in the fact she was a *true* artist.

The hospital was divided into two wards: one for men and one for women. Instead of taking them into either side, the teacher led them through the central corridor toward the back of the hospital, into the teaching area. Of course, artists were not the only ones taking classes here. Doctors trained for years before they were given access to patients, and Ospedale Santa Maria Nuova had one of the best medical internship programs in Europe.

Lamberti shook hands with the doctor waiting for them. "Children," he said, despite the mix of ages in the group, "this is Dottore Savini. He'll be dissecting our body today."

The doctor, an elderly man with a short-cropped beard, barely looked at them. "The ground rules, if this is your first time," he said curtly. "There are close quarters inside the anatomical theater, but you will conduct yourselves with decorum. It is only due to the Accademia's generosity and high standing in this city that we allow these classes to happen. Do *not* be the one who ruins the program. The body will be dissected to our usual standards, and I shall describe what I am doing as I do it. Save your questions for afterward. Dissection is not like a public hanging—it is for education, not entertainment."

"Sketch what you see," Lamberti added. "Move quickly. There will be many interesting revelations inside the theater, and you need to take full advantage of every moment."

They followed Lamberti through a narrow hallway into the anatomical theater. It was a small, cramped room, made entirely of narrow slats of wood standing in concentric, rising circles. It reminded Artemisia of the Roman Colosseum, compressed and sanitized for a new era.

Artemisia and the other artists divided themselves among the stands. Artemisia, wanting a close look, chose the second row, just behind the Accademia teacher. A few minutes later, the doctor reappeared beneath them with two assistants in tow. They set a body wrapped in a white sheet upon the table while Savini examined the row of scalpels and other tools set out for him.

Artemisia had seen death before. When her mother had gotten ill, Artemisia had been the one to sit by her side while her father was drinking his despair away. With tears in her eyes, she had watched her mother's last breath end.

Death was not only in the home; when the most recent plague had swept through Rome, a tenth of the city had died, and bodies had piled up on the streets. Beyond that, there were the traitors left to rot around the city, a constant, stinking warning against crime.

Still, there was something unnerving about the isolated body on the table ready to be exposed in front of so many dispassionate eyes. The doctor seemed entirely uninterested. Did some part of the soul know what was happening to its body? Would it be angry? Ashamed? It was about to be turned inside out to satisfy the curiosity of a room of artists.

Artemisia took a deep breath and tightened her grip on her charcoal. She would learn as much as she could from the lesson. That was the most dignity she could give the person under the sheet.

Savini looked up at the crowd of students above him. "Perhaps I should add that if any of you is squeamish..." He saw Artemisia over Lamberti's shoulder and stopped mid-sentence. "Ah, signorina, this is a workshop for students of the Accademia delle Arti della Magica."

Lamberti, in the first row, turned around and noticed Artemisia. The rows were short, but the stacking put her more than a head above him. "What is this?" he barked. "Who let a woman in here? This is a poor joke."

Artemisia cleared her throat. "I *am* a student of the Accademia."

The doctor blinked. "Are you certain?"

"Of course I'm certain," Artemisia said, lifting her chin.

"Signora, there are monthly meetings you may attend for fun," Lamberti said, "but this workshop is for real artists."

"I am an artist," Artemisia said.

"This is quite inappropriate," Savini huffed. "We allow some accommodations for the Accademia's eccentricities, but—"

"She is not with us," Lamberti said, turning back to the doctor.

Lamberti. Now Artemisia knew that name. It was the artist the Fenzetti had given her sketch to. Had he accepted their commission to finish her work? Had this man corrupted her design?

"Signori," piped up an artist from one of the higher levels. He was not much older than her, with a mop of curly hair. "She was at a workshop last month. I remember her."

Lamberti shook his head, dismissive. "Even if she was, Coccapani, no women are allowed in the anatomical theater," he said. "The Accademia would be a joke. Not to mention your constitution, signora. Would you like to be added to our stack of bodies for dissection? You could lose consciousness and hit your head."

Artemisia crossed her arms. "I would *not* lose consciousness."

"Get out," Lamberti said.

"That's not fair," she argued. "I'm perfectly capable of seeing this, just as the rest of the students are. You think that *child* is better prepared for the sight of this than I am?" The boy in question, who was on the first row beside Lamberti, shrank back into the shadows away from her. "You don't know the things I've seen. I've known brutality like you never will."

"You're wasting everyone's time. Leave so that the rest of the students may witness this dissection before the body rots in front of us."

"But he—" Artemisia said, pointing over the rail at the doctor.

Sighing, Lamberti reached up to clasp a hand around her wrist.

Artemisia lurched backward before he could make contact, slamming her head against the wooden slats behind her. Her pulse was loud in her ears, frantic and unsteady. She shook her arm like she could rid herself of the phantom sensation of his grip. She knew what broad, angry hands felt like.

And if he grabbed her, he would feel the bite of her necrotic amulet. But that hadn't been why she'd flinched.

"Signora," Lamberti scolded, exasperated. "You are not a

member of the Accademia, and you never will be. Stop wasting everyone's time."

"Enough," she said, looking away. "I'll go."

The anatomical theater was silent as she slipped back through the crowded stands and out the door.

It was late.

Her candle flickered, but she didn't look up.

The rejection at the anatomical theater that afternoon had affirmed her fears. She knew she had the talent, but these men would never respect her. Even if she worked every day, even if she painted until her fingers were raw, even if she became the most talented person in Florence, she needed patrons to survive. Without the Accademia on her side, it would be a constant battle to build her career. Knowing her own worth would not put bread on her table.

For every project she was commissioned, two more were declined at the last moment, wasting the energy she'd put into creating the sketches—and, in one infuriating case, part of a painting. She'd been forced to burn the canvas to dispel the magics she'd already layered into the oils. Her single commission from the Medici had not turned the tide of her career in Florence.

The toll of the work with little pay was etching itself into her bones. Her hands, already pained, trembled with exhaustion. Hunger was a constant companion, prodding her awake in the dark and dogging her footsteps.

So drained, she had little energy left to give to her paintings.

Still, she continued to find time late in the night for her personal project. At first, it had felt a bit like a fantasy, an outlet for her bottled, useless anger that she would not truly enact. But as she finalized the sketch, she knew she would not stop here.

If her career failed, she was determined to have this. Her past would continue to haunt her, but she could fight back outside of their rules. It could be one final, gasping success before she faded away. She could make them remember her.

During the day, she worked for her patrons, her focus on the career that always seemed just out of reach. She lived for others, pouring her magics into paintings whose benefits she would never reap. Perhaps one day she would find success in Florence. But she had no guarantee.

Her career was held in place by cobwebs. Perhaps it would find solid ground in the merciful hands of new patrons as she shoved her way into the Accademia and her work in the dark would be unnecessary, her wounds scarred over by time and success. Perhaps.

But she would not trust her legacy to the fickle opinions of others.

Night was the only time for her.

This painting would be more powerful than anything she had created before. She could pray for fame, but she would craft her justice while she waited for God to listen. Both paths would take time—no painting was done overnight—but both could be walked simultaneously. If all went well, no one would ever know of her diversion into the darker side of art.

The design was nearly complete, and she would soon block it out onto her canvas. Galileo had been right—too many paintings of this story were not bloody enough. She had laid out a gruesome tableau—two women sawing off the head of a drunken general.

Could any scene be more apt for her revenge against Agostino Tassi than Judith and Holofernes?

She had not taken Tassi's head in real life. His skin had broken under her nails. She had pulled his hair out. In the end, she had even thrown a knife at him, but she did not have a loyal maid like Abra to give her strength.

No, in the end, Artemisia only had one weapon.

Tonight, she was working on the dark background, using charcoal to black out a night so murky that no virtue would be found inside. For now, she roamed familiar territory. When she finally began to place paint on the canvas, she would need to access a deeper, darker well of her magics. This was no small amulet, designed only to protect herself. After learning to heal since she was old enough to hold a paintbrush, she would need to find the well of power inside her that could kill instead.

She had failed the first time she tried it, pouring too much anger out at once. It seemed that even necrotic magics required a steady hand. Considering how forbidden and secret the process was, it had felt startlingly similar to her healing work. To heal, she steadily drew on a spark in her chest, using that fire to enhance each brushstroke. The necrotic energy was yarn pulled from her darkest, most tangled guts, and she could not control that rage, that hate, the way she could control her other magics. She had never been one for cold revenge, preferring hot flashes of anger like fireworks.

But she would learn.

5

Santa Croce was the most notorious slum in Florence. Ramshackle wooden houses lined the streets, temporary and flimsy compared to the stone edifices closer to the city's heart. Located at the east end of the city on low marshy ground beyond the Ponte alle Grazie, it was vulnerable to the flooding that swept in every spring.

It was late in the evening a few days after the debacle at the anatomical theater. The sun had set hours before, but night barely brought a reprieve from the August heat. Despite the hour, Artemisia was far from the only person on the streets. Rough-clad workers either heading home or venturing out to a bar passed her, many with their hands stained from dyeing fabrics all day. Single women leaned against buildings or stood on street corners every few blocks. Each wore long gloves, high heels that peeked from under their worn dresses, and a bell tucked into their hat. It was a distinctive uniform, and a loud one at that.

The Office of Decency controlled prostitution in Florence. Though the city managed municipal brothels, the prostitutes who worked for them were scorned and forced to live on the outskirts of the city.

And prostitutes were not the only desperate men and women on these streets.

"Signora, some art for your health?" hissed a voice.

Startled, Artemisia looked over and caught an old man's eye. He stood over a blanket stacked with sketches. The paper was mostly torn, likely cheap scraps, and each piece featured a landscape or portrait. In the dark, she could only see the faint suggestions of shapes.

"Buy one and heal your pains," he said.

She shook her head and quickly walked on. She couldn't decide which was worse: if he was a swindler trying to deprive the local poor of their hard-earned money... or if he had the magics but no legitimate recognition, and was now selling bits of his life for cheap.

Santa Croce was an area for the outcast and ignored, the poor and maligned. It was where she would end up if she couldn't get enough commissions to make a living.

Despite her skills, it was clear that she would need more than talent to carve a future in Florence—she needed to be flawless. She did not need the Accademia's training to be the best artist this city had ever seen. She would carve her own path and give them no choice but to see her.

Her life depended on succeeding in Florence, but the fire that truly licked at her heels was defiance. They had tried to ruin her in Rome. She would find success here and destroy anyone who got in her way. She had a back-up plan now, and it gave her confidence. She would fight for their acknowledgement, but either way, she would leave her mark.

She stopped in front of one of the prostitutes, who looked her up and down with tired eyes. "Lost, signorina?"

"I'm looking for a bar," Artemisia said.

"Spit. You'll hit one."

"I'm looking for a specific bar. Or, at least, a specific type of bar. I'm looking for, ah, the type of man who wouldn't need your services. I've heard that there are places where men with certain values might gather."

"There are places like that all over the city, if you know where to look," the woman retorted.

"Say I was looking in *this* area, though," Artemisia said. She pulled a quattrini coin from her pocket and pressed it into the woman's hand. "Where might I go?"

The woman shrugged and directed her to a bar further down the street.

The bar, Il Buco, was tucked away on a side street, taking up the lower level of a building that, from the laundry hanging from a window, was otherwise occupied by tenants. The bar was raucous even from the street, and the noise only grew louder when Artemisia stepped inside. At first glance, Il Buco could have been any of the bars her father frequented in Rome. And though, if the prostitute had sent her to the right bar, her father would not have fit into this particular scene, there were plenty of other artists who would have.

As she entered, she imagined a sneering man telling her to get out, the same humiliation as the anatomical theater. How much more rejection could she stomach?

Despite her expectations, she was not the only woman in the bar. There was a sturdy woman tucked in a corner beside an old man with a long beard chatting quietly over tall cups of beer. A pair of younger women sat on mismatched barstools with their heads close together, a nearly empty pitcher of wine between them. Three black men played cards with two white men, all with blue palms from dyeing wool. Large groups of men in dirt-scuffed work clothes drank enthusiastically while they talked and shoved each other.

In Rome, she had been mostly isolated—her interactions had been with her family or with her father's boisterous friends. Other than her dinner with the Medici, she had not attended any social gatherings in Florence, and now felt smothered by the sudden cacophony of laughter and conversation. She was awkward with new people and too blunt to be good company, and was certain everyone would be able to tell she did not belong. She was no more wealthy, but she was a stranger to these people. This was not a networking event where she had learned to ply rich men with flattery to convince them to commission her.

A few people glanced toward the door when she entered, but most ignored her, which gave her the courage to make her way through the crowd toward the bar which occupied the back corner of the room.

It was not too late to turn around and reconsider. No one would even remember her arrival. But this was her best path forward. She had sent a letter to Galileo for advice after the anatomical theater—not exposing her terrible departure, but asking his advice for understanding the unseen secrets a body held. He was a friendly and fascinating correspondent, and had eagerly told her that observation offered the truth of things. He had, unknowingly, set her on the path to this bar. She just needed to follow through.

She sat on the only free stool and ordered a glass of red wine that tasted like vinegar.

"Careful with your expressions," murmured a low voice from the seat beside her. "The bartender keeps a club under the bar for patrons who get snooty about his swill."

The speaker was in the same rough wool work clothes as most of the crowd. He must have been a decade older than her, burly and solidly built with a jagged scar on one cheek. Beside him, Artemisia was fiercely conscious of the softness of her body.

"But he doesn't mind when people call it swill?" she asked, matching his quiet voice.

The man's lips quirked. "I don't say it to his face, carina." He looked her over. Her skin crawled at the inspection, but he was scornful, not lecherous. "You take a wrong turn out of town?"

"It's that obvious?" Artemisia asked. Perhaps she had been right that they would all sense she did not belong. Yet her clothes were not much better than his, and though she had taken off her apron, paint still stained her hem. She wore a simple green gown over a white chemise, buttoned closed at the front with its sleeves laced on. She removed them so she could paint without dragging fabric through the oils, but never left her home with bare arms.

"I know most of the faces who live around here," he said, "and you're looking around the place like it's a museum. If you're looking for a bit of fun, you're barking up the wrong tree here."

"I know," Artemisia said. "I'm not here for…personal reasons. I'm here professionally."

The man made a skeptical noise and took a sip from his glass.

She looked around the room, considering the other candidates, and then back to him. "I'm an artist," she told him. "A painter. I'm looking for a model to pose for me."

He laughed, nearly choking on his drink. "You really are in the wrong place. Go back on the street and find a prostitute. She'll pose for you."

"Don't be stupid. I already have a female body," she pointed out. "I need a man."

"And there aren't men where you're from? Fancier men?"

"I want someone who can pose for a female painter without

getting…ideas. Other painters have studio assistants they can draw. They can *have* studio assistants without starting rumors. I can't. I need to find a body to sketch without risking myself."

He turned to her, looking at her seriously for the first time. "Maybe you are in the right place," he mused. "You know what this bar is."

"I do."

He huffed. "And you think you're safe here, compared to the men you'd find somewhere else? I'm not a saint just because I don't like women."

It was the first time he had said it so explicitly, and Artemisia felt relief that she was in the right place rush through her like a breeze. "I don't care if you're a saint," Artemisia said. "You just need to want money, and not to hurt me."

"There are other ways to hurt someone, you know. You're not afraid someone will rob you?"

"I won't get the money until I have the model. There would be nothing to rob until they'd already done the job," she pointed out. Artemisia considered his face from an artistic standpoint. His features were more rugged than many artists would have painted, with the crags and rough edges of a mountain. His appearance was striking, though, and real. Artemisia had never painted the waifish women of Raffaello or Caravaggio. Why paint delicate men? "Would you do it?"

He hesitated. "I don't know what 'it' is," he said. "I don't know any artists. I certainly never modeled for them. Believe it or not, you're the first person who's ever asked me. Shocking, I'm sure."

"When I need you, I would pay you to come to my studio and pose for several hours at a time." She cleared her throat and pressed forward. "You would be mostly clothed, or wearing props, but occasionally nude. Thus the need for someone... fortified for that."

"And you're sure you don't want some young man who *will* be overcome with lust? It seems like a convenient set-up for a pretty woman." He glanced at her unadorned hands. "Ask someone in to pose and walk out with a husband."

"Absolutely not," Artemisia said. "I know what I'm looking for."

He thought it over, sipping his wine. "You're offering money? Why not offer me some of your art?"

She laughed, startled. "You would need to work for me every day for a year to afford one of my paintings."

He shrugged. "Then what's the pay?"

"Ten baiocci per day," she said, though she cringed. She needed all the money she had. "I wouldn't be consistent. I don't know what my clients will request, though I'd want you in for a practice session so I could get to know your form. You might end up as one of the Apostles in my paintings, or as Mars riding into battle. I need to know the range of your expressions."

"Make it twenty, and we have a deal."

"Twenty!" Her father had only paid his apprentice thirty a day, and he had been a true aid in the studio.

"Well, you've made an excellent case as to why you need me specifically," he said with an unrepentant grin. "I make ten a day in the orchards. If you want me to do something new, I'll need an incentive. You're free to take this pitch to someone else here, but I guarantee they're less eager to talk to strangers than I am."

The room was full of other options, but it had been a trial steeling herself to talk to this one. "You'd rather be in a field than a quiet studio?"

"Maybe I would, maybe I wouldn't. I'm not doing you a favor here."

"Fine. Fifteen," she compromised.

"Deal. Maurizio Arcuri," he said, holding out a hand.

"Artemisia Gentileschi."

He nodded and waved for the bartender to give him another round of wine. "A toast to new opportunities," he said, and then winked at her. "You're paying, of course."

"Of course I am," she said, shaking her head and throwing another coin on the counter.

6

Artemisia shuffled her feet and straightened the long sleeves of her gown while the senior members of the Accademia delle Arti della Magica mingled around her.

The monastery of Cestello at the corner of the Via di Pinti and the Via della Colonna, at the northeast end of the city, was a small but beautiful building. Several decades ago, the Accademia had been granted use of the temple adjacent to the monastery to host their meetings and art classes. Art filled the room: statues stood along the walls, ranging from the petite busts on pedestals to enormous structures with multiple intertwined figures; oil paintings were mounted around the room, each demonstrating the technical mastery of the members; the ceiling was painted with a swirling fresco featuring angels and clouds stretching up into the heavens. Magics pulsed like an oncoming lightning storm in the room. Skill in design was not inherently tied to magical power, and there were artists who created exhibition pieces without magics, but time put into the craft of art often indicated the same passion in the magics. Here, she knew it to be true—she could *feel* the pulse of life left by the best artists in the city.

Most places that housed a powerful public art collection, like popular churches, did not even have detectable levels of magics.

If the Accademia held such a charge, she could only imagine the power thrumming from the Vatican, which was said to be packed with powerful art from floor to ceiling. Another person likely would not have noticed anything at all, but Artemisia had been trained in magics since she was a young girl.

Though perhaps some of the electricity came from Artemisia's own awe and fear. She had already been thrown from the anatomical theater. Deciding to come here was a gamble. With her own model she would not have to *rely* on their acceptance, but she was not ready to accept failure. Success in Florence began here. This was the heart of art in the north.

Beyond being a teaching facility, the academy had control of all the magical crafts—painting, sculpture, and tapestry—in Florence. In addition to managing who was permitted to join their elite group, the organization controlled the export of art from Florence. Customs officials in the city worked with them to make sure no art by any member of the Accademia was removed from the city without approval. Magics were carefully regulated, and there were questions of legacy if members eventually earned sainthood. When Artemisia sent her works abroad, her paintings were inspected to ensure the canvases were not unsanctioned sales of another artist's work.

Tonight was the Accademia's August meeting. Artemisia, like the other artists hoping for membership, was placed at the edge of the overly warm temple while the members mingled and surveyed the room. Though her father's friend Jacopo hadn't been able to come to this meeting, he had briefly walked Artemisia through what to expect. After the whirlwind first night when he'd introduced her to some of the city's cultural elite, they had exchanged a handful of letters, but the man clearly considered his service to his friend's daughter completed.

Every month, the Accademia invited prospective members to bring in one of their designs. In addition to giving the members a chance to critique and provide advice, a few times a year three to five artists would be selected to participate in the next major feast day. There, the finished art would be displayed as part of the proceedings. The students selected for the honor would be accelerated toward the exclusive membership with the Accademia.

For the students, it was their best chance of being noticed.

However, the members seemed mostly uninterested in the sketches being displayed around the room, instead snacking on antipasti or sipping wine while they chatted. Artemisia watched them eat, feeling her stomach clench. The hunger—physical and emotional—was so intense that her mind seemed to float away from the twisting anxiety in her body, like a crow flying over a battlefield.

Paolo Lamberti, the teacher who had scorned her in the anatomical theater, walked past the students, glanced at her sketch, and then sneered something quietly to his companion. The other artist looked at Artemisia as though she were something unidentifiable he'd found on the bottom of his shoe. She lifted her chin and looked past them—she knew better than to ask for Lamberti's advice.

He had told her she would never be a part of the Accademia. Let him try to stop her.

A pair of members wearing formal dress clothes that could have fit in at the Medici court—with sweat on their faces to punish them for their vanity in mid-August—stopped to talk with the student on Artemisia's left. The boy, a few years younger than Artemisia, beamed at the attention, and his hands shook as he showed them the sketch he'd drawn for a statue. The concept, which the boy had shown Artemisia as they'd taken their spots, was traditional and staid. His Virgin Mary was attractive but looked like stone even in his sketch. He must have spent more time sketching from statues than actually looking at human women. The members gave him a polite critique, pointing out the way he could have made the pose more dynamic and showing him a proportion flaw in the anatomy.

Artemisia straightened as they moved on, but they skipped her in favor of the student on her other side. He had drawn a nearly inscrutable representation of the world's most popular non-religious imagery: a battling griffon and blood drake. The two magical beasts, though rare, ignited every artist's imagination. Half the art in Florence featured one or the other. Griffons, drawn to the healing energies of art, had come to symbolize innocence and justice. The blood drake, which was drawn instead to the toxic pull of necrotic art, represented the dark. During the Grave Age, when the world had turned against artists and their symbols, both creatures had been hunted to near extinction.

As the evening wore on, the same scene repeated as though scripted. Though Artemisia had her own sketch on display, the members of the Accademia looked through her.

Finally, Artemisia had had enough. When the next cluster of members walked past, she stepped forward. "Good evening, signori," she said. "May I show you my design?"

The three men exchanged glances. "Signora," the eldest said with a tone as cloying as honey, "this event is for artists interested in becoming members. We need to focus our time on them."

Artemisia gritted her teeth to keep her smile in place. "I'm also a potential member. That's why I'm here."

Another man shook his head. "Women can come to our

art workshops if they're interested—they're open to all artists." Except the anatomical theater. "But none have ever become a *member* of the Accademia."

"It isn't against the rules," Artemisia said. She knew it wasn't— Galileo and Jacopo had checked for her.

"I'm not interested in a debate," the man said dismissively, already turning toward the next artist.

"If you'll just look—" Artemisia said, thrusting the paper forward.

But the eldest had said something else, quiet, and they had moved on.

"Stronzi," Artemisia muttered. She closed her eyes, just for a moment. She'd known. Of course she'd known. The anatomical theater should have taught her. Here, in the Accademia's heart, no one would give her a second look.

It wasn't embarrassment or defeat that flared to life in her heart. It was sheer, unfiltered rage. She wanted to swear and shout, and tear to pieces the mediocre art of the child beside her. Three years ago, she might have. But she'd learned the value—and the price—of public opinion. Men could afford to be eccentric and aggressive. Until Artemisia made her name, she couldn't.

"Allora, is this your work?"

One of the members stopped in front of her, eyeing the paper in her hand with dark, clever eyes. He was dressed more humbly than some of the other members, though the crest on his lapel identified him as part of the Accademia. He had a mop of curly hair and a familiar, youthful face. It was, she realized, the artist who had stood up for her at the anatomical theater.

Artemisia summoned her smile again and let him take the paper from her hand. "It is," she confirmed.

"It's very good," he said. "I'm Sigismondo Coccapani. Just call me Sigismondo. It's nice to see you again in better circumstances."

"Thank you for what you did," she said, cheeks flushed at the memory of the humiliation he had witnessed.

"I wish I had done more," he said, and then thankfully moved on. "You do good work. This reminds me of Caravaggio."

Her smile eased into a more genuine expression. "He is my inspiration."

"I assume there would be heavy chiaroscuro on this, then?" he asked, examining her sketched scene. "In the background?"

"And on her face," Artemisia said, leaning forward to trace a line down the woman's cheek. "It would be half in shadows, with the moon illuminating the rest."

"Very dynamic!" He tapped the paper thoughtfully, careful not to smudge the charcoal. "Who is she meant to be?"

"Bathsheba." She pointed him toward the shadowed figure watching the woman from the corner. "And David, watching."

"Hm. You have a subtle hand. Maybe too subtle, if you're following Caravaggio's footsteps and cloaking it all in blacks, but it's obvious you have firm grasp on composition. You should step away from his influence and focus on the detail, if you don't mind me saying. So much gets lost in his style, you know?"

"Thank you," she said, accepting the sketch back.

Instead of brushing past her to talk to the other artists, he asked, "How long have you been in Florence?"

"Only a few months," she said, and then added, "My friend told me to come tonight for the meeting. Galileo Galilei—have you met him?"

"A good man," Sigismondo said. "I worked with him on a project a few years ago. I assume he sent you here in search of learning. That's his way."

"Actually, I'm hoping to get membership," she said.

Sigismondo hummed, thoughtful rather than dismissive. "There are no women in the Accademia."

"Yet," Artemisia said.

Someone across the room called his name, and he waved to them before nodding to her. His attention was already divided. She opened her mouth again, but he walked away before she could speak. "Consider what I said about the shading," he called over his shoulder.

Sigismondo was the only one to critique her work. The members continued to drift by and talk to each other, and Artemisia stared ahead.

These fools would never see past her sex, no matter what art she put on display. But Galileo was right—she needed this and could not give up yet. Violence had not made her give up her art, and neither would rejection. She would have to fight for their attention. She would come to every Accademia event for the next twenty years if that was what it took for them to notice her.

At the end of the meeting, the members consulted while Artemisia and the other prospective members waited outside. It was dark, and the warm evening was too muggy to be pleasant. When they announced the three winners, none of the members even glanced in Artemisia's direction.

August bled into September into October. The summer heat broke like shattered glass, and autumn's chill swept through the city with a series of storms.

She had been in Florence for six months now, and progress was slow. There were endless things to be done, all fighting for the next small step forward. Taking one evening away from her work for this meeting seemed a risky indulgence, but breathing the brisk fall air rather than the oil and candlewax in her studio made her lungs feel full for the first time in weeks. She had appreciated summer's long days for their light, but the cloying, unending heat was smothering.

Raised in Rome and taught the basics of safety in a city, Artemisia rarely ventured outside after midnight, though sleep was a rare companion. The city was quiet so late, apart from the wind whistling through the narrow alleys. At this hour, even the bars had shut their doors.

But Artemisia had her amulet, and an opportunity too unique to decline.

After dark, the Duomo at the heart of the city was a hulking black shadow that blocked out the stars and moon behind it. She readjusted the hood hanging over her eyes and approached the behemoth. On Sundays, she attended Mass at the Basilica di Santo Spirito, the church closest to her studio. Its design was simple and symmetrical, leaving grand façades to Florence's other buildings. In comparison, Santa Maria del Fiore was a masterpiece. She'd gone in only once before. As an artist, she couldn't resist the chance to see San Donatello's sculpture and Brunelleschi's dome from the inside, but the church was too grand, too important, for her weekly services. She had not earned her place yet, but perhaps she would soon.

Another cloaked figure was waiting for her at the entrance, staring up at the stars. He didn't notice her approach until she was nearly beside him. "Artemisia," Galileo said warmly. "I'm glad you came."

"You're sure we're allowed inside?" she asked, tipping her head back to take in the magnificence of the church.

"We're not intruders. The archbishop knows we are here. I'm

still in favor with the Medici, though I do not know how long that will last," Galileo said. He looked distant for a moment, and then shook his head. "For now, the city still allows my eccentricities."

It was strange to be inside the cavernous church with only Galileo as company. The cool smell of plaster greeted her as she entered, with faint traces of the dried wax of the church's candles coloring the air. Their footsteps echoed, bouncing from the tall ceiling and rebounding back on her ears. Without Latin chanting and harmonic singing, the space felt empty.

God often felt…removed to Artemisia. Her magics were meant to be a gift from Him, but if He had bestowed any grace upon her life, she had not seen it. Like herself, the church felt cold, abandoned by something mightier than she could imagine. The tall columns seemed like the dried ribcage of a massive skeleton.

They passed through the chancel toward the altar, and she and Galileo both bowed their heads toward the row of relics set to the left. Displayed on velvet pillows were three bones: a finger and two skulls. The finger bone belonged to San Giovanni the Baptist, cousin of Christ. The first skull, ancient and yellowed, to the patron saint of Santa Maria del Fiore, San Zenobius. The second, only one hundred years old, to the saint who had given his statue of San Giovanni the Evangelist to end the Grave Age and start a new era of acceptance for artists: San Donatello.

A hundred years ago, Filippo Brunelleschi had been selected to top the existing church with the most ambitious architectural project ever undertaken: the Duomo. It cemented Santa Maria del Fiore as the heart of Florence.

The spiral staircase that led to the dome overhead was tucked through a door in a transept, which led them to a barer area of the cathedral. Here, things were built for function rather than beauty. The staircase spiraled in on itself high into the air, reaching the base of the dome. From there, the tight circles broadened to the circumference of the dome as they followed the architect's path around and up the structure.

It was an arduous climb, and Artemisia spent most of her days sitting indoors. Sweat dampened her gown, and her breath rattled in her lungs.

Finally, they reached the top. Cool air greeted them as they left the church. This high, there were no buildings to cut the wind from the mountains. A pathway circled the crown of the dome, surrounding the white marble lantern that stretched to its final point overhead, where the Church's golden globe and cross glinted blue under the moonlight. There was no railing, and the sharp decline of the dome started alarmingly close to Artemisia's feet. The dome's iconic red was dulled at night, but its scale was only more impressive up close. It was not art as she knew it, not intricate, personal work, but ingenious design and passion nonetheless.

While she leaned against one of the white marble arches to catch her breath, Galileo revealed what he had been carrying over his shoulder. First, a brass tripod, which perched on the walkway like a spider. Carefully, he slotted a long tube into a catch in the center and tilted one end toward the sky overhead.

"We'll have to sit on the ground," he told her. "I never could convince them to install a full observatory up here, but even so, the view is better than anywhere else in the city. This is the highest point for kilometers."

"Is this where you always come to do your research?"

He shook his head. "If I'm doing precise measurements, I prefer somewhere with my supplies. My home in the country has a decent vantage," he said. "For observations, though, this cannot be outdone. Come, come, sit down."

She sat cross-legged beside him, careful not to jolt the precarious telescope. Though the cold marble immediately leached through to nip at her thighs, the unobstructed view of the sky above and the city spread below was worth it.

The bell tower stood proudly just ahead, pressed alongside the nave of the cathedral. The intricacies of the marble inlay across its surface were lost in the darkness, leaving it the ghost of a pale bone against the night sky. This high, Florence was small and uniform, only broken by the occasional spire, and the twist of the Arno flowing to the west before the rolling hills. The handful of windows lit by candlelight made it seem like the stars overhead were reflecting on the ground.

It was hard to believe that below the rooftops the city was packed with humans sleeping in their beds. From here, Artemisia and Galileo could have been the only people in the universe.

"How are things progressing with the Accademia?"

She sighed and looked out at the stars. "My third monthly meeting was last weekend. It was as bad as the first two. They don't want me there. I'm teaching myself with my new model, finding my own patrons"—few as they were—"and going to the classes they'll let me into, but they still see me as an interloper."

"You would think that artists would be better able to see. You're no less qualified than any of their students, and far more qualified than many." He clicked his tongue. "They will see their mistake. Your art will speak for itself. The truth comes out, in the end."

"If you're sure," she said.

With eyes like Galileo's, he could not miss her skepticism. "It will. You're thinner than when we met, you know."

"What?"

"Your cheeks are growing hollow. Surviving on an artist's

stipend is difficult, and more so for a young woman without a family. The Accademia is failing you by not supporting you."

Money trickled in from her few commissions, just enough to cover her supplies. When her clients were late with their monthly stipends, she had to beg her landlord for an extension in order to prevent him from throwing her out. Gori had complained about her groveling but had seemed pleased to have her under his thumb. It was a desperate position, and her vulnerability horrified her. To know that Galileo could see her struggling scared her, but she was touched by his attention with an intensity that burned her throat.

"Being failed by those in charge is not a new experience for me," she said, and smiled to brush past the awkwardness. "Now, what did you want to show me?"

He put the telescope to his eye and adjusted a knob. "What would you like to see?"

Artemisia looked up at the expanse of stars, all paling beside the moon hanging in the center of the sky. "I hardly know where to start." She was on the Duomo above Florence with the most lauded mathematician of her time. It was not a friendship she had expected, but over their exchanged letters they had become close. He was a good friend, clever and loyal. Finally, he had suggested that if he was going to see her art, she should have the chance to see his. "Show me something you were the first to discover."

"That I can do," he said. He jotted some numbers in his notebook, and then tilted the telescope.

Artemisia hunched her shoulders against the cold. The night wind was sharp, and the marble below her seemed to be seeping through her body. Her hands ached.

After a few minutes, Galileo touched the telescope once more to stabilize it, and then shuffled sideways on the marble.

"Take my spot and look," he said. "Careful—it's perfectly adjusted right now."

Artemisia delicately slid into his spot, readjusting her slightly numb legs, and then set her eye to the end of the bronze tube. She blinked as her vision adjusted to the magnification.

It was the night sky, but not the way she knew it. Instead of the moon or sun taking the attention, the lens was centered on one bright star, which was surrounded by four smaller flecks of light.

"See the brightest spot?" Galileo asked. "That's Jupiter. That, of course, was not my discovery. We don't know when it was first observed, but we know the Greeks and Romans knew about it. My discovery is those four moons circling it."

In their letters, he had mentioned this discovery, along with his more revolutionary theories about the structure of the galaxy. Nothing she'd read, however, could match the passion in his voice. He was as proud of the painstaking searching and mathematics that had shown him new spots in the night sky as she was of her paintings. Even though their subjects were different, they both threw themselves into their passions with their whole hearts. It was invigorating to find such kinship.

"I wrote a book sharing my discovery. I decided to name them the 'Cosmian Stars' after my student, our own Grand Duke. It wasn't until I'd already printed the first five hundred copies of the book that the Grand Duke wrote back and told me that he preferred the name 'Medicean' instead, to honor his brothers too." Galileo laughed. "I had to hand-paste in the corrections to the copies that had already been printed."

Artemisia laughed with him. "Your greatest discovery and he couldn't take the time to answer a letter promptly."

"My greatest discovery so far," Galileo corrected. "I know

there's more out there. I just don't know where the math will lead me next." He sighed. "I'm currently spending my time fighting for a theory that wasn't even mine first, and it's the one people seem prepared to remember me for. Artemisia, there's so much evidence that the sun sits at the center of our galaxy. Copernicus was right. The math is irrefutable. But not everyone is willing to *look*."

Artemisia stared again up at the moons. "I wish everyone could see this view."

Her hand spasmed suddenly, a jagged clench of muscles. She jolted with pain and knocked into the telescope.

She pulled back quickly, but it was too late. The telescope tipped toward the steep edge of the dome. Galileo, with better reflexes than she would have expected from someone of his age, lunged forward and caught the device before it could fall.

He pulled it back from the precipice and leaned against one of the marble columns. Panting loudly, he clutched the telescope to his chest like it was a child.

"I'm sorry. I'm so sorry," she said, twisting her hands together to try to alleviate the ache in her fingers. She stayed sitting still, afraid her lack of balance would send her tumbling from the dome. "My hands don't always react well to the cold."

"You're too young for old joints," Galileo said. The words were light, but his expression was serious and concerned. Carefully, he set the telescope down near the center of the lantern and then stepped back toward her.

"I…" Artemisia hesitated and stared out over the city.

She found, to her surprise, that she wanted him to understand. He was her only friend in Florence. Perhaps she could trust him with this piece of her. She was so damn tired of being alone.

"Do you know why I came to Florence?" she asked.

There was a moment of silence as he sat down beside her again. "I know there was a trial," he said finally. "I did promise not to listen to rumors about you, in exchange for you ignoring them about me."

"That rumor is true," Artemisia said. "There was a trial. For rape." The word hung sour and flat in the air. For something that haunted her every step, she rarely spoke it out loud. "My painting tutor. The court didn't believe my testimony. Why would they? I was a young woman who'd lost her chastity... They thought that I was making up the case so that the man— Agostino Tassi—would have to marry me. They didn't believe that I was unwilling." Her voice broke. Willing? She had tried to *stab* him when it was over. Had thrown a knife at his bare chest but missed. It took physical strength to kill a man, and she could not do it. She was not like him. She could not hold someone down and hurt them. But they both left bleeding that day.

"The court thought I was desperate for his love. At first, we nearly did marry. He convinced me that staying with him, even after what he'd done, was the only way to rescue myself. My reputation was in tatters, and I had nowhere else to turn. He left me desperate. But it did not matter in the end—he was already married, it turned out, though his wife was missing. My father decided to press charges, and the trial began. Roman courts have ways to verify testimony." She clenched her fists. "The sibille. You know the method?" She didn't look at him for an answer. "They wrapped cords around my fingers and pulled. Pulled until I thought my fingers would be destroyed. I knew the answer they wanted to hear. I knew what I had to say to make them stop. But I couldn't let him—them—win. When even the sibille could not change my testimony, they were finally forced to believe me."

"And your fingers?"

She was grateful he didn't ask more about the trial. There was only so much from those months she could bear to relive, even here at the top of the world. "I can use them, of course," she said. "But they ache. The cold makes it more difficult. I wear gloves in my studio."

"Have you attempted to heal them? I know some of the best healers in the city, both artists and doctors. We could find something."

"Not everything is a problem for you to solve, my friend," she told him. "I *could* heal them. But the pain reminds me, and I'm not ready to forget. My fight with Tassi is not over yet."

"Holding onto anger hurts you more than it hurts your enemy," Galileo said gently.

Artemisia hummed. "Perhaps. But perhaps not. I am not powerless."

She had been researching the full effects of the necrotic magics she was planning. Just as artists' healing magics repaired sickness, soothing the dissociation between the humors, dark magics tore the body apart. There were mostly whispers of the details, but the tales suggested that necrotic magics were far more powerful—it was always easier to destroy than to repair. For as long as people had been healing, they had been twisting magics to cause harm. In art, it all came back to blood and life. If she could do one, she could do the other. Galileo respected her for being a revolutionary.

Would he respect this? She did not know.

They did not set up the telescope again. Nor did they continue to talk about the lingering ache in her hands. Instead, Galileo sat with her on top of the dome, and they stared up at the stars together.

*

"I don't understand how you sit in front of a canvas all day. Don't you get tired with only images for company? Do you never want to stretch your legs and *do* something?"

Artemisia pulled another line in charcoal, eyeing the fold in the fabric over the burly man's knee. "Stay still," she scolded.

Maurizio huffed but settled.

She had slowly become accustomed to sessions with her new model over the last three months. During the first sessions, she had sketched him in a dozen positions and angles, familiarizing her pencil with his face. As she had hoped, his heavy brow and strong features fit well within her style. At first it had been strange to have a model, a new person who was by nature intrinsic to her art—which was usually a solitary journey—but she had grown to appreciate his company. Artemisia was able to relax around him with surprising ease. There were no pretenses with him, and she had no need to blunt her tongue for him. In many ways, he reminded her of her father and some of his friends, though that thought threatened to ruin her calm. Confident men without a sense of decorum often blurred other lines when they thought they could get away with it, but he seemed a different type.

"I feel I'm doing plenty," Artemisia added. "I can't think of anything else when I have a brush in my hand. It takes all my focus. You've seen how I am while just sketching; painting creates a real trance. I don't notice I've been sitting still for hours until my hands start cramping."

"Clearly. You already have four new canvases set up since the last time I was in here," Maurizio commented, though he followed her instructions and only moved his eyes to look. "For all your complaining, you seem to have plenty of clients."

"This is nothing compared to an established studio. The ones for pay might take years to finish, and many of these are only practice." When testing new skills, she avoided including even a scrap of magics, which could only be released back to her heart by burning the canvas. Until they were sold, her practice canvases could be either stripped or painted over. One piece of canvas could be used infinitely, with the right tools.

"Practice," he scoffed. "Do you ever take a break?"

"Of course I do. I have to make connections with new patrons somehow," Artemisia said. Though she had continued to force her way into the monthly meetings at the Accademia, she seemed to only draw in one additional pair of eyes each time. Her work—and, sometimes, her life—felt like a fire in an empty hearth, flickering and guttering and desperate for the next bit of tinder to survive another moment.

She had met the buyer behind today's work, a middle-aged businessman, at her second dinner at the Palazzo Pitti. Now that Artemisia was working on a commission for Madama Cristina, she had an open invitation to the Medici dinner parties. Most of the business connections she had tried to make died on the vine, but she had snared several new commissions over the last months. They did not give her the funds to fully support herself, but they were small steps.

This painting was of Salome with the head of San Giovanni Battista. The corpse's head Artemisia would design from memory, but she needed Maurizio as Herod, the looming man in the background who had fetched Salome's grisly prize on a silver platter. With his bulk and strong features, Maurizio was the perfect inspiration.

He snorted. "That's not a break. That's more work, and

probably even more stressful. You make contacts, then you paint and paint and paint some more."

"I can't take a break. I don't have enough commissions yet to keep meeting my rent," Artemisia said, busying herself with shadowing his curls. "I have to make them see me. I'm a woman. I'm young. I'm one of the best painters in Florence, and they still doubt whether I can even hold a brush. I can't stop until I make them respect me."

"Don't you know that respect is the most difficult thing to find? You could unfurl the most beautiful painting in the world *and* cure their gout with a brushstroke and they'd still whisper behind your back."

She ground her teeth. "Even so. I need the money."

"It's absurd you can't afford to feed yourself," he said. "You heal people. You save lives. Pope Clement VII is more than a hundred years old. You should be retiring to the sea with people throwing flowers at your feet, not painting until your fingers bleed."

"The last Pope Clement didn't think so. We're just grateful we're not being burned at the stake anymore."

The story of the Black Death was taught to schoolchildren as regularly as the Bible. A powerful Mongolian weaver, devastated by a wandering husband, had crafted a curse so malicious that its necrotic energies had spread across the entire world. After killing her husband, the new strain of disease had become a contagious pathogen, powerful enough to kill one in every three men. The poison in her heart had spread wide, devastating entire cities and bringing humanity to its knees. Half of the population died. Her necrotic magics were more powerful than any healing in history.

Since then, the plague had swept through Europe in smaller tides, mostly as a natural aftershock of the original disease. No outbreak had been as devastating as the first, though only by a matter of degrees. When the plague came, it was time to pray.

In the aftermath of the first wave, Pope Clement VI had granted absolution to all those who died without their last rites, and declared all artists demons. Across the continent during the Grave Age, artists were beheaded and burned for a hundred years as retaliation for the illness, and protection against new plagues.

"It's been more than two hundred years since San Donatello saved Santa Maria del Fiore," he said. "There have been more artist saints in the last two centuries than there were before the plague. Times are different. They're using your fear to keep you underpaid."

"You're right," she said, putting down her charcoal. "Of course you're right. But I can already barely get anyone to commission me. If I start arguing with the whole system, they'll laugh me out of Florence."

"That's probably what they're all saying. And so no one steps up to help the rest."

"Success takes sacrifice. I barely have room to breathe. I can't fix the world for everyone. First, I need to look after myself."

Maurizio shrugged. "They're probably all saying that too."

7

A fist pounded on the door. Artemisia straightened from where she was leaning over her candle, burning the hair gathered in her brush that night. The smell was acrid, but it was worth it so that no enemy would be able to tie her to magics without her knowledge.

She knew too well the power a few strands of hair could have. She paused by the door, anxious. "Hello?"

"Open the door," said the gruff voice of her landlord.

After pulling on her amulet from where it hung beside the threshold, she obeyed. Gori stood in his usual stance, arms crossed, but there was a new buzzing tension to his shifting feet. "What is it?" she asked.

He pointed upward. She was on the top floor of the small building, and she didn't see anything on the ceiling. "A neighbor spotted it and told me," he said. "I went up to see, but it wouldn't let me get near. There's a law against interfering with one if it settles on your building, but that doesn't mean it's my job to handle."

She frowned, crossing her own arms. "What are you talking about?"

He jabbed upward again. "There's something on the roof for you," he said meaningfully.

She paled. There were only a few types of beasts that were attracted by magic, and only two that could get to a third-story roof. A griffon or a blood drake. With her work, it might have been either. "What is it?"

He scowled. "You think I got close enough to look? I got up there, saw wings, and then the beast hissed at me. I ran back down. It's your problem, not mine. Get rid of it."

It was no surprise that such a despicable man would be immune to the majesty of such creatures. At the end of the Grave Age, endless protections had been put in place to stop the magical beasts' swift fall toward extinction. They were renowned signs of good or evil, even if some close-minded fools like Gori saw them only as pests.

Artemisia had spent her life dreaming of encountering one of the rare creatures. They were rare and shy of humans. Some of her father's friends claimed to have been followed by griffons, and she had seen the winged creatures flying over Rome several times, but she had never gotten close.

Any potential awe was crippled by her fear. If it was a blood drake, Artemisia's life would be over. With their dark scales, lithe frames, and sharp, curled horns, they were at the heart of every artist's depiction of hell. The authorities tracked them to find anyone ill-using their magics. Necrotic magics were strictly monitored, and being found guilty of brewing them was enough to put you on the rack and then a pyre. Her heartbeat stumbled into a sprint.

Artemisia assured Gori she would handle it and he left after a final glare.

The night outside was quiet apart from the autumn winds dancing over the city. A chill had blown in from the west at the end of October, chasing away the last hints of warmth from the air.

She had never used the roof access before, but Gori had left the exit unlocked for her. Like most buildings in Florence, hers had pointed gables of orange shingles, but the hatch door opened to a small flat section she could stand on before it tipped into its sheer angle. She held up a candle to try to illuminate the dark roof. A cool wind off the river threatened to knock her from the unstable perch.

There was something large wrapped around the chimney a few feet away. It looked up when she emerged, its eyes reflecting like coins. She could see a sinewy form, but it was difficult to parse in the darkness.

What could it be but a blood drake called by her sins?

She had known the risks. She would not be a coward. After taking a breath for fortitude, Artemisia called to it softly.

The creature stood and stretched, first its body, which was rangy and lean, no bigger than a dog, and then its wings, which were so large that they blocked out half the stars as they unfurled in the night air.

A griffon. It was a *griffon*. The most renowned symbol of healing magics in the world, and it was on her roof.

Artemisia held up the hand not grasping the candle. Her fingers trembled. Its beak and talons glinted wickedly sharp, but she refused to run from such a noble creature.

It trotted confidently across the shingles, despite their steep angle. There was no reason to fear heights when one had wings. It entered the circle of candlelight and chirped. Its head was covered in dark brown feathers, and its eyes were wide and yellow. At its shoulders, the feathers gave way to rippling amber fur like fallen leaves at the edge of a forest conceding to a grass field. It was young, if the stories about adults growing as large as a horse were to be believed.

"Are you here for me?" she asked quietly. "Or are you simply resting your wings?"

It yawned, showing its sharp beak and a cat-like tongue.

She had been so sure, just as she'd stepped onto the roof, that she would find a blood drake lurking in wait for her. It was the horror story told to all artists to stop them from attempting the magics she was brewing against Tassi. But a *griffon*. Could there be any greater proof that her cause was just?

There had been a time when griffons were as common as dogs, roaming Tuscany alongside their selected humans. That was before the Grave Age, and the universal backlash against artists. Now, it was rare for them to emerge from the countryside and seek out an artist companion.

Artemisia pressed her hand against her chest, overwhelmed by a flood of emotion. The Accademia had ignored her for months, but *she* was the one graced by this creature. To be chosen was an honor far greater than membership in any human fraternity. Gaining a griffon was a sign that God saw your work and deemed it worthy. San Leonardo's griffon was so well known that there was no painting of the saint without his griffon beside him. She had been right—she *was* talented, *was* worthwhile.

There had been a time in Rome she had thought she would never feel powerful again. It was not just the first attack, but the grueling, humiliating trial.

During the seven months Artemisia had sat under the vicious scrutiny of Roman law, and its people, she had been tortured and humiliated. In addition to the sibille, which twisted her fingers until they felt as though they would shatter, there had been constant demands that she repeat her terrible story, skepticism of her motives, and even a painful, intimate physical examination by midwives. She had been exposed in every way. Eyes had lashed her from all sides—the judge in front of her and the stoic angels painted overhead. Though the trial had taken place behind closed doors, the entire city had learned of the proceedings through gossip.

It had left its mark on her—but the mark of her talent clearly shone more brightly.

She felt suddenly and intensely protective of the young beast. As long as the griffon selected her, she was legally permitted to let it. Poachers still collected their strange pelts and sold them in back rooms, and men like Gori scorned them, but the laws were on her side. It would fend for itself without needing her assistance. This was no soft pet like the small animals the ladies of the city pampered. With the wings and talons of an eagle and the spry haunches of an African lion, the griffon would be able to hunt in the forests surrounding Florence. As long as it wanted to choose Artemisia, no one would be able to force it to leave.

But Artemisia was not as safe. Would Gori finally evict her if she failed to banish the griffon as demanded? Did she care?

Would it even choose to stay? Magical or not, it was a wild creature. Perhaps she could encourage it to pick her.

Artemisia darted back to her studio, and then returned to the roof with a small canvas tucked under her arm. She unrolled it in the dark, feeling silly. "Is this what you want?" she asked. It was a practice canvas, but she had accidentally woven in some mild magics. She would have burned it to regain her energy, but this was more exciting.

The painting was of Athena with her owl, both shrouded in darkness and lit only by a single candle, oddly reminiscent of the scene Artemisia found herself in.

She waved the canvas at the griffon, who snatched it from the air with alarmingly fast talons. There was a grating noise as the claws ripped into the painting, and she winced. All that work destroyed in an instant. What had she expected from a beast? Perhaps the stories were just myth.

Then the griffon nosed at the canvas, pinning it to the shingles and rubbing its beak over the center like a cat in catnip. She remembered another bit of lore she'd heard whispered by her father's friends—griffons and their darker counterparts weren't just lured in by magic; they fed on it, supplementing their hunting diets with magics the way humans sipped wine. Could that be true?

Carefully, her candle shaking slightly in her hand, she reached down toward the pointed shoulders of the griffon, waiting to feel the surge of the healing magics spilling from the canvas. Instead, her fingers got nearly close enough to brush its feathers before she pulled back. Whatever it was doing with the magics she'd left inside that painting, the energy wasn't escaping into the air.

She lingered long after the canvas was shredded and the griffon had subsided into lounging on the roof. She stayed standing, worried that too much movement would send it away. The candle lurched in her hand, but she steadied it before it could drop. She had been working late, and her hands were starting to ache deep inside. She wanted to stay, to wring hope from every moment the griffon remained, but her body demanded sleep.

"I... Thank you," she said, knowing it could not understand her. "Be safe."

And she left the roof, certain that it would be gone by morning. Gori could rest easy—this was a blessing, one that would never be repeated in her lifetime. With the entire world beneath its wings, she couldn't imagine the griffon choosing to stay with her.

*

A few days later, Artemisia waited in a grand entrance hall, clutching her bag of sample sketches and paintings close to her side. The ceiling overhead was painted sotto in su, a style which used clever tricks of perspective to make the surface of a ceiling seem endless. These days, most artists used it to make small churches seem larger, giving low, flat ceilings soaring domes made only of paint. This hall was more complex, framing the edges of the ceilings with the bottoms of clouds, and having an array of ancient gods peer over and down. There was Zeus, reaching across the empty space toward his wife, Hera, on the other side, though he kept a nymph tucked under his arm. Aphrodite lounged on a throne of clouds, her hands caressing her bare breasts. Dionysus leaned precariously over the edge of the cloud lip, the wine seeming to spill from his goblet and fall toward those viewing the painting from below.

Since she had moved to Florence, Artemisia had spent time with some of the wealthiest patrons in the city. Still, she was sometimes awed by the art people collected in their homes. The space could have been a museum or church, but it was owned by one man.

She had not recognized the name on the letter when it arrived with the request for her to come to the estate on the west side of the river. Stefano Silvestrini was not a politician, like the Medici, or a renowned businessman like some of her other clients. When she had asked around, she'd learned that he was an older man who had hoarded wealth throughout his life, and, after retirement, began to spend it lavishly.

Even after seven months in Florence, Artemisia's heart fluttered like a bird in a snare when she entered an unfamiliar place. She twisted her amulet with nervous fingers.

She stared at the floor, forcing herself to calm. She was not the helpless girl she had once been, and today's patron would not hurt her. She had weapons she had once lacked—and a true sign of her powerful magics. Despite her fears, the griffon had not left her behind. It had returned every night of the week, greeting Artemisia with purrs and chirps. It felt just as miraculous each time. No matter what the world thought, she tried to remember that she was *special*.

Still, when the doorman returned to the hall to collect her, she jumped at his cough.

She followed him up a broad staircase and down a narrow hall, but she fell behind as she tried to look at all the art they passed. In most homes as grand as this, the displays were carefully choreographed to showcase each piece to its highest appeal. Here, statues littered the floor and the walls were crammed tight with paintings and tapestries. The frames were standardized, likely done by the Silvestrini estate, but the content and style changed dramatically from piece to piece. A light oil portrait of a young woman sat below a vast landscape painting, which was beside a shadowed still life of a dog. Each was done by a different hand, ranging widely in both skill and style.

Then they entered a bedroom, and Artemisia came to a halt entirely. Not because of their destination, though it normally would have tripped her into a panic. The room was so large that it could have been an entrance hall. Dark wooden furniture was polished to a gleam, framing an oversized bed covered in embroidery so dense it was incoherent to the eye.

What caught her attention, though, was the artwork. The clutter from the hallways became riotous in here. The walls were covered by framed paintings from floor to ceiling. Some were standard sizes, but most of the paintings were no larger than a man's head. In addition to the rows and rows of art filling the walls, more paintings, wooden statuettes, rolled papers, and embroidery hoops littered the floor. The clashing colors were like a field of wildflowers against the tile: random, bright, and carelessly strewn.

Surely not every piece of art in the estate could hold magics. It seemed too much for one man. Still, she could feel a thrum of power in the air. It was subtle, a confused haze of different energies that clashed like the sights and smells of a bustling market. Despite the art piled too deep to see, it was less visceral than the energy at the Accademia. If all the pieces did have magics, they were likely tied to someone directly, only spilling into Artemisia's periphery.

It took a rattling cough to draw her attention to the bed. The quilt was so chaotic that she had missed the figure lying beneath it.

The man was older than anyone Artemisia had ever seen outside of Rome.

To the west of the Tiber, wrinkles became far more common than smooth skin. The Vatican was so filled with art from every master in Europe that Church officials lived far longer than the average Roman, drawing their health from the art kept behind locked doors. Though none lived quite as long as Methuselah, the biblical figure famous for living for nearly a millennium, most survived to their hundreds. Pope Eugene III had reportedly lived to be one-hundred-and-fifty years old and had personally ordered three Crusades over the course of his reign.

Most people only lived to be sixty, if they managed to survive infancy and the plague.

"Come," the old man said. The finger he crooked in her direction could have been a bone bleached by the sun.

The servant bowed and left the room as Artemisia approached

the bedside. She perched on the edge of the chair sitting next to the bed. The chair was as expensive as the rest of the house, the wood carved with intricate patterns and the cushion plush and embroidered.

"Lord Silvestrini," Artemisia said. "I am Artemisia Gentileschi."

"I did summon you," he said, voice like rocks tumbling down a well, raspy and distant. "I am old, not senile."

"My apologies," Artemisia said. The room was very quiet.

"Signorina, I am desperate. The artists in this city are simply not making the cut any longer. It sounds mad, but I'm looking for any solution that will work. No one has ever heard of a female painter. Maybe that is the key."

"The key to what, my lord?"

"To life!" Silvestrini exclaimed, and then bent over coughing. The tremors wracked his thin shoulders like waves on the Arno during a storm. "I need art. Powerful art. The Grand Duchess visited me last week and mentioned your work. She's certain that once you unveil your new work for her, you'll be one of the most demanded artists in Florence."

"That's kind of her to say. I brought samples for you to see," Artemisia said, shifting her bag onto her lap.

He shook his head, waving a thin hand. "No, that does not matter to me. What matters are the magics. Have you healed before?"

"Of course," Artemisia said. "I am an artist. A true artist. I learned to tie my magics into a painting in my childhood, the same time I learned how to set a brush to canvas."

"Ah, yes, she mentioned that your father is also a painter. Is he in Florence?"

"No, sorry. Rome."

"Pity," Silvestrini said. "I feel as though I know every artist in this city." He coughed again, just as violently as before. There was a rattle in his lungs that made Artemisia's own chest seize in sympathy. "I need you to paint quickly and regularly. How long does it take for you to finish a miniature?"

Artemisia touched her locket. "For something as small as this, one week." Though the extra energy required for the necrotic touch was far more draining. "For something like those," she continued, pointing to a series of hand-sized paintings on the floor nearby, "three months."

"Pah," Silvestrini huffed.

"Oil has to dry, my lord," Artemisia said, her jaw tightening. He saw her work as something so meager? Something valuable only in how quickly it could be finished? This man would never appreciate her art. "And I have other clients."

"I would pay triple your standard rate for you to prioritize my work."

Her breath stuttered. *Triple?* "Six weeks, then."

"It's a deal," Silvestrini said. "Deliver the first painting in six weeks. My butler will provide you with strands of my hair for the binding—I do not want a drop of the magics to flow into anyone else."

"Of course, my lord." Though blood functioned to tie a work to one client and was ideal for smearing on the base of sculptures, hair was most commonly used by painters.

"This will be a true test of your skills," Silvestrini continued. "Some of the ill get better naturally, with or without your work. There will be no mistakes with me. If your magics do not work, I will know. I'm an old man. If the magics do not keep me alive, nothing will."

"They'll work," she said, raising her chin.

"Good. My life is in your hands, signorina."

*

The next day, Artemisia walked home from the apothecary with a collection of pouches of powdered pigment in a reed basket on her elbow. It was a cold, blustery day, but she felt invigorated. With a griffon on her roof and a commission at triple her rate on the way, things were finally going right.

Her advance from Silvestrini had been enough to replenish her stores, and even buy a small amount of the universally coveted ultramarine. The intense blue was made of precious stones from a desert kingdom across the Mediterranean, imported on trade ships. The color was mostly reserved for depictions of the Virgin Mary—patrons who could commission her iconic blue dress and scarf in ultramarine were considered wealthy. Though Artemisia did not work in such traditional styles, she had an idea to feature the vivid blue against her shadowed designs for a striking contrast.

She passed a group of children in the small alley near her home, gathered in a circle sketching clumsy figures into the dirt with pale chalk. It was a regular sight—kids played artist as often as they played any other game. Perhaps the kids were hoping to discover some latent talent that would bring them glory. Artemisia doubted any of them would be successful. Her father had known early that Artemisia had the gift, and had helped craft it as soon as she was old enough to help crush pigments in his studio. There were traditions and apprenticeships for a reason—art was not as common a gift as people might have hoped. She wondered if the kids would be excited to know she was a real artist.

When she walked up the stairs to her studio door, she found it ajar. Artemisia froze in the dimly lit hall, pulse rabbiting in her ears.

Slowly, carefully, she peered inside. Her studio had been ransacked.

Most of the easels scattered across her studio had been stripped, leaving them standing like bare skeletons. The stretched canvases, many still drying from their last layer of oil, had been stacked carelessly on the floor. Her landlord was in the process of carrying another over to the pile, his fingers smeared with paint.

Artemisia dropped her basket and stormed inside. "What are you *doing*?" she exclaimed, rushing to the pile of canvases. Her paintings were tossed aside like garbage, smearing and ruining months of work. At least one backing frame was broken, tugging the canvas out of place.

"That beast is still on my roof," Gori told her, waving the canvas in his hands for emphasis. "Clicking and cawing and shitting on my tiles. It will scare away new tenants."

"It's *sacred*," Artemisia snarled. "People would be lucky to live near it."

"Artists are deluded. This is my building, and I need tenants," Gori said. "I want it gone."

"We both know it's against the law to harm it," Artemisia said. She imagined her brute of a landlord hurting the griffon and felt her stomach clench. Despite its claws and wings, it was still young. There were no predators in Italy which could harm it, apart from the blood drakes. Would it know how to protect itself from an angry man? "I'll pay you an extra deposit for it," she added desperately.

Gori laughed and dropped the canvas in his hands. It fell paint-first to the floor with a clatter. All her magics. All her work. "With what money, signorina?"

"I'll be getting an enormous payment in six weeks," Artemisia assured him. "I've just gotten a commission from—"

"That isn't soon enough," Gori interrupted, jabbing a finger at her. "This is always the way with you. Promises of future money, but every month, you ask for an extension. Either you give me something now, or you find a new place to live."

It would already take Artemisia weeks to fix the canvases he had stacked, even if they were salvageable enough to not need burning. If she could find the time to spare on them. She had just taken a job that would require all her attention for the next month and a half.

She could not take a break from all those responsibilities to search for a new studio and fight another landlord to allow her to stay. Would Madama Cristina act as a character reference? Artemisia tried and failed to imagine asking the Medici matron to aide her. She needed Madama Cristina to see her as a professional, not as a struggling child. She looked around the studio in a new wave of panic, and pressed a relieved hand to her chest when she saw that Gori had not yet gotten his hands on her commission for the Grand Duchess, which stood tall and dark in the far corner, still drying from her last additions.

Even more fortunate, her revenge was safely tucked behind it, hidden by a heavy drape.

"You could give me a painting."

Artemisia snapped back to stare at Gori. He was looking around the apartment with avarice.

"These have magics in them, don't they? That's why the griffon came to my roof," Gori continued. "One of those could convince me to let you both stay."

"Any one of my paintings takes me months to complete!" Artemisia said, voice rising. "They're worth five times my rent and belong to the men who commissioned them. That *is* my money, signore, and you've just ruined them!"

"Then you have nothing else to offer me," he said, shrugging. "Paint them a new one."

"Starting from the beginning would make me so late that they might cancel the commission together," Artemisia said with the sense of balancing on an uneven tile on the roof. "And I've already spent the stipends on the lost supplies."

"Where will you paint any commissions without a studio?" He asked it as though it were an idle question, but cruelty glinted in his dark eyes. Artemisia knew greed, had seen the pleasure men took in holding power over someone with no recourse.

"You can't do this!" she shouted. "My work does not belong to you."

"Then you'll find somewhere else to live. Tonight."

For a moment, she wished she had not been building her necrotic painting against Tassi specifically. Though she still needed Tassi's hair eventually to complete the final bond, the painting would not harm Gori even if she handed it to him that moment. Her power required patience, but her temper demanded immediate recourse. She longed for the power to crush him the way he had stomped on her art.

But what could she do? She could shout at him, lash him with her amulet, but he owned the building. She did not want to give the authorities a reason to search her flat. If her necrotic painting was discovered, she would lose more than her studio. She would lose her life.

"If I give you this," Artemisia said through gritted teeth, "the griffon stays, you keep out of my studio, and stop threatening eviction every month."

Gori shrugged. "Perhaps."

"No," she said, holding up a finger. "I need your word. This has to be the last time you do this." She pointed toward the damaged canvases. "You'll get a painting, but you can't come in here. I'll pay you each month, but you don't do this *ever* again."

Gori stared at her, small eyes hard and calculating. "Fine," he said. "Pick a painting with strong magics. One that's finished. I know how these work."

"Do you?" Artemisia sneered, looking around her studio. There was only one completed painting in the studio that she had not yet managed to ship off to its new owner, a lord from Spain. She had only just brushed on the varnish that week, and it still sat on its easel to dry. Securing his commission had taken her months of letters and edited sketches. Was this small studio worth sabotaging the commission, her working relationship with the lord, and possibly her reputation?

But what else could she do? Gori could toss her onto the streets without consequence.

"This one," she said, collecting the stretching frame and handing it to Gori. "It's not tied to its commissioner, so anyone who comes into your apartment will feel its effects."

He took the frame, running his fingers over the rough back of the canvas. Had this been his plan from the start? He did not spare a glance for the design on the front. It was a portrait of Mary Magdalene in a gown as golden as the skull in her hands. Like many of Artemisia's portraits of women, it was an image of her own face. Perhaps Gori would feel some sense of shame when Artemisia stared down from his wall. "How long will it last?"

"Considering how many friends you have? A long while," Artemisia said. Unlinked paintings were drained by proximity— Gori would likely pull on its effects for years. Art relied on a cumulative effect, building strength inside the patron to help them get sick less often and less intensely. Fevers would be shortened or not strike at all. As long as the well of magics lasted, he would have the fortitude of, to be precise, a healthy woman in her twenties. Her own energy would propel him onward, granting him a consistency of health a man of his age could rarely find. Like her rent filled his coffers, her life would now fill his veins. "Get out of my studio."

Gori tried to press her for more, but Artemisia was shaking with fury. When she finally shooed him from the studio, she slammed the door behind him. She pressed her forehead against the wood, grinding her teeth. "Stronzo," she swore.

He had won, but she still had her studio, still had her art, still had the griffon. It felt like a small consolation. She took a chair from her kitchen table and wedged it against the door, though it made her feel little safer.

She found her knife and went to the pile of canvases on the floor. Once she separated them, she would have to scrape off any damaged sections, repaint the base with white, and start again—if the magics had not been ruined altogether. She stared down at a crumpled image of her own face, staring balefully back at her over the neck of a lute. It reproached her for not being stronger. At least the griffon had its beak and claws—what did Artemisia have?

She took a deep breath, and got to work.

November rushed by Artemisia in a frantic blur.

With her scramble to finish her first commission for Silvestrini, repairing the paintings Gori had destroyed was slow and painful. The stark white patches where she had scraped off her work and patched a clean canvas looked like canker sores among her dark paintings. She spent all hours at her easel. She might not have tracked the passing of time at all if winter had not clenched its icy fist around Florence. Her visits to the roof to sit with the griffon required bundling herself in layers of clothes and gloves. After everything she had lost to save it, she stubbornly sat on the hard tile beside it until she could not feel her legs. The griffon seemed unbothered by the cold, though its fur had grown paler, dense with a protective layer of downy fur against its skin. Even when she went back into her studio, though, the cold seeped through the walls like poison. There was no escaping it.

Now, it was late in the night, and the world finally seemed still around her. The bells had long since stopped ringing.

With the recent chaos, she had rarely taken nights to dedicate to her private project. Spending time crafting her long revenge seemed like giving up when she had other pressing goals. The design had an ambitious amount of detail, and the seemingly endless scale of the project was intimidating. Now that she had moved into painting her design, she was learning that dark magics were far more draining than those that healed. Sometimes, the magics seemed to be unraveling her guts, leaving her empty in some secret place inside. In comparison to her protective miniatures, which felt like climbing a long flight of steps, this work made her feel as though she had lost a night's sleep each time, aching and hollow.

The moon was high and heavy overhead, and the hours after dark had crept by like the water sludging through the depleted Arno. Sleep had evaded her, and the brief spells she had grasped had scalded her with images of a door clicking shut and heavy hands over her mouth and breast. The dreams had been louder since Gori had broken in. No matter how many commissions she gathered, no matter what necrotic magics she wove into her amulets, she was no more powerful than she'd been at sixteen. Her past would keep haunting her, but she refused to let it win.

She would scour it with fire.

Though her shutters were firmly closed, the winter air bled through the wood and swirled around the empty spaces in her studio. She wore thick, fingerless gloves, a gift from Galileo, but her hands ached still.

Art was not a matter of days, or even months. It would take her another year to complete the work at this pace, especially with how much it drained her energy. She was chipping away at a mountain of marble, crafting the weapon that would finally free her from her past. For her paid work, the wait was to be expected. But for this, the delay was a torment.

Even though Tassi had been exiled from Rome after the trial, she did not trust that punishment to control him. Who knew what horrors he committed every moment he remained alive?

Some nights, that thought haunted her more than her memories.

She had blocked her sketch onto the canvas and was painting in the largest patches of color. As she carefully painted a layer of red onto the border of the canvas, her fingers shuddered. She managed to pull back from the canvas in time, but the brush slipped from her hand and landed on the floor, smearing paint like blood on the wood.

She had only just finished cleaning the stains Gori had left behind.

She paused for just a second, staring, and then stood up and threw her stool across the studio. It struck the wall with a crash.

8

When Artemisia returned to Silvestrini's villa with his first commission, his butler led her again through the vast house to the cluttered bedroom. It was clear that Artemisia was not the only painter in his employ—in just the last six weeks, three new pieces had been added to the pile by his bed: an unframed landscape painted on canvas, a miniature of a comely man, and an ornate charcoal sketch of a blood drake. In stark black lines, the twisting scales and curved horns of the beast were labyrinthine.

"Signorina," Silvestrini greeted her. "You have what I asked for?" As before, he was wrapped with quilts on the bed, more skeleton than man. His skin drooped from his bones as though melting away.

After their first meeting, Artemisia had asked around about the old man. No one knew Silvestrini's exact age. He had been obfuscating it for decades, though no one knew if he was rounding up or down. Either way, it was agreed that the number had passed three digits.

"I finished your painting this week," Artemisia agreed, reaching into her bag to pull out a rolled tube of canvas. "The varnish has just dried." Carefully, she unfurled it and passed it to him. Despite the small size, she'd painted a detailed portrait of Chromatia. Of the twelve Muses, Chromatia, the mythical protector of painting, was one of the most popular subjects in modern artwork. Unlike most representations, which showed a delicate muse floating above a hard-working man, Artemisia had created a paint-stained woman with her curled hair sloppily held in place by a brush. "Despite the time restriction, I believe it's one of my best pieces. I hope you like it."

"Excellent," Silvestrini said, tossing the loose canvas so that it fell among the others.

Jaw clenched, Artemisia watched it settle onto the floor. It blended in with the existing mess, nearly indistinguishable.

"Is there a problem?"

She looked up to find him watching her closely. Despite his age, his brown eyes were sharp.

"No, signore," she said through gritted teeth.

"You can say it," Silvestrini said. "You're not the first artist to be upset. It's the nature of your work—the healing energies come from your dedication to the craft. Without the passion, there's no magic. But your art is a means to an end."

"A means to an end," she repeated, bristling. "Not for me."

"Your part of it is over now."

Artemisia clenched her fists. "Why do you buy art if you don't appreciate it? Why waste my time?"

"I was a healthy young man once. By the time I reached fifty, I had never had more than a sniffle. Then, an artist changed all that." He pressed a hand to his chest as though he were holding himself in place. "I was raised the same as everyone else in the world. I was religious about disposing of the hair from my brushes. Then, I—well, I didn't get lazy. That was never the word for me. But my priorities shifted. They got some of my hair, and that was all it took. I wasn't even in the same city. All it took was my enemy's spite. One day, I was fine. Then, from one moment to the next, I was coughing blood."

Necrotic magics were deeply powerful. At their worst, they created plagues that rippled across continents. The victims, like Silvestrini, cried that the magics were vicious and repellent, unjustified and disproportionate to any claimed sin. The artists rarely lived to defend themselves.

If her work killed her, she could only pray it would kill Tassi first. She would do better than the artist who had failed to finish Silvestrini.

Had Silvestrini deserved the attack? How many artists who used the necrotic magics had a good reason? With Silvestrini's wealth, there were few laws that could touch him. Surely no artist would risk their own death for a petty revenge. She knew its toll. What had Silvestrini done?

"I'm surprised you ever hired an artist again after that," Artemisia said, carefully mild.

"What else was I supposed to do? The body is easy to ruin, but can never be truly healed. The doctors could only help so much," Silvestrini said. "I needed more than medicines—I needed life." And he took it from the artists he paid. Even now, a piece of Artemisia's soul rested on his floor, slowly leaching her energy into his body, attempting to patch the tears created by the necrotic curse so many years ago. "Your craft is your passion, but this is a business transaction. I'll pay you whatever I must for you to accept that and continue your work."

Silvestrini skipped the pretense of valuing her skills, but how many of her patrons truly appreciated her art? How many were more interested in the status symbol or the healing magics than her talent and dedication? If it weren't for the prestige of having a gallery, half of her canvases would likely have been tossed on the floor as well.

Even if she had wanted to hold back her best artistry for the clients interested in her painting itself, she could not do so without compromising the healing magics. Half-hearted effort would spoil an entire painting. He was right—her magics only worked if she gave the work her all, no matter how the end result would be used.

"If you paint me another painting in six weeks, I'll give you an additional bonus on top of our agreed fee," Silvestrini said. "Everyone knows that I only hire the best artists, signorina. If I continue to commission you, your career will only grow. Is that not worth it?"

Could it be worth the money to work for someone she knew did not respect her craft, someone who may have committed unknown crimes? But it was better than ending up on the streets. She needed the work to live, in every sense. It was a compulsion as much as a job.

Even better, if she succeeded here, she could prove that there was more to her than a good eye for composition and detail work. Her magics were as true as any man's. She was an artist on every level.

And the money would only help her standing in Florence.

"I'll have another painting for you in six weeks," she agreed.

Artemisia's favorite apothecary sat across the river in Santa Maria Novella, the neighborhood which orbited the eponymous church. One of the oldest basilicas in Florence, its original façade had been torn down during the Grave Age, but was reconstructed during the artistic revival. The building looked like the flat backdrop of a play with simple geometric patterns in alternating white and green marble.

After an early Saturday morning negotiating for her next batch of pigment, Artemisia slipped through the enormous doors for Mass. The church was draped with the purple accents of Advent, marking this as the most holy time of the year.

At the front of the cathedral, a marble pulpit designed by Filippo Brunelleschi curled around a column, with scenes from the Bible carved in relief and gilded in gold. The famous architect of the Duomo had no magics, but had gained renown for his talented eye. The rest of the church's more replaceable designs—wall paintings and standing statues—would be reserved for magics.

The ceiling over the nave was nearly bare, creating a dramatic effect when it ended at the front of the church, where an intricate stained-glass window hung above the altar, surrounded on every side by a bright fresco. The congregation was surrounded by whites and browns, while the priest would be backed by a riot of heavenly colors. The fresco along the back wall, with clouds and cherubs layered in soft pastels, was an especially gorgeous piece and would certainly have been painted with magics, but it had likely aged past its usefulness. From its style, it must have been a decade old at least. Public church art tended to need replacement more quickly than any other kind. In addition to being a regular gathering place for entire communities, churches were sanctuaries during times of plague. Soon, Santa Maria Novella would need to hire an artist to replace the fresco and invigorate the church with new magics. Though the paintings would not remain on display for long, the commissions paid well and were widely fought for.

Even the basilica was not immune to the cold seeping through the city in the approach to Christmas. The vast spaces of the church were as frigid as their stone walls.

As she looked for a place to stand, she was reminded why she tended to favor the smaller churches near her studio. As one of the pillars of the city, Santa Maria Novella was crowded with people. It was difficult for Artemisia to perform the ceremony of Mass when the press of people on either side of her made her feel as though her skeleton was trying to claw free from her skin.

It had been a long while since she had come through these doors. During her last visit to the church, the preacher Tomasso Caccini had railed at the pulpit about whores who did not remain virgins before marriage, insisting that no woman deflowered before her wedding night would make it into heaven.

After that, she had not come back before today.

Attending Mass at all was one of the concessions Artemisia made to the demands of Florentine society. Even if she wanted to keep working, she had to take time to perform piousness. Bad enough to be the only female painter—she could not be a heretic as well. She would listen to this man say whatever he willed about sullied women or lustful men, keep her face neutral among the flocks of Florence, and then go back to her studio across the river. If she personally questioned the infallibility of a Church that villainized every female since Eve while forgiving the sins of men, she kept it quiet.

Artemisia found a spot near the doors and folded her arms over her chest. She took a deep, grounding breath. The church's strong scents greeted her: warm wax from the candles glowing along the perimeter, the bright spark of incense, and the heady sweetness of white lilies.

After the Latin prayers, Caccini stared over the congregation from his perch inside the heavy marble pulpit. "Sinners of Florence, why do you let heretics spread poison to your ears? Books and pamphlets discrediting the Lord's work have been circulating through the city, treated as points of discussion rather than blasphemous filth," he declared. "Turn away from the heretics who would have you question the Lord's word. Return to God and you will find rest. Repent, confess, and then decide never to sin again! They bring you numbers and drawings and try to reinterpret what God has written in the Book of Joshua. That is the logic of the heretic of the north. Yes, I've heard the claims being made by some in this city. Claims that the sun sits at the center of the universe and the earth—God's earth—is spinning around it."

Murmurs rippled through the congregation. Artemisia flushed with stunned anger. She had expected a standard sermon—she hadn't heard of anyone in the Church addressing Galileo's theories directly. There had been snide comments, but to compare it in the pulpit to Martin Luther was a direct attack. Galileo had been sure that people would realize his logic and accept his findings, but that would be a battle to achieve with one of the most popular churches in Florence publicly scorning him.

"'Say everywhere, "The Lord reigns! The world is established, it shall never be moved."' Psalm 96:10. *That* is the word of the Lord. The world shall never be moved. No number of doodles will change that reality. All of the followers of heretics—all of these so-called mathematicians—are the enemies of true religion."

Glancing around, Artemisia realized she was not the only one made uncomfortable by the bluntness of the sermon. Though some were nodding their heads or listening intently, others were looking away. Artemisia was likely not the only person in the building who had broken bread with Galileo or read his treatises about the world. The Grand Duke himself was immortalized in Galileo's discovery of the Medicean stars.

Caccini was a fiery orator. To hear him speak, Galileo was

the snake in the garden, tempting Adam and Eve with the promise of forbidden knowledge, but offering only eternal damnation. Artemisia clenched her fists in her gown. This man didn't know Galileo's brilliance, much less his kindness. Instead, he proclaimed his ignorant hate in front of one of the largest congregations in Florence.

If there was any question about who precisely Caccini was lambasting, it was made clear at the end of the sermon. "Acts 1:11. 'Ye Men of Galilee, why stand you gazing up in heaven?'" He paused to let the quote sink in, and then continued, "The book of the Lord tells us of those who stood staring up and waiting for Jesus to return while he was ascending to heaven. They were focused only on what they could understand, the things they observed, rather than comprehending that there was a greater force at work.

"And thus, I command you. If you shun the heretical speakings of those on earth who would have you doubt the Lord, you can still placate the wrath of God. Otherwise, I regret to bring you bad tidings." The church was tense and quiet as Caccini said his final words: "There is no place in Heaven for those who would question the word of God."

9

Though much of the value of art came from the healing magics within, the craft was always evolving. An artist could not pour their soul into a painting without passion—one could not be halfhearted with the art without reducing or ruining the magical effects. There had been a renaissance in technique after the Grave Age as artists emerged from hiding back into the public eye, and new styles had continued to develop since then.

There were those who could paint, but not pass along their magics, and those with magics who could never turn it into art. To be a true artist was a gift *and* a craft, which meant practice.

At least once a week, the monastery of Cestello was home to a series of workshops held by the senior members of the Accademia for members aspiring and inducted. Their subjects ranged from the latest techniques for mixing oil paints, to drawing from live models, to exploring the magics inside the artwork. Today, some artists in the classroom were already sketching, with a few others clustered near the front talking to the teacher, Paolo Lamberti.

If she had known he would be their instructor for the day, she would have skipped the lesson. The Accademia rotated among three teachers each season, but she had avoided Lamberti after he had disdainfully thrown her from the anatomical theater.

Artemisia sat with her notebook near the back in the chair closest to the door. She recognized most of the other faces from the monthly meetings, though she had no friends in the room. She set her charcoals in a careful line beside her foot on the ground, and then used one to carefully shade a border onto her paper. She was still thinking of Galileo and the uproar in the three weeks since Caccini's incendiary speech during Advent. Florence had rung in the new year, but the gossip remained cacophonous.

Half the congregation of Santa Maria Novella believed Caccini could do no wrong, and the other half wanted him barred as a radical. Galileo was stuck in his home in the countryside, waging a war of words to defend himself in the court of public opinion.

"Did you hear?" a man hissed to one of their classmates in front of her. There was an edge to his voice Artemisia recognized, the thrill of sharing someone else's bad news. She tensed until he continued with an unfamiliar name. "About Salvatore Vella?"

"The sculptor?" his friend responded, leaning closer. "I haven't seen him around in weeks."

"That's because he's been on trial for murder. He's just been dismissed from the Accademia. Banned for life, if he manages to get out of prison with his neck intact." The first raised his eyebrows, savoring the best news. "They're saying he finished a statue of his ex-lover last month. She dropped dead, vomiting blood, that day."

Artemisia felt as if an icy wind had shot through the monastery, slicing her to the bone.

"Che cazzo?" the other swore. "You think he used dark magics?"

The way he said the words. Horror, disgust, disbelief. Even here, at the heart of art in Florence, necrotic magics were reviled. It was a key tenet of their order, beyond the political or artistic. The Accademia had disavowed Caravaggio after he was accused of killing a man with his painting, though he had later been proven innocent of using necrotic magics. If the Church believed that the politically powerful Accademia permitted the darker side of magic, they would have shut it down. It would be a return to the age before San Donatello, when artists were burned at the stake as demons. The members were instructed only to heal, or else art itself would be in danger.

What would the members say if they learned of her planned revenge against Tassi? She had once imagined awe, or perhaps regret at not seeing her potential earlier, but men rarely changed their minds for the better. Would they see her skill or just use the rules she had broken to justify having never respected her? In crafting her revenge, she was creating a tool they could use to rob her of her legacy.

But playing by their rules had never earned their respect either.

"What else could it be? Keep an eye out for a blood drake next. I'm sure it'll be circling soon. Apparently she broke his heart, stole his money, and ran off with some—"

Lamberti called for their attention, silencing the gossips. Artemisia took a deep breath to calm herself, trying not to watch the two students in front of her. Lamberti surveyed them for a moment, and then launched into his lecture. "Painting is a flat medium, but your finished work should never *appear* flat. There should be depth, layers, and—as we will be discussing today—textures."

Using several of his own oil paintings at the front of the room as examples, Lamberti walked them through his techniques for creating a variety of textures. His focus was on fabrics which, from the lush gray and brown fur on the collar of one of his portraits, were a specialty of his.

After a half-hour lecture, he said, "Try it yourself. You're working with charcoals today, of course, but if you understand the basics, the skills should apply. No magics, unless you want to be stuck burning your pages at the end. By now, all of you should know how to hold that back during practice."

For several minutes, the room was filled only with the sound of quiet scratching. Artemisia was accustomed to charcoals. Her sketches were done entirely in the medium, which allowed her to shade heavily to indicate future dark shadows. Her fingers seemed forever blackened with its dust.

As Artemisia was confident in her skills with silks and wools, she attempted to mimic Lamberti's masterful fur texture across her page. It was difficult—she did not paint many animals—but she liked the result.

The paper was snatched from under her hand and held up above her head. Artemisia grabbed for it instinctively, but stopped herself when she saw Lamberti looming over her desk. Though a narrow man as angled as a blueprint, he seemed to take more space than he should have. "Now this," he said, drawing the attention of the rest of the class, "is how *not* to draw fur."

In front of Madama Cristina's guests, who respected her, or in the middle of a crowd, which ignored her, Artemisia was slowly losing the clawing tangle of fear in her chest her trial had instilled at the threat of scrutiny. But the eyes of her fellow students were mocking, knowing, and Artemisia was frozen in her seat.

"Fur is natural. You, like this woman, may think that fur is simply a row of exact, repeated lines, but that is not how nature appears. I am the first to advocate order, but not in this. Fur must have a sense of movement—and disorder—to be believable. This will not fool anyone, and will take the viewer out of your art."

"I…" Artemisia cleared her throat as Lamberti's frown added to the weight on her shoulders. "Those aren't just straight lines."

"You didn't do enough," Lamberti said dismissively, and handed the paper back.

She stared down at the paper. They *weren't* just repeated lines. Perhaps they were less disordered than he wanted, but they weren't as bad as the student next to her, and *he* hadn't been humiliated in front of the class.

Artemisia sank down in her chair until the workshop ended, and then kept her head down as everyone else packed to leave. They filed out the door without speaking with her.

After everyone else had gone, Artemisia went to the door and propped it open, and then turned back to Lamberti. "Have I done something to offend you, signore?" she demanded. The hallway leading from the classroom toward the center of the monastery was behind her, and she could still hear the footsteps of the other students. The escape route was a small comfort.

"If you cannot accept criticism, you should not be an artist," Lamberti said. He'd finished packing his example canvases and held his bag loosely by his side.

Clenching the doorframe, she said, "You singled me out for no reason."

"Or perhaps you're not as good at drawing as you think you are," Lamberti said. He tapped his fingers on the strap of his bag. "I told you not to pursue membership."

"There's no rule against me trying to join."

"Yet." Before Artemisia could respond to that, he continued, "You are attempting to squeeze your way into Florence's art society. First the Accademia, then the Medici. I expect you're looking to take them down. You are friends with Galileo, after all."

"Galileo has done nothing wrong. If you believe the truth is controversy, that is your problem."

"I'm not alone. Galileo's words are poison. Caccini is a wise man, a holy man, and he's trying to protect this city."

"Caccini is a fool."

Lamberti's face broke into a disgusted sneer. "You are dangerously arrogant. You seem drawn to controversy. It seems to me that you came from Rome with a plan to cause trouble. I heard an interesting story the other day from a renowned artist visiting from there. He had known you well. Paul Bril."

Her heartbeat tripped.

It had been nearly two years since the last time she had seen Paul Bril. He was a well-respected Flemish painter who worked in Rome, known for broad, sweeping landscapes populated in miniature by the figures of mythology. Bril was her father's contemporary, but had fallen out with the Gentileschi during the trial.

He had, after all, been the defendant's teacher.

Agostino Tassi and his old teacher had turned most of Rome's artists against the Gentileschi. Artemisia had won the case, but had lost nearly all of her supporters to their vicious rumors. In the end, even her father had severed ties to save his career.

Artemisia spoke through numb lips. "Paul Bril is no friend of mine."

"So it seemed." Lamberti clasped his hands. "I knew there was something odd about you, and he was happy to tell me the details."

"I'm sure he was," she said, glancing back over her shoulder toward the hallway. She needed to leave. She could not stand here and have this conversation with this man.

"You should not be so flippant. You ruined a man's life."

Artemisia spluttered. It was difficult to form words in her

flood of disgusted fury. Finally, she demanded, "*I* ruined *his* life?"

"I've heard that Agostino Tassi was a good man. You dragged him through the mud for your own gain."

"I was searching for justice," Artemisia snarled.

"He was found guilty, thanks to your lies. Punished by the court. I do not want to see that happen to my colleagues here. Not every court is wise enough to annul unjust punishments."

She froze. "*Annulled?*"

"Exile was a harsh punishment for such a promising artist. Bril fought hard to have his pupil freed."

It had been barely a year. After everything she had suffered before and during the trial, Tassi's exile had been just a short vacation to the countryside.

She felt hot and cold all over, and her hands throbbed to remind her of the lasting damage she would keep from that trial. Why had no one told her? Then again, what allies did she have left in Rome? Had they all welcomed him back with open arms?

"Even if—*if*—Tassi were a good man, whose life was ruined?" Artemisia asked. "Who is here among strangers, among enemies, and who is already back in Rome? Which of us lost their friends and family, and which of us was given a token punishment?"

"Yes, I've seen your suffering," Lamberti said dryly. "You have a commission with the Medici and the ear of Galileo. You're worming your way into influence."

Artemisia's breath caught in her throat. What could she do? Tell Lamberti of her sleepless nights, haunted by a man who had attacked her in the safety of her bedroom? Of the meals skipped to pay rent? Of the silence between her and her father for the past year, dead and unyielding as a crypt? Lamberti had no right to her pain, and would only see it as the penalty she had earned for daring to challenge a more successful painter.

"If you are here to find another tutor to discredit, I feel obliged to tell you to turn your gaze from the Accademia," Lamberti continued. "I have worked my entire life for this organization. I first apprenticed for a member when I was only nine years old. I will not stand for a viper to destroy our work."

"I only ever told the truth," Artemisia snapped. She took a deep breath. This argument was taking them nowhere, and she could not talk to him anymore. She had fought this war already—fought it and won, she had thought. Had none of it mattered? *Annulled.* "I came here for a professional critique, not a personal one."

"Then listen to that instead," he said. "I'm not here to coddle your delicate sensibilities, signorina. Improve, or don't come back."

Artemisia left the monastery, her crumpled sketch still clutched in her trembling fist.

That night, she worked on her Judith until her eyes and hands ached. She pushed aside all thoughts but this: she would have her own justice, no matter the cost.

The candles burned down to their stubs, but she did not move to replace them.

In the middle of February, the chains of winter unexpectedly lifted for a day, bathing the city in sunlight. Some alleys, shadowed, were still chilled, but one would turn a corner onto a sunlit street and be lured forward by a breath of warmth and light. It was a welcome reprieve—and all of Florence agreed, from the press of the crowd around them.

The markets at the heart of the city's squares were bursting with wares. Though they lacked the fruits that would perfume the air in a few months, dried bundles of flowers and herbs dangled from the stalls alongside the crafts the citizens had spent the long winter creating. Intricately woven rugs hung beside glazed earthenware and colorful shawls. The market was set up in the sprawling Piazza Santa Croce in front of the dignified façade of the basilica. The stalls turned the open space into a maze, with some wares spilling into the narrow aisles to create even more cramped quarters.

Artemisia was bundled up in wool, always sensitive to the cold, and turned her face into the sun when she could. Her recent long nights on her Judith were taking their toll, leaving her skin cold and chest hollow. No amount of work seemed fast enough to undo the injustice of Tassi's freedom.

"Are you all right?" Galileo asked, leading her through the market.

"Fine," she said with a brief smile. "You've been busy. I wondered if I'd ever see you again outside of scribbled letters."

"As though Tomasso Caccini could scare me away," Galileo said. She walked close behind him, avoiding the jostling citizens of Florence. She rarely ventured out into such crowds, but she had not been able to turn down the rare invitation from her friend. It had been nearly two months since Caccini's sermon at Santa Maria Novella had ignited a firestorm of controversy in Florence—and she could not spend another day alone in her studio. "Oh, Artemisia. The ignorance that surrounds us is astounding sometimes."

"Always. It seems as though the public is on your side, at least," she assured him. It was a relief, in a way, to focus on Galileo's troubles rather than her own. "He was an ass. Comparing you to Martin Luther. Does he want to get you killed?"

"His own friends seem to think he overstepped as well. The preacher general of Caccini's order wrote me an apology," he said, smirking.

"No!"

"Oh, yes. The Church hasn't quite determined what to do about me, and his blatant attack put them in a position to decide before they are ready."

"That's why you've finally emerged victorious. I'm glad to see it. Tell me, did you burn the letter?"

"I'm sure they made copies to send around to excuse Caccini," Galileo said. He sighed. "The more irrefutable evidence I find for my theory, the more determined the Pigeon League is to smear my name."

The Pigeon League was the derogatory nickname for the group of natural philosophers and religious officials who had joined together against Galileo. The name was appropriate—they picked and pecked at his discoveries, attempting to tear them apart, though they fled at any sign of real danger.

Did Galileo know there were those like Lamberti in the Accademia who sympathized with the Pigeon League as well?

"Are you worried?" she asked. "They're getting bolder."

He shrugged. "The Church will never take their side," he said, pausing to look at a row of scarves. "I've proven my theories with both mathematics and observation. The Church will not deny the facts."

"Won't they?" she asked. "In my experience, people tend to listen when furious men make public pronouncements about one's sins."

"I can only let the truth speak louder," Galileo said. "You wrote that a griffon is still sleeping on your roof? Let me enjoy some good news."

She let him change the subject, though her faith was not nearly so strong as his. "Nearly every night."

"I hope to see it one day," he said, wistful. "Have you been giving it your art?"

"When I can spare it," she said. "Only small pieces—mostly miniatures. It tears into them like they're plump rabbits."

"That should be enough. It's likely also absorbing the excess magics that spill up through your roof when you work. Have I told you I know a man at Padova who researches griffons? Blood drakes may have gotten the name, but there's a blood bond between griffon and artist as well. After long enough absorbing your work, it will stay tied to your magics. It's a connection of the humors. It's supposed to be good luck."

"Good luck, eh? For the amount of magics it has taken from me, its belly is worth a fortune. I've felt like half a fool, some nights, letting it destroy good canvas," she grumbled, though her heart felt warm. Sleep was an elusive companion for her lately—many nights, she left her easel only to bundle herself in blankets and sit on the roof. Every time she glimpsed the tan fur and sleek wings of the beast, it felt like a benediction. She was good. She was skilled. She was worthy. Money was tight, the Accademia was distant, her commissions were a slow trickle, and Tassi was free, but the griffon was evidence that success was in her reach.

Even when she came up directly from handling her Judith, the griffon did not shy from her. What more evidence did she need that her cause was just? Even her companion knew Tassi deserved what came for him.

"Luck rarely comes without a price. You're fortunate to encounter such a creature. It's a rare gift indeed. It was the buzz in a letter I received from one of my friends at the Accademia. Sigismondo Coccapani is seething with envy."

"He seems all right, but I'm sure half of them don't believe it to be true. They still barely look at me during the monthly meetings."

Galileo's pleasure faded. "For such a creative institution, they are stuck in tradition." He shook his head. "They'll learn. I'm sure they will. You have to persevere. Now, let's go in here," he added, gesturing to a stall covered in gauzy fabric across the aisle.

The stall was filled with small metal tins of varying sizes, and from the overwhelming smell of flowers and herbs, it belonged to a healer. Artemisia frowned, following him over. "If you need a painting, you only have to ask. I would make you my top priority."

He shook his head. "I don't need art from the great Artemisia Gentileschi for a small muscle ache," he said. "My neck grows stiff staring up at the stars, and I've found there are salves that relax it. The continued pecking of the Pigeon League has made those small aches worse of late."

Artemisia huffed, arms crossed, as she examined the rows of small tins. "Then go to a doctor," she said. "There's nothing you can't get from them or from me. These things don't work."

"Have you bothered to try them?" a woman asked from behind them.

Artemisia turned, and her cheeks—which always betrayed her—flushed red. The stall's keeper was a woman around a decade older than Artemisia. Her skin was tanned from time in the sun, with fine wrinkles lining her forehead like bent grass in a windswept field. She had dark hair and dark eyes, and was glaring at Artemisia.

"So, you're a painter?" the woman asked, confirming that she had been listening to their conversation.

"I am," Artemisia said, lifting her chin. "I've been training with healing magics since I was a little girl."

The woman scoffed. "So have I." She lifted a tin from the table and removed the lid, letting the waft of lavender fill the stall. "These medicines I make heal more than some painting produced every three years."

Artemisia hummed skeptically.

"Your friend clearly trusts in my work," she said, gesturing at Galileo. "He's been here before."

He nodded. "Your wares are the best in the city. Artemisia, you know I've studied bodies and magics, and the ways we have tried to heal ourselves since the beginning of time. Paintings are the most powerful, but the most unfocused and the least urgent. The energy you lay into a canvas must be a well that can be tapped for months, if not years. A doctor at a hospital might use laudanum to ease a patient's suffering, or bloodletting to reduce a fever. But for the everyday aches, these mixtures help the body do what it wants to do naturally." He reached forward and brushed a finger in the salve the woman was holding. He rubbed it into his hand and sniffed carefully. "Beeswax. Did you know that beeswax, like honey, never spoils? It's one of the few eternal compositions in nature. Even San Leonardo used beeswax in his experiments to create smoother oil paints."

Artemisia peered around the stall. The tins did not look impressive. "I suppose," she said, unconvinced.

The woman put the lid back on the salve and set it down. "You think my work is less than yours?" she asked. "I would rather find small natural remedies for common ills than sell pieces of my soul to the highest bidder. Not all healing has to come at a cost."

Artemisia stared at her, taken aback. She opened her mouth, but then closed it.

The woman was right, in essence. Since she had been young, a toddler wandering around her father's studio, Artemisia had been taught that art was the process of tapping into one's soul and pouring it into a creation. That creation was then sold to the Church or another patron, giving the artist an audience and the money to survive another day.

Even so, it was the work of saints. It was the most noble calling in the world—Artemisia was doing something important.

She tried not to think of the pile of discarded paintings growing on the floor beside Silvestrini's bed.

"Doesn't every job take some part of one's soul?" Artemisia challenged. "A man in the fields sacrifices his body. Even you've sacrificed your time for this."

"Yes, but artists die young," the woman reminded her, unknowingly quoting Artemisia's own father. "They siphon their energies into their work, and feed the elite with their lifeblood."

Galileo was unusually quiet. She wondered if he was waiting for her response, or if he agreed with the shopkeeper and did not want to say.

"Would you say that of San Donatello?" Artemisia asked, pointing at the red behemoth of Santa Maria del Fiore that loomed over Florentine life. "He didn't sell his soul for profit. He saved hundreds of lives."

"Allora," the woman prevaricated, waving her hand. "There are some exceptions. But most is hoarded by those who can afford it, at the cost of the artists—and the people who really need the help. Why should popes live to be one-hundred-and-thirty when there are children dying in villages all throughout Catholic lands? Every famous artist is well-known because they valued their legacy above healing the sick."

The blow hit. Healing was inextricable from art, but it had never been Artemisia's focus. She was no doctor, no selfless martyr—she wanted her skills to be admired, not tucked away in some forgotten town. She flung up her hands. "If you acknowledge that art is so draining, that it takes such a toll on the artist's life, how can you expect us all to donate our work to every person in the world, and starve before we can even run out of magics?"

The healer merely shrugged. "I never claimed to have all the answers."

Artemisia huffed and looked at Galileo, pointing at the woman. "You see?"

Galileo shrugged. "You both have a point."

She narrowed her eyes at him. "You, Galileo, the man who jumps at the opportunity to debate in any forum, says we both have a point?" she asked. "Are you finally learning how to take the middle ground?"

He chuckled. "Artemisia, you know that I value your work. I've been studying the mechanics of art the same way I've studied the sun and the tides. I know the work you've put into building a career, and creating masterpieces of technical skill and creative integrity. But it does sadden me, at times, to know that you are devoting your life to such a select group of patrons, who do not fully appreciate you. And knowing that," he added, turning to the healer, "I know that painting is not the only source of healing. During the Grave Age, there were more than a hundred years where all art was done secretly, and only alternative healing was acceptable. But there was a reason for the renaissance. Art saves life, and they fight for humanity. San Donatello, to use Artemisia's example, died creating his statue. It is too much for any artist to heal the world. But they do what they can, the same as you."

The woman looked away. "Allora. I do not envy the artists' job," she said, and though neither tone nor word implied it, Artemisia thought it was a shade of an apology.

Artemisia glanced around the stall again. "My hands...ache

sometimes," she said finally. "Do you have something you would suggest I try?" The words stuck in her throat, plucked out like comb from honey, but both of her companions seemed pleased by the effort.

The woman glanced down at Artemisia's hands, which twisted under the scrutiny, and then she decisively plucked a small tin from the table. She handed it over, nudging the lid aside and gesturing for Artemisia to smell the contents. Overwhelming, the scent was of mint, though she could also detect hints of the beeswax Galileo had mentioned, along with elderberry. "Rub this into your hands at night," the woman said, "and then tell me that there is no power in nature."

Artemisia and Galileo paid for their respective salves. The baiocci clanged in the woman's apron, and she nodded to them both. Before they could leave, she added to Artemisia, "If you ever decide you want to discover healing without sacrificing yourself upon its altar, come find me."

"I've never been called an angel before," Maurizio commented, settling into the pose she had instructed. Her current commission—one of her rare requests for a male subject—was of the archangel Michael defeating Satan. Many artists portrayed Michael with delicate features, as though he were a pampered prince taking his afternoon riposo. The leader of God's army usually looked as though he wouldn't be out of place at one of the Medici's salons.

Instead, Artemisia had called upon Maurizio to pose. From his work in the summer orchards, Maurizio was built with broad shoulders and thick legs, like someone who could hold his ground and grapple in the heavens against Satan.

Used to her demands, Maurizio was posing against the back wall of her studio with robes draped over his body and a prop stick in one hand. He no longer bothered to pretend to resist the various outfits she laid out for him. During winter, she provided a source of income, and after she'd shown him the result of their first finished painting together, he had decided that he enjoyed being immortalized in her style.

The Accademia still would not allow her into the anatomical theater, and she had found she learned more studying Maurizio than in their other workshops with less chance of encountering that scum Lamberti. She would train herself if they would not.

"Bend your right elbow in, and tilt your head down a bit," Artemisia instructed. "Would you rather I cast you as Satan?" she added dryly.

"It might be more fitting."

She laughed. "I tend to imagine Satan as a bit prettier. No offense."

"None taken. So, to you, Michael looks like me, and Satan looks like a prince," Maurizio said.

"Satan is silver-tongued and arrogant. Michael is the head of an army. Which do you think owns more mirrors?" He chuckled, tilting his head to acknowledge her point. "It doesn't matter for this piece; I'm making Satan a snake."

"So I guessed," Maurizio said, shrugging his shoulders slightly to indicate his posture. She had him half-crouching, as though about to strike the ground with what would become a flaming sword on the canvas. "Besides, I can't imagine you finding a second model."

Artemisia frowned, sketching Maurizio's outline in broad strokes. Were her financial woes so obvious? She still struggled to pay for her supplies and rent, but she was a breath away from finishing her commission for Madama Cristina. It would be her most public piece to date, bringing her fame that a half-dozen pieces for Silvestrini could not offer. "I would hire someone else if needed," she said finally.

"But you'd avoid it as long as you could. You wouldn't trust anyone else in your studio," he said.

"You think highly of yourself."

"You know, this would all be easier if you got a husband."

It would. She could have hired studio assistants and models with no fear for her reputation. Gori would not barge into her studio if there were another man present. All she would have to do was sacrifice the independence she had fought for with blood and pain. "And your life would be easier if you got a wife."

"I'm not picking a fight," he said. "My life would be far worse with a wife. What I am, it's an open secret. These things usually are. Half the men in this city have had encounters with other men—if not more. For some of them, it's simply what's available. Women are not permitted to have sex outside of marriage. Men are. It doesn't take a genius to see the numbers don't match. It's mostly accepted, but the government would prefer for everyone to have sex that creates new citizens."

"Has the Office of the Night caused problems for you?"

The Office of the Night, the judicial panel exclusively dedicated to pursuing charges of sodomy, was more perfunctory than malicious. After the first plague, the city's population had been forced to fight to revitalize, and those not pursuing marriage were seen as not doing their part. With the addition of priests like Caccini who wed themselves to the Bible's most intolerant laws, Florence had been coerced into action.

"It's not the Office of the Night that causes the most trouble. They are just doing their jobs. They know that if they sentenced every sodomite in the city, half the workers would be locked up. They hand out fines and then look the other way. It's more difficult for those of us in my neighborhood than the rich folk, but we survive. The real trouble is the religious fanatics, the hypocrites who want us burned at the stake. They're not the authority anymore. The Grand Duke is strict, but not unreasonable. But men's minds change. If enough people die in the next plague, the consequences may grow stricter. Dear Cosimo doesn't want to rule an empty city.

"You said you saw some of our lovely ladies of the night on your way to find me in Santa Croce. Do you know why this upstanding city has municipal brothels? They know people will find ways to have sex, and prostitution is a sin, but a lesser one than sodomy. It's one they can use."

She frowned. "It's only fines now, but what if they start sending people down to the burelle?" After her trial in Rome, the threat of the dungeons under Florence made Artemisia's stomach twist with fear. "Is there a way for you to hide from them?"

He shrugged, nearly upsetting the gold cloth draped around his neck. "Of course I could hide. I've known men who go their whole lives never acting on their desires. But that seems to me like picking between two miseries. If you could dress as a man to get more work, would you?"

Artemisia considered that, rolling its sour taste on her tongue like a wine. "No. I'd rather fail as who I am than succeed with a mask."

He nodded. "You understand. Though I believe you're living a more hidden life than I. When we met, I assumed you couldn't find a husband, but I know that's not it. You have money, and you're not unattractive."

"As though you would know."

"I prefer men, but I have eyes," Maurizio pointed out.

"My father wanted to arrange a marriage for me when I came to Florence," Artemisia admitted. "Some mediocre artist with no skill or personality to speak of. He thought that I needed a husband to navigate the new city—and to fight back against the rumors from Rome." Like the ones brought to eager ears by Paul Bril.

"The ones you won't tell me about."

"Those," she said. "Look, I would rather be struggling to pay my rent than having a husband I hate in my bed."

"It seems to me that you don't want any man at all in your bed," Maurizio said. "I've known you for half a year and I've never known you to take a lover."

"I'm too busy for lovers." The thought turned her stomach, making anxiety creep up her throat.

"The other artists in the city seem to have them," he pointed out. "Most of them seem to be on my side of things, but there are men who would understand your passion. Women, too."

"I don't want anyone in my bed," Artemisia snapped. "I'd burn my bed in the forest if I could rid myself of the need for sleep."

"It looks as though you've already done that," he said gently. When she frowned, he pointed at her face before taking up the pose again. "You look exhausted, Artemisia. You've lost weight. I'm sure you haven't been sleeping. You're wasting away in front of me."

How exhausted must she have looked for her gruff model to worry? Still, the drain from her necrotic work would be worth it in the end when she succeeded. Her body was a vessel for her art, and nothing more. If it could not keep up with the demand, she did not have time to coddle it. There was justice to be dealt.

"I'm still here," she said. "And I'll stay here as long as I keep doing the work."

"The work is what's draining you. Your hands have been trembling all day."

She looked down. They were shaking, fiercely grasping her notebook and charcoal. The ache in her fingers was a constant companion, but the tremor had gotten worse lately. She had not yet opened the salve she had bought with Galileo in the market. To do so would feel like admitting defeat. She needed to push her way through.

She gritted her teeth and forced the charcoal against the page. When her hands stilled, it sent the tremor up her arm and into her head. She felt as though she were a bell ringing over the city, the clang rattling in the shell of her body. "I'll be fine," she said.

"So you say," he said, and quieted so she could finish her sketch.

10

E vents, dinners, and meetings were held nearly every night of the week at the Palazzo Pitti. Often, the Medici put the city's prime talents in the room with ambassadors from abroad. Recently, Artemisia had shown her sketches over dessert and snared a new patron from Alexandria. Other nights, the Grand Duke hosted philosophers from across the continent to debate for everyone's entertainment. It was always a lavish affair, a silk and gold waterfall that draped the city's influencers in the Medici's favor.

Tonight was the first time Artemisia was the star.

Certain artwork was forced to remain secret as a side-effect of its magics. Untargeted paintings and statues were usually kept behind locked doors until the magics were fully drained by the clients. However, since Artemisia had collected strands from Madama Cristina and pressed them into the last few layers of paint, only Madama Cristina would feel its soothing effects. For the next year—or even longer, considering how much energy Artemisia had successfully infused—Madama Cristina would sleep easily, even if the painting hung publicly in their gallery.

The effects, in truth, had started the week before, as Madama Cristina had confided to her before the party began. It was Artemisia's intent that created the magics, and her intent that declared them ready. Once she painted on the final layer of varnish and sat to write the letter informing Madama Cristina, the magics were released. As with all art, it was a matter of will and purpose. From the kiss the Medici matron had pressed to her cheek when she had arrived, Artemisia knew the painting was successful. Like a farmer, she had spent months toiling before she could enjoy the fruit, but this success could change her fortunes.

With this success, she felt alive in a way she hadn't since learning of Tassi's freedom.

Madama Cristina had suggested the public unveiling. The Medici took any excuse to throw a party. Wine filled every glass around the gallery, as free and lush as Artemisia's pleasure. Liveried servants carried trays of raw oysters, fried artichoke hearts, and pickled vegetables each speared with a small gold toothpick.

The room bustled with the Medici's favorite politicians, artists, and merchants, milling around and enjoying the party. Tonight, they were gathered to celebrate Artemisia, making her truly part of the Medici's collection of favored artists. Once everyone was pleasantly tipsy, Madama Cristina gathered the crowd and called Artemisia to the front. Every eye was on her, but instead of the usual scalding unease, she simply felt a swell of pride as Madama Cristina thanked her formally for the painting. When she pulled aside the cloth to reveal the shadowed figure of Artemis crouched in a wood with her hounds teeming at her feet, murmurs of appreciation rippled through the room.

For too long, she had feared the attention of others. Her trial in Rome had scarred her in many ways.

Here she was respected, *celebrated*. This crowd did not want to tear her down—they wanted to share in her success. It was everything she had dreamed of.

Tassi may have been spared from his exile, but her struggles had not been futile. She was here in the heart of the Medici's power and he was not. Learning of his annulment had sent her scrabbling in the dark, desperate and furious, draining her potential to craft her revenge. In the glittering light of the Palazzo Pitti, that fear seemed far away. She savored the applause, determined to absorb this success as much as she had been branded by every failure.

The weight of the coins on her belt added to her mood. She had earned fifty silver scudi from her work—a small fortune after scrounging for baiocci.

As Madama Cristina left to make her rounds, Artemisia scanned the room, looking for her next target—what better place to confirm more commissions than a party full of Florence's wealthiest patrons, all able to see the proof of her skill? Her career was set to blossom, and she was eager to seize every opportunity.

To her surprise, she noticed Grand Duke Cosimo II standing in the back, watching her. His mother still retained her independence and power, and operated separately from her son on many of her projects. She had seen the Grand Duke in passing during her various meetings at the Palazzo Pitti over the last year, but he stayed distant. The most powerful man in Florence. She was as eager for his approval as she was intimidated by his attention.

When the Grand Duke's presence stopped dazzling her, she realized he was standing beside Paolo Lamberti. Lamberti's expression was shuttered, but she hoped he was seething inside. He had used his power to remove her from the anatomical theater and had gloated about his conversation with Paul Bril, but in the end his scorn meant nothing. He had not managed to stop her from climbing here to the center of Florentine society.

The Grand Duke patted him on the shoulder with a murmured word, and then crossed the room toward Artemisia.

She took a quick breath and curtsied. "Your Grace," she said, hoping her voice did not tremble. "It's a pleasure to meet you."

He nodded, accepting her obsequience as his due. "The Grand Duchess has spoken highly of you."

She was relieved he did not mention Lamberti. "I hope that my work may add some glory to her name," Artemisia murmured.

"Your subject was a bold choice for your first grand piece in Florence. A painting of Artemis by Artemisia," the Grand Duke said, looking up at the display.

She swallowed. Was that censure? "One has to be bold, don't you think? I'm looking to be remembered."

He nodded. "It's a beautiful work. The Grand Duchess seems well pleased. I'm glad to see that her trust was not misplaced."

"Thank you, Your Grace."

The Grand Duke nodded once more, and moved back into the crowd. She stared after him, satisfaction rising like sunlight in her chest. The painting had taken almost a year to complete, impeded by Silvestrini's demands and her own limitations, but all the energy and time she'd funneled into it had been worthwhile for this. *This* was what she had dreamed of when she first picked up a paintbrush. This room full of admirers looking at her work and knowing her name.

Another man approached her at the front of the room with a warm, conspiratorial smile. He was middle-aged with a black moustache and pointed goatee that overwhelmed his face, though he carried the style with confidence. "This is quite the crowd. Everyone is buzzing. You must be quite proud."

"I am," she said without shame.

"Good—it's a gorgeous piece. I've been looking forward to meeting you. Galileo is a good friend of mine. We met in Pisa when he was teaching there. He's told me all about you. I had to see your work for myself."

"It's nice to meet you, Signore...?"

"Michelangelo Buonarroti," he said, taking her hand and brushing a kiss across the back. "Not *that* one, of course," he added with a knowing smile. "The Younger. I'm the cousin of the late artist."

Artemisia blinked. She had met artists of all calibers over the years, but few names garnered the same universal awe as Michelangelo. From what Artemisia had heard, he had painted the entire interior of the Sistine Chapel in the heart of the Vatican. The magics in that room alone were enough to keep the Pope and his cardinals in full health to this day. Though his works in Rome were still coveted so the Church could drain the last of his magics, Artemisia had seen the towering statue of David sitting in the Piazza dei Signori across the river. For its first few years, it had been part of a series of statues that stood in Santa Maria del Fiore beside San Donatello's first, but once its magics had been absorbed by the structure's regular visitors, the statue had been moved to the piazza for the populace to enjoy. In a world where the value of art was tied to its magics, the *David* had become famous for the sheer skill in its design.

Everyone presumed that Michelangelo would be canonized soon, joining Donatello and Raffaello as one of the great artistic saints.

"Are you a sculptor or a painter?" she asked. Michelangelo the Elder had been a rare master of both, though he had infamously preferred sculpting.

"Neither. I'm a poet and a scholar," he said. "I have an eye for art, though, and you have the confident style of someone much older. Is it true that your work used to be mistaken for your father's?"

"It is. He was also a student of Caravaggio's style. I'm attempting to build my own name now, of course." Would her father learn of her success here today? She had not heard from him since she left Rome. She was unsure if he would be proud of her, or disappointed she had not failed as he had expected. He was a stubborn man, and she had defied him in leaving Rome as she had.

He tilted his head. "I do know what it is like to attempt to compete with a talented relative. That's part of the reason I never seriously attempted art. No need to embarrass myself, and I found that I was quite skilled with the written word anyway." He looked around at the gathered faces. "Where *is* our friend Galileo? I was sure I would see him here."

She sighed. "I'm sure you've heard of the current business with the Church. The pigeon Caccini and his friends refuse to stop their pecking. They have involved the Inquisition. Galileo is busy writing letters to Rome to defend himself as well as he can. Their slander grows more outlandish by the day."

"Surely that's a formality," Michelangelo said. "Everyone who knows Galileo knows his faith—and anyone with a mind of their own can know his work. He should have been able to step away from his desk for one party. He was invited, wasn't he? Galileo is close to the family, and they won't be intimidated by gossip. It's not as though Caccini has the full support of the Church. He's surely an outlier."

"Galileo insisted his presence would distract from my success." The disappointment at his absence resurfaced with an ache, so she covered it with a smile. "I pointed out that all good parties cause some gossip, but he wouldn't have it."

"He doesn't give a fig about his own reputation, but he worries about his friends. It's good advice. There's no reason to throw away your career for him if things take a turn for the worse. You're no Medici." Before she could argue, he continued, "I'll be sure to drop by and visit him in person while he works on eviscerating the Pigeon League. I'll feed him grapes or something."

Artemisia snorted. "Considering how often he forgets to eat when he's absorbed in his work, that would likely be appreciated."

"Excuse me."

Artemisia turned. A handsome man close to her age waited beside them. In contrast to Artemisia, who wore the same gown she donned for every Medici gathering, his clothing was nearly art in itself. His green velvet doublet, fashionably cut to his waist rather than draping over his hips in the older style Michelangelo wore, was accented with bead-studded brocade and gold satin ribbons. His strong nose and bright eyes were familiar, but Artemisia was too abuzz from the spotlight to identify him.

"It's good to see you again," he said. "It's been a long time. You've come far since your first night here."

"You," Artemisia said. It was the merchant she'd sat next to the same night she met Galileo nearly a year ago. "Luckily there is no silverware here for me to swoon over."

"I'm sure I can find something else to tease you about," Francesco Maria Maringhi said with a bright smile.

"I'm sure," she said coolly.

Michelangelo gave a quiet excuse and slipped away. Artemisia spared him a quick nod, but Maringhi kept her attention. "Congratulations. A commission from the Medici! I would be drinking wine on the roof."

"In this weather, that seems more of a torment than a joy, vostra signoria," Artemisia said. Spring was starting to fight for its space in the city, but winter was holding its ground. The title—Your Lordship—was an afterthought. After their tense first encounter, she thought him as likely to commission her as the Pope.

"Things can be both," he said. "I get invitations from the Medici regularly, but I've been traveling for work more and more. When I heard what tonight was about, I could not turn it down. You did tell me that you were a painter. I should not have doubted you."

"You weren't alone," she admitted, staring into her wine glass.

"Your Artemis is quite impressive. I could have thought she was prepared to stab me through the heart—or turn me into a deer—for daring to gaze upon her."

"Thank you," she said. "I'll take that as a compliment."

"I'm not sure why you're so determined to take everything I say as anything but," Maringhi said.

She looked at him more closely, cautious. His smile did not seem to be masking daggers. "I'm still not sure you're not making fun of me again."

"I admire you. I tease the people I like," he said with a wink. "You can't take anything I say seriously."

"You don't think there are things worth being serious about?"

"Not that I've found," he said. "Have you found anything worth *not* being serious about? Isn't it time to have fun? You've reached a goal that few ever do, and you defied tradition to do it."

"One big commission isn't my only goal. It's just an early step. I have a lot of work ahead of me. Fun is…" She shrugged. "Unnecessary."

"I know you have friends."

She folded her arms. "Are you going to tell me to pretend not to associate with Galileo too? It seems to be everyone's advice."

"I wouldn't dare to tell you what to do. You seem to know your own mind. Though I can't imagine having a friend worth throwing away my social standing," he said.

"You must not have very good friends."

For the first time, he faltered. His smile slipped, and he blinked. It was as though they had been sword fighting, and Artemisia had struck a sudden blow. Then he recovered, and it was as though the hesitation had never happened. "I must not," he said. "My bank vault, however, has many. On that note, are you still taking commissions, or has fame swept you away?"

"Of course I'm still taking commissions," Artemisia said.

"Excellent. Then can we make a plan to discuss one?"

She blinked, wondering if the wine had gone to her head. "You want to commission me?"

"I like to patronize the best new artists in the city. I've been building my collection. You can't expect me to leave tonight without the promise of a commission from the great Artemisia Gentileschi."

"You can come by my studio, then," Artemisia said, fighting to sound as though she had expected the request. It seemed she had written him off too quickly. "Just ask anyone in Oltrarno for la Pittora"—the lady painter—"and someone will show you the way."

"Tomorrow?"

"So soon?"

"Why not? I want to make sure I beat the others on your waiting list. You're the star tonight, after all," he said. "Besides, I'm not the type to tarry. If there's something I want, I pursue it."

Recovering from her surprise, she nodded. "Then tomorrow it is."

He bowed over her hand. "I'll leave you to the rest of your fawning admirers. This might be the first step in your grand plan, but it's still a step. Celebrate, signorina. And I'll see you soon."

II

True to his word, Francesco Maria Maringhi—"You must call me Francesco if we're to work together"—came to her studio the next morning, far earlier than she had expected. Though she hadn't seen him consume more wine than the others in the room, there had been something about his relaxed smiles that implied a man who stayed up late and woke after noon.

Instead, he was at her studio at the start of the day, bearing a basket of biscotti. "My chef made these yesterday. They're to die for."

Despite his lavish clothing, she had not expected him to be able to afford an in-house chef. He seemed close to her age, and she had never heard of the Maringhi in her research into wealthy local families. "Fancy," she said, eagerly accepting the basket. "Tell me—what is it that you do?"

The scent of the fresh biscotti made her stomach rumble. The wine last night had left her with a headache, but with the final payment from her painting for the Medici in her pockets, the world seemed brighter before her. She felt weightless with the reprieve from her recent woolen cloak of despair.

"I'm a businessman," he said.

"Vague," she commented, setting the basket on the table and plucking a hazelnut biscotto from the top.

He laughed. "I just didn't think you cared about the details. It's not art, after all. I specialize in unique imports and exports. Rare books, exotic fabrics, and the like. My services are highly in demand, with the people who can afford them."

"Like the Medici," Artemisia said. The biscotto tasted heavenly, crisp and sweet.

"Indeed. You and I have patrons in common," he said. He strolled around Artemisia's studio, peering curiously at the canvases that were uncovered. The collected works in progress, of both biblical and historical subjects, showed her range from the poised to the bloody. Artemisia tensed when he stepped close to her Judith, shrouded by a heavy red drape in the corner, but he moved past it without stopping. "Your art is even better in the light of day."

He seemed genuine—more than most of her patrons. "Thank you," she said.

Though he seemed as confident in her space as he was everywhere else she'd seen him, he was also more careful. He didn't touch anything, and kept a respectful distance from both her and the canvases. Still, she couldn't fully shake her tension. No matter how many safeguards she had in place, the presence of someone in her sanctuary always felt invasive.

"You're passionate on the canvas. There's something dark about your art. I appreciate that." When she made a noise, he glanced over at her with a teasing grin. "You didn't think I might have some dark layers under all this? I'm complex, Artemisia." He seemed to enjoy saying her name.

"I was inspired by the great Caravaggio," she said. "I simply made the style my own."

"Didn't Caravaggio paint a man's death? I heard he was being investigated for murder down south. Even that he ended up bonded with a blood drake."

"My father told me that he cut off the man's balls with a knife. No magics involved, dark or otherwise. It was a romantic rival, I think. Blood drakes don't bother artists for that."

Francesco barked a laugh. "Well, that's all right then."

"Maybe not for Caravaggio's victim," Artemisia said, but she laughed too. They sat at the small table near the window and split the basket of biscotti. The morning sun warmed the apartment. "What was the painting you wanted to commission? I assume you want something magical. What are you looking for?"

"Something beautiful. I don't usually get ill, but I like to keep healing paintings on hand for if I pick something up in my travels—and for when the plague visits the city. That aspect is less important to me, though," Francesco said. "The healing magics are finite—the art you create will last forever. I want my collection to be remembered."

"Do you have a theme? Something I should try to match?" She held up a hand. "You've seen my work. I won't paint in a classical style, even for a commission."

"I would never commission a painter like this to create something that looked like a San Giotto," he pointed out, waving at her canvases. "I want your style. Perhaps one of your murderesses? That seems to be a skill of yours."

"I can do that," Artemisia confirmed with a grin.

"How is it that the happiest I've seen you is because of bloodlust?" he asked. "You have an affection for the more controversial women of history. So do I. Women too often are shoved to the side in old tales. I like my women painted the way I've seen them most often in life—eager for retribution and ready to do it themselves."

"Most men prefer those quiet women," Artemisia pointed out.

He winked at her. "Not me. Ovid said, 'The sharp thorn often produces delicate roses.' He was a wise man. I prefer women with fire." They no longer seemed to be talking about art.

Suddenly, their past two conversations appeared in a new light. Was Francesco *attracted* to her? Now that the thought had occurred to her, it seemed obvious. He flirted by teasing, the same way she'd seen eager young men on the street nearly tripping on the heels of the girls they liked.

Most of the men who approached Artemisia were in another camp—the men who lurked and whispered inappropriate comments just quietly enough they could deny having ever said them. The men who left things unsaid because they assumed that Artemisia would pick up on them and make the first move herself, flattered by their coarse language.

It was strange for Artemisia to be approached so openly, so genuinely. She was thrown for a moment, and Francesco's grin slipped slightly. She hated to see him dimmed in any way, but she didn't know how to rescue the moment. Instead, she just said, "Then let's talk payment."

Artemisia had hoped her commission from Madama Cristina would bring her further success, but she could not have predicted it would come so quickly.

In addition to Francesco, she had been contacted by three other patrons, and now had secured a spot in one of the most coveted new galleries in Florence.

"This is the section you'll be painting," Michelangelo the Younger said, leading her into the ornate gallery. The gallery was part of Casa Buonarroti, a new monument to the first Michelangelo and a dear pet project of the current one.

They were both dressed down from their meeting a few

weeks before at the Palazzo Pitti, though Michelangelo's facial hair had been recently sculpted into crisp lines. In comparison, Artemisia's curls felt unruly tucked in a loose chignon at the base of her neck. She'd brought her notebook so she could start to sketch her ideas, and had chosen comfort over style. Michelangelo had already given her the advance on the commission, so all that was left was to paint it.

The gallery was constructed, but mostly bare of art. The walls and ceiling had been carved into rectangles of varying size with interconnected, ornate decoration acting as a frame for each of the discrete sections. Scaffolding sat in various spots, allowing the workers to reach the high ceiling. Only a handful of paintings were already set in place, each a testament to the quality of artist being hired for the project. This would be a hall of masterpieces.

Michelangelo spun to gesture to the entire room. "This hall will be a testament to my uncle's legacy. Each piece will be painted by a different artist, representing one of his attributes or achievements."

She looked around at the paintings already in place. Some were literal, with Michelangelo the Elder sitting beside saints and angels alike. Others, like a long, narrow painting of a battling griffon and blood drake, were more symbolic. It created a sense of unified chaos, all in service to the artist's legacy.

"Your section will be the allegory of inclination," he said. "This is one of the key pieces to the puzzle. I had an idea for the portrait that I knew only you could do. I'd like it to show a beautiful woman holding a compass. That will symbolize the natural instinct at the heart of true artists, the intuition that guides their hands."

Artemisia nodded. "I can do that."

"I know. I saw your Artemis, and I've talked to your

other patrons. And, of course, the word of Galileo Galilei is unquestionable."

She frowned, unable to believe her own luck. "And you've heard no words against me?"

"Of course I have," Michelangelo said easily. "I asked around. I prefer to know what I'm getting into with my artists. But I'd have been more skeptical if you had only friends."

"Paolo Lamberti said something, didn't he?" Artemisia asked. Had he told Michelangelo of the trial? Of Tassi? "He's hated me from the start, you know. He's desperate to slander my name."

"Paolo Lamberti is a talented artist," Michelangelo said, lightly scolding. "I respect his opinion, but everyone has a past— artists more than most. You cannot take professional rivalry so personally. Let your art speak for itself. You're here, aren't you?"

She was. She would prove she belonged. "My work will impress you." She craned her neck up at the ceiling. "I'll need to take the measurements."

"Of course. I originally considered mimicking the Sistine Chapel's fresco style, but my uncle complained so much about painting a ceiling sixty feet into the air that I've coordinated with my architect for the paintings to be done on canvas and then inserted into their slots once complete. As you can see."

There was another artist in the room, assisting the architect and his assistants to place a large painting in the central spot at the top of the ceiling. The scaffolding they were standing on seemed sturdy, but the artist moved on it with far more caution than the other men. When he shifted to the light, she recognized Sigismondo Coccapani, the friendliest face at the Accademia.

"Sigismondo is a fast worker—I asked him for a piece last year when I first imagined this space, and he finished it more promptly than I would have dreamed. It's the heart of the room, and will bring everything together. The three sacred arts—Painting, Sculpture, and Tapestry—are crowning my uncle while the mother of them all, Magic, watches over them. It's quite beautiful."

"A year? That *is* very fast for a work that size."

"Well, this room is free of magics," he told her. "Your piece will be as well. I want this to be an eternal public monument. Soaking it in the magics of every artist in the building would be excessive, don't you think?"

Finally satisfied with the placement, Sigismondo descended the scaffolding with wobbly legs, and then leaned against it for a moment to catch his breath.

"Sigismondo," Michelangelo called, waving him over. "Come meet one of the artists you'll be sharing the hall with."

"Artemisia Gentileschi," he said. "We've met. Good choice, Michelangelo. She's a rising star. Her showings at the Accademia only improve on themselves." He smiled at Artemisia. "I've heard you're also working for Signore Silvestrini? With that, you've entered a rite of passage more trying than the Accademia itself, though hopefully that membership isn't far from your reach either."

"Thank you." To hide her pleased flush, she pointed toward the ceiling. "Your work is fantastic. Excellent composition. It belongs at the center of the room."

"You flatter me," he said.

"Sigismondo is too demure," Michelangelo said. "I've been trying to cure him of it." He gave the artist a conspiratorial smile, which Sigismondo returned with another blush. Artemisia glanced between them again. Perhaps Michelangelo the Younger shared more of his uncle's legacy than he admitted. The rumors in Rome had been that the original Michelangelo had favored younger men as well.

"Good; confidence is key," Artemisia agreed.

"Artemisia, I'll leave you with the architect to determine the measurements," Michelangelo said, waving across the room for the man to join them. "He can move the scaffolding so you can get a closer look at the spot. I need to settle Sigismondo's final payment for his work."

"I'll look forward to seeing what you paint," Sigismondo told Artemisia. He nodded to her, and then Michelangelo put his hand on the small of the other man's back to lead him away. Artemisia looked up around the gallery room while she waited for the architect, envisioning the final collection. Her work was going to be in a building dedicated to Michelangelo the Elder, an artist on the path to be canonized as a saint.

There was no way to know one's legacy during one's life, but perhaps this would help establish Artemisia's place in history.

Perhaps, someday, there would be a building dedicated to *her* work.

"I hear your presentation at the Palazzo Pitti for Madama Cristina was a success."

Artemisia looked up, surprised. She had thought the old man was asleep when his butler had led her into the bedroom.

She was giving Stefano Silvestrini her latest piece, a shadowy portrait of Jochebed. It was a close-up of her face, a warring expression of grief and hope tangling her strong features. For another patron, Artemisia might have included the rest of the scene—Moses in his basket, ready to be sent along the Nile. But Silvestrini wanted speed, and the content was secondary.

"It was, thank you." She hesitated, and then placed her portrait on the pile beside his bed. It was so much more dynamic than the other offerings. A beautiful work no one would ever see.

"I hope you won't forget your standing patrons as your popularity grows."

"Of course not," Artemisia said, smiling with the empty, soothing energy some anxious patrons needed.

He stared at her, his eyes fierce despite the maze of wrinkles surrounding them. He seemed as ill as on her first visit, weak and ancient, but his temper was still sharp. "It has happened before. Artists have no sense of loyalty when new patrons and fame come calling. I need regular deliveries, or my life is at risk."

Loyalty. What *loyalty* did she owe him? He demanded her best work at an unreasonable pace, and her career made no steps forward when her art joined a pile on the floor. If she grew to the point she no longer needed his inflated payments, he would be the first client she dropped. Her art was not an act of charity.

Artemisia kept her voice cool. "I understand that. I complete all my commissions as contracted."

He examined her face. "Have I ever told you how I made my fortune?"

"You haven't." Now would he try to dictate her career? Businessmen had tried before, unable to comprehend the complexities of an artist's life. The advice that worked for traders did not help an artist.

"I was a silk merchant. The most renowned in the land. I had the best material—and the best embroiderers—on this side of the ocean. I was already extremely successful before—" His speech was interrupted by a coughing fit. It was a hacking, wet sound that made Artemisia's stomach turn. She waited while he struggled for breath, repelled but curious where his story was heading. Finally, his breathing settled, and he continued, "I was already successful before I became the primary supplier to the Vatican. Every piece of silk in the Vatican for decades passed through my hands. They grew to trust no one but me. From the cardinals' scarlet mozzettas to the Pope's slippers, it was Silvestrini silk. I was invited into the innermost sanctums. I walked under Michelangelo's Sistine Chapel." He nodded. "I see that impresses you."

Artemisia realized her mouth had fallen open. The Medici had awed her, but the Vatican? It was the heart of life—and death—in Rome. The Roman Church had the most power, the most influence, the most money, of any organization in the world. Europe had been shaped by its will. She had walked past the Vatican's high walls often in her youth, wondering what was inside, but it was kept tightly closed from the public to preserve the powerful collection of art inside.

"I still hold the ear of Pope Clement the Seventh," Silvestrini told her. "And many of the most important cardinals. Even though I had to depart for my health, the business is still mine. I am known as an expert on artists, especially those unappreciated by other patrons. The Vatican is always searching for the most powerful artists to fortify their home.

"You'll have other offers from patrons in Florence and beyond as you grow more popular. But keep me alive, and I'll introduce you to the Pope himself."

Working for the Church would legitimize Artemisia like never before. She imagined returning to Rome with a commission secured to paint inside the holy San Pietro. It was a heady thought. She could return in glory. "Thank you, signore."

"Good. But understand that if I die," Silvestrini said, rubbing his frail chest, "I'll make sure that everyone knows the artists who failed me."

12

Artemisia's incoming commissions were rewarding, but none compared with the bone-deep satisfaction of telling Valerio Gori that she was moving out of his building. With payments from Madama Cristina, Francesco, Michelangelo, and Silvestrini in her pocket, Artemisia finally had the money to find a new studio, somewhere far from Gori and his heavy knocks and greedy eyes. Standing at his door, she could see the art he had stolen from her hanging on his wall. In a place of honor, as though he had earned it.

"You can't leave," he said. "You haven't given me notice."

"We have no contract," Artemisia told him. "As you've so often reminded me. I'm leaving tomorrow."

He folded his arms. "I'll reduce your monthly payment," he said. "Five percent, no more."

She had been expecting a celebration when he learned he would be rid of her. "What, are you hoping to steal another painting from my studio?"

"The griffon has brought in rich new tenants," he admitted reluctantly. "Everyone is clamoring for a place here. They're a sign of good fortune, you know."

Artemisia simply laughed in his face.

With Maurizio's help, she carefully moved her work from

the Oltrarno district across the river to the Via della Fortezza, far closer to the pulsing heart of Florence. Her rent had jumped from fourteen scudi a year to twenty, but it was worth it. The space was as small as her last, leaving her to recreate her hidden cot in a back corner, but the location was far more accessible to the types of clients she wanted. There would be no more Fenzetti sneering at her street when they came for a consultation.

Artemisia was at the center of Florence—and she would stay there.

After she had given Maurizio a coin and a glass of wine for his help, Artemisia climbed to the roof. She had searched a long time for a top-floor flat with roof access. Her new landlord had been skeptical until she had explained her reasoning, and then he had given her a key to the roof. She only hoped it would be necessary.

From the roof, she looked over Florence. From this side of the Arno, the Duomo loomed tall. Nearby, the dark stone of the Palazzo Vecchio jutted toward the sky. In the distance, the mountains were dark and hazy. Orange roofs spread out around her, faded in the dying light. It was nearly night.

Carefully, she crouched and dragged her knife across her forearm. The blade was dull from sawing through canvas, but worked well enough. The pain was bright and sharp, and dark blood welled on her pale skin. The shock of it nearly made her lose her balance, but she steadied herself. With her other hand, she wiped away some of the blood and smeared it onto the terracotta roof tiles.

It was a strange echo of painting, clumsy and ancient.

She scanned the sky. Clouds bunched along the horizon over the river, red and gold with the setting sun. There was no sign of a winged beast in the air.

Using her uninjured arm, Artemisia lowered herself to sit on the narrow roof. Her feet splayed down the steep slope to either side, her dress pooling in the middle. Disappointment clogged her throat.

She did not own the griffon. It was a magnificent, free creature. Attempting to tie it down would take away its heart, and she would never do that. Still, being chosen by the griffon had brought her joy, and had made Artemisia feel she could truly succeed. In the face of scorn from her peers, she clung to a validation most artists only dreamed of.

She had thought the griffon had truly bonded with her, but perhaps it had picked Gori's roof by coincidence. Worse—could the stain of her work on her Judith have finally repulsed it? With so many commissions these days, she rarely had the energy to work on it, but she had packed it up and brought it with her across the river. The annulment of Tassi's sentence continued to haunt her, and she would not abandon the work. She couldn't truly enjoy her success in Florence while he walked free. She would finish it. She had to. Even if it meant losing her griffon.

There was a gust of wind across the roof, ruffling Artemisia's curls. She looked up to find the griffon in front of her, sniffing at the blood on the roof. It cocked its head at her, beak gleaming in the sunset. It had grown since it first came to her last year, its lanky body taller than any dog she'd seen. It stretched its wings wide, and then tucked them along its body.

Relief flooded her breast. "Good beastie," Artemisia said, reaching into her satchel to pull out a sketch she had drawn earlier that week. It was of the griffon in profile, its sharp eyes staring out at her. She tossed it the paper, which it set upon happily.

She leaned her palms behind her on the roof, ignoring the sting of the cut on her arm. She would bandage it later.

For now, she watched the sun set over her city.

*

Since commissioning her two months earlier, Francesco Maria Maringhi had come to see Artemisia at least once every time he was in Florence between his work trips. Ostensibly, he came to consult about her work—he had already commissioned another painting, though the first was barely past the design stage—but they rarely stayed on topic for long. Francesco was easy to talk to, making hours pass like minutes. They bickered about every subject.

Sometimes, she thought he took a contrary view just so she would have someone to rail against.

Today, he convinced her to leave the comfort of her studio to explore the city with him. He led her northwest to the Arno, which sparkled in the early afternoon light. The sky was clear blue overhead, contrasting with the city's red-orange roofs on the horizon. The river's sour scent was heavy in the air, but it was superseded as they passed a gelato shop. Catching Artemisia's longing glance, Francesco insisted they detour inside.

After, they continued along the river, eating their treats and talking.

"Did you know gelato was invented for the last Duke Cosimo? The current Grand Duke's grandfather."

"I met some men in Rome who claimed they invented it," Artemisia said, teasing.

"No, it's true," Francesco insisted. "A man named Bernardo Buontalenti. He was an architect and engineer, and had all sorts of clever inventions. He learned how to keep things cold. The Grand Duke was throwing a banquet, and he asked Buontalenti to create a new dessert for the occasion. And so." Francesco held up his gelato, creamy and soft in the early summer sun. "Ice, lemon, sugar, egg, honey, milk, and just a drop of wine." He winked at Artemisia. "Flavored with bergamot and orange to finish it off."

"He never should have wasted time with anything but desserts," she said, licking her gelato.

Francesco's eyes tracked the movement, and Artemisia gazed out over the river to hide her flush. He still looked at her with those charming, interested eyes, and she still ignored him. Some days, the tension of unspoken words felt as heavy between them as the growing summer heat around them.

After a moment, Francesco continued, "Buontalenti's work with ice is half the reason I can import the things I do. We use the ice cellars at the Medici palace to store all the treats I bring them."

"We're all grateful for it, then," Artemisia said. They crossed Ponte Vecchio and headed north on Via Calimala. "How did you get into the import business? A family trade?"

"Something like that. My father was a nobleman. My mother was not his wife. After I was born, she took me back to where her family lived in Montauto, near San Gimignano," he said, naming a city a few hours south of Florence. "It was a lean life, and I had three siblings from another father. I found a businessman, Matteo Frescobaldi, to apprentice with by the time I was nine. He taught me how to trade, how to make deals. I came to Florence when I was fifteen and haven't been back."

"You haven't seen your family since then?" Artemisia asked. Francesco had been born the same year as her, which meant it had been close to a decade since he had been home.

"My father wasn't a kind man, the few times we met. My mother died the first year I was away. My siblings ignored me. I believe they resented my 'noble' birth, for all the benefits it gave me." His tone was bitter, lacking the light she was used to hearing from him.

"I'm sorry," she said. It was difficult to imagine anyone not being drawn to Francesco.

Francesco just shrugged and took another bite of gelato. They turned to the east into the Piazza della Signoria, the vast square in front of the crenelated Palazzo Vecchio. The same Duke Cosimo I who had been gifted the treat of gelato had ruled from that palace until he moved across the river into the Palazzo Pitti. The square was flanked by the arches of the Loggia della Signoria, which housed an open-air sculpture gallery. As in most plazas in the city during the summer, there was a bustling market in the center of the square.

As they wove through the crowd, Artemisia stayed close to Francesco's side. He managed the crush of people with confidence, dodging between two large families and then walking straight forward to force a cluster of students to part in front of him. Artemisia could follow his path with little trouble, sparing her from the chaos.

It had been months since she had visited the market at Santa Croce with Galileo and met the temperamental healer. Galileo had retreated to his home in the country to continue his war of letters against Caccini and the Inquisition, and she avoided large crowds on her own. Though they exchanged some letters, she missed her first friend in the city. He had celebrated her recent successes in writing, but it was not the same as having him there.

"My chef asked me to pick up some truffles from a stall here," Francesco said over his shoulder. "We'll stop by another on our way out—I know a woman who sells the softest blankets you've ever felt."

"You said that about the shawl you brought me," she pointed

out. "I'm going to stop believing you if you're so easy with your compliments."

He grinned back at her. "Well, was I wrong about the shawl? Perhaps I just have excellent taste."

She opened her mouth to respond, but was shouldered roughly by a passing man. Her amulet lashed him, but he continued on as she stumbled over the uneven cobblestones. The crowd around her was dizzying. Too many people, too much noise.

As she regained her feet, her eyes locked on the terrified face of a pale woman across the square.

Artemisia stumbled again. She quickly looked back toward the woman, and realized it was just the face of a familiar statue in the sculpture gallery—the *Rape of the Sabine Women*. The marble woman was being carried away by two men, their forms twisting on a tall pedestal. The woman's arm reached into the air, as though asking the heavens to pull her from her situation.

"Artemisia?" Francesco asked.

She realized she had been standing still in the center of the walkway. She blinked and tried to focus on his face.

There was a shout nearby, and her head jerked toward it. Someone dropped something ceramic, and it shattered against the cobblestones. There was laughter around her, harsh and grating.

Were people looking at her? There was no way out of the crowd. She would be pushed and shoved and trampled and hurt. She clutched the amulet around her neck, squeezing the metal in her palm.

There was a hiss of pain from nearby, and then Francesco's soothing voice. "Just come with me."

The world seemed to spin. Artemisia thought she was moving, but the only thing she could think was that she couldn't breathe.

Her body was so tense that she was shaking, and she couldn't find her center, find *herself* again. It was as though her soul and body had become disconnected, her spirit trapped inside a sculpture.

She had to breathe. This was her body.

Hers.

Her senses returned slowly. She was sitting somewhere quiet and cool, the sun off her face. She took a deep breath through her nose, and then opened her eyes.

She was in a restaurant, sitting at a table alone. Disoriented, she looked around.

Francesco was standing by the bar, talking animatedly to the bartender and a waiter, seemingly the only two people in the restaurant. He glanced back at Artemisia, and his shoulders slumped with relief. He grinned at the workers, picked up two cups from the bar in front of him, and hurried to her table.

"Are you with me?" he asked, setting a cup in front of her.

She picked it up instinctively and stared at the liquid. It was a white wine, cool against her hand. "Wine?" she asked, at a loss.

"I wanted to get you off the streets, and most shops won't let you use their tables unless you've bought something," he said, putting down his own cup without drinking. "I thought you needed space to breathe. I tried to touch you, but... I couldn't."

He had never activated her amulet before. "You must think me mad."

"You just needed some time. I knew you'd come back to me."

She took a sip of the wine. It was cold and sweet, but cloyingly thick, so she put it back down. "How?"

He tapped his fingers on the table. "I've worked with the same Turkish translator every time I've visited the Ottoman Empire. He fought in their wars against Venice. I've seen him experience...similar reactions. He does not react well to loud noises, in particular. I've learned ways to aid him." He looked at Artemisia. "Would it help you to talk about it?"

"No."

Francesco just nodded. "Would it help to go back to our shopping excursion?"

The quiet stillness of the bar was beginning to grate on Artemisia's nerves. "Yes." She leaned forward across the table. "This wine is terrible," she confided.

"All right," he said. He drank his cup in one deft gulp, and then reached across the table to drain hers as well. He made a face. "You're right. That's horrible."

She laughed helplessly. She'd never felt so secure after anxiety had struck her so viciously. It normally took hours hiding in her studio to become calm, but this strange, delightful man had pulled her from her spiral. "Then why did you drink it?"

"It's rude to leave our drinks untouched," he said, shrugging. He got to his feet, and waited until she had found hers before he led them out of the bar. "Grazie mille," he called to the waitstaff, who waved at him cheerfully.

True to his word, Francesco swept her back out into the busy square without demanding an explanation for those moments when she had lost control of herself. He stayed closer to her than he had before, using his bright smile and broad shoulders to maneuver them through the crowd without trouble, but he kept the conversation on the wares for sale.

He was right. The stall had the softest blankets she'd ever felt.

13

After everything she had been through, she had never expected to feel bored at an Accademia meeting in the heart of Florentine art, but it seemed life had led her here. As she held her sketch aloft at the next monthly meeting, her thoughts were on other work. Another cluster of members passed her by for the fresh-faced boy with a mediocre drawing at her side.

The evening was less awkward than her visit to the anatomical theater, when Lamberti had thrown her out, or that first monthly meeting, where nearly all had ignored her. Some members still overlooked her, but many had grown accustomed to her face both at Accademia gatherings and those hosted by Madama Cristina and other patrons. Artemisia had become a regular in Florence's art society, even if she had not found acceptance here. She was determined to gain entry to the Accademia, but she was no longer desperate. She was proving herself. She would wear them down.

"Ah, Artemisia. This is another beautiful design. You have a real gift!" Sigismondo Coccapani made a point to talk to her every meeting. The artist had a perpetual smile and no hesitations about sharing his time.

"Thank you," she said. Her sketch this month depicted a solemn David sitting over the shadowed head of Goliath. She had laid her charcoal heavy over most of it, showing the deep colors she would use. Only David's shirt—to be a pristine white—and part of his youthful face would be well-lit.

"It's so rare for you to paint the male figure," Sigismondo commented. "You normally keep to women."

"I prefer to showcase all my expertise at these meetings," Artemisia said, a tad icy. "I do have range."

"Of course, of course," he said, holding up his hands. "I was only thinking—your development in that area may benefit from a few lessons at the anatomical theater." He winked.

She stared at him, lips numb. Around them, others seemed to have noticed the tension, and quieted to listen. "Very amusing," she said, unable to conjure a smile for him, despite the eyes on them. It was unlike him to be cruel, but she knew every smile could hide disdain. "You remember my first visit. You were there."

"You know that our workshop teachers rotate every six months. I've been recently assigned as one of them, and have taken over as liaison with the hospital. The anatomical theater has always been a passion of mine. I've spoken with the staff there," Sigismondo said, raising his voice. He knew they had onlookers. "I explained that a woman, a talented artist, has been a student of the Accademia for more than a year without being permitted to attend all our available classes. She has just as much of a right to attend the dissections as any other aspiring member."

"And they agreed to this?" she asked, pulse thudding.

"They did," he said, smiling.

"You can't be serious," Lamberti interjected. He had been standing among the crowd, and his expression was thunderous. "You'll make us the laughingstock of the city. We can't indulge her like this. She should not be here at all, much less shouted about to everyone."

Sigismondo shrugged. "There was no shouting. I explained

that this woman's art is in the Palazzo Pitti and a dozen other galleries across the continent. We'd be fools to exclude her. You are not the liaison anymore, Paolo."

Artemisia's heart swelled in her chest.

"It does not matter if ignorant clients commission her. They don't understand what we do. The Accademia is here to assure the sanctity of art. What is our God-given ability for if we're going to let her stain our legacy? This is meant to be a gathering of artists. Men who could be *saints* one day."

"We don't choose the saints. We're here to recognize talent, and she certainly has it," Sigismondo said.

"I fought to join this group because it meant something," Lamberti said. "This is meant to be the pinnacle of art in this city."

"It is," Sigismondo said. "And that means Artemisia Gentileschi."

There were murmurs from the surrounding crowd now, but few seemed in favor of Lamberti. He turned around to look at them, but they either nodded agreement with Sigismondo or averted their gaze. She felt buoyant, breathless. For years she had fought for herself, but she had never had someone publicly argue for her, especially against his own peers.

"You'll regret this," Lamberti said, jabbing a finger at Sigismondo. He turned to glare at the watching members of the Accademia. "All of you. You're destroying everything we have built here. We're meant to be better than this."

He stepped forward and snatched the sketch from Artemisia's hands. She startled backward. Though he was slender, he seemed to loom over her. When he ripped the paper in half, the sound seemed like a thunderclap in the quiet room. "This isn't over," he said.

She lifted her chin. "I don't need your approval."

When he stormed from the group, no one moved to stop him. His master's robes billowed behind him as he walked out of the monastery and slammed the door. The noise echoed through the small hall and the silence the argument had left behind. Hushed conversation began, the story of the night already being repeated and reconsidered. She could hear the waves of gossip beginning to ripple.

She hoped, for once, the tongues would wag on her side.

"Ignore him," Sigismondo said, stooping to pick up her ruined sketch. His smile was a bit shaken, but there was more iron in him than she'd anticipated. "It's not his decision to make anymore. The next anatomical theater session is next week—I'll expect to see you there."

"I will be," she assured him, voice shaking with intensity. "I will be."

The sunset bathed the skyline in pinks and oranges, lit by a blush of yellow on the horizon. It was bright and lush, the heavy clouds full of the curves and swirls one would find in a background painted by San Leonardo. The flowers in the orchards that lay scattered inside the city's walls had bloomed, leaving the air thick with perfume.

Last autumn, Artemisia and Galileo had slipped to the top of the Duomo to look at the stars. This evening, they were on Artemisia's new roof, several dozen meters lower than Brunelleschi's looming dome. From Galileo's excited murmuring, however, she thought the view was equally appreciated.

The griffon perched on the rooftop beside them, tearing into a small self-portrait Artemisia had brought up for it. She knew it could survive without her help, but she made a point to create extra art for it. There was nothing as satisfying as the way it thrummed with a heavy purr when she gave it new pieces.

Since the griffon hunted during the day and only came to Artemisia's roof at night, Galileo had only a short period to sketch before they were consumed by darkness. His charcoal raced across his notebook.

"Absolutely beautiful," Galileo said again, adding a detailed section of the patch where feather met fur. "I wish I could have come sooner. Caccini and his friends have given me no time to breathe. I don't know where they come up with some of the rumors they throw at me. But this reminds me how much there is outside my quills. What a gift."

"It's hard to believe you've never managed to meet one before," Artemisia said.

"Finding a griffon is rarer than you realize," Galileo said. "They're shy creatures."

"Shy," Artemisia repeated with a snort, gesturing at the creature happily rubbing its beak into her shredded painting, paying no mind to its admirers. The Florentine skyline framed its haunches. Even compared to the towering Duomo and ancient Palazzo Vecchio, the griffon seemed a work of art.

"Normally," he said, sketching the griffon's fierce beak with sharp lines. "Now I just need to track down a blood drake. They're even rarer, and the stigma against them puts them at risk. Unfortunately, I do not foresee befriending anyone capable of summoning a blood drake. No matter what my enemies say, I do not associate with evil."

Evil. Was that what he would think if he knew the truth of what was hiding in her flat beneath their feet? It hurt to imagine his revulsion at a project so important to her.

When she had begun the work, there had been no success—or friendships—to lose. Now, if her dabbling in the necrotic arts was ever revealed, it would burn down the growing scaffolding of her career.

She was distracted by a line of thoughtless humming from her friend as he sketched. It was a mournful melody, something she knew but could not place. The song was like a voice heard crying from another room. "What is that you're humming?"

"*O rosa bella*," he said, naming a common ballad. "O dio d'amore, che pena é quest' amare," Galileo sang. He had a rough voice which hitched on certain syllables like fabric catching on wood grain.

Oh god of love, what suffering is this love.

It was the lament of a man in love with one who did not love him back. No wonder she had not recognized it. She had no time for love songs. Her passions were tied up in her art—what man could change that?

She suddenly envisioned Francesco smiling at her over his gelato. Laughing in the sunlight. Guiding her through her panic at the market.

She imagined kissing him.

The vision was startling in its clarity. She stared out over the sprawling skyline of Florence.

What would it be like to touch him? To trust him with herself, and to hope he did not break her heart? He had flirted with her, but he was an easygoing man. She had seen him flirt with every waitress and vendor he met.

It was foolish to think he would choose her for more than one night.

"Ah, now, before I forget," Galileo said, sparing her from her thoughts. Without lifting his charcoal, he dug into his pocket and handed her a folded pamphlet. Unfamiliar cramped handwriting covered each page front and back, spiky letters like spider legs compared to Galileo's fluid hand.

"As our first meeting revolved around my using you to debate my views on heliocentrism, it seemed only fair for you to have an early copy of my treatise," Galileo said. "This is a letter to our mutual patron, Madama Cristina, to lay out my work directly. She's a respected individual. In addressing her, I will make everyone see the truth of my work."

She opened it, squinting to read the opening paragraph in the dying light.

To the Most Serene, Grand Duchess Mother,

> *Some years ago, as Your Serene Highness well knows, I discovered in the heavens many things that had not been seen before our own age. The novelty of these things, as well as some consequences which followed from them in contradiction to the physical notions commonly held among academic philosophers, stirred up against me no small number of professors—as if I had placed these things in the sky with my own hands in order to upset nature and overturn the sciences.*

Artemisia laughed. "This is good."

"I have scribes making several more copies to be distributed to small circles. Caccini and the Pigeon League can bluster as much as they like, but they will not be able to refute the words from my own quill."

Artemisia wasn't as confident. It seemed to her that all they had done so far was use Galileo's own words against him. He was dedicated to truth, but they had no compunction about twisting his arguments out of context. They were insidious and persistent, determined to stop his mission. It was their word against his, not only in the court of public opinion, but under the watchful eye of the Church in Rome.

From her experience, the truth was not believed easily. She shuddered to imagine him facing the same torture as her.

Galileo dropped his charcoal suddenly, violently, and clutched his chest. His shoulders shook as he struggled to catch his breath.

"Are you *sure* you're all right?" she asked, putting the letter down to watch him closely. This wasn't the first fit of the night.

There was a pause as he gasped for air. "Yes," he said, and, once he was able, "The city air has never agreed with my heart. It has occasional fits, like I've got a bird in my chest. I go through periods like this every once in a while. That's why I was out in the country to write my letters. You can get a lot done when you're trapped on bed rest, dizziness or no."

"I didn't realize it was that bad," Artemisia said. "Maybe you should actually rest instead of working. Take care of yourself."

He finally straightened and began sketching again. "I'd lose my mind if I couldn't let it roam freely, Artemisia. I think you know something of not letting physical ailments get in the way of creating."

She waved a hand. "That does not mean you should need to. I can make you a painting. Chronic complaints like this are the purpose of art."

"Don't worry about me," he said. "Sigismondo Coccapani delivered a painting for me only last month."

"A single painting, even from an Accademia member, cannot fix something instantaneously," she pointed out.

"I'm no Medici who can afford a gallery to keep me youthful. Nor would I want one."

Artemisia flexed her hands and nodded. "Just be careful. If you fall off the edge of the roof, I'll try to catch you and then we'll both die."

Galileo laughed, though the sound was unsteady. "We wouldn't want that. The weather hasn't been helping. It is a ballerina this time of year—jumping up and down, up and down, until summer finally lands."

"Poetic," Artemisia drawled, leaning back against the tiles now that it seemed Galileo had stabilized.

"That's what my eldest daughter calls it," he said.

"Virginia?" Galileo did not talk about his family very often, but she felt guilty for not being sure. When he nodded, she asked, "How old is she now?"

"She'll turn fifteen in August," he said. "I'll send her a gift. She and her sister, Livia, are in a convent just outside the city. They can school two young girls there better than I can." He thumped his chest. "Between my illness and the locusts swarming around my philosophy, I'm not the best father for them."

Artemisia squinted out at the sunset. The city was darkening. "I can't imagine how different my life would have been if I'd been sent to a convent. My father didn't consider it until the end."

"Your career could never have expanded within a convent's walls," Galileo said. "You could have painted, but you never could have found new patrons."

"But you sent your daughters there?"

"Ah, they do not have your dreams."

"Did they ever have the chance to find them?"

Quietly, he admitted, "That's a fair point."

The only sound on the roof was the griffon tearing the canvas to shreds.

Artemisia cleared her throat. "Anyway, my father was not

thinking of my career. At that point, he was looking for any solution that would get me out of the scandal. Marriage was his favorite answer—it would have erased the scandal if he'd managed to make what had happened to me a precursor to a wedding. I could have become Signora Tassi." Artemisia swallowed with difficulty. "I would not have survived life with that monster."

Galileo's voice was tight as he said, "I'm glad your father changed his mind."

"He didn't. It turned out that Tassi's wife was still alive. It would have been bigamy. Even then, I don't think my father truly was disturbed until he realized that the man had also been stealing his art. That was always what offended my father the most; not that Tassi had hurt me, but that he was a thief. My virtue, my father's paintings—those were the things he cared about. The things he owned that Tassi stole."

That was all that had mattered to the court as well. It was not her testimony that had swayed the judge, not truly. Her insistence upon his crimes had been considered vicious and false at first, and then unremarkable once confirmed.

As the court challenged Agostino Tassi's story, they had uncovered that—in addition to assaulting Artemisia—he had planned to murder his wife and steal several of Artemisia's father's paintings. Those crimes were what had swayed the judge against Tassi. Artemisia's real suffering was secondary compared to those planned crimes. Her safety was worth less than a piece of canvas. And even then, his crimes had been pardoned within a year.

"Your father was a fool not to see that your value did not lie with your virtue," Galileo said. "You're so much more than that."

"I haven't seen him since I left Rome," Artemisia said. "It's been more than a year, but... I think I hate him. He never cared about me."

"Fathers make mistakes," Galileo said. "I hope my daughters are gentler with me than that."

"Some people don't deserve forgiveness."

"Your father was not the one who hurt you."

"No, but he was the one who invited the man into our house, left me alone with him, and then blamed me for what happened," she snapped. "I assure you, I'm not misplacing the blame. Every drop of anger I have for my father is magnified a thousand times for Agostino Tassi. Have you ever been so angry that you felt like you would flay your own skin off if it would cause the other person one scratch?"

"Artemisia," Galileo chided softly. "You can't hurt yourself for them."

"Tassi ruined my life," she said. "Ruined my family. I still get so angry, so scared—and he did that to me. He ruined *me*, and I've dreamed for so long about ruining him back. I want to make sure he can't hurt anyone else ever again. Every step I take forward here feels like I'm walking away from the chance for revenge." She ran her hands through her hair. "But I'm so damn *tired* of thinking about him."

"Holding onto that anger is tying you to the past. What happened to you in Rome was not the end of your story."

Artemisia hummed noncommittally, looking away.

"There's so much more ahead for you than there is behind. You're still young, Artemisia... though I didn't believe that at your age either," he said, rubbing his frail chest.

The sun had slipped fully below the horizon, and the bright colors of the sky were fading into blues and purples, dark and soothing. Far overhead, spreading from the center of the sky like glints on spilled ink, stars began to flicker into view. Galileo's moons were out there, and the lights of a million stars yet to be seen.

That night, Artemisia finally uncapped the salve from the healer in the market. The first touch of the mint oil on her aching hands made her hiss, but the heavy scent was one of promise.

She had left the jar on her shelf for months. Not only was she reluctant to be proven wrong about herbal healing, but her explanation to Galileo last year as to why she had never attempted to fix her hands before still echoed. *The pain reminds me, and I'm not ready to forget yet.*

If she wanted to find her legacy, she could not be one of the forces holding herself back. The world was working against her. If she did not take care of herself—who would?

She glanced at the painting of Judith hidden in the corner. Perhaps she did not need to suffer to meet her goals. She would not forget what had been done to her. Why shackle herself further when she could focus better on both her healing and necrotic work without the pain? Suffering was not strength.

She steeled herself and massaged the salve into her hands.

14

"I hope the orchard owners know what a privilege it is that I work for them," Maurizio mused as Artemisia studied the work created during her last trance. It was a sweltering evening, and it seemed as though the oil would melt off her brush as sweat rolled down her back.

"Hm?" she prompted. It had been a productive session, firming her representation of Maurizio's face, but she needed more time alone with the fabric. The texture of the linen was stiff, and it felt unnatural under her hand compared to the silks and velvets she normally painted.

"Mars. Michael. Odysseus. And now Bezalel," Maurizio said. "They have the greats plucking oranges in obscurity." He flipped over his palm for her gaze. During the summer, the sun browned his skin and the thorns of the fruit trees sliced thin scratches along his hands and forearms.

The Bible's first explicit mention of art occurred in Exodus, during the story of Moses. God told Moses to create a tent to house the ark of the covenant, and personally selected Bezalel to paint, carve, and sculpt the décor for the structure. Earlier books mentioned healers and powerful artworks, but Bezalel, as the first named artist, gained a special place in history. God's description of Bezalel was sculpted over the entrance to the Accademia's monastery. "*I have filled him with the Spirit of God, with ability and intelligence, with power and beauty, with knowledge and all craftsmanship, to devise artistic designs.*"

"Maybe you can charge them more for your presence," Artemisia suggested, waving that he was safe to move. Maurizio shrugged, standing from the stool and stretching. "Careful," she hissed, watching the makeshift toga stretch over his chest.

"If I ask for more pay, they'll just find someone to replace me. There's no shortage of men looking for work these days. It's been years since the last plague."

"You say that as though it's a bad thing."

"More people, less work," Maurizio said. "Wages have been on a downswing lately. Frankly, a plague would be a blessing right now."

"Unless you're one of the ones to die," Artemisia said, scrubbing her brushes clean.

"There is that. Anyway, that's why I prefer this job. No one else has this face," Maurizio said, framing his jaw with a hand. Over the last year, Maurizio had starred in many of Artemisia's paintings. Her skill at portraying masculine anatomy had grown with every session, especially now that she was regularly attending the anatomical theater. She'd grown to know the lines of Maurizio's form nearly as well as her own.

"If you ever need a recommendation for a new position, I can vouch for your ability to sit very still for a long period," Artemisia said. "I'm sure I can find someone who is hiring a model. You could get out of picking fruit and doing construction work." During the winters, Artemisia tried to find more paintings involving men she could offer him. Her truly unique skill was in the female figure, though, and securing other commissions was more difficult. Her place in Florence was only just beginning to feel firm under her feet, and she had little room for experiments.

Maurizio frowned, rubbing his beard. He had trimmed it recently, defining his tense jaw. "There are other ways I could get money, you know," he said. "Other ways I have gotten money. In the end, the orchards are safest. Supplemented by working with you, it's a decent living."

"I didn't mean…"

"I don't have any family connections, I haven't trained in any trade. There are only three ways for a man to move beyond his birth: art, crime, or pure luck. I have no artistic abilities in any sense, and luck has never been on my side. But I wanted money."

"Which left one option," Artemisia said. She continued to clean her brushes, avoiding Maurizio's gaze. It felt similar to the first time she'd encountered the griffon—certain one false move would send him flying from her presence.

"I worked in a casino for years," Maurizio said. "The pay was… fantastic. I started as a guard—I was even bigger then, if you can imagine—but I was eventually moved inside to work. It was hidden behind a restaurant near the river, and more than one life was ruined inside its walls. We stacked the decks and threw out anyone who complained. But I could afford an apartment out of Santa Croce and never went hungry."

"What happened?"

"Soldiers came. It was during a movement around six years ago to curb illegal gambling. The only reason I wasn't taken in with the rest of them is that, honestly, I was skiving off in the back with one of the other dealers. What we were doing was also illegal, of course. If we had been caught anywhere else, we'd have been given a slap on the wrist. If we had been caught there, after already being brought in on gambling charges, the law could have sent us both to the dungeons for years, if not the gallows.

You asked me once if I had trouble with the Office of the Night," he said. "They can't punish every man guilty of sodomy. But if they have a chance, if there's another law to give them an excuse, they'll use you as an example to show the Church they're trying."

Artemisia spat to the side. "Stronzi," she said. "Every man in law just wants the excuse to hurt people."

"I have to admit, the Office of the Night does what they can. You know, a while ago, the Church tried to bully them into being harsher. After that, they were *coincidentally* unable to find a single sodomite for fourteen months. They're just trying to get by with the least work possible, same as the rest of us. Only one in five men they try are even convicted, and most of those are never forced to pay their fines."

"You can't trust them," Artemisia insisted. "The laws exist— they can decide on a whim when to enforce them."

"That's why I left the casino. I couldn't risk it. So, yes, my work is hard and inglorious. But it's better than the alternative."

"You—" A knock at the door distracted her, and she swore, looking out the window to assess the shade of the sky. "Is it so late already?"

He had already shed his solemn expression, raising his eyebrows at her. "You have plans?" he asked with insulting skepticism.

She ignored him and opened the door. Francesco grinned at her in greeting. "Artemisia," he said. "You look radiant. I love the touch of green." He gestured to his own cheekbone.

She scrubbed at the skin, feeling the slickness of oil beneath her fingers. "Apologies," she said, remaining at the threshold rather than inviting him inside. "I was painting and lost track of time."

"No trouble," he said. He lifted a basket. "Are you ready for dinner?"

"Dinner?" Maurizio repeated, coming up beside her.

"Maurizio, this is Francesco Maria Maringhi," Artemisia said. "He's a client. Francesco, this is Maurizio Arcuri."

"You're her model," Francesco said, sweeping into the room and shaking Maurizio's hand. "I've seen your face on a half-dozen paintings. Artemisia, you've captured an amazing likeness."

"Do you have dinners here with all your clients?" Maurizio asked Artemisia, though he knew the answer.

"Francesco is also a friend," Artemisia said. There was heat in her face she hoped was not visible. "I lost track of time. You'll be wanting to go home, Maurizio."

"Would you like to stay for dinner?" Francesco offered. "There's enough to share."

She gave Maurizio a bright smile with gritted teeth. "Maurizio should leave before it gets dark," she said pointedly.

"I never say no to free dinner," Maurizio said, returning her smile.

After Francesco cheerfully went to set up the table with platters brought from his chef, Artemisia leaned in to Maurizio. "What are you doing?" she hissed.

"Eating dinner with your *friend*."

"Don't say it like that. And you hate new people."

"You have a handsome client showing up at your door in the evening, calling you by your first name, and bringing you food. What happened to throwing your bed on a pyre?"

"It's not like that," she said, keeping her voice hushed. Francesco was not nearly far enough away for this conversation. The flush was growing. Her hopes that the red would not be noticed were almost certainly in vain. It felt like fire licking under her skin.

"I'm glad that you're not moving to a convent, but Artemisia, men like that? You don't want to sleep with people you work for."

"I work *with* him, not for him," Artemisia argued. "And I can make my own choices. *And* I'm not sleeping with him."

"You want to."

"Red or white?" Francesco called. "I brought both."

"White," Artemisia said, turning from Maurizio. "Let's have white."

The dinner conversation was tense at first. Maurizio was not subtle in his interrogation, though to look at Francesco one never would have known. Artemisia was sure Francesco could make small talk with a mountain if he ended up alone with it.

As the wine poured and the night went on, though, Francesco's endless cheer broke through even Maurizio's thick skin. He was like a stream of cool water on a hot day, able to seep through the smallest cracks. Francesco told amusing stories from his travels, and in return Maurizio shared the antics of his neighbors and friends. Artemisia leaned back in her chair and laughed, warmly pleased to see them getting along.

At the end of the night, after Artemisia had ushered Francesco out of the door, she raised an eyebrow at Maurizio as he followed. Maurizio tilted his head in a show of surprised, grudging acceptance.

Artemisia closed the door and went back into her studio. The half-finished painting of Maurizio as Bezalel caught her eye. What an interesting evening; the model, the artist, and the patron—the beginning, middle, and end of a painting's life—all in the same room.

Until tonight, despite the time they had begun to spend together, Francesco had felt separate from her life. There was a thrill in his company, the unease of exploring new lands, which she had kept for herself. She did not know where their acquaintance was leading, but each meeting was a new discovery. Allowing him to meet Maurizio made Francesco's impact on her life firmer, more real. If he decided to flit away as quickly as he'd come, she would no longer be the only person to know about their relationship.

Francesco was like a boat, unmoored. Perhaps her single bond with him would not keep them together, but maybe creating new ties between him and her friends could.

Smiling to herself, she went to extinguish her candles.

Piazza Santa Croce smelled overwhelmingly of flowers, a bright sweetness that covered the ubiquitous stench of the Arno. It was late enough in the day that there was no shadow from the vast basilica at the end of the square, leaving the sun's heat to reflect from the pale stones.

Crowds still provoked a quiet buzz of fear in her stomach, and today's late summer heat made the press of bodies around her feel even worse. The stalls were cramped, nearly labyrinthine. She wished Francesco were in town. He made everything more palatable.

"Allora, if it isn't the painter Artemisia," drawled a voice.

The herbalist she had met with Galileo was leaning against the front of her stall. There was a man in the small space behind her, handling the tins of salves and tinctures in a proprietary manner.

"Ah, there you are," Artemisia said, stepping under the weak shade of the stall. "I don't believe I learned your name before."

"I didn't offer it before. You're much more polite today. I'm Elisabetta Piperno," the woman said. "This is my husband, Luco."

The man nodded briefly toward Artemisia before going back to his work.

Elisabetta looked her over. "You finally tried the salve," she decided. "And it worked."

"It did," Artemisia admitted. "Not if I push too hard, but most days, the pain isn't as bad. My father always told me that healers were charlatans. He thought art was the only healing worth a damn."

"Consider me shocked," Elisabetta said dryly. "He's not alone. I learned my art from my mother, and she from hers. Women have always been dismissed. Men's craft is the only one worth noticing, right?"

"You'd think I would know better that," Artemisia said, "after how much they've doubted me."

"Allora." Elisabetta shrugged. "You can only fight one battle at a time. So, where's your husband? He was smart."

"He's not my husband. I don't have one." When Elisabetta raised her eyebrows, she said, "Artists can be eccentric."

Elisabetta tilted her head begrudgingly. "I suppose there must be *some* benefits to it."

Artemisia remembered Elisabetta's scorn the last time they'd met, and her haunting declaration that Artemisia was happily spilling her own lifeblood in the service of her patrons. "Your husband wasn't here last time," Artemisia said, changing the subject.

"Luco is a fool, but he's not so bad. He sees the value in my work. Without him, I would not be able to sell my wares so easily. His presence lets me do my work, and I earn our living."

Luco, talking with a new client, either did not hear or paid no mind to his wife's sharp tongue.

"Have you started to second-guess your work? I could teach

you my ways. Herbal healing only takes time and attention to learn," Elisabetta continued.

"Why would you share your secrets with me after I dismissed you?"

"There cannot be too many healers in the world. Besides, it would be years before you could compete with me. And," she said with a shrug, "there would be one less artist working. I do not like art."

"So I gathered."

"You have too much power. I've seen the effects of the plague. I've seen the way it ravages the body, and cannot be healed."

"Art can heal it."

"Art can slow the *spread* of it. And only because art *created* it. Those who get sick still die."

"So, you would have us go back to the Grave Age? Hiding art in the margins, destroying landmarks, killing artists who dare to heal?"

"No," Elisabetta conceded. "But you have to admit that my craft is less harmful than yours."

"This is my calling. It's who I am, and nothing can change that."

"Sure," Elisabetta said, again dryly. "Come. If you're going to be stubborn, I'll get you a larger jar of the salve this time and show you some other items. Maybe my craft can help undo some of the harm yours has done to your body."

In the end, Artemisia left the stall with a lighter purse. There was no harm in trying.

Most people had to save their money to commission artists. It was an expense only possible for the wealthy.

Madama Cristina, however, had one painting in her halls and a second partway through design, but sent Artemisia a letter to discuss yet a third. It was a wonder any Medici ever died.

The note proposed a painting of an Amazon warrior in full battle regalia, a concept Artemisia could not have resisted even without the lure of the Medici purse.

"How have you been, Madama?" she asked as she sat down in her study.

"Well," the older woman said. "We missed you at last week's dinner. It was an interesting event."

"I was putting the final touches on a commission I was filling for a Dutch count," Artemisia said. "The trance had a strong hold on me."

"Of course," Madama Cristina said. Artistic eccentricity was an excuse that worked in every instance. "I know you've been quite busy, though I know you won't forget your existing clients." Artemisia nodded quickly. "Your reputation is growing. There's speculation that you may be the first woman to become a member."

"I hope so, Madama," Artemisia said. After a few more words of complimentary small talk, Artemisia took another sip of wine and cautiously suggested, "Your name has been much heard in conversation around the city this year as well." When Madama Cristina didn't immediately answer, she added, "Have you read it?" With its controversial content, highlighted by the ongoing investigation from Rome and continued heckling from Caccini and his friends, Galileo's letter to Madama Cristina about Copernicus's theory had spread across Florence like wildfire over the past three months.

Madama Cristina laughed and drank from her own goblet. "I haven't," she admitted. "I'm not planning to."

"It's really very—"

The duchess interrupted her. "He's using me as a rhetorical device, Artemisia. He's never discussed these theories with me personally. If he's so concerned about my opinion, perhaps he should have accepted one of my recent invitations to a private dinner, rather than publishing a treatise for the world to see."

"He's been ill."

"He's attempting to force my hand into making a statement. My son is not ready to disavow him—he's loyal to his old math tutor—but my patience runs thin. And not only that. Galileo is making powerful enemies, as I'm sure you've heard. He's tugging the tail of the Church, forcing them to make a choice. That Caccini is a rabid dog looking for some way into power, and Galileo is giving him a target."

"Then is this not the time to support him?" Artemisia insisted.

Madama Cristina shook her head. "The Medici do not rise and fall at the whims of mathematicians," she said. "I know you have no mother to give you advice, so I'll tell you this: you should be careful not to follow in his footsteps. Never be so convinced of your rightness that you're willing to burn every bridge you've ever built."

The mention of her mother stung. How different might Artemisia's life have been if she had survived? Who was Madama Cristina to take such liberties?

"But he *is* right," Artemisia said. "Shouldn't that matter?"

"The only thing that matters is public opinion," Madama Cristina said. "Whether you're a leader, artist, or scholar—it matters what people think of you. You should be more wary than any. You are no stranger to the ways controversy can ruin a reputation. Don't put yourself on the wrong side of trouble and expect people to stand with you."

Artemisia took a long drink of wine to prevent herself from arguing further. Madama Cristina was her most influential client; with or without the Accademia's slow approval, Artemisia needed her. Finally, through gritted teeth, she said, "Thank you for the advice, Madama Cristina."

The older woman nodded solemnly and then clapped her hands. "Come now. Let's talk about your next commission."

After nearly two years, Artemisia had a regular spot during the Accademia's monthly meetings. Many of the other aspiring artists who had been at her first were now fully fledged members of the Accademia, standing in their formal robes and critiquing her work—though she'd seen enough of theirs to not bother listening.

Jacopo da Empoli, back from another trip to Milan, brought over one of his colleagues to see Artemisia's outline for a painting of Medea. The sketch was simple, but she'd carefully detailed the Greek woman's face, the screaming child on her lap, and the dagger glinting in her hand. Medea simmered with the cold fury of a woman driven to madness. Jovially, Jacopo bragged that he had known her since she was born, and encouraged his friends to vote for her design as the best of the night. Artemisia, flushing slightly at the reminder of her youth, thanked him graciously for his support. His friends, who had spoken to her before, seemed genuinely impressed by her sketch.

The winners selected tonight would be given a stipend to complete their art to be displayed at the Accademia's next big feast day, the Feast of San Giotto. After the celebration was over, the art would either be sold to support the Accademia's operation, or would be gifted to one of their more influential patrons across the city.

"An interesting choice," Paolo Lamberti said, stopping in front of her. In the last year, the silver in his beard had begun to overtake the black. After he had ripped up her design in June, she had avoided him as much as possible. Today, his anger was controlled, hidden behind a disdainful sneer. She had seen that his temper was like an earthquake, still until he shattered. "Which murderess is this?"

She held the paper tightly. "Medea."

He snorted. "You think the Accademia will be interested in a portrait of a notorious witch? This has no echo of San Giotto. This is for his feast day."

"If the Accademia want a scene of all twelve Apostles milling outside a temple in his style, they could pick one of the other people here. I can make something the men here can't."

"You'd insult San Giotto? He was the last artist canonized before the plague. His memory endured centuries of people looting and burning any art they could find. His frescoes were beautiful enough that people fought to keep them safe. You think you'll be remembered as he has been? You think *this*," he said, pointing at her design, "will add to the world?"

Perhaps one day she could teach Lamberti not to underestimate a woman's anger.

"Oh, to defy constant demonization," Artemisia snarled. "I can't imagine what *that* would be like. Signore, you waste both our time coming to speak with me—I won't listen to your vitriol."

"You're so arrogant," he said, some of that anger she knew leaking to the surface. "The fact you're still here at all is a sign of the decline of this city."

"A weak city, to be felled by someone like me," she said. Sigismondo was passing at that moment, so Artemisia flagged him down. "Thank you for stopping to speak with me, Signore

Lamberti. Always a true pleasure. Sigismondo, there you are." She turned away from Lamberti, ignoring his seething expression until he stalked away.

"Was he giving you a hard time?" Sigismondo asked as soon as Lamberti was out of earshot. Artemisia and Sigismondo had begun meeting regularly after speaking at Casa Buonarotti. Talking to Sigismondo was often like eating meringue—enjoyable at first, cloying in large doses—but he was a reliable friend.

"Always."

"It's just like him to waste his time on cruelty even when he should be focusing on his own success." At her frown, he said, "You didn't hear? Lamberti is working on the new fresco for Santa Maria Novella. The last one has been drained of its magics for a while, and he managed to secure the replacement job from Caccini."

Artemisia had seen the previous fresco at Santa Maria Novella the day Caccini lashed out at Galileo. It may have been beautiful, but the cherubs were stained in her memory by Caccini's vitriol. All church art drained quickly, but she had not heard the commission was open. As the battle between Caccini and Galileo raged, fought with gossip spread around Florence and letters sent to Rome, she had avoided the basilica.

Artemisia folded her arms and glanced across the room at Lamberti, who had turned his back on her. "I would have thought a project like that would be too big for him."

"Everyone was surprised, to be honest," Sigismondo said. "He's not exactly the best artist in the Accademia, especially with fresco, but he clearly has some in with Caccini. They're trying to make Santa Maria Novella the heart of Florence—though I wish them luck overshadowing the Duomo. Lamberti is no match for San Donatello."

"Or for us. Really, it's never been about his own success. You saw the fit he threw in June. He thinks I'm sullying the Accademia's good name—and his name alongside it."

"Shame on him."

"He's not the only one who hates the idea of a woman being offered membership. They'll regret it someday. I'm making the Accademia notice me." She grinned at him. "Maybe when I save Silvestrini. That old man will sing my praises too loudly for anyone to hear the criticism, and his money will sing even louder."

But Sigismondo only frowned, staring after Lamberti. "Have you wondered what would happen if you succeed?"

"I save a rich old man, he introduces me to the Pope, and I beat Lamberti in the hunt for glory," she said. "I can't think of anything more satisfying. It's worth all the blood Silvestrini drains from me."

"It's only… Have you noticed that the more you triumph, the louder the voices against you grow?"

"Of course," Artemisia said. "They only notice me when I make them. They ignored me for as long as they were able. I have to be too good to ignore. It doesn't matter if they love me or hate me—I need them to talk about me."

At the end of the meeting, Artemisia rolled up her sketch and put it into her bag. She stood with the rest of the group, still chatting with Sigismondo, while the pomp and ceremony of the meeting were wrapped up.

When the senior member called her name as the winner of the contest, Artemisia broke off mid-sentence and stared up at the platform in shock. The rest of the members applauded politely, apart from Sigismondo who clapped like he was at a sferistici match and seemed proud fit to burst.

Artemisia collected herself and waved to the group. She'd

expected that if she were ever to be selected to present her work at one of their feasts, the invitation would come with a grimy layer of reluctance and distaste. Though some in the audience seemed as stunned as she was—and some, like Paolo Lamberti, were red with rage—most were cheering her on. Joy thrummed through her like a wildfire, sweeping from her chest up into a blazing smile.

They had, despite the room of talented male artists around them, voted for *her*.

15

A heavenly scent wafted through Artemisia's studio, overpowering the embedded smell of walnut oil and her raw pigments. It was earthy, like a deep cave, but also sweet, like warm chocolate. Artemisia sniffed, closing her eyes. "What *is* that?"

Francesco, sitting across from her, set his bag on the table and pulled out a metal flask, similar to the wineskins workers like Maurizio took with them to their jobs. He winced and set the flask quickly down on the table, shaking out his hand. "Still hot," he said.

"Something warm in this weather?" Artemisia asked. Her studio windows were open, but there was no breeze to ease the oppressive heat. September had just begun, but the summer refused to bid them farewell.

"It's worth it," Francesco assured her. "I wanted to give you a break from your project for the Accademia. I know you're working hard on it."

She had put aside all other paintings to complete the chosen piece in time for the Accademia's feast. Though they would not pay her beyond a stipend for the supplies, she was determined to show them they had made the right choice. The condensed timeline was another test—which artists could complete a piece so quickly for no fee? Which were dedicated enough to do so?

Francesco gathered two cups—by now, he had easy familiarity with her studio. He raised one in a mock toast. "You're realizing your dreams, Artemisia. They'll have to offer you membership any day now. May you keep flying and never become as stodgy as the rest of the members."

She laughed. "I'll do my best. Don't keep me in suspense. What is it?"

"I had my chef brew it for us this morning. It's called coffee."

"I haven't heard of it. Where is it from?"

"It's very popular across the sea. When I was last in Constantinople, they had shops, like bars, just for drinking it. They've been trying to initiate an export path into our lands for a long time, but the Church wasn't sure whether or not it was satanic. They're still hesitant about anything from overseas."

"Since we're drinking it, I assume they decided it was *not* part of Lucifer's plot?"

Francesco poured a small portion into the cups. "Correct. The Pope tried it last year and opened trade for it right away. He assured everyone it wasn't evil."

Artemisia sipped from her cup, wondering what something that produced such an appetizing aroma would taste like. The answer, apparently, was bitter mud. She swallowed with difficulty. "He was wrong."

He laughed and pushed over a porcelain pot from his bag as well. "Add sugar," he suggested. "It can be overwhelming at first."

"Francesco, it's terrible," she told him. "It can't be helped."

"It's useful. It gives you energy. Overseas, they use it to stay up well into the night, and then to become quickly energized the next morning. It seems appropriate for you. You never stop working."

"Neither do you," she pointed out. "You travel nearly every week."

"I trust the men who work for me, but not that much," he said with a shrug. "I like to have my hands on everything to make sure it's being done the way I would do it. I didn't get where I am by delegating everything important. I need to check on the goods, talk to the traders about pricing, and make sure the transport is smooth."

"I'm not sure how you do it," Artemisia admitted. "Even my ride from Rome to here was exhausting. I prefer staying home."

"I've gotten accustomed to it."

Artemisia tested another sip of the coffee, this time after ladling in half the sugar bowl. It was more palatable, though the hot liquid had not dissolved all the granules. She crunched one between her teeth, enjoying the pure shock of sugar more than she had the drink. "You must spend more time on the road than in your own home. You'll rarely be able to take advantage of the magics I'm working into your paintings."

"I'm mostly commissioning for the beauty of the thing," he said. "I can have an appreciation for both beauty and practicality. Once they've run their course, the paintings don't become useless. They're art no matter what their purpose once was, and I appreciate the finer things."

"Most of my clients are only interested in one thing. I hate making beautiful things for men who won't look twice at them, but the magics don't work if I don't pour my passion into it anyway."

He leaned back in his chair, sipping his coffee without bothering to add any sugar. "We didn't have the funds to travel when I was young. My father had no time for a bastard, and my mother had trouble keeping food on the table already. I was twelve before I even made it up the hill to San Gimignano, which was barely an hour away. I remember walking into the Church of Santa Maria Assunta and feeling overwhelmed. The frescoes inside were like nothing I'd ever seen before. At that point, I'd already started my apprenticeship, and that was the moment I decided to become so successful that I could live with that kind of art every day. Maybe it's because I *didn't* grow up in the center of Florence that I'm able to appreciate it." He gave her the kind of smile he'd given her the night they first met, something as hollow as a mask. "I can't create anything, so I had to make enough money to pay people to do it for me."

"You've created a small business empire," Artemisia pointed out. "You're one of the most powerful men in the city, and you're my age. I would say you've created."

"There's a difference between charming and cajoling people out of their money and creating something real, but I appreciate the sentiment."

"And the new goods you've brought to us aren't worthwhile?" she demanded. "You brought me coffee from across the ocean."

"You don't like the coffee."

"Still."

His brittle smile melted into something more genuine. "There's not much you're not fiery about, is there? You'd even fight for someone like me. I'm surprised you have anything left over for your art."

"If you think I'd waste my energies on just anyone, you're mistaken," she told him, still heated. She leaned across the table and pointed at him. "You're a good man, Francesco. Irritating and irreverent, but a good man."

"That's the nicest thing you've ever said to me," he said with a bright smile.

She refused to let him defuse the situation the way he always did. He poked and prodded her for reactions, but never let them settle. If she didn't know better, she might think he didn't care about anything. But after the last few months, she'd started to wonder if it was too *much* caring he hid behind his smile. "We argue, but I wouldn't invite you into my studio if I didn't think you were worth my time. I like you here."

Francesco leaned forward as though pulled by an unseen string. Suddenly, his face was very close to hers over the small table. The way he was looking at her—it was the way Galileo had looked at the stars on top of the Duomo. It was soft, awed, magnetic, overwhelmed.

Her breath caught in her throat like a bird bundled into a net. Her skin was hot and prickly, over-sensitized in the warm air. She yearned for him. She wanted to wrap herself around him so tightly that he would never walk out of her studio again.

Had she ever felt like this before? The ferocity of her body was unfamiliar to her, wild and ancient.

Catching something in her expression, he moved closer until his face was all she could see. Those bright green eyes were warm, anticipatory. It was as though he were about to let her in on a secret she was only just realizing she'd never known.

She felt the warmth of his breath against her cheek.

It was a familiar sensation. Suddenly, it was not green eyes filling her vision, but the dark brown of Agostino Tassi.

The overwhelming tide of emotion in her chest hardened and cooled, like an ember doused in water. He was too close, too big. She was raw and vulnerable, and he was going to *touch* her. The idea of his broad hands on her skin made her stomach turn. She couldn't let him near her.

She pressed a hand against his chest and pushed.

The magical protection from her amulet coursed through her

palm, fierce, sizzling. He landed hard back in his chair, holding a hand to his chest like he couldn't find his breath. They stared at each other for a shocked moment, and then Artemisia scrambled to her feet. "Get out," she said. Her hands were shaking.

"Artemisia, I didn't—"

"Out!"

Though it was clear from his hunched shoulders that he was still in pain from her cursed touch, he held up both hands in a reassuring gesture. "I'll go," he said. He stood up, losing his footing for a second. He put one hand to his chest again, a frown marring the full line of his lips. "I'll go," he repeated.

As he passed her, she took a step away from him.

From his expression, her reaction was more painful than the magics that had lanced through him. He nodded to her, and then was gone.

She locked the door behind him, the latch slipping from her unsteady grasp twice before it clicked into place. She pressed her hands against the wood, its steady bulk solid beneath her trembling fingers.

The coffee flask was still sitting on the table, propped against the bowl of sugar.

Artemisia wandered the familiar market in front of the Basilica di Santa Croce. It was early in the day, but the sun already beat down from overhead. The morning mists had been swept away in favor of an overwhelming mugginess that blanketed everyone in its heavy cloak. The entire city felt still, holding its breath for a fresh breeze to bring them back to life.

Or maybe that was just Artemisia.

After Francesco left, Artemisia spent the next two days in her studio, working on her commissions at a frantic pace. In the end, even her art could not keep her distracted, pushing her out onto the streets to try to rattle the churning thoughts off her skin.

She dodged around a couple of men striding past, narrowly avoiding an elbow and even more narrowly stopping herself from sending one back. She stomped a foot and turned to glare at their backs. The roiling tension in her chest was quick to turn to anger, and feeling the oily discomfort of her anxiety catch flame was deeply satisfying. "Stronzi," she snarled, but they didn't turn around.

"Allora, Artemisia," came Elisabetta's familiar drawl. "You look as though you could use a drink." She was standing at the front of her stall, watching the crowds as usual.

"Always," Artemisia said.

"Luco," Elisabetta said, looking in at her husband, who was organizing the tins in a sweat-darkened tunic. "I'll be back later. No more discounts, no matter how much the old ladies bat their eyelashes."

"Those old ladies are half of your business," Luco pointed out. "There's no sin in rewarding a loyal customer."

"A loyal customer can pay full price," she said.

He waved a hand at her in submission.

Elisabetta rolled her eyes and pulled Artemisia away. She strode through the crowd like a heavy boat through water, cutting over the waves of people like they weren't there at all. Artemisia followed in her wake, relieved to have a moment without thought.

It was well before the noon bells, but a small restaurant tucked away near the Ponte di Rubaconte was already open. They sat near the door, and Elisabetta brusquely ordered two cups of white wine.

"I prefer red," Artemisia said. It wasn't true, but she could feel her agitation bristling under her skin, eager to lash out and rend something.

"It's too hot for red," Elisabetta said, not changing the order. "Now, tell me what has you looking ready to murder the next man who crosses you."

Artemisia accepted her cup from the waiter and took a long sip. The acrid flavor of the wine was warm and tart, chased by a whisper of ripe cherries. "Why do you care? I don't need more salve already. My pockets are empty."

"I wanted some wine, and you looked like you needed a friend."

Artemisia wanted to protest—she had Maurizio, after all, and Galileo.

And Francesco.

But Maurizio had liked Francesco, and she could only imagine his comments about her ending up in a convent after all. And after Galileo's essay to Madama Cristina had further inflamed the religious community across Europe, he had been feverishly writing rebuttals to the slew of vicious responses. It was rare for Artemisia to see anything of him beyond his handwriting on quick notes. As close as they were, it was difficult to imagine discussing a romantic entanglement with him. He was supportive of her, but old enough to be her father.

Artemisia nodded, lips pressed tight. "I've been having a hard week."

Elisabetta hummed and waved her hand, encouraging Artemisia to keep going.

"I've just been reminded that not all pain heals with time," Artemisia sighed. "And I realized I haven't come as far as I thought. Every time I think I've taken steps forward, the past tugs me backward. It's like a shackle. I never got rid of it—I just moved further down the chain. Now I'm wondering why I even tried." She had worked on her painting of Judith last night for the first time in weeks. Pausing the outpour of necrotic energies had given more energy for her commissions, but she found she had lost ground. Using the necrotic energies used a muscle she had not realized could atrophy with neglect. Working on it again for just an hour had left her trembling and short of breath. Finally, she'd packed up her oils and gone despondently to bed.

"Some days," she continued, "I want to scar over every one of my open wounds and prove that no one has the right to define me." She stared down at the wine in her hands. "Other days, I want to grab that burning rage that's waiting inside me with both hands and let it scald me until I never have the chance to forget what's been done to me. I *want* to burn, because then at least I know it happened. I can't move on."

Elisabetta nodded, tracing the rim of her goblet. "I don't know your past, but we've all been hurt. How long do you want those who hurt you to have control of your life?"

"I can't pretend it never happened," Artemisia said. "It did. If I move on, then I'm saying it didn't break me, but it *did*. How can I be broken and still move forward?"

"You're already moving forward. Life is moving forward. There's no way for any of us to freeze and keep breathing. You're deciding your quality of life now, not whether or not you live it. Why not hunt down some joy and grasp *that* with those hands?"

"Anger is more...reliable than happiness," Artemisia said. "The past won't change. The future can still hurt me."

Elisabetta shrugged. "I didn't think you were a coward." While Artemisia spluttered in offense, she continued, "You were right. I don't know you well. But I think you're a survivor."

"I don't always feel that way."

"You're here, aren't you? If you're already broken, if you're already pressing forward while holding your wounds together with sheer will, I don't imagine anything managing to hurt you worse."

Across the city, people slept in their small rooms, surrounded by their families. Wives and husbands curled together under light sheets. Sheep from small flocks shifted in their pens, resting on the dirt. Birds and insects were tucked in the branches of the orchards inside the city walls, the smell of perfume heavy in the air around them. The summer fruit had all fallen, but fig and pear season was approaching. Autumn was not far off.

Florence stretched out in front of Artemisia, a dark expanse broken by the nearby river, which glistened under the light of the half-moon overhead. The heatwave from the week had finally broken, and a faint breeze off the river played with the loose curls around her face.

The tiles beneath her legs were still warm, radiating the heat of the day through her thighs. Equally hot was the press of the griffon's flank beside her, its coarse fur rubbing against her bare arm.

A shredded portrait rested below its talons, dark oils gleaming under the moon and stars.

"What should I do?" she asked it, voice quiet in the heavy night air.

The griffon glanced at her, its bright yellow eyes dilated wide in the darkness.

Gently, it leaned forward to press its head against her knee. The ridge of its beak pressed against her skin like stone, solid and steady.

Cautiously, she reached up and ran her hand down its back, feeling the transition from soft feathers to short fur. It twitched under her palm, but settled when she ran her hand down the same patch again. Awed and humbled, she pet her companion until her thoughts were soothed enough for her to find sleep.

When the knock came, Artemisia carefully set aside her charcoal and stood up. She had been waiting. Francesco had sent a messenger that morning, requesting a meeting.

She had rinsed his flask out to return it to him, the coffee coming out dark as mud and warm from the summer heat. The smell, which had seemed so seductive at first, was cloying and unsettling after days spoiling in her studio.

She did not want to have this conversation. The possibilities scared her. She wanted to keep her door locked and throw herself so deep into a painting trance that she could forget she'd ever met a charming man named Francesco Maria Maringhi. But she was no coward, so she scrubbed her hands on a towel and opened the door.

Francesco, usually so composed, looked ragged. She'd seen him fresh off a three-week trip across the continent looking more composed. There were purple circles under his eyes, and his dark hair was ruffled over his brow. He looked her over urgently, as though he expected to find her bleeding.

"Come in," she said, stepping aside.

He came across the threshold, but stopped just inside, not making his way to his usual seat at the table. "I wasn't sure you'd let me come over. I wanted to make sure you were all right."

"I'm fine," she said. "I have what you left behind," she added, nodding to the table. In her otherwise chaotic workspace, the flask and delicate sugar bowl were the only objects set out neatly.

He didn't spare them a glance. "I have to apologize. For frightening you."

Artemisia crossed her arms tightly over her chest. She'd never been as skilled at lying with a smile as he was. If she told him she hadn't been scared, he wouldn't believe her. "You could have written that in a letter."

He nodded as though hearing a full paragraph she hadn't said. "I won't come back if you don't want me to."

"I don't give refunds on deposits, if you're canceling your commissions," she told him.

His jaw clenched, a muscle flexing white on the side of his face. "Artemisia, I'm not canceling anything. I wasn't lying when I said I wanted art from you. Our work was never tied to our relationship. I asked you to paint for me because I wanted your paintings, nothing else. About the other thing, I misunderstood the situation. Possibly one of my worst mistakes. I'm usually much better at reading people."

"It's not about you," she blurted. "I didn't… It's not that I…"

He held up his hands. "You don't owe me an explanation." He rubbed absently at his chest. "I got the message."

"It's not about you," she bit out more forcefully. "Nothing could work between us. Go find a nice girl to kiss, someone who doesn't harangue and *hurt* you." She nodded to his chest, and he dropped his hand as though embarrassed to find it there.

"Don't make my decisions for me," he said. "I'm sorry I alarmed you, but I know my own feelings."

She waved a hand. "You don't know me. You don't understand. I wouldn't be good for you, and I certainly wouldn't be good for your reputation."

"Help me understand," he said. "If you don't want to be near me, that's up to you. But don't push me away because you think that's what's best for me."

"Do you know what happened in Rome? Do you know why I came to Florence in disgrace? Why I'm here, unmarried and on my own? Surely there have been rumors."

He shook his head. "Do you want to tell me?" From the way he was watching her, she thought she wasn't holding onto her composure as well as she'd hoped. It was the way someone watched a glass on the edge of a shelf, unsure whether it was about to fall.

Did she want to tell him? He didn't need to know. He wasn't pushing her for an explanation. If she told him to leave again now, he would.

But the past was like bile inside her. No matter how many times she tried to expel it, to channel it, it lurked in an empty hole behind her heart.

"I was attacked, when I was younger. Someone I thought I could trust came into my bedroom when I was alone and…hurt me. It's been four years, but I don't do well with…being touched. It's not just you. It's anyone. Even here, in my space." She laughed, and it felt like being punched in the stomach. "Maybe especially here. So, it's not about you."

"Who hurt you?"

"My tutor," she said. "An artist from Rome who worked with my father."

"And where is he now? Was he ever punished?"

She realized he wasn't simply curious. There was something in his eyes, something dark and calculating. He was collecting intelligence, like a general surveying a battlefield. "He was," she said. "The trial was long and…horrible. You will never understand what I went through. In the end, they believed me."

And within a year, Tassi had been freed from his sentence.

Artemisia couldn't articulate that. Her rage at that newer injustice was still an ember in her throat, threatening to burn her again if she gave it air.

"It shouldn't have taken so long. You're one of the most forthright people I know. They should have believed you," Francesco said. He clenched his fists, but when he noticed Artemisia watching his reaction carefully, he released his hands so they hung loosely at his sides. Francesco was always aware of the people around him. At parties, she'd seen him defuse tense situations with an easy word, move between conversations and morph himself to stand out in each one.

This was the first time she'd seen him try to make himself seem smaller.

"I won't hurt you," Francesco said. She'd thrown her story at him, and he'd caught it so that it became a tether. It was still monstrous, still haunting, but she wasn't trapped alone with it. "I wouldn't. You can make me leave, but I'm not him."

"I know you're not, but…" She shrugged. "I can't be what you want me to be."

"I want you to be you," he said. "Like I said before—if you don't want me, just tell me. But don't make my decisions for me."

"And if I don't know? If I'm not sure I can do this? How much are you willing to leave uncertain?"

"Nothing is ever certain, Artemisia. If we don't try, we'll never know how it might have gone," he pointed out. Seeming to sense that she was wavering, he held up his hands in a plea. "I wouldn't ask anything of you that you did not enthusiastically want to give. I don't want to torment you with my affection. I simply…want your company."

It wasn't what Elisabetta had suggested it would be. She didn't feel brave, like a knight charging into battle while ignoring an injury. She felt raw, exposed, bare. It wasn't strength she had to find, but the softness to open the hands she'd kept so tightly clenched over her past. There might never be a way to cleanse it completely, but with Francesco standing in front of her, she thought she could try.

Artemisia took a deep breath, and then tilted her head at him. "My company is all you want?"

He hesitated, examining her expression like a man testing flooded streets for a secure path. Delicately, he said, "Hopefully not all."

She closed her eyes, letting herself feel the emotions that zipped through her like fireflies sparking through an empty field. There was fear—of course there was. It was the dark night against which her other reactions stood out. There was the warm flush of attraction she'd felt for Francesco since the beginning, along with a new bubbly sensation of knowing that he wanted her too. The thrill of it was heady, and offered to push away the lurking darkness.

Francesco was flighty and witty, not someone she ever would have expected to become a stabilizing force in her life, but he'd started to lighten the load she carried on her shoulders every day. He was a sculptor chipping away at the excess that surrounded her to start to reveal the truth that waited underneath.

And she wanted him.

She opened her eyes. Then she pulled off her amulet and set it down carefully on the table.

He stepped toward her, but waited for her to close the gap between them. In every moment, it was her decision to move forward. Even when part of her wanted him to take the faltering flag of her courage and carry it for her, she was grateful that he made—*let*—her set the pace.

She was in his space, pressed against the front of his body. Artemisia was tall for a woman, but Francesco was taller yet, just enough that she had to look up to meet his eyes. She barely had to lift her face in order to meet his lips.

The brush of skin was dry and chaste, but she felt sparks jumping from their single point of contact to thrum throughout her body. One warm, broad hand fell to her waist, and another gently cupped the side of her face. Francesco's head tilted, and the kiss deepened.

Francesco was an observant man. He used the skill in every facet of life, from parties to his trade empire, and he used it now. He kissed carefully, experimenting with each new step, each alteration, to see what worked.

She fell into the sensations, letting him sweep her higher and higher. Her mind felt so light it might drift away, but she was grounded through the slick press of their lips. The hand on her face moved to her hair, brushing through her thick curls before cupping the back of her neck. Gently, he encouraged her to tilt her head so that he could trail kisses down the length of her neck.

"Francesco," she murmured.

He pressed his lips to each ridge of her collarbone, and then lifted his face to meet her gaze. "Artemisia," he said, as though savoring the combined taste of her skin and her name on his tongue.

Artemisia felt the way she did when a storm rolled low and warm over the city. Electricity hummed in the air between them, and it seemed as though swollen clouds were primed to finally let loose their bounty. It seemed as inevitable as breathing, but she didn't know what the conclusion would bring.

"Don't stop," she said quietly, and let the storm sweep her away.

PART II

OCTOBER 2, 1615–MAY 14, 1616

16

Artemisia sipped a cup of wine and plucked a marinated olive from the table, letting the breeze lift her curls without protest. When Sigismondo had asked for her company, she had insisted they meet at an outdoor bar near the Accademia. As October began, Artemisia clung to chances to enjoy Florence's piazzas. From the crowds, it seemed the whole city had remembered that winter was oncoming.

Nights were cool now, but that brought her less dread than it once had. If her fingers ached, she had her salve from Elisabetta—and Francesco to help warm them.

"You and I should talk seriously, Artemisia," Sigismondo said. Despite his words, he leaned casually in his chair and surveyed the piazza beyond their café. "I believe I'm meant to be the centerpiece for Casa Buonarroti, and yet from the Medea you did for the Accademia, I imagine no one will be able to look away from your work."

Though her work had been displayed at the Feast of San Giotto, only inducted members of the Accademia were permitted to attend the Mass and subsequent feast. She wished she could have seen it in its place of honor. "Flatterer," Artemisia said. "Your piece is stunning."

Sigismondo saluted her with his cup. "I hope you're well? You do seem a bit tired, if I'm to be honest. I've never thought it fair we don't pay our prospective members for the work we benefit from."

She shrugged. "It's not just the Medea. I feel as though half the blood in my body must belong to Stefano Silvestrini at this point. It will be worth the exhaustion in the end for his favor, if either of us can save him," Artemisia said.

"Perhaps. Though I hope I do not look quite as wan as you," Sigismondo said, softening the comment with a fond smile.

"I haven't had much time for sleep. My work keeps me up all day, and, honestly… I have a new lover to keep me up at night." It was thrilling to talk of Francesco like that for the first time. Sigismondo had once asked if she had someone. It felt somewhat like joining a private club to admit she did now.

"Oh, good for you, Artemisia. You deserve some fun."

"I'll have the chance to sleep tonight, at least. He's away on business," she sighed. "I hate when he's gone. Not that I can complain—without his money we never would have met."

Sigismondo rubbed his chin. "You're seeing one of your patrons?"

She frowned. "Don't look at me like that."

"I'm just saying—that's a delicate road to walk."

"What about you and Michelangelo?"

A blush spread over his cheeks. "Ah, Michelangelo and I are not as…close as we once were. He's a good man, but self-centered. He rarely thinks of anyone but himself—or his uncle."

She winced, but said, "That's nothing to do with me. You don't know us."

"There's no reason to be like that," he said. "Take my advice, borne from experience—it can be difficult to determine where the patronage ends and the romance begins. Patrons… They can feel like they own you."

"Francesco isn't like that," she said.

"I only care about you. But I trust your judgement. I didn't mean to scold you today." He put his hand on hers, earnest. She was grateful she had begun leaving her amulet at home for their sessions. She was growing comfortable without it more and more. "You do so much work for so little recognition. You know, I still think about that day in the anatomical theater. I've always thought of myself as someone who stands up for what is right, but I failed you that day. I should have spoken more loudly on your behalf against Lamberti."

"You tried," she pointed out. "You were the only one who said anything."

"I should have walked out with you. I knew from being in the workshop together that you were skilled, that you deserved the same education I was getting. But I was afraid to argue." He pressed on before she could reassure him again. "Over the past year, I've seen your skills, and I've seen your dedication to the craft. You deserve the chance to stand with the rest of the artists in the city."

"Thank you," she said, pressing a hand to her chest.

"So," he pressed on, a smile tugging at his lips, "when the vote came through after the feast, I insisted they let me be the one to tell you—though Jacopo da Empoli nearly had my head for it."

"The vote?"

"Artemisia Gentileschi—would you like to be a member of the Accademia delle Arti della Magica?"

The initiation ceremony to the Accademia was all pomp and ritual. After so much time working for the invitation, the night arrived with disorienting speed. Everyone wore their formal clothes to gather in the monastery, hiding their forms in dark velvet and stiff wool. It was the first time Artemisia had been to the building without the other aspirational artists shoving for space and attention. There was a charged atmosphere tonight, a buzz of excitement and tension about their newest member.

They had voted to induct her, but the decision had not been unanimous.

Everyone in the room had been given matching black leather masks for the ceremony, which made them seem like a mob of eyes in the night. The paintings and statues that crowded the edges of the room held the only faces she could see, making the experience even more like a dream. Candle-laden sconces were littered around the room, but with sunset occurring earlier in the fall, even the candlelight wasn't enough to suffuse the whole room. The monastery smelled of burning wax and the damp must of plaster.

When Artemisia stood on the dais to complete the ritual, she stared out at the crowd of faceless eyes. She was not wearing a mask, and felt viciously exposed. It was like a scene from one of her nightmares—but the eyes here weren't judging and finding her lacking. They had found her *worthy*. She was being welcomed, not scorned. Respected, not belittled.

The long hours of work had been worth it. When she arrived in Florence, she had nearly starved, bleeding herself dry. But finally the most elite organization of artists had recognized her value and welcomed her into their ranks.

The Accademia's official robes were uncomfortably tight across her breasts, and draped loosely across the rest of her body, but they announced her belonging.

She repeated the ritual phrases Sigismondo had taught her the night he told her about her acceptance. The ceremony was about the sanctity of art, encouraging the members of the Accademia to elevate the artistic integrity of the craft in everything they did, to bring both beauty and health into the world.

Her voice did not waver as she swore to never use her magics for harm.

No one needed to know about her Judith.

At the end of the ritual, a large statue was unveiled on the dais. It was carved in Michelangelo the Elder's distinct style. Artemisia should have expected it—Michelangelo had been one of the first honorary superintendents of the Accademia. Before his time, artists were part of the guild for doctors and apothecaries, the Arte dei Medici e Speziali. He had worked with the Medici ruler of the time to establish a new guild for artists alone. The statue depicted Apollo, the Greek god of art, magics, and healing.

Artemisia guessed the end of the ritual before it was explained. The marble in the center of Apollo's chest was faded slightly from dozens of hands brushing against it.

She placed her palm in the center and felt the rush of magics sing through her. She had expected the movement to simply be ritualistic—unbonded magics rarely lasted even a decade—but this statue was kept locked away except when it was brought out to induct new members. The great artist's power still sat inside like a gift waiting to be unboxed.

Magics were often a subtle sensation, layered onto the air like the most transparent oils. Michelangelo's magics felt like floodwaters. If there was nuance in the power of his art, it was lost to the bright intensity. If all his work had such heft, perhaps it was why he was on the road to be canonized.

"May the blessings of our craft be upon you," the superintendent announced. "You are now a member of the Accademia delle Arti della Magica. Your eyes are now opened to our brotherhood."

Around the room, the masks lifted from every face, revealing the other artists of Florence.

With that, the ceremony was over, and the rest of the gathering's matters could proceed. Artemisia mingled with a line of men congratulating her on her acceptance. Many she had met during her time as an aspiring member, but some had never spoken to her directly before tonight. An older weaver commended her heartily, calling for her to be given another drink.

Paolo Lamberti shouldered past her, hissing in her ear, "I hope you're pleased you've made a joke of the Accademia." She stared after him, distressed, but even he could not ruin her night.

Artemisia searched the room for Sigismondo. She had spotted him in the crowd earlier despite the mask—his curls were distinctive no matter what covered his face. He visibly restrained himself from hugging her, and instead clasped her forearm. "Congratulations," he said. "Interesting ceremony, isn't it?"

She glanced back at the dais, though Michelangelo's statue had been covered up again already. It would be moved back into storage soon. "That statue was powerful. It must have touched hundreds of people over the last century," Artemisia said. "And I could still *feel* it."

Sigismondo shrugged. "It's Michelangelo," he pointed out. "He could do anything. He'll be canonized any day now."

Artemisia looked at her hands. She was part of a legacy now, tied by magics to the glorious history of Florentine art. She'd expected to feel as though she had crested a peak, but had only found a full mountain range ahead. Would her work be remembered as Michelangelo's was, or would her standing fade with her death?

"Come," Sigismondo said, steering her toward the snack tables. "Let's drink to your success."

They were both on their second cup of wine, the room a pleasant swirl of lightness around them, when Jacopo da Empoli approached them, his own wine in hand. The black mask was dangling from his wrist, tied there with a satin ribbon. "Congratulations," he said, beaming. "What a triumph! I was sorry this kid took my chance to tell you the great news. Your father must be so proud."

"Of course," Artemisia said, smile stiff as wood. Someone would surely send her father a letter about her initiation—he had other friends in the Accademia—but he had not contacted her. If he'd had his first choice, she would still be in Rome, wedded to Agostino Tassi. If he'd had his second, she would be in a convent in the countryside.

Though he had trained her, she refused to give him the credit for her triumph.

She had succeeded in spite of him. This victory was hers.

After the ceremony, she took a private coach to Francesco's home. She normally walked, especially on a mild fall evening like this, but with the wine and triumph swirling in her head, she did not trust her feet. The coach rattled beneath her.

Francesco lived in an unassuming villa north of the Duomo, its plain stone walls masking the lush interior he had cultivated within.

The entrance hall was breathtaking, even after so many visits. Gilt accents and a mirrored ceiling added a sparkle around the set of murals on each side wall, which had been done by one of the best traditional artists at the Accademia. They portrayed a lush forest scene, peopled by an array of regal gods and goddesses, including a plump Venus holding a golden apple.

When Artemisia and Francesco were not tucked away in her studio, as they often were, they stayed in Francesco's personal quarters, where her own paintings lived. No matter how often she visited palaces like those of Francesco and the Medici, Artemisia would never be able to see a building so lavish as home, and Francesco was of the same mind. He had spent too long in poverty to feel fully comfortable surrounded by gold. Away from the gilded entry halls he used for hosting events, he had a set of cozier rooms to sleep in. His wealth was a front just as dazzling and distracting as his smiles.

"Artemisia," he greeted as he emerged from the adjoining study. "I'm glad you came. I thought you might want to celebrate with the Accademia all night."

"Of course I came. I know you leave again later this week, and I'm not missing a night with you," she said, pulling him into a kiss. She felt as though she drowned in him when he was in Florence, clinging as much as possible before he had to leave for work again. He held just as tightly, coming to her studio even more often than she came to his villa. Despite the lavishness of his home, he always seemed content in her small space.

"Good," he said. "Look at you. An official member of the Accademia. The first woman in their history. You astound me."

"You told me at my reveal at the Palazzo Pitti that I should have been drinking wine on the roof. What do you say we make that a reality?" she asked, grinning.

"Certainly," he said. "Congratulations, my heart. You've earned this."

17

Autumn winds swept through Florence. The trees on the rolling hills around the city turned yellow and red with the changing season. As they fell, the leaves swirled down the Arno under the bridges at the heart of the city. The fall was mild, easing them into the inevitable winter. Artemisia's hands warned of the coming cold, seizing up during her long nights in front of her canvas.

"It's coming along splendidly," she commented as Michelangelo the Younger led her through the soaring gallery. He had sent a letter earlier that week inviting her to see the progress. Over the last six months, half of the other frames had been filled with their paintings. Happy cherubs now framed Sigismondo's centerpiece, and further scenes of Michelangelo's life or symbols of his success were scattered around the room. "I recognize this style," she added, stopping to examine one painting. In it, a clergyman examined a set of architectural plans with a magnifying glass as Michelangelo the Elder fiercely explained the details. There was a hint of Caravaggio's style—dark curtains framed the scene—but the realistic faces and perfectly detailed fabrics spoke of a more familiar artist. "I didn't know you had commissioned Jacopo da Empoli. He's an old friend of mine."

"A good man. Enjoys his treats, he does. I had to give him a bottle of nice red wine for him to get me this painting on schedule," Michelangelo said, shaking his head. "This scene is the moment my uncle gave his model of the façade for the Basilica of San Lorenzo to Pope Leo the Fourth. It would have been an impressive design."

Artemisia tried to remember the story. "But he never did it, did he?"

Michelangelo huffed, folding his arms. "He was invited down for an even more important task, one with magics. The Pope preferred to have my uncle paint the ceiling of his own chapel instead. The magics are said to still be at work in Rome." He waved a hand at Jacopo's painting. "It is still an important moment in my uncle's life."

"And a well-done painting," Artemisia assured him.

"Indeed," Michelangelo said. He paused, staring up at the centerpiece. "Difficult to surpass the first, of course. Have you seen Sigismondo lately?" Michelangelo did not meet her eyes, poorly feigning nonchalance. "Does he seem well?"

"As well as can be expected," she said carefully. Sigismondo avoided talking about their failed relationship, and she believed he was already seeing someone new.

He glanced at her, and then forced a smile. "Good, good. I suppose you're both in the Accademia now. Is it all you dreamed?"

"It—well, it's more tedious than I expected," she admitted. "The biannual elections were last week."

Other than the superintendent, who was appointed by the Grand Duke, the rest of the officers of the Accademia were voted on twice a year. Most positions were limited to senior members, and varied greatly in prestige. There were consuls of painting, sculpture, and tapestry. Beyond that, the Accademia had a secretary, a chancellor, a treasurer, three workshop teachers, and an official visitor to the sick and poor. The last managed the membership dues that went to support artists who were struggling with their health or finances. Aid was available to anyone who applied, from established members to their assistants to visiting foreign artists. That had been a surprise to Artemisia— there had certainly been no mention of aid during her early years in Florence. Apparently such help only applied to men.

Beyond the positions for senior officials, there were a variety of smaller roles that even newer members could fulfill: clerks, treasury assistants, customs representatives, and more. For each position, the names of all eligible candidates were scrawled onto scraps of paper and put into a bag. Then the superintendent drew three out at random, and the assembly voted to select the final appointee.

"Ah, bureaucracy," Michelangelo said. "The heart of every organization, no matter how esteemed. My uncle was the first superintendent of the Accademia, you know."

"I do know," she said, amused. She was sure there was a portrait somewhere within the gallery depicting his inauguration. "My first appointment is not so glamorous."

"You were elected?" Michelangelo asked.

"I'll be working with Florentine customs," she said, unable to suppress a proud smile. "One of two representatives from the Accademia. I'll be helping to make sure important art isn't sent outside the city walls."

"Vital work," Michelangelo said. "You would not believe the people who tried to sell my uncle's art abroad. Florence was his home. Every piece that leaves the city dilutes his legacy."

And the impact of the new gallery, of course. Michelangelo the Elder had split his time between Florence and Rome, but Casa

Buonarroti—and the Accademia—still claimed him as their own. When Michelangelo was inevitably canonized, Florence would celebrate for weeks.

"So, do you like it?" Michelangelo asked, turning with his arms spread to encompass the developing gallery. "I hope to have it completed by next spring. Your piece is coming along soon, correct?"

"It will take a few more months, at least," she said. With her regular deliveries, Silvestrini continued to absorb a large portion of her energy, and unlike the old man, it would not kill Michelangelo to wait a bit longer. "I'm sure it will be ready for your planned opening."

"My uncle was a very punctual artist, you know." Michelangelo raised his eyebrows meaningfully. "The Medici have already promised to attend."

"It will be done on time," Artemisia insisted. "I'm looking forward to the opening. I think we can finally drag Galileo from his work in the country for something as big as this."

Michelangelo looked away. "Perhaps Galileo will not want to attend."

"Not want to attend?" she repeated, surprised. "Half the artists in this room are his friends."

"Well," Michelangelo prevaricated. "If he is still making so many enemies at that point…"

Artemisia stared at him. "You're the one who was disappointed he did not come to my unveiling at the Palazzo Pitti in March."

"Matters were different in March," Michelangelo said. "The Medici still loved him then."

"Sure, Madama Cristina is frustrated, but her son still supports him."

"For now," Michelangelo hedged. "I'm worried he'll be forced to go to Rome to talk to the Church soon. He should be thinking about how this fight will impact his work—and his friends. He's asking for trouble by pursuing this."

"So you're going to cut your ties with him?"

"Only in public, of course. I'm just not interested in sparking gossip. This is to be my place in the Buonarroti line. This gallery is my *legacy*, Artemisia. I can't risk its reputation at the opening. You should be careful with Galileo too. The Accademia won't appreciate your split loyalties."

"The Accademia trusts me. Have a little faith, Michelangelo," Artemisia said. "Galileo knows what he's doing. We made friends with a genius. He doesn't make plans based on politics. Only on truth. He may be a bit arrogant, but he's *right*. The world will see that."

Michelangelo sighed. "I hope you're right."

Over the centuries, the city walls of Florence had spread out from the central Piazza dell'Esedra like ripples, expanding with the population. The current wall encircled the entire city on both sides of the Arno, and though nearly three hundred years old, the stones still stood sturdy.

Artemisia had not left Florence since she arrived from Rome. Standing in front of them again, she remembered the terror and elation she had felt when she first saw the imposing city walls. Her dreams of acceptance in Florence had been a desperate hope after what she had left behind in Rome. She had been ready to fight for a new life.

She could never have imagined that the next time she approached one of the city gates would be as a member of the Accademia delle Arti della Magica.

The Customs Service operated out of a large building beside the southern gate, just below the newly built Forte di Belvedere. The Medici crest, that ubiquitous circle of balls, was inlaid on one side of the door, with the city's crest, the Florentine lily, on the other.

The guard at the entrance had been expecting her. "You're that female painter?" he confirmed. "The one who joined the Accademia? I've heard about you."

She preened, satisfaction warming her chest like a hearth fire. She had truly made history. "That's me."

How far had the news spread already? Were they talking about her in Rome? If so, she doubted it was with praise. Rumors were rarely pleasant, and there was no one in Rome willing to defend her. Still, they would know she was finding success without them.

The guard led her through the narrow halls to a small room stacked with crates and leather tubes. Each was stuck with a slip of paper marking it as in need of inspection. The crowded space smelled of wood shavings and old must.

Artemisia and her partner, Giuseppe Nardella, were assigned to help the customs official examine every bit of art being exported from Florence, with a single goal: to prevent the unauthorized distribution of pieces by nineteen key artists. All the saints of Florence were included, along with more recent artists like Caravaggio and Il Bronzino. The goal was to keep Florence's best art inside the city walls unless its export was specifically approved by the Accademia. Florence was already hemorrhaging artists to Rome or scattered to the various courts across Europe, and they were desperate to keep the existing art in place. She had been briefed on her task by the previous customs representatives alone. Nardella had been a member of the Accademia since his youth, and with such a long tenure had cycled through the Customs Service more than once. With only a six-month election cycle, longstanding members of the Accademia often repeated the same positions.

A clerk briskly walked Artemisia through her section. "I'll be assisting you. If any of the items need confiscation, we'll mark them for removal. Otherwise, I'll mark them as free to go. There's a bit of a backlog with the transition. Your partner has already started." He waved across the room, and Artemisia noticed Nardella standing over an unrolled canvas.

Artemisia looked over the room, astonished. Was this how much art was traded out of Florence every two weeks? There were dozens of boxes. It was no wonder she and Nardella were expected to come at least once a week.

She took a breath and set to work looking through the first box.

She lingered over each painting. It was a slow process, but pleasant. Searching for the work of nineteen specific masters among every piece of art—magical or not—that was sent from Florence was like searching for a single rose in a sprawling meadow of poppies. Many modern artists completed commissions for patrons abroad, and there was a steady stream of older art passing to new hands after it was drained of its magics, presuming the artist had enough prestige. Before long, her fingers began to subtly tingle. Much of this work was infused with untied magic. She inhaled deeply, feeling the power drift through her. It was a subtle sensation—no one who had not spent the past two decades living and breathing art would notice. This was why the customs service needed the Accademia to assist them.

She spotted works by fellow members, deciphering their signatures or recognizing their style. She sneered over one from

Lamberti. It was technically skilled, but his brushstrokes offended her. The painting was tied to some foreign patron, but this close she could feel some of the energy pulsing out. His magics had the bland grit of an underripe pear.

She peered into a crate and brushed a thumb over the smooth marble of a small cherub. Only three sculptors were monitored by the Accademia: San Donatello, Michelangelo, and Giambologna. Though the cherub was well done, she knew at a glance it was not the work of a master.

Across the room, her partner harrumphed under his breath as he examined a rolled canvas. He seemed to be going through them far more quickly than Artemisia.

She moved on to the next piece, a painting of a woman in red over a soft, blue-green landscape. It had no spark of magic, but the technique was impressive. She examined it for a long moment, fingers hovering over the portrait's delicate features, and then squinted at the details in the background. "Signore," she called, waving her partner over.

A plump, ruddy man in his sixties, Nardella moved with all the urgency of melting ice. "What is it?"

"There's something about this painting that seems familiar," Artemisia said. Nardella leaned over to peer at it. "Do you recognize the artist?"

Though Artemisia had seen examples from most of the artists they were searching for, some were still too cherished to be revealed to the public. Not every artist was as prolific as Michelangelo—there were allegedly only fifteen paintings attributed to San Leonardo, though each was powerful enough alone to secure his sainthood. She hoped someday for Madama Cristina to let her see the *Primavera* by San Sandro that was hidden somewhere in the Palazzo Pitti.

"No," Nardella said, standing back up.

"You're sure?" Artemisia asked. He had barely glanced at it. The clerk hovering alongside them did not hesitate, sliding it back into its travel case and updating a piece of paper to verify it could be taken from the city.

"There was no signature," Nardella said with a shrug.

"Someone could have cut it off to hide the original artist," Artemisia pointed out. "The edges of the canvas were tattered."

"Then they'd be cutting away the piece's worth," Nardella said. "You have a lot of art to get through. Focus on pieces with a magical energy. That one is dead."

"Even pieces from the saints could have lost their magics by now," Artemisia said.

He shrugged. "Unless you want to spend the next year in here, you'll learn to prioritize." He turned for the door.

"You're done already?" she asked.

"As I said, you'll learn to move more quickly." He hesitated. "I'm sure the Accademia appreciates your dedication, but don't kill yourself over this. It's rare to find anything of interest. New members are always overeager."

"Oh," Artemisia said. "Thank you."

He nodded to her and left.

She felt a pang of disappointment—she wanted to help the Accademia, prove her worth—but there was an undeniable flush of pleasure at his final words.

New members are always overeager.

Perhaps she could have been embarrassed, but Artemisia had joined the legacy of artists in Florence. She was stepping in footprints left behind by a generation of the city's top creators. She was a member of the Accademia, just like the others who had come before her, and the others that would follow. Even this small job was a symbol of her belonging, and her enthusiasm a sign she was meant to be here.

Smiling to herself, she went back to work.

Artemisia slumped over Francesco's chest, her loose curls licking over his skin like flames. She kissed his collarbone. He smelled of thyme and mint under the salt of sweat. They were in her studio, which was less insulated than Francesco's house, but he'd slowly been gifting her thick furs and silks for months. Tucked together on her cot, surrounded by soft fabrics, they had created a pocket of warmth.

"I'm glad you're back," Artemisia told him quietly.

The feel of his body against her was a comfort she had never hoped to have. When she came to Florence, she had expected to wear her amulet every moment for the rest of her life. Instead, Francesco had become *part* of her, body and soul.

The amulet had another side-effect which had only now become relevant—there would be no child in her womb. It would not suffer another person to exist inside her. In a way, it was a relief not to worry about a pregnancy out of wedlock. And yet— she thought Francesco would make a good father.

"It's good to be back. Zürich is beautiful, but already deep in winter. I thought my fingers might fall off." Francesco wrapped his arm around her waist, warm and secure. With regular meals, she had gained back the weight she had lost during her first year in Florence, and more. Surrounded by Francesco's arms and gifts, she felt like one of the lush women in her own paintings. "I'm sure you barely noticed I was gone," he continued. "There are a half-dozen new canvases here. I see being an official member of the Accademia has made its impact already."

He was right. Artemisia's client list had continued to flourish, expanding internationally as the Accademia put her in contact with several members of the French gentry. She was constantly rotating among different paintings for her current clients, including another addition from Madama Cristina. Training with the Accademia had expanded her art in ways she had never imagined, unlocking the next level of her artistry. Her magics, too, were stronger, flowing from her with less drain on her soul.

But he was also wrong. "I notice when you're not here. I miss you," she told him, pressing up to capture his lips with hers.

She often wondered where Francesco was, and who he was with. He shared his smiles and laughter so easily. She wanted to hoard his light for herself, but they were both devoted to their work. She would keep painting, and he would keep traveling. It felt as though her heart were tied to his, and the further he went from her side, the worse the pull.

O dio d'amore, che pena é quest' amare.

Oh god of love, what suffering is this love. Galileo's song rang true.

He kissed her back. "I doubt that, carina." He brushed a thumb over her cheek. "You look exhausted."

"Sweet talk will get you nowhere, vostra signoria." The honorific vostra signoria—Your Lordship—had morphed into an intimate shorthand between them.

"With the amount of healing you do here, you should be able to afford a mansion," he continued. "You should be paid as a doctor, not like this." He waved at the studio around them, at the small nook of her bed tucked on the floor.

"No one will pay a worker who *needs* to work," Artemisia said. "I would paint even if I were unpaid, living as a hermit in the wilderness. If I protest and charge them more, they will find one of the other artists desperate to work. Why should they pay me well for something I would do without them?"

"Because they're reaping the benefits," Francesco said. "You give yourself away for so little."

"You seem to like my self," Artemisia said, rolling away from him.

"I do," Francesco said, following her and keeping his arm over her waist. His fingers stroked her soft stomach. "Very much. I just worry when I'm gone."

"I'm sure there are plenty of beautiful women to keep you company," she said, scowling.

He pressed a kiss against her hair. "I don't see any of them. When I'm away, I only have my hand to keep me company."

She hid her smile. "Then I'm jealous of it," she said, lifting the hand from her waist and kissing his palm. "I'll create a self-portrait for you someday. I couldn't spare any magics, but, well, that wouldn't be the purpose."

"I certainly wouldn't protest that. Or...perhaps next time you could come with me."

"Come traveling with you?"

"Not for long. I know you're busy," Francesco said. He was talking quickly, airily, into the crook of her neck, which meant this was important to him. He masked his vulnerabilities with casualness. "One of my business partners has a villa in Prato he said I could use if I was nearby."

Artemisia hummed. "Are you going there for work?"

"Well, no," he admitted. "I thought maybe we could just go together."

She rolled back over and propped herself up on an elbow. He looked handsome with his hair mussed by her hands. "A vacation?"

"I think I've earned the time off." She snorted at the understatement. It seemed all he did was work. "And I know you have. Come with me, Artemisia. Three days without the demands of Florence to separate us. Just you and I, our own private villa… It's the birthplace of the biscotto, you know. And we could hike Monte Retaia. It's meant to be gorgeous."

"You may have an empire of underlings to keep your business running, but my work cannot rest on my laurels," she said. "Days I don't paint are days I don't earn money."

"Your stipends will not halt if you take a small break. I'll pay for the whole trip. You're doing me a favor, getting me away from my work. I'd owe it to you."

Sigismondo's warning about being involved with a patron tugged at her mind. "I don't need you to pay for me."

"I want to," he said. "Indulge me. I have the money."

It was true. She had seen his villa, and the army of servants who lived within its walls. "Yes, that we've lived the same number of years and yet you are so far ahead of me has not escaped my notice."

"We can't be compared. I've created nothing myself. Only taken what belongs to one and sold it to another." He shook his head. "I had no money growing up. Now I do, and I want to spend it. On you. Let me, Artemisia."

Artemisia looked out through the gap in the heavy curtain that surrounded her cot. Her studio was filled with commissions to finish. Even now, they all beckoned for her to come from her warm sanctuary and fall into the work again. Her griffon did not require her magics to survive, but she was not eager to abandon it either.

In the corner, covered in a drape, necrotic magics still festered inside her Judith. She had not set her brush upon it in weeks.

Between Francesco and the Accademia, it had never seemed the right time, but it was a mission she had to finish.

But the promise of Francesco's time was irresistible. He wanted her company during his travels. Perhaps he did enjoy the company of dozens of strangers while he worked abroad—but he wanted her to come with him. With the entire world before him, he turned back to pull her alongside him. Was it wrong to let him distract her? She hardly cared. It was the first time she had ever felt so happy.

She turned and kissed his cheek. "Replace the hike with more biscotti, and I think we can make this work."

"I'll feed them to you myself," he said, and captured her lips again.

The next week, Francesco and Artemisia took his private coach up to Prato. The carriage rattled uncomfortably, but the ride was brisk and easy compared to the last time Artemisia had traveled, the week-long journey she had taken early the previous year to leave Rome.

The public coach had been crowded with bodies. Everyone wore linen to fight the spring heat outside, but a sweaty stink had settled inside the wagon. Artemisia had sat hunched, legs set on either side of her bag to protect it from thieving hands. She had been striking out on her own, leaving Rome along with every person she had ever known. Regrets had crackled through her thoughts like wildfire. It had been a miserable week.

Now, instead of looking over her shoulder toward the past, she was anticipating her destination. Francesco chatted while Artemisia looked out the window, watching the city fade away in favor of rolling yellow hills and dark green cypresses. Drawn by a pair of dark horses, they left after breakfast and arrived just in time for lunch.

The villa was painted a rich ochre, sitting on the ridge like part of the landscape. The view of the shadowed blue mountains was breathtaking. She stood on the balcony with her hands on the rail, breathing deeply. The stench of Florence was only surpassed by that of Rome, even in early November. The oils and candles in her studio were a stringent and temporary mask. She could not recall the last time she had smelled nothing but fresh air.

"Beautiful, isn't it?" Francesco asked, coming from behind to wrap his arms around her waist.

"Magical," she said. "I hadn't realized how much I had grown accustomed to Florence. It's the city of my heart, but there's another world out here. I forget, sometimes, that there's life beyond the city walls."

"Exploration is good for the soul," he agreed.

"I understand now why you travel so much. It's astounding you ever come home, vostra signoria."

"It's not all like this," he said, pressing a kiss below her ear. "Spend a week on a boat to Egypt with a seasick bunkmate and you'll realize home has much to offer. Besides, I have someone waiting for me in Florence now."

Artemisia turned and met his lips. They had no responsibilities calling their names, no pounding city to draw their attention. They spent the afternoon between the bed and the balcony, leaving the windows open so that the mountain air joined them in the sheets.

Despite Artemisia's protests, Francesco convinced her to hike with him the next morning. "We can stay in bed in Florence," he pointed out. "You'll regret not taking advantage of the space while you have it."

The morning air was crisp in her lungs. Leaves crunched under her shoes, yellow and brown and red. Only the Tuscan cypresses held onto their green despite the changing seasons, dispersed throughout the mountain like stray brushstrokes.

Halfway up the path, Artemisia called for a rest and leaned against a tree, panting. The bark of the cypress was rough against her shoulder, and the crisp smell of resin flooded her senses. She wore a lightweight dress, but sweat slicked down her spine and under her arms. The forest had been mostly quiet around them, other than the birds and the crunch of brush under their own feet. In comparison, her own heart was loud in her ears.

"Aren't you glad we came out?" Francesco asked. Barely out of breath at all, the bastard.

Artemisia just glared at him.

He laughed, clearly at ease. He was in simple clothing, for once leaving behind the velvet and embroidery he loved in Florence. A straw hat perched on his curls, shading his eyes from the sun. "Just think—you could be working right now. Enjoy the time off."

"I like working," she pointed out, voice thready with effort.

"You like painting," he corrected. "You can't pretend to like the rest of it. Talking to patrons, shelling out money on overpriced pigments—not to mention dealing with the Accademia. All of that takes you away from what you want to be doing."

She shrugged. "It's not what I…I love, but I'm an officer with the Accademia now." Though her heart was pounding, her lungs were slowly coming back under control. "They need my help."

"Yes, of course. Who *will* be guarding the gates of Florence from thieves and smugglers without you there?"

She ignored his teasing tone. "They only need me once a week. It's not as though we're digging through boxes ourselves, you know. The officials pull out any art that tries to pass through and lock it away until we have the chance to review it."

Francesco whistled. "Those poor bastards," he said. "I can't imagine how many legitimate shipments are delayed because of that policy."

She straightened up and looked out over the ridge. In the morning light, the landscape seemed to stretch into a misty haze. She would not admit it, but she understood Francesco's fondness for hiking. There were views that could not be found without an effort. "We've had some complaints, but it's a necessary process," she said. "That art belongs to Florence."

"Oh yes, I've heard the city of Florence is quite the collector. A truly passionate patron of the arts. I'm lucky I have an in with the Accademia representative. At least I know you wouldn't let them ruin my business like that."

She frowned at him. "I can't give you special treatment, Francesco."

"Of course not," he said. "I was just kidding. You always take me too seriously."

"I take everything too seriously," she said. She was irritated by his flippancy, but reined in her annoyance. "Look, let's keep going. Once we finish this hike, I want those biscotti you promised me."

"You'll be disappointed to learn there's not a bakery in the wilderness," he teased as they started back up the path.

"Obviously. I meant—"

"Luckily for you," he continued, "I got some in town yesterday while you were napping. They're in my bag." She looked over at him, hopeful, and he winked. "I wouldn't make you hike without giving you a reward."

"You *do* know me," she said, smiling.

A branch cracked nearby, and the undergrowth rustled.

Artemisia glanced over, and then screamed. She bit down on the sound quickly, but it was left ringing in the forest, bright as spilled paint.

Standing in the underbrush, half hidden by the brambles, was a wild boar.

Its bristled gray fur made it blend in with the shadows, but its black eyes were bright. A streak of ivory jutted on either side of its wet nose. Tusks. It was twice her size, sturdy and squat with a torso like a wine barrel. It was standing only a few meters away, just down the incline. Its gaze was intent on Artemisia.

Her pulse lurched back into a butterfly rhythm, rapid and fragile. Her breath was caught high in her throat, unable to reach her lungs. The splitting note of her scream still resonated in her mind.

Artemisia's only experience with cinghiale was slow-roasted, but she had heard the stories of the beasts in the wild. They were vicious creatures. Hunting them was a common sport of nobility, and many lords had been gored by their prey. If the blood loss did not get them, infection did. Even a castle full of the best doctors and art were often not enough to heal the wounds, and Artemisia and Francesco were far from aid.

Francesco grabbed her arm. "Stay calm," he said. "We need to back away slowly. There was a boulder behind us down the trail. We'll climb it until it leaves."

"Francesco." Her voice was barely more than a whimper.

"Quietly," he said, and tugged her backward.

She kept her eyes on the beast, and, trembling, took a step away.

The boar squealed, a ferocious, feral noise, and lunged up the incline toward them. Artemisia screamed again and turned away, colliding with Francesco in her terrible, desperate scrambling. Her skirts clung to her legs, slowing her retreat even as Francesco dragged her down the trail. The world spun around them, and Artemisia had no thought but for finding safe ground.

A wild screech split the air, and then a crunch and crash echoed as though the entire forest were falling apart behind them. A bellowing growl, a feline hiss, a scream of pain. The sounds were incomprehensible. She glanced back, and then skidded to a halt, pulling Francesco alongside her.

Wings stretching from one side of the path to the other, a griffon stood on the mountain trail. Its amber haunches and swaying tail were lit in a spotlight through a circle of broken branches overhead. Beyond it, the skittering blur of the retreating boar was visible for just a moment before it vanished into the undergrowth.

"Artemisia," Francesco breathed. He let go of her hand and carefully stepped in front of her, putting himself between her and the griffon. Climbing a boulder would not be enough to save them now. Griffon attacks were exceedingly rare, but brutal when they happened. Though few in number and skittish near most humans, griffons were only below wolves and blood drakes as the most dangerous creatures in the region.

The griffon huffed and looked over its shoulder at them, bright, intelligent eyes glinting in the dappled light. Its beak was open, and its sides heaved as it panted.

"That's mine," Artemisia breathed. "My griffon."

"Are you sure?" Francesco asked.

"I've sketched every inch of that creature," Artemisia said. "I know it as well as I know my own face." Francesco was stiff beside her, but she squeezed his arm and took a step forward.

She clicked her tongue, and the griffon tilted its head. "Hello, carino," she greeted. "You're far from home."

The griffon glanced back at the empty trail beyond, and then folded its wings and turned. Compared to the squat, vicious boar, it was large and regal. As big as a wolf now, it stood on the mountainside like it belonged there. Its tail swished, and its pupils were dark and intent. Blood stained the talons on its front right claw like spilled wine.

"How did it find you?" Francesco said. "You haven't done any painting here."

"It must still be able to smell me. We're bonded by blood from my art. It must have followed me up when I didn't come home last night." She held out her hand.

The griffon ignored it and instead pressed its beak into her stomach, nudging her with its feathered forehead.

"Should you let it so close?" Francesco asked, hovering behind her.

"It's not going to hurt us," Artemisia said. "It's chosen to stay with me for more than a year."

"I'm not the artist," Francesco pointed out. "It has no affinity for me. I've seen enough beasts in my travels to give this one a wide berth."

"You've seen other griffons?" Artemisia asked. She kept a hand on her companion's neck, feeling its warm feathers beneath her skin. After the scare of the boar's attack, the sturdy, lanky presence of the griffon was stabilizing. "There are so few in the wild. Too few."

"Rarely near here. I saw a mated pair in the mountains in France, and, once, a blood drake flying over the Black Forest," he said.

Between their appearance and apparent taste for dark magic,

blood drakes had been nearly hunted to extinction during the Grave Age. In Rome, she had seen a booth claiming to sell powdered blood drake scales as a way to protect the body from the plague—curing a poison with a taste of its source. Artemisia's father had scoffed at the eager salesman, of course; even if a blood drake's hide were able to cure the plague, the elusive animal was as rare as snow in Rome. If the salesman had actually managed to find some of the substance, he would not have been selling it by the pound on the middle of the Campo de' Fiori.

"The Grave Age changed the face of Europe. Their numbers are low here, and those clever enough to survive learned to avoid humans." His tension eased slightly as the griffon closed its eyes, leaning into Artemisia's hand scratching against its neck. "Abroad, there are more. In Jerusalem, packs of griffons hunt in the deserts. You can hear them shrieking from the city. In Cairo, they have serpopards—I'm sure you've seen sketches. Their bodies are something like a leopard, if its neck was twenty times as long. There's a hood around their heads that flares like a cobra, and most people say their bite can suck the life from you. It's better to not get near one at all. When you take a boat down the Nile, your guide is as much there to keep you safe from the hippos and crocodiles and serpopards as to get you to your destination."

"Galileo has a theory about those," Artemisia said. "He thinks all these creatures are the balance to our art. God has a creature for everything, after all, and artists have a power not seen in nature—it makes sense for some to crave it as much as others crave flesh. Griffons are drawn to healing magic. Blood drakes come to dark magic. Serpopards skip the art altogether—they can draw that spirit out from a person's blood."

"All animals are prey, companions, or predators," Francesco

said. "If your griffon chooses to be our companion, I am very happy."

"You could give it a pat," Artemisia suggested, a bit wry.

Francesco hesitated, and then slowly reached toward the griffon's forehead. The griffon opened one yellow eye and stared at him. He snatched his hand back. "I'll leave that to you," he said. "Do you think it would walk with us up to the top of the mountain? Maybe if I feed it a biscotto, it will change its mind about me."

"It would work on me," Artemisia said. "Let's see."

The griffon took off back into the sky when they restarted their hike, but they found it sleeping on the balcony of the villa when they returned, tired and sweaty. It glanced over at them, fluttered its wings, and then fell back to sleep.

Artemisia had never had a vacation like their time in Prato, a true reprieve from daily life. Her father had taken her and her brothers up to Assisi once to pay homage to the great San Giotto, but the trip had been a trial of wrangling her brothers during the long, steep walk up the mountain. By the time they had reached the Basilica di San Francesco d'Assisi, they had all been tired and frustrated. After that, Artemisia had been eager to return to Rome and her work in her father's workshop.

Transitioning from a truly restful break—wild boar aside— to return to the intensity of work in the city was less appealing. It took less than two days for her commissions to absorb her again, and within a week she experienced a frustrating night of insomnia. Rest evaded her as the sun set, and continued to stay far from her grasp as her candles burned. She yearned for the peace her vacation had given her.

Francesco was asleep in his villa across the city, so neither his embrace nor more energetic activities could distract her. She missed him with a fierceness that startled her. He had become integral to her life with unexpected swiftness, changing the fabric of her days.

She continued work preparing a new canvas, letting the methodical application of the astringent rabbit-skin glue occupy her hands while her thoughts wandered. Unlike the painting process, the initial canvas work didn't require magical input, though it was nearly as important; the glue base would tighten and protect the raw canvas from both the oils and the elements.

Despite the work, her sleeplessness was like a fungus in her mind, warm and heavy and spreading.

Deep into the night, her heavy gaze fell on the covered painting of Judith.

How long had it been since the last time she had worked on it? Weeks, at least. With the increase of commissions after her Accademia initiation and the heady rush of exploring intimacy with Francesco, adding to her Judith had slipped from her mind.

None of that was an excuse, she chastised herself as she put aside her canvas prep and mixed her oils. There may have been no patron hounding her for this work—but justice was a responsibility. She removed the drape and took in the painting anew. Without the usual clawing need to coat the work with her revenge, she could see that it promised to be some of her best work. It would never grace the halls of a powerful monarch or gain compliments from her fellow Accademia members, but it could bring her another type of glory. Even with tired eyes, she could see its potential.

She mixed oil into a dark red pigment. In the candlelight, it looked appropriately like fresh blood. She lifted her brush and took a breath. She looked to her heart, reaching for the well of fury from which to draw her necrotic magic—and coming up dry.

Slowly, she set her brush against the palette. She focused more carefully, searching for the roaring fire that usually sat so close to the surface. She could only claw at scraps, like unearthing low embers that glowed anew with the disturbance.

This inability to focus had interrupted her regular work before, though fortunately only rarely. There were tales of artists who lost their connection to their hearts and never found it again. It was a horror story whispered among the Accademia.

Only, Artemisia had never before lost her ability to tap her necrotic energy. The first time she had tried, it had been *too* much, a splurge of lava impossible to direct. Then, it had seemed as much a part of the terrain of her soul as her name was.

This was startling, a missing limb she somehow only noticed in its absence.

Even if she could occasionally lose her healing focus, how could she misplace her rage at Agostino Tassi? The memory of his name made her stomach turn—but the magic still would not come.

She tossed her palette down and paced to her window. It was shuttered against the late November weather, which, though not quite freezing, was enough to irritate her hands. She rapped her knuckles on the wooden slats. The Artemisia Gentileschi of last year would have been horrified by this sudden lapse. There had been little on her mind but this.

But that Artemisia had also not achieved her goal of gaining access to the Accademia, or fallen into the arms of Francesco Maria Maringhi. She'd had nothing else to live for, but now her heart was full.

She turned from the window and set about cleaning her work station.

The disconnect would not last forever, just as her healing magic had always returned with rest and refocus. There was no cause for alarm.

Like all magic, necrotic art required intent, and tonight she could only muster idle obligation. She simply had to return to this painting when the time was right.

Perhaps it was a sign that she was meant to save her energy for paying work until she felt fully settled as a member of the Accademia. Art took time—she could not rush through the final layers of this painting. It was more important for it to be done right than done quickly.

She went to bed with less trouble than she anticipated, and slept solidly through the night.

18

Though Artemisia was thrilled to contribute to the Accademia's legacy, she had to admit she had expected a bit more glamor in her first job. Though she had insisted on its importance to Francesco, idly scanning her half of the most recent haul of art at the customs office made her wish she were back with him in the mountains. After nearly a month, Artemisia had not yet found a single piece of smuggled art from the Accademia's nineteen masters.

She paused to look at a marble bust of Medusa. The serpents on her head coiled close to the skull, a sign of a sculptor cautious of breaking pieces. The crate was destined for St. Petersburg, so she could not fault the caution, but it was a stagnant design. Artemisia was no Michelangelo, skilled in both sculpture and painting, and she couldn't help feeling more affection for her own craft. Physics did not limit painters.

"Please inform the trader that the Accademia is confiscating this one," Nardella said, his voice a surprise in the quiet, stifling room.

Artemisia looked at him, eyes wide. He was directing the clerk to wrap a painting. She glimpsed the edge of a dignified profile before the portrait was rolled up and set aside. "You found one?"

He nodded. "Finish up your review and then we'll take it

back to the Accademia. It's time for you to see the next part of the process."

She rushed through the rest of her pieces, her mind already on the confiscated portrait. Who might the artist be? San Raffaello? San Sandro? She was electrified by the possibilities.

It would only take a half-hour to walk back across the city to the monastery of Cestello, but Nardella hailed a hack to carry them. Artemisia gritted her teeth against the rocking of the carriage as they trotted over the bridge. Compared to the smoothness of Francesco's private coach, the hack rattled them like dice in a cup.

Artemisia had never been inside the monastery headquarters outside of workshops and meetings. It was strange to be there alone, the place empty. Only the art on display around the temple saw them—blank marble eyes and the darting gazes of two dozen oil portraits.

"There are three ways to handle the art we confiscate from customs," Nardella said, leading her through the center aisle. It was the most energized Artemisia had ever seen the old man. "If it's lost its well of power, or if that power was tied to a patron and can't be unleashed, there are aesthetic collectors we will gift it to. It's always wise to flatter the city's biggest patrons. If it still has power..." He gestured around the room. "Most of this art was donated directly by our members for display. They get to leave their mark on the Accademia, and the magics help keep us well. The rest are pieces we found being illegally exported. The original owners lost their rights by trying to send them out of the city. We bring the art home where it belongs."

They went through the temple to the platform where the superintendent and other senior officers conducted their meetings. Artemisia glanced back over the room from the new vantage point—would she ever be elected to one of the primary positions? She imagined herself as a senior member, an established painter in her fifties, presiding as superintendent of the Accademia. It was a heady thought. She would be one of the most respected artists in the world.

"Now, there are also some pieces that would not work for display," Nardella said, picking up a candle from a small table and lighting it. "We only have so much space, after all, and an academy for design can't be overly cluttered. It needs to look impressive. That's when we utilize this." With a flourish, he opened a door at the far end of the platform.

The candle revealed a set of wooden stairs leading down into a windowless cellar.

Carefully, Artemisia followed Nardella down the steps. The temperature, already glacial, dropped as they went belowground. She clutched her shawl around her shoulders with one hand, the other ghosting over the splintered rail.

They stepped onto the stone floor, and Artemisia gasped as the candle illuminated glints of marble and bronze, the sheen of oil, the rough backs of canvases. The room was stacked with endless works of art, more even than in Silvestrini's bedroom.

"This is stunning. How big is this place?" Artemisia asked. The darkness seemed to stretch forever.

"The cellars run all under the monastery," Nardella said, sounding pleased by her reaction. "Old art is stored in the other rooms, but anything with magics goes under the temple. There's a radius effect with open magic, you know. Up as well as around. We're directly under our meeting space right now. This close, our members can feel the effects. Welcome to the Accademia's greatest gift."

Artemisia had noticed the amount of ambient power in the

monastery, but had attributed it all to the pieces on display. This treasure trove flooded their headquarters with magic. It must have been building for decades, ever since the Accademia was founded. It was stronger down here, now that she knew to feel for it. It crackled in the air like an incoming lightning storm.

Nardella opened the leather travel case and pulled out the rolled canvas. He led them through a narrow path in the stacks of art, and then set the canvas against a wooden crate. He stood up and nodded to himself, satisfied.

Artemisia waited, and then prompted, "Can I look at it?"

"Oh," Nardella said. "Of course, go ahead."

Eagerly, Artemisia unrolled the canvas. There were fresh magics in the oils. It must have been kept isolated after its completion to retain so much of its well. The portrait was stiff and formal, showing a weak-chinned man staring off to the left. Unless the candle was masking some subtle detail, the background was a simple black. Though it had magics inside, the painting was far from masterful.

"Who painted this?" Artemisia asked. She searched in the candlelight for the signature, but the edges of the canvas seemed to have been sliced. If it had been signed, the signature was lost now.

"It could be a Caravaggio," Nardella said.

Artemisia scoffed. "A Caravaggio? This?" She refused to believe even his earliest work had been this staid.

"The merchant cut away the signature," Nardella said. "They were clearly hiding the artist to get the painting through customs."

"When I suggested the same thing, you didn't think it was worth noticing," Artemisia reminded him.

"Well," he said, pointedly, "*that* piece had no magic."

Artemisia looked back down at the painting.

Nardella had never thought this was a lost piece from one of the nineteen masters.

"We only take what we need," Nardella said. "The customs service has faith in the Accademia, and we cannot break that trust. After all, who is to say this is not a Caravaggio?"

"But this…" Artemisia trailed off, horrified. "None of this art belongs to us. We keep all of this for ourselves? What about the churches? A cellar like this would be a blessing during the next plague."

"In a church, the magics wouldn't last long enough to matter," Nardella said. "They have gatherings with hundreds of people at least three times a week. Even this much art would only last a single church a handful of years. The Accademia has only a few dozen members."

"Still—" she began.

"We are not the Vatican," Nardella said, an edge of frustration in his voice. "We are not hoarding art to give ourselves long lives. This art gives us the chance for a *normal* life. When is the last time you saw an artist live past seventy? The cellar is only counteracting what we give with our art. Without this, we would lose more artists than we already do."

Artemisia stepped forward to examine a frame set against a statue of a faun. Her mind was racing.

The cellar had been a shock, but how many artists had she seen die too young? Her father and his friends in Rome lived fast and loud, fully expecting to drip the last of their lifeblood into their paint at any moment. The Accademia was meant to protect its members, helping them hone their craft, find commissions, and deal with legal struggles. Why should it not also make sure the healing energy did not only flow out?

Perhaps her monthly visits to the Accademia had quietly stopped her from painting herself to death when she had been juggling her first commissions and the dark magics of her painting of Judith.

Nardella himself was one of the oldest artists Artemisia had ever met. What good had he been able to do for the world with the extra years gifted by the Accademia's aid? Elisabetta took her own herbal tinctures. Doctors certainly treated each other. Why should artists be condemned to give and give and never receive?

"Do you understand?" Nardella prodded.

Artemisia looked around the dark cellar, this miracle of the power of art. "I do," she said.

Artemisia's acceptance to the Accademia had led to a flood of new commissions from patrons both in Florence and beyond, and the tide was only rising. Between long hours at her easel and the creeping chill of winter, Elisabetta's salve could only do so much to help the ache in her hands. When she brought a new piece—a miniature of a boar, in gratitude—up to the griffon, she was only able to pet its head briefly before the cold drove her inside. She already longed for another vacation with Francesco, though neither of their work schedules would permit it. There was simply too much to do.

Still, when Elisabetta and Francesco teamed up to force her from her studio to participate in the Feast of San Donatello, Artemisia could not resist. Elisabetta had been demanding for months to meet Artemisia's lover, and the feast was a perfect excuse.

The feast day celebrated the day of San Donatello's martyrdom, when the energies he poured into his statue finally killed him. Florence had several saints close to their heart—especially their patron saint, San Giovanni—but San Donatello was the city's favorite.

After the Accademia's official Mass, Artemisia slipped away to Santa Croce, where one of San Raffaello's paintings of the Madonna was carried around the city through streets strewn with sweet herbs and flowers at the head of a procession led by priests decked in gold. Musicians and dancers followed the priests ahead of the crowd of citizens close behind, all hoping to feel the touch of San Raffaello's magics. The crowd swelled as it left Santa Croce, with people coming out of their homes to join the group. At the end of the parade, the painting would be displayed at the Duomo near San Donatello's statue, and celebrations would kick off in the square around the church and baptistery.

The late November day was cold and crisp, but lacked the vicious bite that true winter would bring. Still, she was grateful when the procession left the windy path by the Arno and turned onto the more protected streets toward the Duomo.

She and her companions—Francesco, Elisabetta, and Elisabetta's husband, Luco—walked at a more sedate pace than some of the other citizens. Artemisia knew that no matter what miracles San Raffaello's paintings had performed in the past, this smaller piece was likely drained of all its magics by now. There were stories that his most famous painting of the Madonna, in Milan, still healed all visitors, but it was difficult to know where a saint's miracle ended and rumor began.

Francesco regaled them with entertaining stories, always at his best with new people to perform for. Elisabetta let him ramble and then unsubtly pulled Francesco forward for a quiet conversation. Francesco gave Artemisia an exaggerated look of fear, but went along without resisting, leaving Artemisia to walk with Luco.

They walked in companionable silence, listening to the cheers and music, while Artemisia watched Francesco and Elisabetta confer ahead. "What are the chances your wife makes him cry?" Artemisia asked idly.

"High, but it's good for his character," Luco said, making her laugh. He spoke slowly, in measured beats, so his jokes were always a delightful surprise. "How goes your work?"

"Really well," Artemisia said. "I'm busier than ever. Joining the Accademia has truly changed my place in Florence."

"Congratulations," he said. "What's next for you?"

She faltered. What *was* her next step? She had achieved what no woman in history had by gaining membership with the Accademia. She had enough commissions to support herself without scrounging for food. She had invitations to mingle with the greats of Florentine society. "I want to be remembered," she said finally. "That's when I'll know I've made it."

He was silent for a long moment. "Artemisia... You can't allow others to shape how you value yourself."

She glanced over at him. He was avoiding her gaze, looking at the dried flowers and branches strewn across the streets and the decorations hanging from the windowsills they passed. He was more reserved than his wife, but it did not mean he had no mind of his own.

"What other goal can there be for an artist?" she asked. "I make art to be seen. I need others to see me."

"Many people have the power to give us many things," he acknowledged. "But our own work is all we can control."

He fell silent, allowing her to contemplate that.

Luco walked as slowly as he talked, so Elisabetta and Francesco had to circle back around to find them after a while. Artemisia clucked her tongue as Elisabetta returned Francesco to her. "Are you done tormenting him?"

Elisabetta shrugged, unrepentant. "Maurizio had the chance to meet him," she said. "It's only fair that I got to, too. Maurizio liked him, but he is easily swayed by a handsome face."

Artemisia tucked her hand in Francesco's elbow, laughing. "That's not true, and you know it. Maurizio is grumpier than you."

Elisabetta rolled her eyes. "Maurizio is too kind. I've seen those hideous costumes you make him wear. No self-respecting man does that unless he has a soft spot for his friends."

"I do pay him, you know. Why were you and Maurizio talking about me?"

A few months ago, Artemisia had taken Maurizio into the markets to test different fabric colors against his skin to prepare his next costume, and had introduced him to Elisabetta along the way. The two had become unexpected friends, their rough edges sticking together like two burrs.

"He likes to gossip, and you're our favorite subject," Elisabetta said, waving her hand.

"My life can't be that interesting."

"It's more now that you've gotten this man," she said, pointing at Francesco. "Awfully eager to please, isn't he?"

At her side, Francesco blanched, and then smiled. "Signora, is it so wrong to want to impress one of my dear Artemisia's closest friends?"

Elisabetta raised her eyebrows at him. "You're doing it again."

Artemisia patted Francesco's arm. "Don't be mean to him," she said to Elisabetta. "He's scared of you. I've told him all sorts of stories."

Elisabetta laughed. "If he's with you, he must not mind a mean woman."

"Now that may be true," Artemisia allowed, and Francesco stroked a hand over hers.

Tucked inside her small group, Artemisia was protected from the buffeting crowd around them. The noise, however, was overwhelming as they reemerged into the square in the shadow of Santa Maria del Fiore.

Streamers waved overhead, linked from the various statues and windows of the Duomo across to the surrounding buildings. The bright colors in the air were mirrored on the ground, where dried flowers and ribbons covered the square until the dirty cobblestones were nearly invisible. The smell of bread, pastries, and meats were thick in the air, the smoke from the latter winding around them like a blanket.

When Elisabetta and Luco left to examine the food and drink lining the square, Artemisia turned to Francesco. "I really do hope she wasn't too mean to you," she said. "I've felt the lash of her tongue before. Elisabetta spent our first two meetings telling me how she thought art was a terrible profession, and that I needed to leave before it sucked out my soul."

"She was fine," Francesco said, craning his neck to look for Elisabetta in the crowd. "Do you think she likes me?"

Artemisia shrugged. "She can be hard to read," she confessed. "You don't have to try so hard to impress her."

"I want your friends to like me," Francesco said, stubborn.

"Francesco, my heart, you want everyone to like you."

He ducked to pick up a dried poppy from the cobblestones and offered it to her. She tucked it into her collar. It was bright against the muted wool. "You're not wrong," Francesco admitted. "People need to like me. I'm a businessman—I operate on favors, and most of my deals are made over dinner. But I'm not trying to make a deal with Elisabetta or her husband—or Maurizio. I want them to like me because they're important to you." He shrugged, looking over the milling crowd. There was music playing nearby, loud and tinny. "Your friends don't put on the same pretenses as mine do. With mine, I can never tell who appreciates me because they all pretend they do. With your friends, I can't tell if they like me because they seem to enjoy acting like they don't."

Artemisia put a hand on his arm to make him turn toward her. Despite the crowds, despite the chaos of the day, she had left her amulet at home. She was there with her friends and would rely on them to look after her rather than risk one of them taking an accidental injury from it. After she had lashed out at Francesco when he first tried to kiss her, he had given her amulet a wide berth. Unlike Galileo, he did not understand the necrotic magics that made it work, but he knew that it had hurt him. She did not like to see him anxious.

"My friends show their affection in ways other than words," she said. "I trust that they like me because they spend time with me, when they both prefer to be alone. Elisabetta wanted to meet you today. She is protective of me, but she knows that I make my own choices. If she didn't like you, she would say. Even if she didn't like you, I would fight to keep you. She would have to accept it."

"I wouldn't want to make you choose between me and your friends," Francesco said.

"That is one of the reasons I adore you," she told him quietly, aware of the press of people around them. Artemisia's reputation was well-ruined, and as a successful businessman, Francesco's reputation could likely only be improved by being sighted with a young woman around town, but the public setting made her feel exposed. "As long as you make me happy, my friends would not make me choose between you. Not these friends. They may use some strong words to protect me, but they don't make my decisions for me."

"I need to make better friends," Francesco mused. "I need one of them to talk to you about breaking *my* heart. It very much seems to be the one in danger between us."

"Or perhaps you just need to learn to stick up for yourself," she said. "Make your own threats, vostra signoria. Like this: break my heart, and my friends will be the least of your problems."

"Maybe it's just me, but that sounds more like a warning than a lesson. You might not make the best teacher."

"I teach by example," she told him, leaning against his side, no longer caring about the crowd around them. Let them see. He held her weight easily, his arm moving to wrap around her waist.

Elisabetta and Luco returned, both holding bread trenchers stacked with food. There were savory street foods, as well as a zuccotto for each of them. The pastry, a sponge cake shaped like the Duomo and filled with chocolate syrup and dried nuts, was a staple of the holiday. Luco handed a plate to Artemisia, and Elisabetta handed her second one to Francesco. "Eat up," she said. "You're too thin."

Artemisia gave Francesco a significant look, and they dug into their meals. The meat was plump and cool from being outside, and the olive-studded bread was rich and dense. Streamers waved in the breeze, arcing across the blue skies, leading up to the vast Duomo.

19

Artemisia watched from the stool in her studio, bundled in the scarf and gloves Galileo had given her, while he collected his scattered papers from around the room. He had left behind piles of notes during various visits, and Artemisia had liked having the scattered evidence of her friend's presence filling the empty corners of her studio. Now, the debris of their friendship was being examined and packed away. "You must be joking," Artemisia said, feeling hollow. "You can't leave."

"This isn't going away with me sending letters from Florence," Galileo said, unrolling a paper to check its contents before rolling it up again and sticking it into his bag. "If I'm not there to defend myself, I'll never be sure if they're seeing the truth. The Inquisition is out for blood, and they don't know me. You heard what Caccini did with my letters?"

"Of course I did," Artemisia said, and cursed him. "Stronzo." As part of the Inquisition's deposition, Caccini had sent a heavily doctored set of Galileo's letters, exaggerating his claims and including blatantly heretical content. If Galileo had not been able to produce the originals, the sentence would have already struck down from Rome like lightning.

It had been a year since Caccini had first taken to the pulpit to speak against Galileo. After the reflexive apology the Church had been forced to send, Caccini had learned the art of subterfuge, and Galileo was battling lies and gossip from all sides.

"I need to make sure they're hearing the truth, not the bullshit the Pigeon League has concocted. Caccini has been summoned as well, and it will be my word against his." Galileo set down his bag and turned to her. "Once they see my evidence, they won't be able to avoid the truth any longer. The Church can't deny that the sun is at the center of the solar system. They will be made to look the fool when the truth eventually comes out—which it will. Our understanding of the world is only growing. They need to accept it before they make a proclamation that goes against the nature of God's universe and make the Church seem fallible."

"Men are fallible, my friend," Artemisia reminded him.

"The Church is God's mouthpiece on this earth," Galileo countered. "He will not allow them to convince the world of a lie. Copernicus was too afraid to write his theories down—he worked for the Church. He could not go against their assumptions. But we can't stay silent about the truth."

"Copernicus was afraid because he knows as well as you do the punishment for heresy," Artemisia said. "If they decide you're doubting God, you won't die easily. They'll burn you at the stake, Galileo."

"I've done nothing wrong," he said.

Artemisia sighed. "Just be careful. I know the courts of Rome. They'll stuff their fingers in their ears before they'll admit that they're wrong."

"Then let's hope no decisions have yet been reached," Galileo said.

"Do you know when you might be able to come back?"

"Within a few months, I'm sure. The Grand Duke has assured me that I'll still have a place here—presuming I win my trial."

Artemisia frowned. "And if you don't?"

"I'll have larger things to worry about," he said. "Not everyone has been even as supportive as Duke Cosimo. You'd be better off seeming to forget I exist while I'm away."

"So everyone keeps telling me," Artemisia said. "I'm not any more prepared to throw you to the wolves than I was when this started. You're my friend. My first friend in this whole city. I have no plans to turn my back on you."

He smiled at her. "Don't let them dampen your spark."

As they stood together by the door for their final farewell, he lifted a hand toward her, but he pulled it back before it came close. She tugged at the edge of her collar to show she was not wearing her amulet. Then she held out a hand.

He grasped her forearm and put his other hand on her shoulder. His smile was heavy. "I'll miss you," Galileo told her. "Don't forget to write me."

"Never," she promised.

Sometimes it hurt to hand her work over to its new owner. She was rightfully proud of her art, and wanted to cling to the canvas. In this piece, San Donatello was working on his sculpture for Santa Maria del Fiore, the artwork that had brought Florence out of the Grave Age. The hunched, fierce figure of the sculptor toiled in the darkness to redeem art, though light caught on the delicate marble under his chisel. It was *good*.

Her work for Silvestrini needed to be done quickly, and that let her experiment with new designs more easily than her work for patrons who cared for the art itself. As long as she finished on time, Silvestrini didn't care about the design. Still, she regretted that the piece would never see the world beyond this room.

Her work for Silvestrini was not as glamorous as the rest, but his inflated payments were a security she had grown to rely on. With the Accademia now under her belt, his promise of introducing her to the Pope felt closer by the day.

"Have you noticed anything?" Silvestrini said abruptly, in the jarring way some old men did. It was as though he expected her full attention even when he barely gave her a glance.

"Hm?" she prompted, still watching the painting in his hands.

"I haven't coughed since this morning," Silvestrini said proudly. It was true—usually he greeted her with a hacking cough, but he had been silent. "I have little else to do in this room, you know, other than feel the ebb and flow of the magics keeping me alive. Most cannot notice those small changes, but it is the pulse of my heart, the cycle of my breaths." Silvestrini eyed the canvas in his lap. "I'm growing stronger. Those who said I was wasting my fortune on art will be proven the fools. I was smart to add you to my retainer."

"Thank you," she said, startled. He was so stingy with his praise that the barest hint felt monumental.

"I haven't felt so strong in...years," he said, staring at San Donatello and almost speaking to himself. "Since my wife died."

Artemisia hadn't known he had been married. "Your wife?"

"That was when the artist did this to me," Silvestrini said, rubbing his chest absently. "My wife was killed by her lover. Hot-tempered bastard. I'd never liked him, but I didn't begrudge her the dalliance. When she decided to leave him, he killed her. He wasn't an artist—a blade works cleaner and quicker. I knew the men I needed to know to have him drawn and quartered on a public square within the week for it. It didn't bring her back, but his screams... They were some small comfort." Silvestrini's wizened face was shrouded with the pull of memories long past.

"I tried to move on with my life. In my grief, I was less religious than usual about disposing of my hair. I didn't know the man's brother was a painter."

"He cursed you?" Artemisia asked, the words quiet.

"Yes. I didn't know who had done it at first. He tried to cover the work, but nothing could hide his skeletal frame. The rushed magics drained every ounce of fat from his body. His neighbors noticed and turned him in. His punishment was far more gruesome than anything his brother endured. Unfortunately, I was too weak to witness it."

She had seen during her trial in Rome the way that men could excuse their friends' worst behaviors. They had said Tassi had not taken Artemisia's virginity, that she was promiscuous. But if he had, it was not unwanted. But if it was unwanted, she had deserved it. They could weave tapestries in their minds to excuse any action. The artist who had attacked Silvestrini must have done the same. His brother had been a murderer, but he had died to avenge him.

She had learned the hard way that dark magics pulled even more energy from the artist than healing. Could she have survived the completion of her painting of Judith? She had not gone back to it after the first failed attempt. She could not know how much of her weakness during those early months in Florence had come from the shackles of poverty and how much had been drained into the canvas. To another, would her self-destructive revenge against Tassi seem as tragic as the painter who had thrown away his life to hurt Silvestrini?

"Since then, I have not had a day's peace. But these paintings," Silvestrini said, nodding to the canvas, "may bring it yet. And you and the other artists will be remembered forever for this."

He dismissed her, setting the canvas on the floor with the others. She tried to cling to her pride. It did not matter if the art was appreciated—she was working a miracle on Stefano Silvestrini, and it would open the door to the Vatican.

And, perhaps, it would bring an old widower a moment of relief.

Between her work for Silvestrini, her next two pieces for the Medici, and the incoming commissions from patrons all over the world, Artemisia was in front of her canvas at all hours through December. She rubbed Elisabetta's salve thoroughly into her hands twice a day before putting on thick gloves. They made her clumsy, so she worked with delicate slowness.

When he could pry her away from her work, she spent long nights at Francesco's house, wrapped in his soft sheets and letting him distract her. She treated his body like a canvas, something she needed to map and draw and understand inside and out, and he did the same. It was a frigid winter, and Francesco's thick stone walls and lush fabrics kept her warm. For a night, she could be somewhere else, and then she would go back to her studio and work more.

He traveled often, and she ached for his return each time. The letters they exchanged warmed her, though they could not replace a night together. She felt invigorated by his company, like dry tinder being thrown onto a desperate fire. She craved him with an intensity that alarmed her, and despaired when he was gone. After years keeping herself distant from everyone, she was now overwhelmed by longing.

When she got word at the end of the month that Francesco would be unexpectedly leaving again after only a few days home, she cleaned her brushes and went across the city without bothering to send another messenger ahead of her. She could not wait another two weeks to see him again without saying goodbye.

After so many months, the walk to Francesco's villa was as familiar as the journey to her own studio. Her breath fogged in the crisp morning air, and her stiff joints seemed to be turning to marble in the cold.

The butler, a stoic older man named Giacomo who was accustomed to Artemisia's visits, unlocked the door for her and ushered her inside without question. She reached up to unclasp her cloak, but Giacomo shook his head. "You'll need that still. The signore is about to depart," he told her. "He's in the back preparing his cart."

"Ah, I was hoping to stay out of the cold for a moment," she sighed. "Grazie, Giacomo."

It took her a few false paths to find her way to the back door of the villa. The hallways, each grander than the last, were labyrinthine. The architect behind it had clearly been more interested in presentation than functionality—though perhaps the disorienting maze was meant to add to the sense of awe as one walked through.

Out back, Francesco was working with one of his servants, a man named Carlo, to carry a large roll of fabric to a large cart stacked with layers of them. Ahead of it, horses stamped against the cobblestones of the courtyard. Francesco's private coach was also prepared alongside to travel with the shipment out of the city.

"Francesco," Artemisia called as she approached. "I'm glad I caught you before you left."

"Artemisia," he said, turning and pulling her in for a kiss. "I didn't think you'd be able to make it. Yesterday, you seemed wrapped up in your new commission."

"I took a break to see you. I can't believe you're leaving again so soon," she said, kissing him again. His breath was warm against her skin, a welcome respite from the winter air around them. "Bavaria does not deserve you. I'll miss you, vostra signoria."

"I'll miss you too, my heart."

Carlo swore—he had lost hold of the heavy bundle on his own, and part of it unrolled onto the ground. It was not, as she had first expected, a tapestry or rug.

It was a painting.

Carlo dropped to his knees, trying to roll it back into place.

"Careful," she said, stepping around Francesco. "You'll crack the paint." She frowned, tilting her head. The portion of the painting she could see showed a clay statue, partially hidden behind a pink curtain. The style was classic, so smooth and well-lit that it seemed waxen. It showed more mastery than most of her fellow Accademia members could display even on their best days. "Who painted this?" she asked, nudging the rolled canvas with her foot slightly to unveil more.

A youth sat in the center, staring out at her. Like the background, his face was smooth and clean, his skin more like that of a plump infant than a man. His perfect hands, one of the hardest aspects to paint correctly, were poised delicately over an open book on the table in front of him. The style was undeniably familiar, a stoic and reserved hand she had been trained to recognize.

"This is a Bronzino," she said. Agnolo di Cosimo, better known as Il Bronzino for his dark skin, had been a popular—and powerful—artist fifty years ago. He was one of the nineteen artists Artemisia had been searching for at the Customs Service for months. This was true art, unlike the false Caravaggio. She clenched and unclenched her fingers, focusing on the sensation from where her fingers had brushed the canvas. "There are still magics in this. Nothing of his should still be active. Where did you get it from?"

"It was a lucky find," Francesco said. "A collector had it in his vault, and his heirs only just uncovered it. I had to offer a good price, but I got it. Why don't we go inside? I have time for a coffee before I have to leave."

"I can't believe I didn't hear about this," Artemisia said. "It will be the talk of the next Accademia meeting."

"Allora," Francesco prevaricated. "It's about to leave the country. No reason to be excited."

Francesco's cart was filled with rolled rugs, nearly identical to the canvas from the outside.

"Let's go, Artemisia," he said. His smile was the bright, impenetrable one she'd seen him use on recalcitrant waiters and diplomats and business partners.

"You were smuggling this out of the city," Artemisia said. She didn't know how she'd spoken. Her mouth felt numb, like she had become one of her paintings. "This export wasn't approved by the Accademia."

"Why should the Accademia decide what I can sell?" Francesco said, still smiling. "I got this legitimately. This way, the collector's family and I get a fair share of the money." He stepped forward, lowering his voice conspiratorially. "You know how the Accademia is. They want to control everything and everyone in this city. You've seen that. Their cut is ridiculous."

"And the artist?"

"He's dead! He's been dead fifty years. Nothing that happens to his art matters now, and I'm putting it in the hands of someone who will appreciate it."

"It's about the principle. What about the other artists? Do you think I'll believe that this is the only time you've done this? How much art have you smuggled in and out of the city?"

"Smuggling is a harsh word. I'm liberating it to those who want to purchase it," Francesco said.

"Don't pretend to be a hero," she snarled. "You did this for the money."

"Of course I did," Francesco said. "I've told you how I lived without it for so long. When I first went to that church in San Gimignano, I realized that there was one way I could make it out. Art is what sells. It contains the things everyone wants: health and prestige. I would be a fool to ignore the market."

"A fool? I am the fool here." She stilled. "Have you sold any of my paintings?"

"Of course not," Francesco said.

"Why would I believe you? You can lie to me without even flinching," she said. She jabbed a finger down at the canvas, at the figure staring up at her. "You've been doing this the whole time. Smuggling art while you were with me. Lying every day about what you did."

"I never lied."

"You know how to lie with your silences," she said, voice rising. "I've always known that about you. Why did I ever trust you to be honest with me? You're a liar. That's who you are. You've lied to everyone I've ever seen you talk to. I thought you were showing me a different side. I was wrong."

"You *are* different," Francesco said urgently. He stepped forward, and Artemisia did not cede her ground. She had to tilt her head to meet his eyes. He lifted a hand to stroke her face, but she batted it aside. "I knew you wouldn't like what I was doing," he said. "You wouldn't have stayed."

"So instead of telling me—or *stopping*—you lied to me," Artemisia said. She finally stepped back, shaking her head. "I didn't come to Florence to be *managed*, Francesco. You don't respect me *or* the work I do."

"I respect you!"

"If you did, you wouldn't smuggle art like it was blood drake scales! Art is *important*, Francesco, and you're treating it like another product to sell."

"It *is* a product, Artemisia. It's a business, one you built your life on. If someone wants to pay money for something, I provide it. That's what I do. I couldn't do this if there wasn't a demand."

"I don't care if half the world is demanding stolen art," Artemisia snapped. "I don't care about them. I care about you. Or I thought I did. It seems I never knew you after all."

"You can't be serious."

"Can't I?"

"My business has nothing to do with you. We're happy, aren't we? Why does my work matter? Artemisia, this is just business."

"And all the lying? This, between us, isn't business. You can't treat me like a stupid buyer you're trying to sway. I'm not some child so...so *desperate* for your attention that I'd let you treat me like an idiot."

Even in the simmering heat of her anger, the words were difficult to say. Her relationship with Francesco had shown her a new world, one where she could touch and be touched, love and be loved. She *was* that desperate. What had made her believe that it could be real?

"Go to Bavaria," she said. "Don't expect to see me when you get back."

"Don't do this," Francesco said, as she turned and walked back into his house. "Artemisia, wait!"

She didn't answer.

When Giacomo let her out of the front door, he did not comment on her red eyes.

20

The transition between that year and the next was the coldest on record. Ice crackled along the edges of the Arno. Frost coated the cobblestones. Icicles hung from ledges. The griffon abandoned her rooftop most nights, spending the harshest weather somewhere safer from the howling winds.

Artemisia holed up in her studio alone.

She had thought perhaps Francesco would come apologize to her. He had been the one to pursue her, the one to seduce her. He had made her believe he cared about their relationship.

Neither of them sent a letter to the other in the two weeks after their fight. Had Francesco already forgotten her? Or did he, like Artemisia, wonder if it was worth abandoning his work for them to be together? They both lived for their careers, even if she did not approve of his.

She missed him with a fire that scorched her from inside.

Still, Francesco and smugglers like him disrespected the Accademia, which disrespected the craft she had dedicated her soul to. Despite the Accademia's initial skepticism of her capabilities, despite Lamberti's sneering, despite their marriage to a tradition that had sought to exclude her, Artemisia trusted in the Accademia's mission. She had given everything to become a member.

Art was her blood, and her blood was art.

With every step she took to secure her legacy, she *helped* people. Silvestrini's health had been on a steady incline since she had joined his retinue. His cough had turned to heart palpitations, but he had grown strong enough to sit up on his own.

She was stretching the limits of how long a man could live, and would change the face of art forever.

Still, a brush against canvas could not compare to the contact of two bodies in love. She had hoped that with Francesco she had found a happiness that let her embrace her career *and* her heart. What a foolish dream.

With her mind heavy, she finally sent a letter to Elisabetta, hoping for distraction. Most of the time Artemisia spent with Elisabetta was at her herbal medicine stand, but now that the holidays were over, the January cold scared away most customers from the open-air markets. The other woman invited her for dinner at her house immediately, with the promise to show Artemisia her workshop.

Elisabetta and Luco lived in Oltrarno, the neighborhood that sat on the west bank of the Arno. Their small home was tucked near the northern edge of the sixth city wall. Less crowded than Artemisia's bustling city center or Maurizio's densely packed slums, their neighborhood was humble and quiet. Located on the opposite end of Oltrarno from the sprawling Medici palace, most of Elisabetta's neighbors were craftsmen or artists. They were not far from where Artemisia started in Florence, before she had gathered the money to move across the river and out from under her landlord's thumb.

It was a small house, but comfortable. Elisabetta managed the space here as confidently as she did her stall in the market, certain of her dominion. She gave Artemisia a brief tour, and then led her into the workshop tucked in the back of the house.

It was as cluttered as Artemisia's studio: hanging bundles of dried herbs and roots, empty vials and tins, sturdy pots and pans, a stone mortar and pestle, bags of salt, heavy blocks of wax, pouches of seeds, and more. A small table and chair were crammed in beside the door like the final bastion before the chaos.

"Someday I'll give you a lesson in brewing," Elisabetta told her. "Put those hands to real use."

"I'd like to learn," Artemisia said honestly.

"Of course you would," she said with a sniff. "Now go keep my husband company while I finish making dinner."

Artemisia sat with Luco at the small square table in the kitchen while Elisabetta worked over a fire in the corner. The peaceful domesticity was a far cry from Artemisia's last fortnight alone in her studio. Her smiles felt false at first, but warmed as the night wore on. Even without Francesco, Artemisia was not alone. She had built a life in Florence beyond him.

Luco, always taciturn in public, was more relaxed in his own home. Though still quiet by nature, he asked Artemisia about her day, and told her of their troubles in the market. "There's a new herbalist with a stand in Piazza Santa Croce," he told her. "Giulia Rosetti."

"Fucking Giulia Rosetti," Elisabetta snarled from by the fire.

Luco nodded his support. "We petitioned for her to find another market—there are dozens inside the city walls, and winter hours are already limited—but she has a friend on the city council that oversees assignments. They're on her side. It's causing some, ah, tension."

Elisabetta snorted. "'Friend.' I bet she slept with him."

"My dear," Luco said, sighing.

"Don't you defend her again!"

"I'm not defending her, wife."

"Her products aren't even good," Elisabetta continued, ladling their dinner into three mismatched clay bowls. "They all smell terrible, and are far too oily. I doubt they even work. She'll give us all a bad name."

Elisabetta set one bowl in front of Artemisia, the weight of it clunking against the wooden table. Bright strands of green herbs wrapped around blobs of ravioli and egg in a sea of light broth. The steam wafting from the top was visible in the cool air and smelled delicious.

"Quality speaks for itself," Luco said.

Elisabetta and Artemisia exchanged an eye roll. "Politics silence quality," Elisabetta said, giving Luco his bowl before sitting down with hers.

"She's right," Artemisia said. "It's always about who you know." Francesco used to say that as well.

Luco shook his head. "They'll see that my wife is the best healer in the market. Giulia will not last."

"You're sweet, but you're a fool," Elisabetta said, patting Luco's hand.

"He is right, Elisabetta. You are the best healer," Artemisia said.

Her father had mocked any form of healing outside of art—herbal medicine was women's work, and doctors were arrogant frauds. As though leeches could ever compare to the power in a brushstroke! However, in just six months, Elisabetta's salve had saved Artemisia from the clawing ache in her broken hands.

Perhaps it was the same men who claimed a woman would never be a painter who also decreed that art was the only legitimate form of healing.

"You're a fool too, Artemisia," Elisabetta said fondly.

They drank from the bowls. Luco lost his conversational energy, focusing on his dinner while Artemisia and Elisabetta continued to gossip about her competitors. The soup was as good as it smelled. As she sipped the savory broth, a lump of cheese-filled ravioli would bump her lips, and she would slurp it into her mouth. The pocket of dough and soft ricotta was a welcome break from the broth, chewy and sweet.

After dinner, they settled in a small sitting area. Elisabetta sprawled unabashedly on the couch beside her husband, leaning against him with easy confidence. Artemisia sat in a chair against the wall, hands resting over her full stomach. They chatted for a while more, idle and easy.

"So," Elisabetta said, "how are you doing, Artemisia?" The weight of the words left no doubt she was asking about Francesco. Artemisia had mentioned briefly in her letter that their relationship was over in the hope it would ward off any questions about him.

"Perfectly fine with good friends and good food to keep me company."

Elisabetta scoffed. "Liar."

"She doesn't wish to dwell on it," Luco told his wife.

"Nonsense," Elisabetta said. "Nothing cures heartbreak as surely as complaining about it. And you, carina, are heartbroken."

"Are you hoping to remind me that you warned me about him?"

"After I met him, I believed he loved you," Elisabetta said.

After the feast day celebration, Francesco had gone back to Elisabetta's stall more than once to buy armfuls of her products in his attempts to win her full approval. Elisabetta had confided to Artemisia that his mission had worked, but the healer had kept that information from Francesco so he would buy even more.

"We can't always predict who will hurt us," Elisabetta told her. Then she clapped her hands brusquely. "Is there a plan? I have a recipe for a drink that will make him shit his brains out for a month. My herbs do more than heal."

"I don't want revenge. I couldn't stand to think of him hurt. I can't stand to think of him at all. I just want him to disappear from my thoughts and my heart." She shook her head and stared up at the low wooden ceiling. Tears heated her eyes but she refused to let them fall.

"It will pass," Elisabetta said. "It always does."

"When? I can't move on. I had him, and then suddenly everything I thought I knew was a lie. I'm…lost. The last time I was this stuck, I at least had…" She had worked on her Judith to heat her with the fire of revenge. Now, she only felt cold. "Well. I had a plan. I knew how I'd make my enemy pay. That's what I need. Action. A purpose. But Francesco is not an enemy. Not like that."

"Hm. And what revenge could one like you carry out?" Elisabetta's gaze was intent.

"It doesn't matter," Artemisia said. "I didn't finish it."

For a long moment, Elisabetta only watched her. "Do you know why I don't let you sketch in my stall?"

Artemisia kept a notebook and charcoal with her no matter where she went in the city, in case she was struck by inspiration, or wanted to capture a moment. During one of her early visits to Elisabetta's market stall, she had sat on a stool and pulled out her sketching materials. Elisabetta had instructed her to put them away, her tone brooking no questions. Artemisia, aware of the fragile newness of their friendship, had complied.

"Because you're stubborn?"

"Because I don't trust artists."

Artemisia felt exposed. She should not have admitted anything. She had been too upset to manage her tongue. "I can control when I put my magics in. And if I made a mistake, I could burn it afterward. That cleanses any leftover energy and gives it back to me. I would never hurt either of you."

"My herbs I can control. They can hurt people, of course. There's poison all around us, and I know how to use it. But they cannot start a *plague*. I help heal patients during the outbreaks—did you know that? I go into the quarantine areas, I lance boils, I watch people die in pain."

"Elisabetta," Artemisia said weakly. Fear was like ice in her belly. If Elisabetta chose to accuse her publicly of using dark magics, soldiers would turn her flat inside out—and the hidden painting of Judith would be waiting for them. She looked at Luco, who was impassive as always, and back to her friend. "I don't curse people."

Elisabetta let out a slow breath. "When I was young, people started to die in my village."

"Elisabetta, I'm not—"

Elisabetta raised a hand to silence her. "It was a bloody death, quick and violent. We thought it was a pestilence at first, but none of them had the usual symptoms. They would just die. I was fifteen, and felt that I knew the world. I didn't understand the terror overwhelming the town. We all knew death, and this was just another brand. I thought they were being delicate. And then my father died." She shook her head. "It was…terrible. I had already started working with my mother to learn the healing herbs by then, and had helped her with a dozen births, a half-dozen deaths. Nothing compared to my father's blood betraying him, scalding him from the inside."

"A blood curse," Artemisia murmured. "Necrotic magics."

"None of us knew the signs. It's so forbidden that it's not even spoken of in small towns. By the time we realized what was happening, twelve people were dead. It seemed contagious, focusing on the most powerful men in the city. Why are evil magics so much more powerful than the rest? What single healing artwork could do as much?"

"It's easier to break something than to fix it," Artemisia said quietly.

Elisabetta clicked her tongue and continued, "That's when someone realized that the new tapestry hanging in the town hall had been gifted there just when the deaths started happening. Everyone who walked into the building died within two days.

"When we realized what was happening and tracked it to the weaver who lived on the edge of town, we found a blood drake waiting outside her home. Her son had been executed the year before, but no one had believed she would go so far in revenge. I wasn't in the attack party, but I had followed, furious and determined to make sure justice for my father was done. I saw the blood drake, lit by the torches and the moon. It was horrifying. It had enormous wings, but it moved like a snake through the air. It was larger than any animal I'd ever seen. It ripped two men in half before they managed to pierce its scales with their spears.

"Once it was dead, they pulled the screaming witch out of her house. She was so thin that one man could have carried her. Her face was like a skull. She had already lost her blood drake, but she was still furious. She was screaming at us when they burned her. If she could have cast another curse with her words instead of her weaving, she would have." Elisabetta rubbed her hands briskly over her arms, though the kitchen still warmed the small house.

Was that how Artemisia would have appeared if she had finished her curse on Tassi? A ravening, hollow witch too far gone to see her own demise looming? She had the weaver's same drive for revenge, that willingness to burn herself and everyone around her to get at her enemy. The intensity of the darkness simmering inside her heart, waiting for a chance to boil over again, terrified her.

"I would never hurt you," Artemisia said. "Either of you."

"I know. And there are times when revenge is necessary. But necrotic art kills the maker as surely as the victim. You must promise me never to turn to it."

She took a deep breath, torn.

Her quest for revenge had been justified. Her rage and despair had been too vicious to repress. Back then, she would not have listened to anyone telling her to stop.

But she had also had no friend who cared enough to try. Perhaps it was time to truly decide to put her Judith away for good. Surely this life she had built was worth protecting, even without Francesco.

Finally, she said, "I swear."

Luco squeezed Elisabetta's knee and then stood up. "If dinner is settled enough, I bought some bruttiboni for tonight," he said. Artemisia perked up.

"You don't need to buy dessert every time we have a guest! You're wasting money!" Elisabetta called after him as he went into the kitchen. It was a relief to see her return to normal. Despite her obvious concern, Artemisia did not think Elisabetta would report her. Her fear was *for* Artemisia, not for her potential victims.

"Don't discourage him," Artemisia said. "I love bruttiboni." With meringue and nuts warping their shape, the chewy cookies were aptly named: ugly, but delicious.

Elisabetta rolled her eyes. "Get your own husband."

"I don't believe marriage is in the cards for me," Artemisia said. Her voice was less flippant than she'd hoped.

"You deserve better than Francesco Maria Maringhi," she said. "Too much money does things to a man."

"I think it was the lack of money that started it," Artemisia said. "Look, the bruttiboni," she added as Luco came back into the room.

Elisabetta shook her head, but allowed the conversation to move on.

When the messenger came to her door the next day, Artemisia could not stop the leap of hope and fear in her chest that it would be from Francesco. Her disappointment was only short-lived, however, when she recognized Galileo's familiar handwriting, which swirled deftly across the page like a dance.

It had been more than a month since Galileo had left for Rome, and the rumors of his trial were slow to trickle back to Florence. She had sent him a letter not long after his departure, but had not been hopeful of him finding time to respond.

Cara Artemisia,

I have arrived in Rome, and I must say my fondness for the city has waned. I hope you'll forgive me for speaking ill of your birthplace. Being here, I think often of the young woman who left the only home she knew to pursue independence and greatness in a new city.

It's an ambition I recognize in the mirror. We are of a kind, my dear. We cannot imagine conceding our battles, even if it's a bloody, empty field around us. There are times when that tenacity will see us through.

But take this from an old astronomer—meteoric rises lead to meteoric falls. The more success one finds, the more others will search for a way to tear them down. Perhaps my trials here in Rome are already beginning to chip away at my walls. I dearly hope your success is kinder to you than mine has been. I have not had the decisive victory I hoped for—I imagine this will take much longer than I'd hoped.

I begin to regret not spending any of my youth traveling abroad. I always thought there was enough to keep my mind busy on the peninsula—and in the stars—but now I may never know.

I often feel as though I am attempting to teach simple mathematics to children in the courts here. Perhaps worse—it is to children already convinced that two and two is three, and that four does not exist at all.

Tomasso Caccini of Santa Maria Novella followed me here from Florence. Without his incessant vitriol, my voice would be heard more clearly, but he will not be silent. His dream is to destroy rather than create—a far simpler goal than mine.

This is a dual battle, and each front complicates the other. I must convince them that all evidence points to the sun at the center of the solar system. I must also convince them that such a belief is not heretical, when they have believed for their entire lives that it is. Worse, I must convince them of my own faith. So few understand the marriage of science and religion.

I had never attempted to contradict His words—only support them. For what truth could I uncover that He did not place there for my discovery?

Ah, Artemisia, I feel at times as though I spin in circles.

The truth must be heard.

*

A nobleman from England had recently contacted Artemisia for a painting of Daphne, a commission which she could not resist. Not only did it come with a robust payment, but Artemisia had long been fascinated by the subject. Perhaps it was a presumption on the patron's part—that the female artist would only paint women—but she knew she understood Daphne better than any other artist in Florence.

The Greek legend told of a river nymph pursued by the god Apollo. Daphne had pledged herself to Artemis, foreswearing all men, but Apollo denied her refusal. When he chased her down and seemed ready to catch her, Daphne begged the gods to save her. In an instant, she was transformed into a laurel tree, her vulnerable flesh forever protected by firm bark.

Artemisia's portrayal captured Daphne at the start of her transformation. Her gaze looked back over her shoulder, desperate and terrified. Stretching out ahead of her, reaching for salvation, her fingers were elongating and sprouting green leaves. One of her feet already was setting down roots, stopping her mid-flight to secure her forever.

She was sketching the design in red chalk, testing angles for the most dynamic approach, when there was a firm rapping against her door.

The sun was setting outside—it was too late for unannounced visitors or messengers. Thus far, her new landlord had not followed in Gori's aggressive footsteps. She glanced at her amulet hanging beside the door. "Who is it?" she called.

"Artemisia."

She put down her chalk and stood up, hands trembling. His voice had more effect on her body than his beloved coffee could ever hope to achieve. "Francesco," she breathed.

It had been three weeks since she had stormed out of his villa, and not a word had passed between them since. What would Elisabetta say if she knew Artemisia's first instinct was to fling herself back into his arms?

She steeled herself. "Go away," she said. "I have nothing to say to you."

"Then I'll talk," Francesco said. He knocked on the door again. "Let me in, my love."

"You're not setting foot in this studio," Artemisia told him.

"Don't be absurd, Artemisia," he said. "We should have this conversation inside."

She snorted, crossing her arms tightly.

He did not let the silence rest long. "Artemisia, please," he said. There was a thunk of something hitting the door. From his next muffled words, she thought it might have been his forehead. "I've been dying to speak with you. It's all I've thought of for weeks. You have to let me see you."

"Keep dying," Artemisia drawled.

"I'll give my speech out here," he said. "The entire building can listen if they'd like."

"Bother my neighbors and my landlord will throw you out on your ear," Artemisia said. "Leave, Francesco. Just go."

There was a heavy sigh, and then the faint tread of boots back down the stairs. Artemisia stood still, heart hammering. She wanted to call him back. She wanted to cover her ears and pretend she had never sat down beside him that first dinner at the Palazzo Pitti.

He had left so easily. She had never seen him give up on anything this quickly. Had he only come to confirm that they were over?

She scrubbed her hands over her face. She should sit back down and continue blocking out her sketch, but it seemed an impossible task. Everything she had done in the past weeks had been dancing on a rickety scaffold hastily constructed over the ruins of her heart. With a handful of sentences, Francesco had kicked those fragile beams down.

A sudden clatter against her window drew her attention. She was on the third floor of the building, and it was not storming. The noise clanged again, so she stalked over and heaved open the shutter. The evening air shot through her wool dress and scraped icy nails down her skin. The January nights skirted on the edge of freezing, often hovering just enough above to leave them with frigid rains and blistering winds. The sun was pressed against the roofs beyond, retreating in a riot of orange and pink.

Francesco stared up at her from the cobblestones, grinning despite the cold.

"What are you doing?" she demanded, raising her voice to be heard. A few passing folks glanced between them, but hurried on their way. It was getting dark, and no city was without its public fights.

"Your landlord does not own the street!" Francesco called up to her.

"You arrogant bastard," Artemisia retorted. She clenched the windowsill, digging her nails into the wood. "Not everything is a game for you to win! Why can you not leave me alone?"

"I'm not letting you throw us away over something so small," Francesco said. "You know me, Artemisia. You love me!"

She laughed, hoping it would wound him. "Do I?"

He opened his arms. "Artemisia. We're good together, aren't we? I've never known a woman like you. This can't be what separates us. It's nothing."

"Nothing? *Nothing?*" she repeated, voice growing louder. "Would you like to explain why it took you more than three weeks to come have this conversation? Because I'd guess those three weeks were the exact amount of time it takes a private coach to get *back and forth from Bavaria*! You couldn't come apologize earlier because you were too busy *selling the goddamn Bronzino!*"

"You haven't turned me in!" Francesco said without apparent care that he was on a public street. "If you truly hated me, you would have by now."

She could have. She should have. Standing in the customs office by the south gate once a week and reviewing the art they had collected, she had thought a dozen times about announcing she had found a smuggler. Francesco had not been trading some unknown artist—he was depriving Florence of the work of Il Bronzino. How many pieces slipped out of the city without ever being seen by the Accademia's customs representatives at all? Francesco had declared the canvas as a rug, and had likely not been questioned twice.

It was her duty to report him.

And yet. She was far too aware of the vicious laws of the land. Francesco might only be slapped with a fine, one he would be able to pay without a thought. But if the Accademia took offense—if there was a long line of lost art that could be traced back to him—the punishment could be vicious. The thought of Francesco mutilated or strung up outside the Palazzo Vecchio turned her stomach.

"You love me!" Francesco repeated.

"How little do you think of me? You thought you'd come back and smile, and I'd change my mind so easily? You compromise with every breath. I do not."

"Artemisia, let me come inside. We can talk about it."

She snatched a mug from a table by the window and threw it down. It cracked at Francesco's feet, shattering against the cobblestones. "Come back when you've changed your ways," she said. "With what you do, you've been laughing at my dream for years. I cannot be with a man like that. *Laughing.*" She scoffed and looked up at the darkening sky overhead. "It's always the way with you. You never know when to take a thing seriously."

"I take you seriously, Artemisia," he said, all joviality gone from his expression. "I always have."

"Prove it," she said, and slammed the window closed again.

21

With so little structure in her days, the Accademia meetings on the second Sunday of each month had quickly become an anchor for Artemisia. There was comfort in pulling on her formal robes and affixing the pin that declared her status as a junior member. They were symbols she had fought hard to earn.

She had chosen her art, her career, the Accademia. She had to believe it was worth losing Francesco.

A slap of cold wind met her when she left her building, and she tucked her hands into her sleeves. It rarely snowed in Florence, but she thought a storm might be building.

As a member, Artemisia participated in the opening ceremony at each monthly meeting. Before the aspiring artists were admitted, the superintendent and his council led a recitation of the Accademia's principles, made announcements, and introduced the foreign artists the Accademia was hosting that month. Being part of the Accademia's daily workings still thrilled her. Even the mundane minutiae were intriguing.

Once the opening remarks ended and the doors opened to the young artists searching for guidance—and membership—Artemisia stood to mingle and explore the snack table. It was no Medici spread, but free food was a comfort she could never decline. She grabbed a goblet of red wine and a slice of castagnaccio.

The chestnut cake was far more plebeian than the Medici's famous marzipan delicacies, but it was dense and hearty.

She chatted with some of her fellow members. The casual inclusion was a sharp contrast to when she had been only an artistic hopeful, fighting for scraps of attention. Now, men moved to welcome her into conversation groups, and even more thrilling, asked her opinion on art, or suggested which of their patrons she should meet. This camaraderie was what Francesco refused to understand—no artist could truly work alone.

Today, everyone was buzzing about one of the Accademia's guest artists that month. The court painter to the Archduke of the Netherlands stood with the superintendent at the back of the temple, nodding politely to the members as he was introduced. He would be teaching a guest workshop later in the week that everyone was clamoring to attend. She would attend—to believe the gossip, this Rubens was the premier painter north of the Danube.

She slipped away to do a circuit of the room, offering critiques of the sketches on hopeful display. She had stood alongside many of these boys only months ago, but they listened to her guidance with an open ear. Her robes and pin gave her authority here.

She made sure to talk to every person in the room, no matter their level of talent. There were all ages and skills on display, but she knew the pain of being overlooked. Artemisia was in the Accademia now—she would not close the door behind her.

As Artemisia stepped away from the last aspiring member, Sigismondo approached her and bowed with a flourish, holding his own goblet of wine.

"Sigismondo," she said. "I hope you're doing well."

"As well as anyone," he said, waving a hand. "Have you heard from Galileo?"

"I had a letter from him two weeks ago," Artemisia said. "I was disappointed—but not surprised—by his struggles. He has too much faith in a broken system. I have to fear for him."

"That Caccini is a piece of work," Sigismondo said. "He left behind Santa Maria Novella to fight Galileo in Rome. The church doesn't even have a fresco right now—it's under commission with Paolo Lamberti. If a plague comes, Caccini will have left his flock untethered. No preacher, no art to help them."

"They are fools to trust in him," Artemisia said.

"Perhaps, but innocent fools. Caccini claims to care for them, but he seems to truly believe ruining our friend is his greatest cause."

"Galileo is upsetting his delicate understanding of the world. The facts would change what Caccini knows about his place in the universe. How he sees himself, how he sees his future, how he sees his legacy. There are few things more dangerous than a man at risk of that."

"You do have some knowledge of such things," Sigismondo said wryly, making a small gesture to the Accademia milling around them. Lamberti and his poisonous gaze was surely nearby.

Artemisia shrugged. "You could say I've seen it before."

"I'm sure. It's all difficult to bear on top of the news of Silvestrini." She sighed. "What now?"

"You haven't heard? Artemisia, he's dead."

The words seemed to ring. "Stefano Silvestrini? Dead? That can't be right. I was healing him. It was working."

"It wasn't enough," he said gently. "He died yesterday."

She pressed a hand to her chest. She had put so much work into the art for Silvestrini. It was supposed to take her to the Vatican. Her mind whirled. "That can't be right."

"I was just at his estate earlier today. His lawyer is settling the last of his outstanding accounts. Silvestrini had requested that all his open art commissions be submitted to his estate upon his death, even if they were unfinished. They will pay us the rest of the commission fee when we hand it over. I'm sure they'll be in touch with you soon. They'll have to work through many of the artists in this room."

"Of course they will," Artemisia said, bitterness welling inside her. All that work, and she was a footnote in Silvestrini's list of artists. He had only made her feel special to encourage her to work for him. "Why do they want the art? It's all already tied to him. It won't be of any use to his heirs."

Sigismondo sighed. "They're burying it with him," he said. "All of it, even the pieces that have been drained for decades, even the pieces he bought that weren't tied to him. It was his standing request in the event of his death."

"All of it?" Artemisia repeated. "There are hundreds of artworks in that house. Thousands. He's commissioned the greatest artists alive. They could make a gallery dedicated to him that would be bigger than Casa Buonarroti."

"I know," Sigismondo said, rubbing his forehead.

"I could burn my art and pull that power back," Artemisia said. "If I let them have it now, that would be weeks' worth of energy going to waste. Even the rest of the commission price isn't worth knowing my magics are going to be buried alive."

"I said the same thing," Sigismondo said. "His lawyer was insistent. You won't be surprised to learn Silvestrini is his best-paying client, even after death."

"Not at all." She flexed her fingers. Even with Elisabetta's salve, the cold and her long work hours left an ache in her hands. How much of her life had she given to Silvestrini? Not just the hours spent on his commissions, but the time lost on other work, the magics poured directly from her heart onto his floorboards instead. "So we have no recourse."

"None that I could see," Sigismondo said.

Who would attend the old man's funeral? In all her time in his service, she had never seen anyone in his house other than his butler. His wife was long dead, and the ripples of her murder had left Silvestrini a broken, angry man. Perhaps there would be a gathering of artists watching their years of work get sealed into a marble mausoleum.

Silvestrini's grave would look quite a bit like the cellar beneath the Accademia.

Even on the steps, she could feel the faint pulse of power under her feet from all the art—donated and ill-gotten alike.

Was there ever a possible world where people did not hoard artists' magics like gold? It was a power like any other, concentrated among the wealthy and powerful. The Vatican, Silvestrini, the Medici, the Accademia—they could collect and collect art no matter the cost.

And all Artemisia could do was her job.

She pressed her eyes closed. "I thought it would be worth it. I thought I was making a difference."

"He was an old, old man, Artemisia," Sigismondo said sadly. "Even art cannot stop death."

Rain pummeled the terracotta roofs and cobblestone streets of Florence. Wind whipped through the narrow alleys, driving the bitter rain to slash like needles. Artemisia clenched her cloak under her chin, hunching her shoulders. The wool was treated with beeswax from Elisabetta's supplier, but nothing could repel the freezing rain.

January had passed and February was nearly over, but there was no relief from her misery. The Arno was swollen with the constant rain, and icy air seeped in through every crack. Florence's citizens stayed inside or huddled under sodden cloaks. If she had not needed more walnut oil for her work, she would not have ventured out at all.

As she approached her apartment building, she stopped in her tracks. A familiar private coach sat in front. The bay horses were nearly black with the rain, their flanks quivering in the cold.

She shook her head and stalked past, the chill replaced with a flood of heat through her veins.

"Artemisia, wait!" Francesco fell into step beside her, holding a woolen cloak over his head. "We need to talk."

"You can't keep coming here," Artemisia said, striding toward her door. "It's over."

"I just want you to hear what I have to say," Francesco said. He jogged and put himself in front of her. He looked exhausted. The confidence he had shown calling from beneath her window was gone. She had never seen him so subdued. He was as gray as the stormy sky overhead. "After that, you can walk away again."

She looked past him to the door of her building. Her empty studio awaited her. Her *work* awaited her.

She would be wet and cold and alone, but fueled with the knowledge Francesco was the same. She could leave him as miserable as she'd been these last weeks.

But suddenly, she wanted anything but more silence.

"Fine." She stalked to the carriage and clambered in. Rain drummed on the roof overhead, but it was quieter than it had been on the streets, especially when Francesco followed and closed the door behind him. The interior of the carriage was shadowed, the small windows letting in only a weak light.

"Thank you," he said quietly.

"It's been almost another month," Artemisia said, arms folded tightly over her chest. "Where have you been this time? Selling a Michelangelo in Muscovy?"

"No," he said simply. He dug a folded blanket from under his bench. "Would you like to dry off? You must be freezing."

She did not move to take it. "I don't plan on being here long."

"I know," he said, a brittle smile flitting across his face. "I just wanted to let you settle in before we did this."

"You always liked things to be easy."

He leaned forward, elbows on his knees. "Artemisia, I legitimized my company. It was time. I had the money, and there's more to my business than the art. I spent the last month cleaning it up."

She faltered. "What?"

"We're stepping away from the smuggling business."

Artemisia struggled to swallow. "Truly?"

A smile flashed across his face like lightning, sharp and painful. "Not that I expect you to believe me. I've not been quite trustworthy, I know. But I respect your work, if not the Accademia's management." He spread his hands. "I say a lot of things, but I rarely admit when I'm wrong. In this, I was wrong."

"How much of your business is—was the smuggling?" she asked. For too long, she had let him be vague and flippant about his work. She had never cared to press him. Her work was the product of passion, part of a long legacy of magics that had shaped the world. Francesco's business was only about money. Somewhere in her heart, she had believed that meant it was less important.

"I knew when I was young that I wanted to leave Montauto. My mentor, Matteo Frescobaldi, taught me the basics of business, but I saw that most merchants never made it past their city gates. It would be too easy to fall through the cracks into obscurity. I became known as the best source for items that are difficult to find. The more I satisfied the requests of my wealthiest clients, the more I learned what people would pay the most to have. There's power in the rare and exclusive, and what could be more of both than art?"

"I've worked with customs for months and haven't seen a single piece of restricted art come through," Artemisia pointed out. "There can't be that many pieces for you to sell."

"The key to smuggling art is to never go through customs in the first place," he said. "There is more art being passed from hand to hand than you can imagine. But I do not live solely on the art trade. Over the years, the legitimate side of my business has grown more and more. Oysters, coffee—there are always things that are difficult to acquire. But the art brought large payments, and I was the best at getting pieces in and out of the city. I couldn't let any aspect of my business slip when it could build instead. Poverty seemed just around every corner. Cutting any income loose was a risk I couldn't take."

"You never feared being caught?"

He shrugged, a small ripple in the dim carriage. "There are few things a well-placed bribe can't smooth over."

She shook her head. "Of course. To think of all those hours I've wasted with the customs office. There are people who can hand over a bag of gold scudi and skip any process or punishment."

"Isn't that the way with everything?" Francesco asked. "Smuggling art will never end. It's too powerful, too profitable. But my men and I won't be a part of it. I have proof back home—letters, documents. It's over."

"You lied to me," Artemisia said, her voice unsteady. "You made me feel like a fool for trusting you."

"I know. You told me to only come back if I changed. I want to, for you," he said. "You've always managed to make me want to be a better person, Artemisia. I never cared before. I needed to protect myself. What did I care about society and its rules? But since I met you, I wanted to deserve you. I don't know if I ever will, but… it's the only thing I've ever found worth trying. I've never been steadfast. Compromise is too easy for me. But I will do whatever it takes to be worthy of you."

She wanted to fling herself at him, to trust his pretty words, but she held herself back. "Show me this proof."

He rapped the front of the carriage, and the horses were spurred into motion.

At the door to the villa, Giacomo took Artemisia's cloak without comment. Francesco was nearly vibrating with tension beside her as they walked through the halls. It was the same as it had ever been, luxuriously built on years of business dealings both legal and illegal.

In his personal quarters, he showed her angry letters from art dealers and his partners, all ranting at his decision to leave a profitable business. His trading was even more extensive than she'd expected. Though he had been its creator, the machinery of his business was large and complex as a clock tower. There were a dozen people to contact to grind the illegitimate arm to a halt. Francesco's coffers would not be the only ones damaged by the loss of that income, but from the responses, his announcement had been uncompromising.

She flipped through the letters, noting the names and locations. Dark had fallen outside, and she held the paper close to the candle to read them. They came from all over; several were in languages she did not recognize. Francesco did work all over the world, and was educated far beyond the Roman and Tuscan dialects she knew.

"There are still some responses to come, especially from across the sea," Francesco said, hovering beside her. "There's no getting a letter to and from Sweden in a month, much less Mongolia."

"This was a large undertaking—the art smuggling *and* the dismantling. Some of these letters are very angry. Are you not afraid of a backlash?"

"Let them try," Francesco said. "I have information that no one would want me to reveal. They won't want to test me."

Artemisia set the letters down, dragging her fingers along the paper. "You did this for me."

"I did," he said. "My heart, there is little I would not do for you."

"I said I could not forgive you," she said, not looking at him.

There was a quiet sigh. "I know."

She swore, and then grabbed his shirt and pulled him into a deep kiss. Her hands dragged over every bit of him she could reach. The contact raced through her like a storm, lightning and thunder and a sweeping of cleansing, drowning rains. It was human and mythic at once, bigger than the collision of flesh and breath.

"Lie to me again and there will be no second chances," Artemisia growled in his ear.

"I know, I know," he said, and pulled her back in for another kiss.

She felt devoured, taken apart from the inside. Their damp clothes dropped to the floor without ceremony as they fell into bed, refusing to let another moment pass without the touch of skin on skin.

She had yearned for this with all her heart, and had not believed she would have it again. They clutched each other tightly, anchors in the darkness. The rest of the world would wait. She let the warm press of hands and heated kisses take her away.

Afterward, they stayed tangled together, warm under a layer of soft furs.

＊

Artemisia was used to holding onto grudges like lifelines. It had taken her a harrowing eighteen months to put aside her Judith even as it ate her alive. She expected to feel adrift forgiving Francesco so quickly—but she only was relieved to wake in his arms.

He convinced her to spend the weekend in his villa, unable to stand the separation for another moment. The silks and furs draped on the bed were expensive and lush, a welcome comfort in winter, and his bedroom was dark and cozy.

Her favorite feature of the bedroom was the pair of familiar paintings mounted by the door like guards. Both were done in Artemisia's own hand.

The first was a dark, moody portrait of Jael, cloaked in shadows. The woman was crouched over a sleeping man, the leader of an opposing army, a tent peg and hammer lined up with his temple. From the upward swing of Jael's arm, the scene captured the moment just before the assassination.

The second painting was lighter, still shadowed but full of lush, rich colors. It depicted Danaë, a pale woman draped over a velvet chaise, looking up at the rain of glinting gold coins falling from the ceiling. In the myth, Zeus impregnated Danaë with the coins—one of his more creative guises. When Artemisia picked the theme all those months ago, she had said it was a dig against Francesco, teasing him for his assumptions that his wealth was so seductive.

In hindsight, painting a nude woman stretched beneath a shower of coins for her patron had been an obvious flirtation.

Francesco was a smart, ambitious businessman. She'd once imagined him marrying the young daughter of a trade partner, someone quiet and dignified who could make his empire grow. He made most of his connections for the political benefit, and Artemisia would be no use to him, especially now that he had left smuggling behind.

But from the first day they'd met, Francesco had made it clear that he had no interest in a partner who couldn't challenge him. He'd chosen Artemisia, and she had chosen him. Her mark on his heart was on his walls.

Breakfast was a simple affair. They picked from a platter of breads, olives, and cheeses, drinking white wine and Francesco's beloved coffee respectively. They seemed small in the massive dining room, flanked by standing servants who watched to be sure their mugs never ran low.

"We should have eaten in your quarters," she commented. "I feel we're being watched."

"I own the house," Francesco said. "We don't have to hide away."

Artemisia gave him a solemn look. "It's unsettling."

"My servants don't care," he insisted. "They like you, you know."

"I meant the cherubs," she said, pointing upward. On the fresco that covered the whole ceiling, pale, fat cherubs danced on pastel clouds, clanging goblets, playing instruments, and engaging in lewd behavior. One looked like it was peeing down into the room. "There's a reason we never came into this room before, isn't there? You were hiding your true artistic preferences? That mural is quite something, vostra signoria."

He smiled at the nickname, reaching to brush his hand over hers. "I knew you'd say that," he said. "I bought the house before I'd developed an opinion about art. I asked around for the most popular artists and brought them in to do as they wished. It may be time to replace them. The magics are long since gone. Have you thought about doing frescoes? I'd pay well."

She snorted. "I don't take jobs that require scaffolding or plaster. Luckily, I know many artists you could commission for it. We can scrub those cherubs from existence."

"I believe it will be quite easy with your connection to the Accademia. You know, I wouldn't trust them half as much if you didn't vouch for them. I've never been a fan of that much bureaucracy."

"Of course," Artemisia said, smiling tightly.

She thought of the hidden cellar beneath the Accademia of art hoarded away from the rest of the world. Of the patrons who demanded so much life from artists that they collapsed young, milked dry. Of men like Silvestrini who would hide her art even after their deaths. Of the flawed and prejudiced men that set the organization's rules and the standards for art in Florence.

She had taken a stand against Francesco to defend an organization in which she was slowly losing faith.

How could she ever explain that the Accademia was flawed, but that she still believed in its mission and found smuggling to be an abhorrent evasion of important rules? Francesco's betrayal had carved a divide between them that could not be erased even by forgiveness. She could not tell him her doubts without fueling his disdain for the institution that had become her life.

"We should look around the house to see what else you think needs painted over. I'm happy to take your advice. I would love for some to be done by you, but I swear to only ask you for paintings that can be done on solid ground," Francesco said. He added another spoonful of olives to her plate.

"Thank you," she said, and leaned into his side.

She would deal with the rest in time. For now, she had Francesco again, and that was enough.

22

Their much-needed respite from the chill and rains of winter did not arrive until the beginning of April.

Following the lead of most of Florence's residents, Artemisia left her studio to explore the city under the golden light of the sun. The cold would certainly come again, but the push toward spring had begun in earnest, and no one wanted to miss a moment of it.

She had spent much of the past month at Francesco's villa, but her work never stopped. He had suggested building her a studio in one of his unused rooms—of which there were many—so that she would be able to work there some days, but her art was not easily transportable. She needed not only a dedicated space, but her oils, pigments, canvases, brushes, glues, and her works in progress. Instead, she spent her days at her studio, and then went across the city to spend most nights with Francesco. Their break-up had, in the end, strengthened their relationship. After seeing the cost of losing their love, they both held onto it more tightly.

Between her healing with Francesco and dedication to the Accademia, Artemisia had not been able to find as much time for her friends. Sigismondo was busy with his own work, and they mostly spoke at meetings. Galileo was still fighting for his life in Rome. She had seen Elisabetta on occasion, stopping by the stand soon after her reconciliation with Francesco. Elisabetta had taken one look at Artemisia's face and known. Her friend had grumbled about Francesco's unworthiness for Artemisia's entire visit, shaking her head and looking up as though God would explain Artemisia's choices. Maurizio, modeling for Artemisia and doing odd construction jobs while waiting for the orchards to begin hiring again, was the most vocal, complaining about Francesco's monopoly on her time.

This week, Francesco was traveling to Pisa. He had limited himself to two- or three-day trips since February, but she knew his work would require him to travel abroad again soon. For now, he seemed as unhappy leaving her as she was to be left.

Still, she did not need to be alone even without Francesco.

However, when Artemisia knocked on his door, there was a delay before Maurizio answered. When he did, he only poked out his head. "Artemisia?"

"Maurizio," she greeted with a smile. "I thought we could go for lunch today. My treat. It's too pleasant outside to do anything else."

"Maurizio? Who is it?"

Artemisia raised her eyebrows at Maurizio, and he sighed and opened the door all the way to reveal another man in his apartment. "My friend, Artemisia. Artemisia, Gabriele."

Gabriele was a slender man close to Artemisia's age. In contrast to Maurizio's stone-hewn face, Gabriele's features were delicate. He had unusually light green eyes under a mop of sleek black hair that made Artemisia's fingers itch for a paintbrush. She may have preferred painting rougher men, but Gabriele could have modeled as the angel for whom he was named. "The artist!" Gabriele said, coming to the door. "I've heard so much about you!"

"It's nice to meet you," said Artemisia before looking at Maurizio with raised eyebrows.

"My neighbor," Maurizio said gruffly. "Aren't you supposed to be with Francesco?"

"He's traveling this week, and I couldn't stay inside on a day like this. I see the two of you have not had that problem."

"My God," Maurizio grumbled.

"Allora, I should leave you two alone," Artemisia said, suppressing a grin. "I just wanted to see how you were, but I don't want to interrupt."

"Thanks, Artemisia! We should get a drink together sometime," Gabriele suggested. "Maybe you can show me some of the paintings you've done of Maurizio. I've heard you're a wonderful artist."

"Maurizio said that, did he?" Artemisia grinned at him even as Maurizio ushered her out of the apartment. "We will certainly talk more."

Still laughing to herself, Artemisia left and walked back through Santa Croce. She would have to bring Gabriele by her studio, and make sure Maurizio knew just too late to stop them. She had multiple sketches of Maurizio in togas—and, often, without clothing at all—that she was sure his cheerful new friend would appreciate. She was glad that Maurizio had found someone to spend time with. Considering how vocal he was about her love life, he kept his own affairs quiet. If he had found any other lovers over the year they'd been friends, Artemisia had never known.

Still hoping for some company, Artemisia turned toward the eponymous basilica at the heart of Santa Croce, and the market spread beside it.

The square was bustling with the residents of Florence

enjoying the mild day. As spring fully bloomed, there would be more stalls in place selling fresh flowers, fruits, vegetables, and herbs. The winter fare was leaner, though the market never fully died. Artemisia made her way through the familiar maze, but there was an unfamiliar stall in Elisabetta's usual spot. A hunched older woman stood by a table stacked with candles, pale and slender as bones.

"Excuse me," Artemisia said. "Where is the woman who normally runs this stall? Elisabetta the herbalist."

"She hasn't been here in a week," the woman said, her voice raspy as the wind. "They offered me her space while she is away."

"Where is she?"

The old woman shrugged and went back to arranging her candles.

"It's her husband," called a voice from across the aisle. The man who sold scarves across from Elisabetta had a thick white beard that bristled like a cloud. Artemisia had exchanged a few words with him in the past—he occasionally requested Elisabetta's help monitoring his stand while he took short breaks. The longstanding members of the market in Santa Croce had a complex structure of alliances and rivalries. He waved Artemisia over and said, "Luco is ill. The signora is home taking care of him."

"All week?" Artemisia asked, alarmed.

He nodded, his frown nearly hidden by his beard. "I have never seen Elisabetta away from her stall so long."

"Thank you," Artemisia said.

"If you see them, tell them I'd like to have them back soon," he said, eyes crinkling. "That new one's not good company."

Artemisia went quickly through the rest of the market, and then walked across the river to Oltrarno with a lighter purse and a heavy basket on her arm.

Elisabetta opened the door at Artemisia's knock, looking haggard. Her dark curls were tucked at the base of her neck in a sloppy bundle, and her skin was pallid and greasy. "This is not a good time, Artemisia."

"I heard," she said, and held up the basket. "I brought supplies. Food and drink and fresh linens. How is Luco? What ails him?"

"He's been stricken with an ague," Elisabetta said, leaning against the door and staring up at the blue sky. "Hot then cold and back again, over and over. Every time he climbs a mountain he seems to tumble straight into a pit. He has chills that threaten to chatter his teeth from his head." She folded her arms across her chest, a muscle in her jaw clenching. "It's been a week, and he's only growing worse. Some days… Some days he's not even coherent."

"Elisabetta," Artemisia said.

The herbalist held out her hand. "Thank you for this. It will be helpful."

"You won't take him to the hospital?"

She snorted. "And who would pay? Besides, I trust my herbs far more than theirs. I would not accept Luco in anyone's care but my own."

"Can I help?"

Elisabetta jabbed a slender finger at Artemisia's face. "I've told you there will be no magics in my house. No matter the circumstance."

Artemisia wanted to argue. What was the point of being friends with an artist, an elite member of the Accademia, only to ignore the healing they could bring? But, truly, what could Artemisia do for a fever? It was an acute illness. She did not store completed, untethered art in her studio. Even if she did, a single painting would not be powerful enough to reverse the course of a severe illness. Art relied on a cumulative effect, building strength inside the patron to help them get sick less often and less intensely.

"You're the one who wanted to teach me herbal healing," Artemisia pointed out. "Could you not use an extra set of hands?"

Elisabetta searched her face. When was the last time Elisabetta had accepted help? Finally, she said, "I could, if you're offering them."

Artemisia nodded. "Let's start."

Elisabetta did not take Artemisia to see Luco, and Artemisia did not ask. He did not deserve her intrusion—she was there to help, not to gawk. Still, she could hear quiet whimpering as they passed the cracked door.

A window sat open on the far wall of the workshop, inviting in the mild spring air. Since her last visit, it had grown even more cluttered with the addition to the rows of wares ready to be sold when Elisabetta returned to her stall. Every day Elisabetta spent caring for Luco was a day's sales lost to the new candlemaker.

"If my foolish husband had gotten sick in the summer, I'd have far more plants to work with," Elisabetta said, frowning at the room. "Almost everything is dried or preserved."

"What can I do?"

"I'm bleeding Luco as much as I can. That's the best thing we know to stop a fever like this. But I also want to give him a favorite tonic of mine. If I walk you through the instructions, I will have to trust that you do it correctly. I don't have time to sit and teach you."

"I'll try my best. I recognize most of these tools in my own work," Artemisia said.

She spent her days creating her paints, using oil to mix the salt, dirt, and root pigments from around the world. Though her craft was brushed onto a canvas, the process was not dissimilar from Elisabetta's. They were connected in this, despite Artemisia's early prejudice.

Elisabetta was a gruff teacher, and left twice mid-sentence to check in on Luco. Finally, Artemisia assured her she understood the instructions and ushered her to go sit with her husband. It was telling of Elisabetta's stress that she obeyed with only a quiet grumble.

The first brew was a decoction of dried elderflowers and coriander. It would be months yet until the flowers bloomed again, but Elisabetta had rows of dried plants dangling from the ceiling like dark clouds.

Elisabetta had repeated a dozen times that the stems and seeds of the elderflower were poisonous, so Artemisia carefully plucked the petals before using the mortar and pestle to grind them in with the coriander leaves. The dried plants crushed to flecks and powder under the round edge of the pestle. Artemisia put her nose close to catch its subtle scent, which was overpowered by the chaos of smells in the room. She mixed the herbs with water, then brought them to the low fire in the kitchen.

Elisabetta sat by Luco's bed, and Artemisia could just hear her quiet murmuring over the crackle of the flames. "Goddamn you, Luco, wake up," she said. "I can't do this without you, you bastard."

Artemisia's heart ached, but Elisabetta would not appreciate the intrusion. She quietly hummed to herself as she waited for the herbs to boil—the song Galileo had sung, O rosa bella.
Oh god of love, what suffering is this love.

When the mix finally came to a boil, Artemisia covered the

pot to let it simmer. It would sit for half an hour before she could strain it and hope she had created something useful.

She slipped from the house to refill the water from the public well. Artemisia had been spoiled by her time with Francesco—he had a private well in his courtyard, used only by his household. Her heart twisted as she hauled the water up. Elisabetta had been doing this all on her own.

Artemisia had been young when her mother died, but she would never forget sitting alone by her bedside and watching her life fade away. Her father had not been able to handle the stress, and had consoled himself with wine and friends while his wife died.

She would not leave Elisabetta by herself in this.

By the fourth day, Artemisia had found a routine.

Her paintings were left in stasis as she spent dawn to dusk at Elisabetta's house. By their nature, the paintings were not urgent beyond the requests of her patrons. Luco, on the other hand, was growing worse by the hour. She feared he was not long for this world if she and Elisabetta did not work quickly.

She was not only helping brew more medicines, but had elbowed her way into cooking meals as well. Elisabetta, it turned out, had been subsisting on hard bread and broth, and the latter only because Luco needed easy food. Artemisia was no great cook, but as she stood over the fire monitoring different teas and tonics, she added meat to another pot to make a thick stew. Getting Elisabetta to actually eat it was a task in itself, and she implemented her friend's usual bullying tactics to get her to at least take a few bites.

Elisabetta eventually graduated Artemisia to slightly more complex tasks. After lunch, she set to trying to finish a salve

Elisabetta thought would help clear Luco's lungs. The fever was still the worst of it, rattling his bones, but Elisabetta said that as he slept, his breathing tended to stop and start as though he were laboring under a great weight.

Artemisia had spent the last day beginning to create a pair of herbal oils—one infused with mint, the other with rosemary. Many of Elisabetta's medicines were a long process—there was a row of tinctures at the back of the room that had been settling for a month. Fortunately, Artemisia would be able to finish this salve today now that the herbs were fully infused. Luco did not have time to wait.

She took one of the bars of beeswax from Elisabetta's local supplier. It was a hefty chunk, solid and beige. She wrapped the bar in an old cloth, and then smashed it into small chunks with a sturdy hammer. After days in the quiet house, the noise was startling but exhilarating. There was still life here, even if Elisabetta and Artemisia had to pry it forth with their fingernails.

Using one of the workshop pans, she melted the wax over the fire. She had accidentally swapped a kitchen pot for an herbalist one on her first day, and Elisabetta had nearly had her head.

It was mesmerizing to watch the irregular shards of beeswax melt into a slick cohesion along the bottom of the pan. She stirred with a copper spoon, the motions familiar from years of mixing oil paints. There seemed to be no world beyond the kitchen. It was meditative, entrancing. Slowly, she poured in a dash of each essential oil, blending them thoroughly.

Once the salve was fully mixed, she pulled the pan back into the workshop to pour its contents into a waiting set of glass jars. She worked smoothly and methodically, filling each jar evenly before scraping out the last bits from the pan with her spoon. As soon as it cooled, it would be ready for use.

Artemisia set the pan aside, feeling reality come back into place around her. She blinked and stared down at her hands. There was a slight tingling at the tips of her fingers, a barely noticeable buzz of energy.

She had not fallen into a full artist's trance, but the sensation was similar. The herbs had siphoned some of her energy, just as her oils did. It was on a far smaller scale—the magics pulled accidentally from an hour of preparation were infinitesimal. Still, there was power here.

Galileo had told her that San Leonardo experimented with beeswax for his oil paints.

Was there anything truly unique about art, or was it simply the task most suited to a dedicated person pouring in a steady stream of their magics? If salves were to take years to brew rather than hours, would herbalists have a table in the Accademia? So much of what she understood came from years of tradition— but she knew personally how much tradition overlooked.

"Artemisia," Elisabetta said, coming into the workshop. Artemisia put her hands behind her back, as though Elisabetta might scent the dribble of magics. Elisabetta would be much less excited by her discovery. "He's lucid. He's asking for you."

"For me?"

"Just go and keep him company for a second. I'll make sure you haven't destroyed my workroom."

"The salve just needs to cool," Artemisia said. "You're…sure he wants me to see him like this?" She always avoided witnesses to her moments of weakness, especially after the trial in Rome. People were too eager to see others in pain, too intrigued by suffering when it was not their own. She would not be anyone's entertainment. She had been careful to avoid the bedroom while helping Elisabetta, not wanting to add to Luco's suffering.

Elisabetta scoffed and waved her on. Artemisia pulled off her apron and cautiously went into the small bedroom. Luco was propped up and covered in thick quilts despite the mild weather. He had lost weight in the past two weeks. His skin was sallow, practically waxen, and dark hollows carved space below his cheekbones.

He was more ill than she had ever seen even Silvestrini, though he was less than half that man's magically bolstered age. It was not fair.

"Artemisia," he said. He took a deep, quavering breath, as though even that single word had drained him.

"Luco," she greeted, sitting in the chair beside the bed.

"Elisabetta says you've been helping," he said. His small smile was slow, but familiar. "I wanted to thank you. I know she won't."

"No thanks are needed," Artemisia said. "We only want you well."

A visible shiver ran through him, quaking under his skin like the rattle of thunder. His teeth clattered for a moment, and then he pulled the shaking under control. "Take care of Elisabetta. Please."

"Luco…"

"She will need someone," he pressed on. "She tries to stand on her own. She's stubborn, my wife."

"I know she is," Artemisia said. "Right now, she's using that stubbornness to make sure you get better. You need to heal from this, for her. She…" Artemisia swallowed. "She loves you very much."

He did not respond, only stared ahead.

"Luco?" she prompted.

He frowned, face scrunching as he squinted at her. "'Betta?"

"She's in the workshop," Artemisia said carefully.

He did not react. He did not seem to truly see her any longer. "'Betta? I'm cold." He folded his arms over his chest, shoulders hunched. His voice fell to a mumble. "Mamma?"

It hurt to see such a stoic, kind man peeled vulnerable by disease. He was suddenly delicate, and there was nothing she could do to help. She squeezed his arm and left the room to find Elisabetta.

Her friend was sitting at the table in the workshop, staring at the wall. She didn't seem to hear Artemisia enter.

"Elisabetta, he's…"

"Lost again?" she asked, and pushed herself to her feet. She immediately tilted to lean against the wall like standing straight was more than she could bear, nearly crushing a dried bundle of sage under her hand. "He's been confused more and more. It happens sometimes when someone has a fever this high for this long. A good thing, maybe, that he's not here to feel it."

Artemisia's heart twisted. "I'm sorry."

Elisabetta closed her eyes for a long moment, and then nodded to herself. "He needs another bleeding. Find me if you need me."

"How is Luco?" Francesco asked that night when he arrived at her studio. Without asking, he had begun spending his nights with her rather than waiting for her to come to his villa. Her studio was closer to Oltrarno, and she had no energy for extra travel after her long days with Elisabetta.

"Still poorly. The only changes have been for the worse." She was reclined on her bed, propped against her pillows. She could not neglect her art for much longer, but she had no energy to spare. The work would hold another day. After coming home, she had gone to the roof to sit with the griffon. She had not had anything to feed it, but it had stayed beside her. There was something soothing in the rise and fall of its sleek feathered chest, its wild musk, and the flutter of wings as it settled itself. It could not know the exhausted turmoil in her mind, and it did not need to. It only wanted her company. They had sat in quiet comfort until sunset drove her inside, back to the helpless waiting.

"I'm sorry to hear that. You're sure she won't let me help?" He had offered to buy additional supplies for them, even volunteering his own time, but Elisabetta had refused.

"Very sure. She's stubborn. She told me she'd throw me out on my ear if I tried to have my rich lover swoop in."

"I'm capable of following orders," Francesco said. "I wouldn't try to take over the situation."

"She values control. She's lost enough of it as it is," Artemisia said. "We need to help on her terms, or we'll just do more harm."

He sighed, running a hand through his hair. "Between you and Elisabetta, Luco is in the best hands in Florence. Hopefully my aid would have been excessive anyway."

"I'm no saint," Artemisia said. "My magics aren't any use here. Luco's only exposure to art is in the Basilica di San Spirito. They attend Mass twice a week, and it's a small church without a steady stream of new art. Even if I could hand him a painting tied to him tonight—which would be impossible even if Elisabetta had not banned me on pain of death from offering—it would not help." If she could drag him across the city to the vault under the Accademia's monastery… But no, at this point even *that* rush of art would not save him. "Art is a steady drip, pressed into layers of oils one stroke at a time for months, and absorbed nearly as slowly by its recipients. It changes lives, not moments."

"And Elisabetta's herbs are more fast-acting, but not as powerful," he said.

"Well, that's not entirely true. Francesco, I felt magics in Elisabetta's workroom today."

"What do you mean?"

"I've done this long enough to know what it feels like for my energy to siphon into my work. I felt that today. I don't know what to think. Could there be magics in every craft? Only not enough for them to make the difference art can?"

Francesco shook his head. "I'm no expert, but I've never heard of such a thing. Maybe artists can just find a way to instill magics into anything. It could be *you*, not the craft."

"There's so much we don't know," Artemisia said. "This was why Galileo wants to study art. We listen to the past and we don't look more closely. What if there was some way for me to save Luco if I only knew more? What if I could *help*?"

"Artemisia," he said. "You're doing the best you can. You cannot blame yourself for tools you don't have. That no one has."

She pressed a hand to her forehead, forcing a tide of tears to subside. "I feel so *useless*, Francesco."

"You're not useless," he said, coming over to kiss her cheek.

She pulled him down alongside her. "Let's not talk about it anymore," she said. "I just need to know you're here with me."

He obliged. Her cot was not as lush as Francesco's bed, but it only mattered that they were together. They had learned to play each other as musicians played their instruments, plucking sighs and murmurs with deft fingers.

His touch felt like coming home. There was comfort in being known, in being held. She tucked herself around his warm body in the darkness and tried not to think of the world beyond.

✳

The next morning when Artemisia arrived in Oltrarno, Elisabetta was sitting on her doorstep, drinking from a flask of wine. She stared at nothing. The lines at the corners of her mouth had deepened, like land worn down by the incessant flow of water over time.

When she saw Artemisia, she shook her head.

"Oh, Elisabetta," Artemisia said, standing awkwardly on the dirt street. A basket of fresh supplies dangled from her fingers, useless now.

Elisabetta took a long drink from the bottle. "He got worse in the evening. I called for a confessor. He was gone by midnight." In Florence, everyone was guaranteed a confessor, unlike other cities where only the wealthy could afford their final absolution. Luco had likely been too disoriented to make a final confession, but the ritual would still have cleansed his soul before he parted. It was a small blessing, but didn't help their grief.

She loathed to imagine only Elisabetta and a stranger at Luco's side as he died. Only a stranger left to witness Elisabetta's grief, when her friend did not trust the world with her soft heart.

"You could have called for me," Artemisia said.

"Can artists stop death with a single glance now?" she returned, then took another drink of wine.

Artemisia just watched her, her heart feeling hollow. "I'm sorry you were alone." Words seemed inadequate.

Pressing the back of her hand to her forehead, Elisabetta turned away for a moment. Her face clenched in agony before smoothing out again. "I have cleaning to do, Artemisia. Arrangements to make. You should go home."

"No," Artemisia said simply, and finally approached the door.

"It's over. I don't need any more help. I'll survive. Just as I always have," Elisabetta said, voice strained. She gave a weak laugh. "You and I are the same, in that way."

"I'm not leaving. I brought food. I know you haven't eaten."

"I have this." She waved her wine. The bottle was close to empty. "And my neighbors will bring food later, I'm sure. They'll come for the funeral. So will the other merchants from Santa Croce. They all—" Her throat caught, and she took a steadying breath. "They all liked Luco."

"He was a good man. Elisabetta," she said firmly. "I'm staying."

"Fine, if you're so sure." Her expression softened even as she shook her head. "You're a stubborn one."

"You and I are the same, in that way."

23

When the knock came, Artemisia shot to her feet.

She had been waiting anxiously all day, barely able to focus on her work. After she had helped Elisabetta with Luco's funeral, she had returned to her paintings, making her excuses for the delay without fanfare—Elisabetta was more important than any work. Michelangelo the Younger, who was opening his gallery soon, had not been happy, but she had smoothed it over.

But for today, he could continue to wait.

Already smiling, she crossed to the door and revealed Galileo Galilei at her threshold.

"Artemisia," he greeted. "It's been far too long." Half a year had passed since he had left for his trial in Rome. He looked tired but whole. His face was a balm after the past weeks.

"Galileo," she said, letting him kiss her cheeks. "I feared it would be even longer."

They sat at her kitchen table to share pasta and wine. Artemisia had moved well past her days of relying on bread and cheese. She was able to eat as she wished, and was spoiled even more when she visited Francesco. For the first time since Luco had died, her chest felt light. Galileo's company was like a breeze after an oppressive heatwave. After so long fearing that he would lose his trial and end up in a dungeon or on a pyre, it was a relief to have him across from her once more.

Galileo told her of his trial as they ate. It had lasted nearly as long as Artemisia's own, though it had been far less brutal. She had worried he would end up in the sibelle as well, but he assured her they had not touched him. "We had debates that lasted all day and night. The Inquisition, with that fool Caccini on their side, was determined to drag my name through the mud. In the end, they couldn't agree to condemn me, but the theories of Copernicus have been formally deemed heretical. All books on the subject are now banned. I was ordered not to teach or defend the ideas—or even admit I believe them. They're trying to erase the theory from the face of the earth."

"I'm just grateful they did not destroy you with it," she confessed.

"I fear it was close for a while. I have managed to hold on to just enough prestige that I was spared. I still have friends in high places. They were not prepared to lose my work, despite everything. Once the decision was made, they were all courtesy itself." He shook his head. "You've never met a more two-faced group, Artemisia. If things had not gone my way, the same men would have publicly jeered at me. Instead, I met with the Pope."

"You did?" Artemisia asked, leaning forward. "What was he like?"

"The oldest man I've ever met," he said with a shrug. "Everyone in the Vatican is old. They have more art in their halls than anywhere else in the world. Still, meeting him feels like meeting Methuselah. It would be an exaggeration to say that he *apologized* for the trial, but he did emphasize that the Church is grateful for my discoveries. He told me that, during his lifetime, I should feel quite secure in his good will and that of the Church. As long as I cease my promotion of the heliocentric universe, I will be permitted to continue conducting research. The alternative was left to his underlings to explain."

"That's all? You think this is the end of it?"

"Oh, Artemisia," Galileo said. "I think this is only the start. It will be a miracle if the Inquisition doesn't burn me in the end. When this pope is gone, the next will not have such sympathy for me. I smiled and made my promises, but we both know the truth. No Inquisition can tell me that my math is false. Truth is truth. If I stopped my research because they told me to, I would be unable to live with myself."

"I understand," she said. Galileo could no more stop looking at the stars than she could stop painting.

He sighed. "At least I know Caccini will be looking for a new fight. Who knows where he will turn his eye next, but at least I am done with him."

"You don't think he'll keep his focus on you? He won't like losing."

Galileo shook his head. "It was never about me. It was about taking down someone whose fall would help him rise. I've proven a more difficult opponent than he wanted. He won't try again. He cares too much about his position."

"They shouldn't have underestimated you," she said, toasting him.

Once their stomachs were full and their heads light with wine, Artemisia sat back and considered her friend. "I've been thinking," she said slowly, "about the saints. The artists that were canonized after the Grave Age."

"Yes?" Galileo asked. His face was ruddy from the wine behind his beard, and his smile was easy.

"Galileo. Are we truly supposed to believe that San Donatello *happened* to make that statue just in time to save Santa Maria del Fiore in 1415?" Artemisia asked. "Statues take years to complete."

He frowned. "We've all heard the story—you probably more than I. The bishop was given a message by God to trust San Donatello's offer. His speed and strength were the miracle for which he was canonized."

"So they say," she said, tapping the edge of the table. "It's been on my mind. I think it's more likely that the Church kept commissioning artists to save their own skin while condemning them to the rest of the world. Even during the Grave Age, popes and cardinals were living to be one hundred or more. You think that was just because they're holy? There's no threshold at the gates of the Vatican that offers long life. That comes from art."

"That's quite an accusation," Galileo said slowly.

"*You* wouldn't accuse me of heresy, would you? Not for simple curiosity."

Her theorizing was far from the most unlawful activity she had done, but it paid to be careful with her words. If someone found reason to question her, her Judith was still covered in the corner of her studio. She could have burned the painting, preventing anyone from ever finding it and absorbing the unfinished magics.

But she had not.

Galileo waved a hand. "I would be hypocritical to, my friend."

"Donatello's skill did not come from the air, and neither did his marble. He must have been taught."

"Artists were still working, just in secret."

"I'm sure they were. *I* would have been. Nothing can stop a true painter from creating. I'm also sure that even after the plague, people with enough money would keep hiring artists no matter how illegal it was." In another life, she thought Francesco would have done so. "There are so many places the Church keeps hidden from the rest of us. No outsider has been in San Pietro for centuries. I used to visit that side of the river when I lived in Rome. You said you saw it, too. Have there ever been such long-lived men as those in the Vatican? The art comes from somewhere."

He stroked his beard thoughtfully. "If all this were true, why ever confess to having an artist helping them? Why not keep Donatello and the rest a secret?"

"Maybe they decided it was finally time to bring art back. Maybe they were tired of keeping it hidden. Maybe Donatello threatened to reveal the secret himself."

Galileo looked thoughtful, those sharp eyes intense despite the empty bottle of wine between them. He was the smartest person she had ever met. There was no one else to whom she could have suggested this theory that had been burning in her. The other members of the Accademia would be horrified. Francesco needed no fuel to doubt the Church. Elisabetta, unfortunately, had been part of the catalyst for her musings. Why had Luco died in his forties and Silvestrini in his hundreds? If Silvestrini had spent his private fortune on art, surely nothing would have stopped the Vatican, the most powerful and secretive organization in the world, from doing the same.

"Or," she pressed, "maybe they decided that the best way to keep art controlled by the Church was to turn artists into saints. All miracles have to be approved by the Church—if other artists can do them too, what's so special about their saints?"

"Artemisia," Galileo said, finally truly shocked.

She shrugged, looking away. "Maybe you shouldn't spend so much time with 'revolutionary' people if you're afraid of questions."

"We will never grow if we do not ask questions. But you are an artist. You must see God's hand in your work."

"It may be in my work, but it is not in my patrons. While the rich and powerful hide in their homes with bits of our souls, people are dying in the streets. *Dying*." Artemisia folded her arms tightly. "Art is a commodity in our world. It is not above the faults of men."

"Nothing is, though, is it?" Galileo asked.

"No," she said quietly. "I suppose nothing is."

As Artemisia settled back into her work, she found more and more that she missed the quiet solitude of that villa in Prato.

Art was her passion, her calling, but her arms and eyes grew sore after long nights in front of her canvases. Luco's unnecessary death haunted her, as did her questions about the purpose of art. The Vatican, Silvestrini, the Medici, the Accademia—art was hoarded across the world, giving impossibly long life to certain men and leaving others to die slowly.

But what could Artemisia do? She could not change the entire world. She could paint, or she could not paint. Beyond that, she was powerless.

With enough time, she hoped to gain more influence inside the Accademia and shift matters from the inside. She was slowly gaining a collection of influential friends and patrons. They valued her work, and she would make them value her opinion.

One day, her voice would be heard.

In the meantime, she insisted on regular drinks with Elisabetta, even if nothing would ease her friend's pain. Without Luco, Elisabetta had needed to hire a girl part-time to manage her stall some days, which gave her more time to focus on her brewing— and to meet Artemisia at their favorite bar for a weekly distraction. They were both absorbed in their work, but Artemisia made time for her friend.

She was blocking out the sketch of a new painting when she

heard her door open behind her. The sketch did not pull her into a magical trance, so she was aware enough to call, "Francesco?" without looking back. Only one person had the key to her studio, and her lover was scheduled to arrive back in the city from a short work trip.

"Hello, my heart," Francesco said. He draped a garland of flowers around her neck and kissed her cheek. She put down her charcoal and lowered her gaze, lifting a heavy pink lily from her breast. She inhaled slowly—the sweet scent cleansed her nose of the smell of her studio's candlewax and walnut oils.

It was the final day of Candelmaggio, the annual celebration of the first day of May. From the noises Artemisia heard from the window of her studio, the parades and games had been raucous. The laughter had a heady tone, the joy of the approaching summer in every voice.

"Don't tell me you haven't gone outside at all," he chided. "The party is in full swing just blocks from your door. Come dance with me, darling. You deserve a break after everything, and it's the best holiday of the year."

"I need to work on this. I'm still catching up on everything, but I'm almost done blocking out the design," she said, letting the lily fall back and picking up her charcoal to finish her thought. "You can duck back out if you want to enjoy the holiday."

"I'd rather be here with you." He came to stand beside her and moved the garland of flowers to kiss her neck. "What's this you're working on?"

"The Madonna and her child," Artemisia said, tilting her head at the rough black lines on the canvas. "Or it will be." It was softer than her usual works, a gentle moment between the Virgin Mother and her son. She was planning to use less shadow than was her wont, leaving both of the figures mostly in the light.

Caravaggio's chiaroscuro may have been truer to the reality around her, but she suddenly longed to bring a glint of light into the world.

She made one final mark, and then put down her charcoal; the outline was as finished as it needed to be tonight, and Francesco had been busy with his own work lately. Now that she had him in her studio, she did not want to waste their time together. With all of her doubts and questions, Francesco's company brought the rare gift of peace.

"I'm sure it will be beautiful."

"Thank you, my heart," she said, pulling him into a kiss.

He met her, but then pulled back, a small smile on his lips. He rubbed a thumb over one of the petals around her neck. "I love you."

"I love you, too," she said. She trailed a hand from his hair down his neck, tugging gently at the collar of his shirt. He was wearing far too many clothes for her purposes. "I missed you."

"I thought of you the whole time I was gone," he told her. "I always do. I never imagined I would meet someone like you. Beautiful, passionate, talented, brave, clever." He paired each word with a small kiss, tracing her skin from her cheekbones up her nose to her forehead.

"Flatterer," she said.

"I want you in my bed," he told her. "I want you at my breakfast table. I want to hike with you, and feed you biscotti to make up for it. I want to travel with you. I want to see every step you take with your art."

"I want those things too," she assured him, pressing up for another kiss.

He reached into his pocket and withdrew a small gimmel ring that glinted warm and golden in the candlelight. The surface was intricately carved, an ornate work of art in miniature. "Then, Artemisia Gentileschi," he said, lingering on her name like a poem. "Marry me."

She stilled, staring at the ring. Marriage? Artemisia had nearly been married twice before. If Tassi had not already been wed, she might have been forced to marry him to save her reputation. If her father had gotten his way, she would have been married to a stranger when she arrived in Florence. No one had asked her opinion either time, and certainly not in such a gentle, conspiratorial tone.

When he just waited, she said, "We were fighting only a few months ago."

He huffed a quiet laugh. "And we'll fight again. Marry me, my love."

In the dim candlelight of her studio, it was difficult to read his expression. It seemed languid but intent, soft but sharp. "You know that with my amulet, I'm not pregnant. I may never be."

He reached up to put his hand against the side of her face, his thumb rubbing along her cheekbone. "Marry me, Artemisia. You don't need to talk me out of it. I want this. The question is—do you?"

There would be more obstacles in their path, both trials they had encountered before and others they could not predict. Even if they clung to happiness together, she had seen at Luco's bedside the ways that deep love could bring deep pain.

Artemisia had spent years fighting for the glory she wanted as an artist. She had been willing to overcome any obstacle to realize her dream.

Why not fight for this love as fiercely as she had fought for everything else?

"Yes," she said. "Yes, yes."

His expression melted into a wide smile—she had not realized that he was hiding his anxiety until it was gone. He slid one ring onto her finger, and she slid its twin into place on his.

After that, there was no chance that Artemisia would return to her work for the night. She traced her fingers over Francesco's body, leaving dark charcoal smears across his olive skin. He clasped their hands together. She could feel the band of his ring against her fingers.

Once they fell sweaty and tangled on her cot, she lifted her hand so the candlelight caught the details on her ring. It was slender and gold, decorated with a single hand stretching toward half a ruby heart. The hand's sleeve was studded with small emeralds, specks of bright green. Francesco's had a mirror pattern. At their wedding, the halves would be hooked together so that the two hands would clasp into one ring for Artemisia to wear for the rest of her life.

"Lie to me ever again, and you'll regret it," she murmured, admiring her ring.

"I swear I won't."

"I'm not going to stop painting when I'm your wife."

"I'd never dream of asking you to. I know what I'm asking for, Artemisia. I want you as you are." He ran a hand through her hair. "I'm not perfect. I'll still need to travel for work. I'll be gone often."

"That's all right. You can bring me back gifts," she said, patting his stomach.

"I love you," Francesco said, as though it had been punched from his chest.

"I love you, too," Artemisia told him.

*

Michelangelo the Younger was beside himself with anxiety before the unveiling of the Casa Buonarroti gallery. He paced just inside the door, peeking through the keyhole at the gathered cultural elite. Artemisia and the other featured artists were with him in the entry hall. Most were fellow Accademia members, though there were a few international artists showcased as well. Artemisia had seen the hall during the rehearsal. It would truly be a gallery worthy of a saint. Sigismondo hovered nearby, clearly twitching to help Michelangelo, but held back. Their break-up had been relatively amicable, but according to Sigismondo they had not seen each other often since.

Instead, Artemisia stepped forward. "Breathe," she told Michelangelo briskly. "You've done all your work. It's our art on display."

"You're right, you're right," he said. "And they will love it."

"You're damn right they will," Artemisia said. "It's time to let them in."

Finally, he opened the doors. The crowd was small—exclusive, as Michelangelo said—and limited to the patrons and influencers Michelangelo trusted to appreciate his work and get the word out to other elites. The Grand Duchess, the Grand Duke, and the duke's wife were in attendance, standing slightly separate from the rest. Perhaps they thought they were above everyone else. Even with the most powerful family in Florence in attendance, her eye was drawn inevitably to Francesco. When he spotted Artemisia—seeming also to be drawn to her face in the crowd—he winked. The engagement ring felt bright and heavy on her finger.

As soon as the first patron stepped through, Michelangelo's demeanor morphed, sloughing off the anxiety like a blood drake shedding its skin. He ushered them inside the monument to his late uncle, leading the group of appropriately awed men and women through the grand hallways and into the gallery, which was both the centerpiece of the evening and the space for the celebration.

Following Michelangelo's careful instructions, Artemisia followed the group into the gallery and positioned herself below her piece of the ceiling. Her painting had been laid in place at the last moment, the canvas set carefully into the wall so as not to brush against the drying varnish. Michelangelo had not been pleased with the delay, but the result was undeniably one of her best works.

The effect of so many different artists' styles on display at such close quarters, each framed by the wall's uniform filigree, was that of a sprawling farmers' market. The textures and styles were so diverse that the full effect was overwhelming, but pleasing.

Artemisia preened under her work. In a room full of intricate paintings, her allegory of natural talent stood out for its simplicity. It was one of the most brightly lit portraits she'd done in years, showcasing a nude woman perched on a cloud throne, a compass in her hands. Unlike the women in some of the world's most famous paintings, such as San Sandro's *The Birth of Venus*, Artemisia's figure did not use her hands to cover her own body. Instead, both of her hands were holding the compass. The effect was of a casual, confident innocence, as unaware of her own nudity as Eve in the garden. This woman was free from the constraints of womanhood in Artemisia's era, and could live freely in her art.

The face was a self-portrait.

The guests milled around the gallery, observing the tributes to the elder Michelangelo while they sipped wine. Sigismondo, with his enormous painting in the center of the room, was enjoying the lion's share of the attention, which he accepted with a gracious flush.

Everything was proceeding as Artemisia had dreamed. Her commission for the Medici had led her here, and the presence of her art in this place would lead to bigger and bigger commissions. Public commissions for the Church would not be far behind. Her work would finally pay off. If there were still things she hoped to fix about the art world in Luco's memory, how better to do so than as one of its most valued members? She could make change happen.

"I should create a gallery like this," Francesco said, coming to stand beside her.

"Do you have a theme in mind, or were you planning on dedicating it to yourself?" she asked. "I would like to secure the allegory of self-importance."

He grinned at her. "Nothing wrong with knowing one's own worth. You do as well," he said, pointing up to her painting. "Immortalized forever. I wish you'd shown me this one earlier."

She rolled her eyes and nudged him with an elbow. "You've seen it all before."

"Yes, but—"

"Is that *your* face?" interrupted a man she'd never met before. From the detailing on his doublet, he must have been one of Michelangelo's wealthier patrons.

"It is," Artemisia said.

He scoffed. "Are you not ashamed? A painting like *this* in public?"

"My art is in the most important new gallery in Florence," she pointed out. "I am far from ashamed."

His jaw dropped. He must have been accustomed to people

groveling to him. "Don't you find it arrogant to include your likeness in a gallery dedicated to Michelangelo?"

Artemisia smiled, and it felt like a knife. "This gallery is supposed to hearken back to one of the greats. What artist has not immortalized his own face in his masterpieces? You do know that San Raffaello included portraits of himself and all his friends in his *School of Athens* mural back in Rome, don't you? Including our beloved Michelangelo the Elder."

Francesco hid a snort behind his goblet, though he didn't try to mask the mirth in his eyes.

"You shouldn't be so flippant," said a gravelly voice.

She turned and swallowed the quip on her tongue when she saw who had spoken. Grand Duke Cosimo II stood behind her, his expression tight.

"Pardon me, Your Grace," she said. "I was simply..." She trailed off. She didn't regret her words, and hoped he would not make her pretend she did. This was a night for her success, not false humility.

Thankfully, Madama Cristina stepped forward. "Your Grace," she said, addressing her son formally for the public, "Signore Lamberti was asking to speak with you."

The Grand Duke gave Artemisia a cold look. "You'll make enemies," he warned her, and then strode across the room. Lamberti had been invited as a guest, as he was not one of the artists on display, and was standing in another corner as though he could not see Artemisia. If the Grand Duke was friends with him, Lamberti was surely poisoning his ear against her.

Madama Cristina hesitated only for a second to look up at Artemisia's painting and give her a quick nod before leaving as well. Though she wouldn't contradict her son in public, she clearly was not as offended by Artemisia's boldness.

The man who had confronted her had drifted away when Florence's leaders approached, leaving her and Francesco alone in their pocket of the gallery. He pulled a quick face at her, mocking the Grand Duke for a moment so brief that no one else in the room would have noticed.

She laughed, the tension of the moment ruptured.

"Heaven forbid you paint a beautiful woman with a beautiful face," he said wryly. "That's usually just the sort of thing they enjoy. It's not as though we're lacking nude figures across this city. I saw Michelangelo's *David* at a formative age," he murmured.

"I'm sure it didn't have anything to surprise you," Artemisia pointed out.

"Only the scale," he said, and she laughed again.

The rest of the evening flew by in a rush of wine and praise, and Artemisia put the incident from her mind.

"I'm looking for an African woman to model for my next commission," Artemisia said as soon as Maurizio was inside her studio door. After her success at Michelangelo's gallery opening last week, she could afford to hire another model. The final payment for her work had been substantial. Her fingers itched to learn another face. "I'm painting Bathsheba with her attendants. David will be off the canvas, so you won't need to pose for it. Do you know anyone who might be looking for work?"

Maurizio was still standing by the door, looking more hesitant than she'd ever seen him.

"What? Come on in. You know we're working on the painting of Lot today. I have your toga ready. Tell Gabriele he's welcome in advance. I know those are his favorite paintings of you."

"Artemisia, have you been outside this morning?"

"I've been preparing for today's session. It takes all morning to blend the pigments." She frowned at his expression. "What's happened?"

"You need to hear what Tomasso Caccini was saying in his sermon yesterday."

"Caccini? That bastard," Artemisia said. "Galileo was acquitted. What good does he think it will do to smear him more? He's probably just glad to be back at Santa Maria Novella where his followers have to listen to his nonsense."

"He wasn't talking about Galileo," Maurizio said. "He was talking about you."

"*Me?*"

"You," he confirmed, gesturing for her to sit at the kitchen table. Unsteadily, she did so, and he joined her. "Apparently, he spent half the sermon raving on the subject."

"I don't understand. Why me? I've never met the man. Is it because I'm friends with Galileo? At this point he should drop that grudge. He failed in Rome and Galileo was acquitted."

"If it is because of Galileo, he didn't say it. He's been to Casa Buonarroti. He thinks your painting there, the nude, is some sort of sin. He told everyone in attendance that art should be reserved for rational and pious men, like the clergy."

A laugh burst from her throat. "Oh, is that so? How many artists has he met? How many clergymen? Ridiculous."

"When has reason mattered to men like that? He said that letting you 'pretend' you have one of God's rarely given artistic gifts is heresy. There was…also something about you defiling Michelangelo's legacy, staining it before the man could reach sainthood."

She could not stay seated. She stalked to her window and looked down at the narrow streets below. She wrapped her arms around her stomach and asked, "And the Accademia admitting me into their ranks means nothing?"

Maurizio grimaced. "I believe there was talk of trickery, bribery, and seduction."

"That bastard. How did you hear of all this? I know you don't attend that church. Who do you even know who goes to Santa Maria Novella still? They should have left after what he did to Galileo. Let Caccini have his little platform. He's just lashing out."

"Artemisia—it's not just the people who go to that church. It's all anyone is talking about today. Gabriele heard it from one of our neighbors."

Artemisia closed her eyes. She tried to stoke her fury, the burning ember of righteous anger at her core, but a wave of helpless fear threatened to drown it. How quickly could her reputation change? She'd been here before, targeted as a harlot by men in power. Last time, it had ruined her. It had taken her clients, her family, her friends, her health.

Artemisia flexed her fingers, feeling the phantom of the sibille.

"He's full of shit," Maurizio declared, jarring her from the terror clawing at her throat. She looked back at him, and he shrugged. "You were right. He wants everyone to think that artists are pious? Give people two minutes to think about it, and they'll realize they aren't and never have been. Your own Caravaggio spent more nights in bar fights than he did sleeping. Most famous artists are scoundrels. You're a saint in comparison."

Artemisia laughed. "People are blind to men's sin. The standards are different for me."

"Maybe they are," Maurizio admitted, "but you have people on your side. Things will move on soon. I just wanted you to know."

"I hope so," Artemisia said.

*

Once Maurizio left, Artemisia climbed to the roof. She rarely went up during the day. The griffon tended to hunt with the sunlight and come back to sleep at night, so she didn't expect it to be there, but she found it sitting by the chimney, staring out over the city.

The creature was striking in the light, with the sun glinting off the sable feathers of its head and neck. It stretched when it spotted her, bowing down over its front claws and pushing its sun-warmed rump into the sky. Its movements were languidly feline as it loped over to greet her.

It had grown substantially in the last eighteen months, its body finally matching its large back paws. Though still lanky with youth, it was less rawboned. It now stood tall enough that when it headbutted her in greeting, its forehead bumped into her chest. Its coat was healthy and shiny—her art kept it well nourished.

It was a sweltering day, the air still and heavy, but Artemisia felt cold. She sat on the narrow ledge at the peak of the roof, with the steep edge tumbling into space in front of her. The height did not scare her.

Caccini was out for her blood. His accusations were enormous. How would the city react? Galileo's fall from grace had shown how quick even friends were to turn when the Church selected an enemy. If the most lauded natural philosopher in Europe was not immune to the whispers of heresy, what chance could she have?

The specter of her trial in Rome pressed down on her shoulders.

Her torture at the hands of the court had been brutal, but was only a standard part of questioning. The punishments for a

guilty verdict of heresy were public and merciless. The rack was
the least of the tortures they would subject her to before finally
killing her. She had seen the bodies hanging from the windows
of the Borgella, rotting in sight of those passing through the
square below. The heads of those decapitated were often hung
as well. Worse, for a crime as abhorrent as heresy, she could be
burned alive.

She shuddered, imagining the flames licking her skin and
the smoke flooding her lungs.

Perhaps Maurizio was right. Caccini enjoyed stirring trouble,
grasping for relevance by attacking anyone he thought was
vulnerable. She had never even met the man. His attention would
move on soon. She had done no wrong.

The griffon sat beside her, watching her curiously. When she
didn't acknowledge it, wrapped in her own thoughts, it lay down
and put its beak in her lap, closing its eyes.

Absently, she stroked its feathers. They were soft, and warm
from the sun.

PART III

JUNE 2–OCTOBER 23, 1616

24

Any optimism Artemisia tried to cling to was quickly snuffed out over the next two weeks.

"I wanted to tell you in person," sighed Signore Orlandi, folding his hands on the table. He was a patron she'd met through the Medici, a merchant who specialized in metalworking. They were sitting in the study of his large flat to the south of the Duomo. The servant who led her inside had avoided her gaze. Compared to her last visit there, when she'd been handed a hefty sack of silver scudi for her advance, the welcome was frigid.

"You're canceling your commission," Artemisia said, clutching the glass of wine she'd been given. Considering how much wine she'd been plied with during similar conversations over the last fortnight, it was a miracle she was ever sober.

Orlandi nodded. "I decided you should hear it from me."

Artemisia's smile felt sour. She had received a half-dozen letters since Caccini's declaration of war, and a handful more personal invitations like this. She preferred the letters. If she didn't have to force a smile, she could stomp and rage until her throat was sore. "I've been working on your painting for six months. Surely it's not worth canceling. I can't repay you for the stipend—I've spent it on the paints already."

"I don't need the money back," he said. "I simply can no

longer work with you. Caccini has a vendetta against you. He's spent weeks dragging your name through the mud. I can't go against him."

"I didn't know you were so pious," she said with a naïve blink. "You attend Santa Maria Novella?"

"I'm between churches," he admitted delicately, "but those who *do* attend Caccini's church won't do business with those of us still paying you. If they saw a piece by you in my gallery, I would lose my standing here. I'm sure you understand."

"I'm the same painter I was when you hired me. I'm a member of the Accademia."

"The Accademia's word isn't worth much now either. They don't have strict enough rules as to who gets initiated. They encourage artists to make secular art instead of sacred art." More of Caccini's rantings. It was astonishing watching Caccini's statements ripple across Florence, repeated as though they were new thoughts. No one in this city had a mind of their own.

"I was painting a biblical story for you," Artemisia reminded him.

"Right, but…" Orlandi floundered. "Look, Caccini has the ear of the Medici, and they have the ear of the merchants. I'm not willing to stand against that."

"The Medici were my first patrons in the city. They won't condemn me."

"So you say. I'm sorry, signorina. I'm not the man to make a stand."

After she made it back to her studio, she found his half-completed canvas on its easel, depicting a shadowed Delilah holding a fistful of Samson's hair. She had been adding a layer of magic and paint only the night before, and the oil still gleamed wetly in the morning light. The painting had been crafted for

Orlandi, awaiting the addition of his hair to seal the bond. Even if she attempted to change course now, the work would not bind to a new owner. Art was a long process, and failed without consistency. Heart heavy, she gathered her iron and flint.

It caught fire beautifully.

Her breath caught as the magics welling inside the oil were released into the air and rushed back into her soul like filings launching toward a magnet. Incomplete and unmoored, her magics were freed from the tentative anchor of the painting. It was a shame that fire was the only way to dispel magics. It could have been a beautiful piece.

The bitter catharsis only lasted until the next morning, and the arrival of another cancelation. The news of Caccini's attack would be rippling across Europe soon, and she was certain the letters would continue to arrive from even further afield.

How quickly the world was ready to turn on her again. More than two years building a life in Florence, and it only took one man's accusations to topple her work like it had been built with splinters. Her hands already felt bloodied by the demolition.

When she arrived at the monastery of Cestello for the Accademia's monthly meeting, she walked with a spine of iron. It was her first truly public appearance since Caccini had begun his attacks, and she was certain every eye would be on her. If they wanted weakness or fear to sip on like leeches, they would not find it.

Sigismondo greeted her as soon as she stepped in the door, making a quiet demonstration of welcoming her as usual. He kissed both her cheeks and murmured words of encouragement. Since the first day at the anatomical theater, he had stood by her side. Jacopo was not far behind, though his performance was less subtle. He had always enjoyed drama. He had brought her into Florence's art world in a rapid whirlwind, and now swept back in as though he'd been by her side throughout, making sure the gathered artists knew she still had his support.

She was deeply heartened, though it was not entirely unexpected. Jacopo had been one of her father's few friends to take her side against Tassi during the Roman trials, and that had been with her open admission of her ruination. In comparison, an antagonistic priest smearing her name now was hardly a barrier for him to crash through.

The surprise came from the rest of the Accademia. Though there were many that kept their distance from her, glaring from across the room and speaking in whispers to each other, most acknowledged her, taking her side. Despite Caccini's slander, she was still one of them, just as she had fought to become.

"Terrible what that priest is saying," an artist Artemisia had never spoken to said. "If all artists were expected to be saints, it wouldn't be such a celebration when one was canonized, would it? I expect the preacher general will be handing you an apology soon. He did for Galileo, didn't he?"

He had. And Galileo had still ended up on trial in Rome. Instead of dampening the moment, Artemisia simply nodded and let Jacopo sweep her forward.

Lamberti was one of the most obvious exceptions. He watched her with a vicious smugness that made her grind her teeth. He was working on the new fresco for Caccini's church. She wouldn't be surprised to learn he had painted the target on her back for his patron. She itched to yell at him, but she needed the Accademia's sympathy.

Eventually, they settled into the seats for the meeting, but when the Accademia's superintendent stood up to speak, the mood of the room darkened. "There are a few newly passed laws that we need to be aware of, for they will impact all of us greatly," he said. "A new ruling has been passed on the export of paintings from Florence, both by Accademia members and non-member artists. The Church will now be in charge of approving all sales, led by Tomasso Caccini at Santa Maria Novella."

"What?" Sigismondo hissed to Artemisia. "He can't do that."

"Why would the Grand Duke agree to that bullshit?" Artemisia asked. "Caccini wouldn't understand art if someone shoved a brush through his eye."

"Furthermore," the superintendent continued, holding up his hands for quiet, "a law has been passed to regulate the work of artists. All initiated members of the Accademia will need to do work for the Church in equal measure to what they have been commissioned for by private citizens. Existing commissions with the Church will be paid in full, but future commissions will only be given a stipend to pay for supplies."

The uproar across the chapel was even louder, rippling like thunder through the crowd.

"A stipend—"

"Do they understand how long it takes to—"

"Do they expect us all to starve while—"

More than one pair of eyes flicked to Artemisia accusingly.

"Why would the Medici agree to this?" Artemisia asked Sigismondo, pulse fluttering. "They commission half the art in this city. They can't believe this is a good idea."

"It doesn't matter what they think. Look at what's happening. They're afraid Caccini will be the next Savonarola," Sigismondo said. "They'll be doing whatever they can to make sure that this time, the Medici aren't kicked out of the city again."

A famous prophet who had taken over Florence at the end

of the Grave Age, Girolamo Savonarola had swayed the entire city with his words. His rise to power had been meteoric. Even after he had been put to death, there had been a cult around his name. Though his body had been burned to ensure there were no relics left to worship, there were still those who said his name with reverence. He had worked with the French to overthrow the Medici, and it had taken nearly one hundred years for the family to claw their way back to power.

"I've heard him speak—Caccini is no Savonarola," Artemisia said. "He has no great mission. He's only doing this because he wants control." She shook her head. "And he's using me as an excuse to do it. He's been telling everyone for weeks that the Accademia was fooled into letting me in. He's been undermining their authority since he got back to Florence. He couldn't beat Galileo, so he's turning on us."

After answering a series of questions about the new laws, the superintendent reminded them of that weekend's funeral for one of their recently passed members, and asked the gathering if anyone had additional issues to bring up at the end of the meeting.

Artemisia could feel eyes heavy upon her. They stung like gnats, and she gritted her teeth. The new laws would put pressure on them all, and it was clear that Caccini was behind the changes. He wanted her out of the Florentine art world, and would continue to attack the Accademia as long as they supported her. It would be a matter of a vote to kick her out.

Her patrons had been disassociating from her. Perhaps her entire career was about to die.

But no one spoke up. She was still one of them and, for now, that seemed to matter.

"I didn't know that artist who died well," Artemisia admitted to Sigismondo as they left the monastery. Her formal robes were heavy in the summer heat, worse now her skin was sticky and sensitive after sweating nervously throughout the meeting.

"He was young," Sigismondo said. "I hate to hear it."

"Art is draining for the best of us." It would be her first funeral as part of the organization, though she had known some of her annual fee went toward the funerals of the members. Once someone joined the Accademia, it became their highest obligation and deepest affiliation—they would be interred in the artists' chapel, rather than their family mausoleums or the potter's field. "Maybe we'll be lucky and Lamberti will be next."

Sigismondo gasped. "Artemisia."

"It's true," she said coolly, but he didn't falter.

"Lamberti isn't a monster simply because he doesn't like you," Sigismondo pointed out. Artemisia shot him a glare, and he shrugged. "It's true. Even the worst men in history have had wives, children. Lamberti believes it when Caccini says that you're a sinner and a whore because he believes that he's neither of those things. Or he is, and he wants to think that you're worse."

"Sounds monstrous to me," Artemisia said. "Men can do terrible things to people they think are below them."

"Oh, Artemisia," Galileo said as he sat at her kitchen table. He coughed hoarsely and rubbed his chest. He had only come into Florence from his house in the country that morning, but the travel and city air aggravated his lungs. "I'm grateful you could make the time to see me. I've been thinking of you often."

"You're always welcome when you're in the city. I wish you could come more often. I expect the rumors have slithered their way out to you?"

"Of course," he said. "I still have many friends in the city. Sigismondo dedicated an entire letter to the troubles. I was surprised I did not hear from you directly."

She shrugged. "After you only just escaped Caccini's ire yourself? I couldn't ask for your help."

He set his fist against the table. "If I had my way, I would redirect his arrows back to me to spare you from this. He is a master in spreading hatred. He's like a poison, corrupting whatever he touches." He shook his head. "I wish he had not discredited my opinion. I will argue for you as loudly as I can, but no one will truly believe that I fight *for* you rather than *against* him."

"I appreciate that. You know as well as I do that being a revolutionary means shouldering a large target," Artemisia said, tracing a line of woodgrain on the table. "I fear I will not fare as well as you did."

Galileo nodded solemnly. "I can't fault you for your nerves. You once told me that you had little faith in the court. I believed that the truth would always win. But though I may have escaped with my life from Rome, they buried the truth deep. There are those who don't care about what is true."

"What do I do?" she asked, voice trembling.

"Lies are louder, and there are an endless number of them. They can be deafening. I've seen the ways Caccini uses hate and fearmongering to obscure the truth. But what *is* the truth here? What does he *want*?"

"He left his post here to chase you to Rome, and then failed to have you condemned," Artemisia said. "He must be looking to reestablish his name in Florence. With his gossip against me and the new laws he's convinced the Medici to pass, everyone is talking about him again. The Accademia is furious about the new restrictions."

Galileo tapped his fingers on the table. "He picked *you* for a reason. Why?"

"You did warn me he would go after an easier target once he found his footing in Florence again. Maybe I'm the Accademia's weakest link."

He scoffed. "Artemisia Gentileschi, an easy target? If he thinks that, he's even more a fool than I thought. And I'll tell you I've long thought him the worst kind of fool."

"He must have been, to argue mathematics with you." Her laugh felt scraped from her throat. Francesco was away traveling for work, and she had found little cause for laughter in the past weeks.

"You have achieved things thought impossible for a woman. You are one of the city's most affluent and powerful artists, and the world knows your name. Not only that, but you have friends in many places. He should be careful choosing you as his enemy."

She sighed. "I wish everyone had such faith in me."

He smiled gently. "The most important person is yourself. You've stood on your own before. Don't forget what you've been through to get here."

Francesco had been traveling for the last month, ignoring the press of summer heat and venturing deep into the pulsing heart of Egypt. She had gotten letters from Alexandria and Cairo, and had imagined the scent of scorching sands and ancient monoliths still lingered on the paper.

At the end of his last letter, he had written, "Though I am far from your side, my heart is still with you. Remember me one thousandth as much as I remember you, and I am all yours."

He had always had a way with words.

Her letters back had been short and sparse. With the growing tensions within Florence, it had felt as though writing any longer would break open the dam inside her, and she would not be able to stop her quill until the inkwell and her heart had been bled dry.

She addressed every letter to V.S., a shortening of the honorific *vostra signoria*. The formal address was quickly undermined in her writing, because even when she was so reticent about her life, her pen stroked out the words 'my love' as easily as breathing. She knew her phrasing was uncouth, but she tried to show him her heart.

At the end of the letter, she wrote, *Come home soon, V.S.*

Then she tore off that last inch of the paper, and instead signed her name along the margin. She would handle this without begging for help from anyone.

25

I t had been more than a month since the start of Caccini's attacks, and Artemisia's commission list was down to a small handful of loyal patrons. Despite how it dredged up memories of her trial against Tassi, she was holding her own better this time. In Rome, she had been abandoned by all of her supporters, with her own father attempting to convince her to marry Tassi to smooth over the scandal. Here, her colleagues had declared themselves her allies, in spite of the new laws restricting their movements. Though they were all struggling with the new sanctions and the ripples of Mario Ricci's death, she was still one of them.

Florence was hers, and Caccini would need to pry it from her nails to take it from her.

"Ciao, Michelangelo," she said, greeting him with a kiss on each cheek. He had asked her to come to Casa Buonarroti in a note that morning, and she had appreciated the excuse to leave the lingering anxiety that plagued her inside her studio. She had last seen him the night of the gallery opening, glowing from the praise as his monument was finally unveiled and free of the anxiety he had felt before the doors opened. He had thanked her profusely as she left with Francesco, face flushed and teary-eyed.

The anxiety, it seemed, had not stayed away. He was pale and jittery, unable to meet her eyes.

It was early evening, and Casa Buonarroti was closed for the day. He led her to the gallery, which was as stunning as it had been the first time Artemisia had seen it. This would be a collection that lasted the ages. She glanced up at her own piece with a small, private smile. Despite the trouble it had caused, it was truly some of her best work. After years of heavy shadows, it was satisfying to see her skill in light and clouds.

Her appreciation was short-lived. Michelangelo sighed heavily, for the third time since she had arrived.

"What's wrong?" she asked. "Are you okay?"

He avoided her gaze in favor of looking around the gallery. "I made Casa Buonarroti as a monument to my uncle," he said, stepping away to examine the painting of an angel reaching down from the ceiling with a long, slender finger to bless the figure of Michelangelo the Elder below with inspiration. "He owned this house, even though he never lived here. He changed the world— and my family. He's going to be canonized, and everyone will remember him. I have my own accomplishments, but I'll never be my uncle. This was going to be what tied us together beyond our names." He turned to her, face solemn and drawn. "Tomasso Caccini is telling people that your painting here is sinful, and that I should never have commissioned you for this hall."

"Tomasso Caccini is a bastard," Artemisia pointed out.

"A bastard with influence," Michelangelo said. "Attendance has dropped dramatically already. It only just opened, and it's already threatening to disappear. No one wants to give money to the gallery that commissioned your painting. It's becoming a scandal."

"This storm will pass, and the house will still be here," Artemisia said. "Caccini can't ruin your uncle's legacy. The Church wouldn't stand for that."

"No, but he can ruin *mine*," Michelangelo said. "We just need to appease him. I need him to stop telling his congregation to avoid this place. I don't want to end up like the Accademia."

Caccini had interfered with a dozen attempted sales by members already, claiming that only the export of religious themes would be approved going forward, for the sake of Florence's reputation. As though the foreign buyers hadn't specifically requested their secular art. When artists had protested, the Medici had supported Caccini's decisions. The new law gave him the authority.

Artemisia folded her arms. "I don't 'appease' men like Caccini. The night we met, you told me I was right to stand by Galileo."

"I'm not disavowing you. If you would just paint over the nudity, you can stay as a part of the gallery. He'll stop attacking us."

Artemisia's jaw dropped. "So that is why you've asked me here? You want me to censor my work to satisfy Caccini?"

"You have to admit that it's provocative," Michelangelo said.

"The subject was your idea. It's not even the only nude in this gallery!"

"It's the most obvious," he pointed out. "The others use their hands to cover themselves. Your painting is...uninhibited."

"She's an allegory of talent. You expected her to be shy? If a man had painted that, people would call him bold. Look at Titian! His Venus is as naked as my work, and she's seductive. My figure is simply living! There are no bedsheets. If you see her as provocative, that's your problem."

"I'm not the one who is bringing up the issue. Caccini is convinced that this work is obscene. It's sent him on a rampage. It started all of this. I don't want to be in the way. This isn't my fight."

Fury roiled in her chest. "Coward."

"You know," Michelangelo said, voice high and clumsy, "he says you put yourself into the painting to set yourself on my uncle's level. And I wonder if he's right."

"In honor of your uncle's style, maybe I should have painted the woman as a man and stuck on oranges for breasts as an afterthought," she snarled.

Michelangelo flushed, the color mottling purple and pink. "If you won't paint a modesty cloth over your figure, I'll hire someone who will."

"You have to be joking," she said. "That is my *art*, Michelangelo. *My* art. You don't get to cover it up because you're feeling anxious! One man, one slimy man, speaks against me, and you're willing to destroy my creation by letting someone else paint over it?"

"It is my art now," he pointed out, face flushing. "It's in my gallery. I paid for it."

"Of anyone, I thought you would understand artistic integrity. You would never let anyone do this to your uncle's work."

"My uncle is being canonized. *He's* not being called a heretic," Michelangelo pointed out.

"Bullshit. That's all just labels, and you know it. If he had been born during the Grave Age, he'd have been burned at the stake. My art is just as important as the great Michelangelo's." He started to argue, but she talked over him, voice rising to a shout. "I spent a year on that painting. That work is an allegory of natural talent. I have that. You have no right to damage my work! A *modesty cloth*? Do you hear yourself? That," she said, jabbing a finger at her work, "is my creation. Don't you dare ask me to paint over it, and don't you dare let anyone else touch it."

"Stop shouting," he snapped. "You know, this is why people don't hire women."

"Your esteemed uncle was famous for his temper! Caravaggio

cut off a man's balls! Neither of them was ever accused of femininity. All I've ever wanted has been to paint without idiot men like you getting in my way. How dare you try to censor me after our deal was done? I thought you were my friend."

"And I thought you were mine," Michelangelo said, jaw tight.

"You will have trouble finding an artist who will do this for you. I'm a member of the Accademia, just like the rest of them. We're all having to fight against Caccini's influence."

"I've asked another artist already, and he said yes. I was hoping you would agree for your own dignity, but I see that it was a futile hope."

"Don't turn this back on me," she said. I'm not the one being unreasonable."

He shook his head, jaw set. "You should go," he said, pointing toward the exit.

"Who agreed to do this?"

"I can't—"

"Tell me who."

"Paolo Lamberti."

Because Michelangelo was a disgusting coward, Artemisia managed to demand an address from him before she agreed to leave the gallery. She might not have been able to sway him to leave her painting intact, but he wasn't working alone.

Her journey across the city seemed to take only moments. *Paolo Lamberti*. The syllables clanged in her head. Her vision was blurred with fury. The rage swelled inside her like a blister, teeming and sour and ready to burst.

It was getting late, the summer sun low over the city.

Paolo Lamberti lived by the river, not far from Ponte Vecchio.

It was a far nicer building than the one Artemisia lived and worked in, though he was a fraction of the artist she was. He didn't deserve this place. He didn't deserve anything he'd been given.

She only needed to ask one person passing the hall to be directed toward Lamberti's studio. They seemed proud to live near the artist.

Meanwhile, the entire city was disavowing her.

She knocked on his door hard enough to rattle it. Lamberti raised his eyebrows when he saw her but did not seem shocked.

Artemisia, arms crossed tightly over her chest, said, "We need to talk."

The artist stepped aside and let her in. His studio was a sharp contrast to her own. Where she was chaotic, with half-finished canvases scattered around the room like toadstools, his workspace was meticulous and precise. He kept his pigments and oils in neat jars, and the palettes she could see boasted a precise rainbow of colors, moving from dark to light and back again.

A familiar face caught her attention from the corner of the room, tucked away by a long painting of an intertwined griffon and blood drake. On a pair of canvases were mirrored busts of the Grand Duke and his wife, the Archduchess. Artemisia frowned, unease rolling through her like smoke. When had Lamberti become the artist of choice of the Medici? She had seen him talking with Cosimo before, but had not known their alliance went so far.

Artemisia wondered if he was also painting a portrait of Madama Cristina. Surely her first true patron in the city had more loyalty—didn't she? An hour ago, she had thought Michelangelo was her friend. What else would she lose?

She turned to face Lamberti, who was still standing by

A PORTRAIT IN SHADOW

the door and watching her. He appeared exhausted, and his slenderness seemed to be turning to skinniness. She hoped he wasn't sleeping.

"I just talked to Michelangelo," she said. "He told me that you agreed to help him desecrate my painting. I know you don't approve of me, but even you have to realize that this is too much."

Lamberti strolled toward her, unfazed by the attack. He looked at Artemisia as though she were a child throwing a tantrum at the market: irritating, but ultimately not his problem. "It is not truly art, though, is it?"

She gritted her teeth. "What do you mean?"

"None of the paintings at the gallery are imbued with magics. Isn't that correct?"

She shook her head. "No, but that does not mean it isn't my art. Even if there are no magics for you to undermine, the concept, the technique, and the product are *mine*. You should not have agreed to censor them."

He shrugged. "Can any of us turn down a paying job?" he asked. "I will be true to your original vision. It will barely be noticeable."

She pointed at him, her finger trembling in the dying light. Her emotions refused to stay under her skin, all spilling out. "Stop acting like this isn't personal. You've hated me from the second you saw me. You've been a spoiled child about it ever since. Michelangelo *loved* that painting until that scum Caccini tore me down."

"If you simply finished your commission, Michelangelo would not be forced to pay me to fix it."

Artemisia bristled. "Finish it? He requested a woman to represent natural talent. I painted it. I painted it *perfectly*. No artist is commissioned to continue to edit at the client's every whim for the next hundred years, especially when it is not even the *client* who wants the change."

"Your client is the one who approached me," he said, lofty. "Signorina, we are in the business of selling pieces of ourselves to those who can afford them. Once that piece is gone from us, it is no longer ours. It's his choice. And fabric texture is a specialty of mine." A small, smug smile curled his lip. He was enjoying her distress.

"It's not his choice. He's been poisoned by Caccini, just like everyone else in this damned city." She pointed across the room at the portraits. "Just like the Medici. I'm surprised they're wasting their time on you."

"The Grand Duke and I are long-time acquaintances."

"Then I assume it's you who's been poisoning his ear against the Accademia? Strange that the Grand Duke's friend secured a fresco in Santa Maria Novella. I'm sure Caccini loves that his new pet has a connection with them. It certainly wasn't your art that sold him." Cosimo de' Medici was renowned as a patron of the arts and culture, but not as a particularly devout man. There had been Medici rulers over the years who had embraced their religion more publicly—including several who had become popes—but Cosimo II had always been more focused on the internal workings of Florence than the universal workings of God. His laws were fair, but loose. Allying himself with a monster like Caccini went against everything Artemisia had thought she had known.

"Caccini is right—about you and the Accademia," Lamberti said. "The Grand Duke is wise to follow his suggestions. The Accademia has lost its path. It selects its members for political reasons, not skill. That's the only reason you were allowed in. It was supposed to be an honor to be initiated, but now everything I worked so long for has been turned into a joke."

"Those new laws are destroying us. The Church can't decide what we do. Caccini is going to *ruin* the Accademia."

"It's already been ruined. Caccini will do a better job preserving the sanctity of art than the Accademia ever did."

"He's a preacher, not an artist. How would he know how to manage art in Florence?"

"He's a man with *standards*," Lamberti said. He rubbed at his brow, which was dotted with a sheen of sweat. There were dark circles under his eyes, and his face grew paler the longer they spoke. She felt no pity for him. "That's what we need. Art has lost its way. It's supposed to be a holy craft. Michelangelo the Younger is taking the first step in the right direction."

"You've been threatened by me since I came to Florence," she sneered. "Do you really get all your self-worth from being better than others?"

"I worked and struggled for years to become an artist. This is a calling. I've drained my *soul* for it." His veneer of calm superiority was finally cracking. With his gaunt, tired face, the fury made him seem unhinged. She was viciously glad he was finally showing that was not unaffected by her.

"So have I!" she shot back.

"You're a perversion. Your paintings should all be *burned* so we can move on."

"Burned?" she repeated, horrified. "My paintings have saved lives."

"Like Silvestrini? I've heard that you were one of his little stable of artists. I could have warned him he was putting his life in the wrong hands." His expression shuttered again, turning cold and distant. "And you're still here. You shouldn't be. Caccini and I first spoke after Coccapani invited you to the anatomical theater. We knew that was the beginning of the end of everything we had built. We're doing something important at Santa Maria Novella. He cares about the future of art, just like me."

"My work never had anything to do with you, either of you!"

"Art is my life. Everything you do affects me. Do you know the difference between us?" He stepped forward and tilted an easel for her to see. It was a familiar scene.

Judith stood in the center, her expression placid. She was wearing a lush white gown, which stood out like a candle against his dark background. Beside her, still only sketched in with loose brushstrokes, was an old woman—Judith's maidservant Abra. In Judith's hand, held near the bottom frame of the canvas like an afterthought, was the severed head of Holofernes.

"This is a commission I'm working on now," Lamberti told her. He tapped the edge of the canvas, careful not to smudge the drying oils. "Judith's face? That is the face of a model I hired.

"*This* is the type of work artists should be producing. Biblical scenes, important scenes." His finger drifted to hover over the severed head of the general. "And do you recognize this face?" Of course she did. It was a self-portrait of Lamberti. "You'll see that here the artist is not the murderer. Unlike your Medeas and Delilahs. There's a reason you can put your face on so many villains. It's always women."

"Villains, you say," she said. "You call her a murderer? You barely show it. Look at this—it's stale." Artemisia gestured at his Judith, letting her finger get dangerously close to the wet oil. She was tempted to smear it, to see his face as she ruined *his* work. "Judith should not look like a woman you would see at the market, picking from a barrel of apples. Where's the passion? This is a woman who has just committed murder to save her country." Her finger drifted down toward the severed head.

"And if you can paint yourself as Holofernes, then you cannot possibly understand this story. He was the invader."

"Of course you would defend her," he said. "This has always been the problem with you. You look at sin and see something to celebrate."

"If you don't understand Judith, you shouldn't paint her. You know nothing about her, or any woman's struggles."

"What, now you believe I should be limited to paintings of men?"

"If *this* is the best you can paint women, then yes," she said. "Leave Judith to those who understand her. And leave my art to me."

"Why am I not surprised to find that Judith is your hero?"

"I made a mistake like yours when I was younger. My first Judith at least had a sword, but it was boring. I was too focused on copying the style of dull old men. But I've grown as an artist, and I am much younger than you are. My career stretches ahead of me. I'll still be painting when you're dead. You and Caccini can't stop me." She pointed at him fiercely, jabbing the air. "When I paint Judith, she is covered in blood, as she should be. I am tired of her story being used as an excuse to paint a delicate maiden in a pristine gown. Women have had their hands drenched in blood since the beginning of time. The blood of men. I'll make sure everyone knows that."

Lamberti did not bother to try to stop her when she stalked from his studio. She was still shaking with rage when the door clicked shut behind her.

She reached up and grasped the amulet around her neck so hard that she felt the metal edges cut into her skin. Lamberti, Michelangelo, and Caccini thought they could erase her. Thought they could erase anyone they wanted.

She would prove them wrong.

*

Artemisia paced inside her studio, unable to contain her frenetic energy but even less able to venture onto the streets where she might expel it. The walk back from Lamberti's apartment yesterday had been fraught. She had been so wrapped up in her thoughts that she'd nearly been knocked over by passersby twice. Public opinion about her would undoubtedly only be growing worse. She could do nothing right.

As the night had gone on, her fury with Michelangelo for betraying her had turned inward. Why had she grown so complacent, so eager to rely on fickle supporters? She had been so pitifully desperate for stability that she had forgotten a lesson she had learned with blood and tears; no one could be trusted when adversity knocked.

It had been three years since she'd left Rome behind, and the foundation she thought she had been building in Florence turned out to be so much tinder. The patrons she'd amassed, the standing she'd built, the friends she'd trusted, were all dandelion seeds blown away by Caccini's breath.

She'd feared this when she first came to Florence. It had seemed as likely as not that she would fail to establish her career in the city, and that her legacy would be ash.

Then, she'd made a plan.

She had started one last painting, something of her own that would assure her that she had made a difference in the world, even if her career was forgotten. A way to secure the revenge she'd fought for so fruitlessly in Rome. Her conversation with Lamberti had rekindled a fire that had been left to die by a passive, content hand. As she had grown settled with Francesco, supported by Elisabetta, Maurizio, and Sigismondo, accepted in the Accademia, she had let herself lose her connection to her necrotic magics and had decided to stop trying. Though she had been only steps from the finish line, she had failed to take them out of fear of what she might lose.

She'd been a fool to believe that she could step into her future before she had truly scourged the past.

A knock on the door startled her from her pacing, and she nearly collided with a standing easel. Collecting herself, she opened the door and let in Maurizio. Perspiration darkened his shirt at the center of his chest and under his arms, a sign of the long day of work he had just finished in the orchards.

He smiled, but his expression fell as he examined her. "What's wrong?"

"Who says something is wrong?" Artemisia asked, stepping away to pour them both a cup of water. She stared at the earthenware, trying to steady her breathing.

"Your note said it was urgent, and you look... well, carina, to be frank you look terrible."

"Calling me sweetheart doesn't lessen that blow," Artemisia said. The familiarity of their banter helped her finally school her expression, and she looked back up at him. "Maurizio, I need a favor."

"The type where I wear another toga?"

She shook her head. "It's the type where I need your connections."

"You're the big artist. You have far more connections than I do," he pointed out.

"I wouldn't be so sure," she said. "I need the type of assistance I can't get on my own."

He sat down at her kitchen table, his large frame overwhelming the small wooden chair. "How can I help?"

She explained what she needed, and how he might find it. It was a delicate balance to tell him enough so that he could follow her instructions, while not so much that he would refuse to help. In the last two years, Maurizio had become a dear friend, but this was more than she would ask of anyone else. She had seen Elisabetta's reaction to the idea, and that had been when her plan was firmly in the past.

Finally, Maurizio leaned back in his chair. "Rome. That's a far trip, and I've never been before."

"You don't personally need to go. There are men who could be hired if you can help me find them. I have the funds." With her canceled commissions, her finances would drain quickly, but that no longer mattered. She would do what it took to finish this, no matter the cost.

He held up a hand. "I would never give this to someone else. You asked for my help, and I'll see it done right."

"You can't risk that. You told me the consequence for you breaking the law."

"I'm not leaving this in some stranger's hands. There are too many factors. I wouldn't even bring Gabriele with me. You're sure about this?" he asked. "I don't know much about what you do, but this…"

"I'm sure. I'm running out of time. I need to do this. Otherwise—what have I accomplished?"

He examined her. His expression, which so often settled on unimpressed, was solemn. "I've gotten to know you over the last few years. Maybe as well as anyone I've ever known. I trust you. If you say this is necessary, I believe you."

"Thank you, Maurizio," she said, exhaling. "Be safe."

26

When Francesco returned to Florence after his travels, he always brought her gifts. Sometimes, they were as simple as jars of olive oil from the southern isles off the peninsula. Other times, when he visited more exotic locales, he would find handwoven rugs, mosaic tiles, or rich chocolates that melted on the tongue, leaving faint traces of berries or peppers.

After a year together, Artemisia had learned to live around Francesco's absences. His trading empire was massive, and ever growing larger, even without the smuggling business. He was not content with limiting his influence to nearby cities. He traveled far and wide for the best products—and his patrons paid him well for it.

With his easy charm and irrepressible confidence, Francesco could make connections with anyone, no matter their cultural or linguistic barriers. There was a reason that he had been one of the first to bring coffee beans into the city. While others stumbled over the obstacles of Turkish insulation and Florentine skepticism, Francesco simply barreled over objections with a smile.

In the first heady months of their relationship, Artemisia had felt his absences like ulcers, like abscesses eating into her flesh. She was vulnerable in front of him, and those flayed sections of her soul felt exposed even when he was gone. He was off traveling the world, likely being gawked at by beautiful women, while she was alone. Without him there to hold her steady, she was forced to once again shove her broken pieces into a semblance of composure and move along without his help.

After their separation and reconciliation, though, she was more secure when he left town. Their initial relationship had been a wildfire, burning through brittle tinder and brushing past any obstacle with sheer momentum. Artemisia had waited to be scorched. Instead, the wildfire had banked into something like a flame in a hearth—still strong, but fed steadily by an attentive hand, and growing stronger with a base of thick logs that burned low and deep.

Francesco entered the studio using his key, and she turned from her easel to face him. Luckily, she was not in one of her painting trances tonight. Even she needed a break sometimes from the necrotic drain, and she was grateful he had not stumbled into it. She was not sure he would approve of her work.

Instead, she was preparing a new canvas for a future commission that might never come. Her rabbit-skin glue base had dried, so she was in the midst of spending months layering the cloth with lead-white paint, polishing the surface once it had dried, and then repeating. In the end, the canvas would have a glossy finish onto which she could place her thin layers of oils without fearing that a crosshatch pattern would push through. It was mindless work. Her fury with Michelangelo, Lamberti, and Caccini continued to tug her away from the process. Would each new painting be subjected to future censorship, covered up by the paint of a stranger to mollify her enemies? She could no longer trust the durability of her work, and it added a hesitancy to her hand she had not experienced even in the early days after Rome. Everything seemed a waste of time.

Francesco set his bag down on the floor and approached her with her gift, but his gaze was sharp on her face. She had never been a good liar, wearing her emotions in plain view. Francesco, always attuned to those around him, could read her easily.

His expression fell with the force of his concern, but he pulled her in for a gentle kiss. She closed her eyes and breathed in the scent of travel, of lands far from the ruddy roofs of Florence. The scent of salt—sweat and the sea air—was thick on his clothes and skin. He must not have stopped at his own house first.

He pressed a gift into her hands. The cold metal of the engraved copper bracelet heated quickly against her skin as though the warmth of the desert sand had waited to rise at her touch. It was carved with a familiar pattern—a griffon and blood drake intertwined. She let him place it on her wrist and press a kiss to her palm.

"Are you all right?" he asked as they settled onto her cot.

Her cot was small, but covered in lush fabrics and embroidered pillows—more gifts from Francesco—it was the most comfortable she'd ever owned. Francesco, still wearing rough-hewn traveling clothes dusted with sand, lounged among the colorful fabrics like a bird in its own plumage.

Quickly, clumsily, Artemisia recounted the events of the last month. Though she had shouted at both Michelangelo and Lamberti already, endless rage churned inside her. Even in the soft light of her studio, in Francesco's warm arms, the bile of her anger threatened to explode, a volcano pulsing under a thin layer of broken stone.

"Bastard," Francesco growled when she finished her story. "I should buy back your painting from that worm, and then take away every grain of standing he's gathered in the city. Surely no one wants to collaborate with a curator who would betray his artists."

"More patrons than just Michelangelo have cut their ties with me. He was just the only one who dared to ask me to change my work. I'm sure there are Artemisia Gentileschi paintings in garbage heaps across the city. Or they'll hide them in back rooms until they've drained the magics from them, and *then* destroy them," she said, voice shaking with venom. "These men, these rich, powerful men, paid for pieces of my soul, and then abandoned me at the first sign of trouble."

"Then they never deserved your work."

"That's just it—they didn't. So why did I do it? I thought if I put enough of myself into it, they'd value me. But there's no loyalty in this business. If I had killed myself giving too much, they would have shrugged and moved on to the next artist. But I need them—don't I? How can I build a reputation without clients?"

"I'll talk to them. They can't treat you like this."

Artemisia shook her head. "This isn't something you can solve for me."

"I could," he argued.

"You haven't even been here," Artemisia snapped. "You've been laughing and smiling with a hundred strangers."

"You know I have to travel for my work," Francesco said.

"Your work," she repeated. "So important to you."

"Why do you say it like that? It's not as important as you are. You know I stopped the smuggling business for you. I would be here if you needed me."

"Would you?" she asked, but continued before he could answer. "This is something I will not *let* you solve for me, even if you could. This is my art, my reputation, that they are attempting to erase. If I don't settle this on my own, then I am giving my legacy to other hands."

Francesco sighed. "Just because you *can* handle these things on your own doesn't mean you have to," he reminded her. "I am not trying to control your legacy, but if I can help, I want to." He took her hand between his. "I have money and influence, but they mean nothing to me if I can't use them to do as I wish. I'm not your keeper—I'm your tool. Why not use me?"

"You're not my tool. Soon you'll be my husband," she said. "Besides, there are other weapons in my arsenal. I have my own tools. These men will not crush me, even if I have to destroy them first. I have a plan."

"Then tell me what I can do," Francesco said.

What could he do? She reached out to put her own hand over his. "Distract me," she pleaded. "Please." She used their tangled hands to pull him toward her, over her. His weight was warm and familiar, and inside the curtained alcove surrounding her cot, she could pretend there was no world beyond his touch.

"Of course," he agreed, and leaned down to capture her lips again.

The city's heart was quiet in deference to the heat, even so close to sunset. Most citizens were tucked away in the shade of their own homes. Workers out in the city sipped from leather wineskins at their sides, letting the warm liquid wash away the dryness in their mouths. The orchards were in full bloom around the city, plump fruit dangling heavy from some trees while from others flowers coated the air with a thick perfume.

Artemisia walked alongside the vast Duomo alone, and the echo of San Donatello's legacy seemed to ring in her ears with the noon bells.

Would anyone remember Artemisia Gentileschi one hundred

years from now? Would they even remember her in ten? She was losing everything she had fought so hard to earn.

News came in nearly every day about Caccini's grab for power. His influence was only growing. When he spoke out about Galileo, he had been swiftly reined in by the others in the Church. The preacher general of the Dominican order had quickly sent the letter of apology to Galileo. That was when Caccini had found a way to be more subtle, and brought the Inquisition to Galileo's door. Since Caccini's return from Rome, he had been amassing his influence within the city. It likely helped his standing that instead of attacking a beloved astronomer who had brought glory to Florence's rulers, his target now was a woman. Beyond that, she was an artist with a scandalous history, someone who had already gone through the trials of public opinion and would be haunted by rumors forever. After Rome, Artemisia had hoped that facing public scorn was like the firing of an earthenware pot. She thought the first flames would have hardened her, altered at her core to be less vulnerable to future heat. Instead, her past had left cracks that her new attackers used as weaknesses to cut deeper.

At that Wednesday's sermon, Caccini had praised Michelangelo for revealing the new version of her painting on his ceiling. Artemisia had been banned from Casa Buonarroti, but she was told that Lamberti had painted two strips of fabric, one heavy and blue, the other gauzy white, to cover her figure's exposed breasts and groin. According to Caccini, it was the first step in preventing a soiled woman from corrupting the sanctity of art. With his help, the Accademia would be set upon its rightful track and they could pretend Artemisia had never existed.

Artemisia had not given up entirely. She still had her allies, and those were the people whose opinions mattered to her. She hoped they would last longer against Caccini's campaign than Michelangelo had.

Despite the wealth of the residents, the Medici palace was sweltering like the rest of the city. There were, however, servants bearing platters of chilled drinks and small treats, and the Medici were protected from the summer pestilences by their galleries of art. Wealth had a way of mitigating discomfort.

Artemisia made it to the study at the top of the vast palace, sweat drenching the small curls at the edge of her hairline. When she was alone in her studio, Artemisia wore her shift only, and left the windows wide to tempt in a breeze off the Arno, but she could wear no less than her embroidered gown to meet the Medici matriarch.

Madama Cristina had a glass of chilled white wine waiting for Artemisia on the desk, and though she was wearing her usual mourning blacks, even she had abandoned her more formal headpiece. The sunset bathed the room in an orange glow.

"Hello, Artemisia," she said.

She had aged since they'd met. The lines by her eyes and mouth had deepened. Artemisia had once seen her as immutable. Madama Cristina was a strong woman, and had not faltered even under the weight of her husband's death and with the responsibility for a region on her shoulders. Still, even with the constant presence of healing magics from the artists she patronized, Madama Cristina was not immune to the effects of time. From Silvestrini to the Medici, even the rich would meet death.

"Thank you for seeing me, Madama," Artemisia said. Madama Cristina gestured for her to sit, and Artemisia did not waste time. Her tension was a living thing under her skin, and it ached to burst free. "You must know why I'm here. You've heard the attacks against me."

"Tomasso Caccini seems eager for an adversary," Madama Cristina said dryly. "I presume this was not what you hoped for when you wished for your name to be known by all of Florence?"

"Not quite," Artemisia said, trying for a smile. "Caccini is not the first man to question whether or not I deserve to be an artist. He's not even the first from the Church. Most of the complaints came before I had proven myself in this city and earned my spot in the Accademia. Now, his attacks should be too late. I am already an artist. My work sits in the halls of the greatest families in Europe, like your own."

Madama Cristina nodded. "Your influence has spread far."

"Right," Artemisia said, eagerly. "Now, I need my illustrious patrons to stand by my work. I only found success as an artist with your benevolence, and I find I need it again to remain one."

"Artemisia, you know I have always wanted to support you. From the moment that Jacopo da Empoli told me of a girl who rivaled her own father, I wanted to have you in my court." Artemisia felt hope flutter like a bird in her chest, but the woman's next words speared it. "Unfortunately, I do not maintain the singular influence you believe I do. I will do what I can for you, but I cannot publicly support you."

"Why not?" The words stumbled from Artemisia's mouth, quiet with hurt. "You're the Grand Duchess Cristina de' Medici. If it's the Church you fear, they are not in agreement yet. I would not ask you to speak against the Pope, but I'm on trial with the *public*. Caccini is gaining influence by the day, but there are still others in the Church who oppose him as a radical, another Savonarola. None of us want that. It's not too late to stop him."

"He won't be a Savonarola, because this time the Medici are on his side."

Artemisia gritted her teeth. She took a deep breath, trying to remain diplomatic. "Surely you don't support that man."

"My son has found that he respects Caccini's guidance."

"What changed? He's supported Galileo through his trials against Caccini, and he's never seemed…" She broke off before she could say 'pious.' She could not risk accusing the ruler of the city of atheism. The conversation was already slipping away from her, like everything else these days.

"I believe my son is feeling the weight of his responsibilities in a new way. I have always been here to lighten that load, to help him stand strong without fearing the consequences, but things have changed recently. He envisions a Florence with a more equal balance between our family and the Church."

"And this is the way to do that? By letting an enemy of art and philosophy control the Accademia's every move?"

Madama Cristina sighed and rubbed pale fingers across her forehead. "To be honest, I don't understand it either. My son has never been…tied to the Church. Now he does everything Caccini says. There are more laws on the way to solidify that bond. The Grand Duke seems only to stand strong against me, afraid that I will contradict him against Caccini and split our authority."

"But you won't," Artemisia realized, betrayed. She had come looking for an ally, but Madama Cristina was just as she appeared. A weak, old woman, who, despite her title, allowed her son to rule.

Madama Cristina's eyes flashed, reminding Artemisia of her griffon when it spotted a flicker of a dove's feather across a rooftop. "I do not stand against my son," she said coldly, "because I value the reign of the Medici over any single law he may pass. This family has ruled Florence for more than two hundred years. I will not be the one to undermine our authority, even if I disagree with the specifics."

"What is the point of authority at all if you hand it to scum like Caccini?" Artemisia demanded.

Madama Cristina stood up, leaning on the desk. Though her arms were thin, her expression was fierce. "As long as the Medici remain at the end of the day, anything can be repaired. I have learned to compromise. It's an important skill for someone in my position. No matter what happens, the Medici will rule Florence, and we will not be questioned."

Artemisia stood as well, feeling as though she were balancing on a cliff's edge, staring at an abyss beyond. Still, she barged forward. "If Caccini gets me burned alive for heresy, that cannot be undone when the Grand Duke comes to his senses!"

"If I support you, I will either shatter this family with my actions, or my son will do so for me. I have already become convinced that he means to retire me to the country soon so that Maria Maddelena can be the Grand Duchess. I have worked too long for this position to lose it over a single artist."

"If you let your son betray your values, you've already lost your position," Artemisia told her.

"You overstep, Artemisia," Madama Cristina said. She pointed to the door, her finger unsteady. "Leave."

"But, Madama—"

"Leave," Madama Cristina repeated, brooking no argument. "You told me when we met that your scandals from Rome would not follow you here, but it seems that you bring trouble with you." Artemisia pressed a hand to her chest. The words felt like a physical blow. "And do not bother to finish your last commission. We will no longer be needing your services."

Artemisia left.

The summer sun continued to beat down.

27

"You look terrible," Sigismondo greeted, stepping aside to let her into his studio. Sigismondo's assistants had gone home for the night, but he and Artemisia were long past the formality of needing others to chaperone their meetings. She had nearly ignored his invitation, too drained to be good company, but when she saw his smile she was grateful she had agreed. As she lost patrons like dying embers, it was a relief to have a friend.

"Thanks," she said dryly. "I'm sure you've heard what Michelangelo has done."

"I have," Sigismondo said. "Stronzo. He's always thought more of himself than anyone else. But really, you are pale. You're sure you don't want to go out for dinner?"

"I'm not interested in getting more lectures from strangers," she said.

He ushered her to his dining table and pressed a goblet of wine into her hands. "People are confronting you on the street?"

"According to Caccini, I'm the new Jezebel. His flock wants me out of this city," she said. "They didn't say anything when I was out with Francesco, but with him gone again, they feel no shame in speaking their minds. I'm lucky they didn't form a mob. I fear what will happen if the rumors fester much longer."

"Gone? Now?" Sigismondo had met her fiancé a handful of times, and they had flowed together like a river. "What was he thinking? You're in a fight for your career—maybe your life."

"He had urgent business in Venice. They sent him three letters before I managed to shove him out the door to make him leave," she said. "I won't let him throw away his business for me. He can fend for himself, and I'll fend for myself."

"I'm unmarried, but I'm not sure that's what that ring is supposed to mean," Sigismondo said, nodding to her hand.

"Allora," Artemisia prevaricated. "You don't look great yourself, you know."

"These new laws to control art are draining. I'm already being overwhelmed with requests for free art from the local churches—we all are."

"I haven't gotten a single request," Artemisia said.

"Well," Sigismondo said, awkward. "No, I guess you wouldn't have. That's one benefit, I suppose?"

"A *benefit*," Artemisia snarled, and then held up her hands when Sigismondo flinched. "Sorry. I know it isn't you behind this."

"I assure you it's not a gift, Artemisia. They're trying to grind us down. We're all being threatened and worked to the bone while they tell us they're righteous. They act like art is a sin, but unlike the Grave Age, they want to use us for all we have."

Artemisia sighed. "Isn't that the Accademia's mantra too? They want us to be proud for digging our own graves. This is just more of that. What nobility is in death?"

"Ask the martyrs," Sigismondo said.

"I would, but they're all dead," Artemisia said. "Our work isn't just tiring—it can kill us. How can we be proud of dying and losing the chance to do more? Any of us could die for our patrons, and Florence would cheer."

"And it's worse than ever. I feel like a pheasant trying to dodge a group of hunters," he said. "First the Accademia, and now these anti-vice laws." After taking control of the Accademia's work, Caccini had pushed through another set of laws. It was as Madama Cristina had warned her—the ties between the law and Caccini's vendettas were growing closer and closer. He was increasing pressure for the Office of the Night to find and punish sodomites, and added restrictions on the municipal brothels through the Office of Decency. He had even instituted harsher punishments against public drunkenness and immodest dress. "Caccini seems out for my blood. Oh, sorry, Artemisia."

No matter how many new laws Caccini pushed the Grand Duke to pass, it was still Artemisia who received his vitriol at his weekly sermons. "It's like losing to Galileo has driven him mad. He was undercut in Rome, so now he's taking complete control of Florence."

"He wants to take us back to Savonarola's time," Sigismondo said. "If not the Grave Age."

"Savonarola had the people on his side. Caccini has the Grand Duke in his pocket. Maybe people are spreading his gossip, but he's not beloved. Some are afraid their businesses will end up like the Accademia if they don't comply, but many are resisting so many sudden changes from a man who has been out of the city most of the year." It was easier to comfort Sigismondo than it had been to soothe herself. She did not want him to share her misery. "We're still fighting. He's coming for all of us. We just have to stand together."

"Artemisia," Sigismondo said cautiously, "that's why I wanted to meet with you tonight."

When he hesitated, she prompted with a curl of dread, "What do you mean?"

"No one wants to be under Caccini's scrutiny. The Medici are rolling over for his every demand, and are pushing the blame back on the rest of the city. The businessmen are blaming the Accademia for sparking this backlash. And the Accademia is blaming…"

"Me."

"Not all of us. I've been fighting against it at every turn. They're all hiding in the shadows, meeting at bars and exchanging secret letters. They think that they can reason with Caccini, make him see that they are trustworthy, that they're as human as he is."

"Fools. At best, he'll think of them as individual exceptions. They can't change his mind about artists."

"They claim they think they will, but I don't believe them. I don't think they care whether they save anyone but themselves. Lamberti has been a strong voice, and the tide in the Accademia is turning against you." He shook his head. "I wanted to warn you."

"It wasn't enough for Lamberti to paint over my work at Casa Buonarroti? They're kicking me out?"

"Not yet. They have nothing to hold against you. They can't expel you for no reason. At the September monthly meeting, there will be a vote on your membership."

"And by then, Lamberti will have convinced every member that I'm the cause of all our trouble," she said. "Everyone knows he's never liked me. Can't they see this is an excuse?" She scoffed. "As though they're saints. You must know of the cellar beneath the monastery. The Accademia clings to power as much as the next mortal."

"They're scared. Caccini has gained too much power too quickly. Churches are demanding free work. He can block any of us from selling art abroad. Most of our patrons come from outside Florence. The Accademia is looking for any way to save themselves." His lip trembled as he continued, "I plan to resign if they do throw you out."

"Sigismondo," she said. "You don't need to do that."

"I do," he insisted, taking a deep breath. "You've fought twice as hard as any artist to find recognition. It's not right, what they're doing."

Finally, she understood Galileo's attempts to distance them during the early months of his trials. Sigismondo was kind, but too soft for the ordeal to come. He did not have what it took to survive this. "You're lovely," she said. "But if you quit because of me, I'll personally drag you back by the ear to undo it."

"Artemisia," he said, startled, but she held up a hand.

"The Accademia is cowardly, but with Caccini controlling their actions, they'll need someone on the inside helping resist," she said. "I'd like it to be you. You're the best of us, Sigismondo. Art is relying on you. Besides, one of us has to be noble, and it's certainly not going to be me. I'm sure you'll handle your setbacks with far more grace than I could. I fight dirty—I'll find my path no matter what it takes. You can be the symbol for art in this city."

Her smile felt shattered, a glass in jagged pieces in the dirt, but he leaned forward to embrace her. "I won't let you down. You'll see."

Hopefully, she would.

But she would not bet on it.

Artemisia worked.

They had not taken that from her—yet. She might have no patrons, no standing, but she had her brushes. Even the torture in Rome had not stopped her from using her hands, though her recent stress had caused them to cramp once again, twisting and aching at unexpected moments. Holding a brush made fire throb in her joints. What tortures would condemnation for heresy bring? If she survived them, would she ever be able to work again?

The candles around the studio flickered, low in their dishes. It was late, so late that it was nearly morning.

But she still had a mission. Carefully, her face close to the large canvas, she added highlights to the intricate bracelet high on Judith's wrist. The cameos on the gold chain depicted Athena, goddess of war and wisdom, and Artemis on the hunt, her bow in hand and hounds at her feet. Symbols of power and death watching as Judith completed her kill. As Artemisia completed hers.

It was close. So close.

It should have been finished months ago. How had she let herself become so distracted from her revenge? She had been swept away by her small successes, and by Francesco's love. She had taken the coward's route and stopped.

Now her time was running out, and her revenge was unfinished.

Still, all the distractions had given her an unexpected gift. Her training with the Accademia had heated her power like a blade in a forge, making it stronger and sharper than ever, and that strength was not limited to her healing magic. The necrotic magic drained her quickly, pulling from some place deep inside her that cringed to be touched, but she was powerful enough now to finish this.

Even if it killed her.

28

Artemisia came down from spending time with her griffon late one evening to find a shadowed figure by her door. The hallway was dark at night, and the flame of her candle had gone out while she was sitting on the roof, looking over the city with her fingers tangled in the griffon's feathers.

She stilled on the last step of the ladder, her hand grasping her amulet. It guarded against physical attackers, but it was not infallible.

"Artemisia?"

Her body slumped, tension dropping like a heavy sack from an overworked shoulder. "Maurizio! I didn't know you were back." She moved forward to unlock the door and let him inside her studio.

She never left candles burning when she was gone, even if it was just to the roof. Her life's work was made of oils and cloth, all so flammable that it seemed sometimes as though they were reaching for the flames. Blindly, she found the closest candle and then lit it with flint and steel. The small fire cast an orange glow over the studio.

Maurizio followed her inside and closed the door behind him. "The word is that Florence has changed since I left."

"It's been a dark time. The anti-vice laws have been coming

hard and fast. Have you heard from Gabriele? Is he all right? I wanted to reach out to him, but association with me would… not help, these days."

"He is. I just came from our flat. He's been afraid to go out, but he was safe. I wanted to come here right away, but I had to make sure he was all right," he said. "I'm sorry. I knew you'd be anxious for me to get back. And to hear of my success."

Her breath caught in her throat. "You were able to get it?" she asked. She had told him to only bring her news in person. Letters, even the explicit ones she exchanged with Francesco, were essentially public property considering the number of hands that they would pass through on their way across the land. "Did you have any trouble?"

He shook his head and picked up another candle for her to ignite with the burning wick. "No trouble. I was careful. And I did my due diligence. I asked around—subtly, of course. I trust you, but I wanted to know what I was facing."

Her breath caught. "And?"

"And there were many stories to be heard about Agostino Tassi and Artemisia Gentileschi," he said.

Her hands clenched into fists, and brittle nails bent against her palms.

"I needed to know what I was doing, Artemisia. I'm not a fool. I'm no artist, but I knew what you were asking. I've heard the whispers just like everyone else. Never let an artist get a strand of your hair, or you'll be a blood drake's next meal."

"That's not how it works," she said.

"There's a reason people burn their loose hair, no matter how shit it smells," Maurizio said. "These magics terrify people."

"If you asked around, you heard the stories about him. About us," Artemisia said, voice shaking. "I'm doing what I have to do."

"I know," Maurizio said. "Tassi is scum and deserves what's coming to him—even this. Someone should have done it earlier, honestly." He scoffed. "Though it's a shame you can't take Caccini down too."

"Believe me, I've thought of it. But I've been crafting this painting for Tassi for years. It's too late to undo what's there, and each painting can only have one target. It's the first rule I learned in art."

"So why finish it now? This is a chapter from your past—and you have far more to worry about here. Why this sudden urgency to complete it? If Caccini finds out about this, he will have all the more leverage against you." When Artemisia hesitated, he said, "I just want to understand. I'm in this too."

"Caccini is trying to ruin me, and I have to decide what legacy I am leaving behind," Artemisia said, speaking slowly. It was the first time she had ever spoken of her plans out loud, and they seemed too empty in the dark room. "I can't die with nothing to show. If nothing else, I can damn well know I destroyed my first enemy. The court's punishment was a joke. If I don't do this, he'll stay free. Maybe I'll even save some other women in the process. I'll make a difference, no matter what Caccini does to me."

Maurizio hummed thoughtfully, face shadowed.

"So, did you get it?"

He stepped forward and handed her a small glass vial. Inside were a spiky cluster of gray hairs. "I did," he told her. "I hope you make it hurt."

A smile unfurled on her lips, and it felt cold and hard between her teeth. "Thank you, Maurizio," she said, accepting the vial. "It will."

*

Deep in her painting trance, Artemisia saw sections of the canvas in flashes.

Her brush was coated with the palest color she would be including in the painting, a muted cream. The fold of a rolled sleeve. A highlight on a bundled sheet. A gleam on gold jewelry. A glint inside a shadowed mouth.

The painting would take the time it needed to take, but every day seemed to last longer. It had been three days since Maurizio had brought her the hairs to complete the binding. Now, it was just a matter of finishing it.

A brisk rapping on the studio door jarred Artemisia from the haze of her trance. "Artemisia? Artemisia!"

She blinked, and then grabbed the velvet drape. Her hands trembled, but she covered the easel without smearing it.

Feet unsteady, Artemisia opened the studio door. "Elisabetta?" In her trance, she had not recognized the sharp, feminine voice.

The healer was standing outside her door, arms crossed. "You missed our drinks tonight."

What day was it? She had a standing weekly outing with Elisabetta, but surely it was not Monday again already. Her days had been a haze since she resumed work on her Judith. "Sorry," she said, unable to muster an excuse.

"You look like hell," Elisabetta said, shouldering her way into the studio. Artemisia lurched sideways—she was wearing her amulet, and did not want it to lash Elisabetta with her magics. Her friend noticed the movement and motive. "You're wearing that thing inside your locked studio now?"

Artemisia turned and went to the kitchen table. "Come in, if you're going to."

"Allora," Elisabetta said, clicking her tongue. "I was just making sure you were still alive. You forgot to come get your monthly supply." She put a jar of salve on the table as she sat down. "I thought something had happened."

"Has something happened? Haven't you heard? Florence is being run by my enemies. There's a new law passed every week."

"Don't tell me you're letting that priest's bullshit get to you. You've never let a man's opinion change you before."

"Haven't I?" Artemisia snapped. "You don't know me as well as you think you do. The stupid, narrow opinions of men have run me out of town before, and they're trying to do it again."

"You're a member of the Accademia—the first woman in their entire history. What can a fool like Tomasso Caccini do to you?"

"The Accademia is under his thumb now," Artemisia said. "He's controlling what we can sell, what we can do. Everyone is furious. They'll be kicking me out at this month's meeting. They have no choice. The Grand Duke has handed Caccini everything he needs to ruin me."

"The Grand Duke? What happened?" Elisabetta asked. "The Medici used to be your biggest supporters."

"The pressures of his position, or so his mother says," Artemisia said. "She's sure he's still growing into the leader he'll be—no matter what happens to me while he's learning who that is."

"Sounds like he's growing on the path of roots," Elisabetta sneered.

"I should never have trusted them. Politicians are greedy and small-minded. History is repeating itself. These men, they think they can erase me. Erase my legacy." She ran a shaking hand through her hair. She felt oil paint smear across her forehead, but did not bother to wipe it clean.

"So you're working yourself to death to prove them wrong?" Elisabetta asked. She narrowed her eyes at Artemisia's face. "You've lost weight. You look…gaunt."

"You told me once that I can't let what's been done to me define me," Artemisia said. "The horrible things they've all done to try to control me, to break me. But none of them have ever paid for it. I have *suffered*, and they're all free. Caccini is just the last in a long line. I'm going to destroy them before they can destroy me. I'm going to end this."

"You're declaring war, but you're no warrior," Elisabetta said.

"I am," Artemisia snarled. "I can be."

"You're not," Elisabetta said. "You're cleverer than this, Artemisia. The past is the past, and the future is not yet set. Caccini is three blocks away, and you're letting him talk bullshit about you without arguing back. Make your voice heard—don't hide away while they control the story. You're young, you're beautiful, you're talented. They're old men."

"Old men are who people *listen* to," Artemisia said. "There's no punishment for people like them. There never is. I've experienced it. Maurizio agrees with me. There's no one to stop them."

"I know," the healer said quietly. "I know. But you can't stop trying already."

"I'm not giving up," Artemisia assured her.

Elisabetta rapped her fingernails on the table. "I'm leaving town for a week or two," she said abruptly. "You'll be here when I get back." It wasn't a question.

"You're not staying for a drink?"

"You're not good company right now," Elisabetta said, more gentle than insulting. "Get some sleep and then rise to fight tomorrow. Your story isn't over yet." She gave Artemisia a firm nod. "Don't forget to use the salve."

When Artemisia shut the door behind Elisabetta, the studio felt still and empty without her presence. Artemisia's breathing was loud and jagged.

29

Santa Maria Novella was only a few minutes' walk from her studio. She had taken pains to avoid the building since the vicious sermon about Galileo that cold December morning, but her feet remembered the way. The white and green church was bright in the early morning sun, austere and forbidding as dried bone.

That replacement façade was a standing reminder of the Grave Age, when a mob had destroyed the original design. The fear of artists was still stained on the heart of Florence, screaming from ancient buildings carved bare. People had worshipped artists, and burned them at the stake. Favor was always fickle.

Morning Mass would be ending any moment. She had spent the morning debating her plan, and had finally forced herself from her studio just in time. She had put her hair up and picked a modest gown too heavy for the heat. From outside the heavy doors, Artemisia could hear Caccini's voice echoing off the high ceilings. "...will make Florence more glorious, more powerful and richer than ever, extending its wings farther than anyone can imagine!"

The streets around Artemisia were quiet in comparison. Those who were awake were mostly at services in the churches scattered around the city, listening to men in robes telling them what to think and how to behave.

Though it was another sweltering summer day, Artemisia was cold. The fire that had been swirling inside her chest since Maurizio told her of Caccini's first attack—the fire that had stayed burning under her skin since she left Rome—had drained away, leaving her feeling like an empty shell of herself.

Perhaps she had worked too late last night, poured too much of herself into her work.

No matter. When the doors opened and she spotted Caccini just inside, saying farewell to the departing crowd, the embers caught once again in her chest and ignited her fury. Artemisia was still alive. She could still win. She watched and waited as the congregation filtered through the broad doors. Beyond the tall arches, she could glimpse inside the church.

It had been more than a year since she had last been inside Santa Maria Novella. Like most churches in Florence, it followed a classical structure. The façade was at the base of a large Latin cross, a testament to God built into the very design of the building. Over Caccini's shoulder, she could see Lamberti's in-progress fresco. It was too dim to make out fully, but she could see rich colors and deep shadows. It would likely be a striking work of art.

She prayed that one day *she'd* be hired to paint over it.

When the crowd had thinned enough that she risked the preacher turning back inside, Artemisia shouted, "Caccini!" and stepped forward.

Tomasso Caccini looked the same as he had during that Mass. He was wearing his order's distinctive bright red robes and a matching hat to cover his entire head, and his face was flushed nearly the same color by the heat. His plump, clean-shaven face was average, forgettable, especially surrounded by the loud trappings of his order. He was younger than he had seemed in the pulpit—likely no more than forty.

Though she had watched him speak and he had slandered her name across the city, they had never met before. His cold eyes scanned her face before recognition set in. He spread his arms and raised his voice, not attempting to hide their confrontation from the remaining members of his congregation. "Artemisia Gentileschi," he said. "I did not think you would attend one of my sermons."

"I wouldn't. I was waiting for you."

"Were you?" he asked. "I don't imagine we have much to say to one another."

She snarled at him. "I do not know why you picked me as a target, but you're wrong. I am an artist, just like the others in the city who you have insulted. You have made me into an enemy, but we've never spoken before. It's time we talked, since you won't keep my name out of your mouth."

"I do not need to speak to every sinner to know that is what they are," Caccini said. "I've seen your art. That is enough."

He turned back toward the church door, but she called after him, "Then let's talk about my art." He looked back at her, eyebrows raised. "What makes my art so different from that you've seen of others? I'm classically trained. I'm talented. These days, it seems like you hate all of art, but mine especially."

"Not the art, but the artist behind it. There's still time to save the Accademia. I'm trying to give them a chance for redemption," Caccini said. "But no woman should be an artist."

"I *am* an artist," she pointed out.

"Yes, we've all seen your work." He gestured to the small crowd around them, who had lingered to watch the argument instead of dispersing.

"Have you? Or just the version Paolo Lamberti painted over?"

"Is that what has you so upset?" Caccini smiled beatifically.

"We are in the process of painting over the fresco above our altar, as you may have heard. It is common practice for church art to be replaced once it has been drained. Paints and canvases and plaster are not immortal, and neither is art. Perhaps you are too young to understand that."

"That's different. You haven't claimed the last painter wasn't a true artist and tried to erase their entire legacy. My art exists. I paint. I *heal* people. What else is there to being an artist?"

"You *claim* to have healed people," Caccini said. "Often that is difficult to determine, is it not?"

"You're accusing me of being a fraud?" she demanded.

"Aren't you?"

She reached up to grab the amulet around her neck, holding it so tightly that the metal creaked under her grasp. Her other hand jerked toward Caccini, but fell before making contact. If she touched him, he would know she was truly blessed with magics—because he would feel the necrotic lash of her amulet. She would hand him evidence that she worked with dark magics on the streets of Florence in front of his loyal congregation. The desire to hurt him was only outweighed by the desire to prove herself, and she could do neither.

Instead, she forced her hands to her sides. "Art is a slow and steady process. An artist who claims to cure the plague in a single stroke is lying. Our work isn't so visible. My patrons can vouch for my skill."

"Ah yes, the plague. The prime example of art in the hands of someone who did not deserve it. Everyone knows the story of the first outbreak. A woman lost her temper and killed millions. Besides, even if we could trust that your feminine temperament would not break and compel you to release your own plague, your healing art needs to be relied upon in the face of death.

There has been no record of a female artist successfully healing as the great artists do. Who would put their life in your hands?"

The crowd around them was undeniably hostile to her, muttering approval of Caccini's arguments and sneering at her words. It made her feel as though she were standing in a small closet lined with poison-laced needles. One wrong step and she would be skewered on a hundred deadly barbs. In Rome, she had seen the way men could play crowds, stirring their agitation and then calming it with the simple direction of their voices.

"My clients are satisfied. The Accademia brought me among their ranks—which are still lauded no matter what you do to stop them."

"I've heard your last client died. What was his name: Stefano Silvestrini? He trusted you to heal him, and you failed."

"Silvestrini was old. No one could have saved him," Artemisia said, though she could hear murmuring from the crowd around them. "But there's proof. I have a griffon. It lives in my roof—people have seen it. It chose me for my art."

"That's only artist superstition. I'm not surprised you attract pests," Caccini said carelessly.

Artemisia's hands were shaking. "What right do you have to question me? You're not an artist. You are just a little priest so desperate for attention that he has to attack those of us actually *creating* within the city. I'm not the first innovator you called a heretic."

Her words were mostly falling on deaf ears, but some were moved by her last argument. Galileo was still a controversial figure, even within Caccini's own flock. His fight against the astronomer had failed despite his constant public outcry, and it was a stain on his reputation.

"I speak in a pulpit in service to the Lord in a church filled with pious art meant to serve him and His purpose," Caccini said. "Next week, I'm hosting every leader of Florence here in my church. Art and government and faith will always be connected. As for Galileo, I do not believe he's won yet. He'll be watched closely."

"Only because small-minded men like you can't see the truth. If your philosophy can't bend to new discoveries, then it was fragile to begin with. I *exist*." She waved at the sky, bright overhead. "The moons around Jupiter *exist*. Your denial doesn't make us disappear."

Caccini sucked in a sharp breath, his nostrils blanching white for a second. "I had heard you had delusions of grandeur, but it's more extreme than I expected. Not only are you to be compared to the great artists of our world who have been canonized by the Church, but you compare yourself to the celestial bodies. Next you will tell me that to attack you is like attacking the Pope."

She folded her arms. "I'm only saying that I'm an artist of the Accademia."

"The Accademia has waned. There hasn't been a new artist saint in years. Michelangelo may be the last—the same man whose legacy you tried to corrupt with that painting of yours. A true saint has to be beyond earthly limitations, and the Accademia is certainly not that. They were fooled by you. Paolo Lamberti told me how you wore them down, infected them from within."

"I've been patronized by people across Europe. You think I've deceived all of them?"

Caccini raised his eyebrows. "I do. You are an actress, but your true nature comes out when you hold your paintbrush. You're a fallen woman with no remorse, and your mockery of the most sacred arts is unforgivable."

"No artist has been a perfect person. We're humans, just like the rest. Most artists just use the gifts they're given by God the best way they can. My sins are no greater than any other artist, *including* your saints."

"Is that so? I visited Casa Buonarroti. I, like many of the clergy of the city, was invited to view the new gallery honoring the great Michelangelo. Obviously, I was horrified to see your painting. A nude woman painted *by* a woman? It's indecent."

"I am not the first artist to paint a nude figure!" Artemisia nearly shouted, exasperated. "You can find them in churches throughout Europe. The human body is not something to be ashamed of. You all seem to love looking at naked women as long as a man holds the brush!"

"Male artists cannot put their own faces on the female figure. Women are descended from the original sin," Caccini said. "How do you even paint such figures? Do you bring a mirror into the sacred studio of the artist? Is your painting a self-portrait from head to toe? Lamberti has told me who you truly are. He's heard stories from those who knew you before you darkened Florence's doorstep." Artemisia felt cold. Sour bile sat heavy on her tongue, like her body knew what was coming before her mind did. Caccini leaned forward, but his voice still carried to those standing around them. "Is that how you painted in Rome? Is that why Agostino Tassi was tempted to have a taste?"

Artemisia lurched backward as though she had been slapped. The eyes of the crowd felt like lashes against her skin.

The phantom weight of a broad hand seemed to close over her mouth.

Caccini stared at her, unflinching. "You will not continue your work. No matter what it takes I will make sure that the world knows not to commission you. Art is a sacred calling, and you and the Accademia will not sully it any longer."

Her breath was racing as though she had been sprinting rather than talking. She couldn't do this. The unexpected mention of Tassi sent her spiraling back five years to another day, another crowd, another man.

No. This was different. Caccini was not Tassi. He was not.

But he was just as primed to see her fall. He fought for her demise with an inconceivable passion, dragging her from the sky like a hawk barreling into a dove. She was helpless once again, and her only recourse had been to struggle and scrape for a revenge three years old while a new enemy set up his camp in her foyer.

Her fear and rage burned like a wildfire, scalding her blood from the inside.

She clenched her amulet so hard that the chain snapped. She flung the necklace away, and it disappeared into the dirt at the crowd's feet. Shivering with fury, she stepped closer and grabbed Caccini's collar with a clawed hand. Her grip felt weak, and her skin looked pale against the cardinal red.

"Let go of me, you demon," Caccini gasped, eyes wide.

"She's mad!" someone exclaimed.

Hands descended on Artemisia, pulling her back. She stumbled at the disjointed manhandling, nearly losing her balance. She shook off the grasping hands and found her feet. She glared blindly at the crowd pressed around her, unable to parse a single face.

"Get her out of here!" Caccini ordered.

She did not have the mind for a parting comment. She just pushed her way through the crowd before anyone could try to touch her again, elbowing people aside if they were in her way. Her vision blurred with tears, and she broke into a run.

Her hands stayed clenched in fists at her sides.

30

It was almost done, but she could not rush these final touches. A painting was only as strong as the passion that went into it, and she would not let anything falter now. It had to work. It had to.

Through the haze of exhaustion, her necrotic magics were shallow and still. She had to reach deep inside her soul to pull them free, and they clung like warm ashes to her mind.

Elisabetta had cautioned her not to act rashly without trying to speak to Caccini, but Artemisia had been right—it was too late for her to succeed in Florence. There was no hope left. It had been foolish to try diplomacy. He had publicly humiliated her.

In the week since, she had scarcely moved from her easel. Her remaining commissions had been set aside. They would surely be canceled soon anyway, and she could not waste her time on them. She was too close.

A tremor wracked her hand, but she tamed it with a breath of stillness. The new jar of salve from Elisabetta waited on her counter, but she did not want to step away for long enough to open it.

She was nearly too absorbed to hear the footsteps approaching her door, but a jagged blade of nerves slashed her with panic at the sound of the lock rattling. She blinked, and then blinked again. There were shadows in her mind threatening to cover her vision.

Fingers stiff and aching, she grabbed the velvet cover and draped it in place over the canvas just as the door opened.

"Artemisia?" Francesco asked, stepping inside. His trip to Venice had taken longer than planned, and she hadn't expected him back tonight. "Lord, it's dark in here. Did you forget to light your candles?"

From the gray light at the window, it was dusk already. How long had she been painting? Was it still the day she last remembered, or had she painted through another night and day? "I didn't notice." Her voice croaked with disuse.

"I sent you a half-dozen letters, but the messengers said no one answered the door. I was wondering if you'd left town," Francesco said as he went around the studio, lighting the stubs of her candles. He turned to her, blinking in the new, dim light. "Love, are you well? You're pale."

"I'm fine," Artemisia said. She leaned against her stool, letting it support her weight.

He stepped forward and took one of her hands. "You're freezing. Do you have a fever?" He put a hand against her forehead, frowning. "You're cold all over."

"Just overworked," Artemisia said.

"You should take a break. You'll drain yourself dry at this rate." He peered more closely at her waxen face. "It seems as though you're well on your way."

She pulled her hand away, though she immediately missed the scalding heat of his skin. "I'm fine," she repeated.

"When was the last time you ate? You're shaking."

"I have work to finish," she said. Her voice sounded weak as a guttering candle.

"I haven't seen you in weeks."

"Whose fault is that? You've been traveling the world while I'm fighting to not be run out of town," she said, voice hoarse. "What do I matter to you? You have an entire life to live without me."

"You *told* me not to help," Francesco pointed out. "I *wanted* to. You're the one who pushed me away."

"Leave," she said. "I can't do this."

He took a step toward her. "Talk to me. What's going on with you?"

"I confronted Caccini about what he's been doing. We argued. He won." Artemisia's words were harsh and clipped. "The Grand Duke is on his side. The Medici dropped my commission. The Accademia is abandoning me. New laws are being passed every day to give Caccini more power. He's going to destroy me. He's well on his way."

"Not while I'm alive," Francesco said.

"Don't you see? I've already lost."

"It's not over yet, love. You still have friends, and you still have me. We—"

A bloodcurdling shriek ripped through the air, so close it seemed to be on top of them. The sound manifested the rage and helplessness from Artemisia's soul and released it in one devastating screech. Artemisia and Francesco both jolted and looked up as one.

"Your griffon," Francesco breathed.

They ran. The sun had dipped below the horizon, and the hallway to the roof was swathed in shadow. Artemisia crashed into the wall as she left her room, jarring her shoulder, but was still directly on Francesco's heels up the ladder.

When she scrambled onto the roof, she was immediately pulled back by Francesco. They both nearly lost their balance on the precariously steep angle, but he steadied them. Artemisia barely noticed—her eyes were locked on the roiling mass of limbs and sharp teeth in front of them.

A slick, scaly monster was twisting around the griffon, lashing and clawing at her beast's golden sides. The griffon's expression was frantic as it fought its attacker, eyes wide and beak open. The smell of blood was thick in the air, and heavy streaks slicked the tiles. There was only a faint whisper of the setting sun still lighting the air, and the haze of dusk merely added to the confusion of the scene. The full moon overhead was an empty shell, not bright enough to aid them.

With a breathless curse, Artemisia knelt to pry a tile loose from the roof. Francesco's light hands on her waist kept her from falling.

The griffon's blood stained her palms.

She stared at the fighting beasts for a long moment before throwing the tile as hard as she could. There was a solid thunk as it collided with flesh, and an eerie hiss from its victim.

The griffon used the moment of distraction to lurch away from its attacker and take to the air. Its left wing was ragged and torn, dark with blood, and its movement against the sky was stilted. In moments, the night enveloped the griffon, and it was gone.

The other creature hissed again at the retreating shape, and then turned back to Artemisia and Francesco. Blood-smeared teeth filled a long, thin snout under yellow eyes that glinted in the darkness. Curled horns framed its head like a crown. Its flesh was covered with dark scales, and wickedly sharp claws tipped each foot. A pair of enormous, leathery wings stretched in the air, the narrow veins in the thin material visible from the faint backlight of the dying sun. Far larger than the griffon, it seemed to block out the emerging stars.

There was no mistaking it. Its visage was in every symbol warning of evil since the carvings of ancient Egypt.

Swiftly, the blood drake twisted like liquid across the roof toward them. It stopped just in front of them, its breath hot on Artemisia's face. She clutched Francesco's hands, which were tight around her waist, and stood as still as she could. The beast stretched its long neck forward and pressed its snout against her chest, and then inhaled deeply. The sound rattled in the silent night air.

For several beats, the blood drake simply breathed in her scent, and then it stepped back. Its scales rustled on the tiles as it wrapped its long form loosely into a ball. It settled down, belly draping over the sharp incline of the roof without fear, and exhaled a thin spiral of smoke toward the sky.

Artemisia tapped Francesco's hands and then tilted her head toward the still-open roof door behind them. Carefully, they slipped back down the ladder, leaving the creature, blood-smeared and content, resting overhead.

They walked back into the studio in a tense silence that felt like the long drag of flint before a spark ignited. The candles Francesco had lit were waiting for them, flickering with the movement of the door.

Wringing her bloody hands, Artemisia went to the window to peer out at the dark night. "Do you think the griffon will survive?"

"Artemisia," Francesco said, voice slow and deliberate. "Why is a blood drake on your roof?"

"I don't know," she said. "We'll need to find a way to get rid of it. And soon. I'll be killed if anyone sees it."

"What have you done?" he asked, voice hollow.

She turned to find him standing in front of the painting she had been working on before his arrival, staring at the velvet draped over it with a frown. He glanced up at the ceiling, and then reached forward to grasp the fabric.

"No, don't!" Artemisia cried, but it was too late.

The velvet drape billowed through the air before landing in a heap on the ground, the same color as the blood spilled on the roof.

The painting underneath was almost finished.

Three figures dominated the center of the canvas, framed by blood-stained white sheets below and dark shadows above. Struggling on the bed, futilely fighting for his life, was the general Holofernes. Above him, Judith and her maidservant, Abra, were in the grisly process of sawing through his neck. Though his arms were still in the process of pushing away Abra, his head was pinned against the sheet by Judith's hand, fist entangled in his hair. Blood sprayed from his neck, betraying his imminent death. Judith, expression determined, had rolled up the sleeves of her golden gown before she began, but the arc of the blood was making its inevitable way toward the pale fabric.

Judith's face had been painted from a mirror.

Francesco winced, pulling his hand away from the canvas. Even though it was not his hair laced through the paint, the waves of unreleased dark magics pulsing from the painting would scald anyone so close. "What is this?"

In answer, she stepped closer and pointed toward the contorted face of Holofernes. "That," she told him, "is Agostino Tassi."

Francesco was silent for a long, still moment, and then he cleared his throat. "A plague?" he asked, voice very quiet.

"Of course not," she said. "I'm not a monster."

"The blood drake came because of this."

"Maybe."

"It's *killing* you. Can you not see how far you've fallen? Are you so obsessed with a revenge five years old that you'll throw away your life? I know he hurt you, I know he was an evil man, but *look* at you. These types of paintings destroy artists. You're already skin and bones. If you do survive finishing it, the blood drake will lead the authorities straight here. Is hurting Tassi worth your life?"

She jabbed toward the painting. "He *took* my life," she snarled. "It's not over, no matter how far I go from Rome. He's still haunting me. And he's just the first in a long line. If I can't beat them, then I can at least know that I've taken them down with me. I won't be helpless. I won't be erased as though I was never here."

"This is madness. You're angry at Caccini, and you're fixating on the past. What will this fix? If you die, they win."

"I'm not mad, Francesco. I know Tassi isn't my most pressing enemy." Artemisia shook her head, and hovered over the spray of blood arcing from Holofernes's neck. "The face targets Tassi. But here, I also wove in the hair of Tomasso Caccini."

"*What?*"

"That day in front of his church, when I realized I had lost this fight, I grabbed his robe and took away a strand of his hair. Only one, but it will be enough. I realized I was letting my past distract me from the enemy of my present just because it was the only path I thought I had. Maybe I'll never grow past what Tassi did to me. But I could not do *this* and let Caccini walk free in the meantime." She tapped the base of the easel. "Not when I could end them both."

"Two targets for one painting, and Caccini only added in

NICOLE JARVIS

this past month? Artemisia, I'm no artist, but I know that's not possible."

"Everyone tells me they know what is possible or impossible," Artemisia snapped. "How do they know? Have they *tried*? How much are we bound by the ignorance of the past? Painting is guided by emotion. I've directed plenty enough toward Caccini. And I'm stronger now than I've ever been before. What has all this training been in Florence—in my *life*—if not for this? I'm more powerful than anyone knows."

Francesco scrubbed a hand over his face. "You're playing with magics no one understands. How do you know it's safe? For you, for the *world*. Who knows what these magics will do?"

"I thought you believed in me," Artemisia said.

"Artemisia, please. It's not over," Francesco insisted, stepping toward her. "You can end this now. We can still win."

Her hands were shaking, though she wasn't sure whether it was from shock, anger, fear, or simply the unrelenting drain of the necrotic magics. "You don't get to tell me it will be all right. You've never faced a person—a *mob*—that wanted to ruin you. You don't know what it is to be unmade in front of a crowd, but I *do*. They're trying to erase my legacy. I have to do something they can't change. There was a time I wanted this to be a quiet revenge, a secret I could tuck away if I moved on to my successful career. Not anymore. My career is over, and this is my only chance to show them that I *am* powerful, that they never should have tried to stop me. When I die, they'll still say my name forever."

"This is how you want to be remembered? Using your magics to kill?"

"I'll be remembered as a woman who got revenge," Artemisia said. She pointed at Judith steadily decapitating her enemy.

"Maybe someday a new female artist will paint *me* in my bloody glory!"

"Judith was saving her city by killing Holofernes," Francesco shot back. "Who are you saving?"

"Caccini is destroying Florence. And I'm not the only woman Tassi ever hurt. During the trial, they found out he was planning on killing his own wife! He's a monster. You think that he's spent these last years reformed? I can't trust the law to protect anyone. They tortured me with a seven-month trial. He was freed from his sentence in less time than I was interrogated. Where is the justice? Who will punish him if not me?"

"I know, but you'll be burned for this, if not worse. I'll lose the only woman I've ever loved," Francesco pleaded. "There's no mercy for dark magics."

"There doesn't seem to be any mercy for me anywhere," Artemisia snarled, pointing to the window. "Caccini was going to destroy me for trying to live my life. I might as well do something worth punishing." She stilled and met his eyes. "Will you turn me in, Francesco?"

He hesitated for a long moment, but then shook his head. "I'd rather see you become a murderer than be responsible for putting you back on trial. But I can't be with you if you do this."

"I've been working on this painting as long as you've known me."

"I don't believe you," he said. "The blood drake only came now. You haven't been pouring your life into this. I would have seen it. I *know* you, Artemisia."

"I let myself be pulled away," she admitted. "I started it just after I came to Florence, but I stopped for a time. I couldn't find the magics." She scoffed, still furious with herself. "I wasted precious time with distractions."

"No!" Francesco replied. "*We* were not a waste. Happiness is not a distraction from revenge. Which fights back against what they did to you better—stooping to their level or living a good life in spite of them?"

"What good life? I'm running out of time, Francesco. My enemies will see me destroyed," Artemisia said. "I have to do this."

"You will be destroyed, but I don't believe it will come from outside." Expression wretched, he said, "I can't watch it happen."

"You'd leave me alone in this?" she demanded. "You said you loved me."

He closed his eyes, took a breath, and then turned away. "That's why I can't watch you throw your life away."

Artemisia raised a hand to call him back, but let it fall without speaking. She watched him collect his bag and go to the door.

He looked back over his shoulder. "I hope you change your mind, my love."

She looked at his face as though she were examining a lost San Sandro painting. She wanted to remember every line and shadow, even though his expression was creased with heartbreak. It was a beloved face, the source of a joy she had never hoped to know.

She had not expected betrayal from this source. She should have known she would be on her own in the end.

"Goodbye, Francesco," she said.

Slowly, he took the gimmel ring from his finger and set it on the table.

The studio door shut behind him, and the gust of air killed the flickering candle closest to the entrance. The wax puddled low in its dish, melted away. There was not enough wick left to relight it.

31

The blood on her hands had not yet dried.

Artemisia paced her small studio. The remaining candles were low, stuttering with their final breaths. The light flickered in dramatic shadows against the walls, adding new angles to the paintings scattered on easels around her. A dozen sets of painted eyes watched her.

Abandoned by her lover, betrayed by her patrons, stalked by a monster on her roof, and all with the final work unfinished.

Would Francesco change his mind and report her for the dark magics? How quickly would the blood drake be noticed? Her griffon had mostly stayed on her roof at night—perhaps this, too, would stay hidden in the darkness.

How far had the blood drake traveled to find her? They were rare in Tuscany, hunted to near extinction in the Grave Age and now born with a fear of humans. It took powerful magics to call them into a city this crowded.

Like griffons, blood drakes were bonded to their artists. Even if Artemisia snuck out of her building and moved away tonight, it would follow her. She remembered Elisabetta's story of a mob surrounding a weaver in the country, slaying the blood drake and then dragging the artist to the pyre.

She pulled her ring from her finger, where it had sat since

Francesco's proposal, and flung it at the wall. It clattered and fell, but the tension boiling under her skin did not ease.

Part of her had thought Francesco would be on her side if he ever learned what she was doing. She had told him what Tassi had done to her, and he had seen the chaos Caccini had caused in her life. Maurizio had guessed her purpose when she sent him to collect Tassi's hair, and he had encouraged her. How could her own lover turn his back on her?

If the authorities came at dawn because of the blood drake, she would not have time to finish the painting before she was arrested. All that remained were some small highlights and the final layer of varnish, but the oils were still wet and gleaming in the dim light, and she could not add more until they dried. It was nearly done, but she could not risk a mistake when she was so close. She needed another day.

If Francesco would not use his influence to help her, she had to find another ally, someone to confuse the authorities while she finished her work. If her career—likely even her life—were already over, she would fight with her last breath to finish her final mission… but she was running out of time.

It was still early when she slipped out of the building and made her way across the city. With the horrors of the night—of the past several weeks—she had expected it to be well past midnight. It was strange that the city could be so alive around her when she was so withered. With the summer heat acting as a warden during the day, the citizens of Florence waited to leave their homes after sunset. Patrons from bars spilled into the squares, laughing and chatting. There were couples walking by the Arno, heads pressed together in quiet intimacy.

Artemisia moved like the hands of a clock, compelled forward without thought.

A man plucked a lute in Piazza Santo Spirito, and a haunting melody drifted over the terracotta rooftops. She stopped in front of the sprawling Medici palace. In the dark, the broad building loomed like a fortress.

A liveried guard shook his head as she approached. "Artemisia Gentileschi," he said, voice rumbling like a growl, "you've been taken off the entry list."

She summoned a smile. It was a guard she had seen often before, though she had never learned his name. "Signore—"

"Move along. You're not welcome here."

"I need to speak to Madama Cristina," she said.

"I told you—"

"Tell her I'm here. She'll change her mind." She hoped. Their last conversation had been a mistake. Artemisia shouldn't have challenged the Medici matriarch when she knew the woman was hanging onto her power by a thread. She needed to flatter her, inform her that her patronage would be the only thing that could save Artemisia from the misunderstanding the blood drake would cause. Surely Madama Cristina would not believe that Artemisia had earned the blood drake's presence with her actions. Though they had fallen out, Madama Cristina would probably not want to see her falsely arrested—for the Medici's reputation if not Artemisia's sake. Artemisia could use that. She just needed enough time to complete the crime for which they would charge her.

The guard was unmoved. "Madama Cristina is not in residence."

Artemisia blinked. Though it was early for most people, the aging Medici matriarch rarely went out to evening events these days. "Where is she?"

"San Piero a Sieve," he said, naming a town a day's ride into the country.

"So far?" Madama Cristina had said she was afraid her son

would force her to retire soon. Had she been sent away already? If the Grand Duke were willing to take away his mother's long-held title, he had been more corrupted by Caccini than Artemisia had realized. Cosimo had once been a fair and cultured ruler, but he had clearly fallen into paranoia. Madama Cristina had always worked to support her son's authority, even above her own wishes.

There was nothing for Artemisia here. There was nothing for her anywhere.

Perhaps she could instead convince Cosimo directly that Caccini was the only actual threat to his power. The priest had been hoarding influence for years, using his attack on Galileo as the foundation of a legacy of religious fervor. Caccini was building a cult of personality within the city. The Grand Duke was being overpowered, not strengthened, by his cooperation with Caccini.

At this point, Artemisia would try anything. She just needed one more day and she would complete her legacy. "Then tell the Grand Duke that I am here," she said.

"The Grand Duke and Archduchess are not here either."

"Are they in the country as well?" Artemisia sneered, out of patience.

"They're somewhere you have even less of an invitation to attend than here," the guard said.

She folded her arms. "I had a standing invitation to this palace. You know that as well as I do. Who revoked it?"

"His Grace does not permit any artists to come inside anymore," he said. "He was very explicit about the rule. He does not trust your kind. Paolo Lamberti is the only artist who has been inside these walls in a month."

"Of all the people to trust," she exclaimed. "Paolo Lamberti?" She knew they were friends. Lamberti had said as much when she saw his portraits of the Grand Duke and Archduchess at his studio. They likely fawned over Caccini together, the bastards. "For someone who isn't speaking to any artists, he's been making plenty of laws regarding the Accademia."

"He's protecting the city. We all know the powers of artists," the guard said darkly. He was eyeing her with renewed suspicion. How obvious was her pallor in the light of the torches? It had been obvious to Francesco that something was wrong.

But it could not have been that. The average Florentine did not know the impacts of necrotic magics. Besides, she was no paler than...

The last time she had seen Lamberti, before she had fallen back under the thrall of her Judith, she had been furious, distracted, but he too had been gaunt and pallid. She had always known him as a thin but hearty man, but even in his moment of triumph, he had seemed quite weak.

The Grand Duke's behavior had begun to change when Caccini returned from Rome. Madama Cristina had believed it to be shame or fear that motivated him. But was that not the same time he had commissioned Lamberti for the new bust portraits of him and his wife? Perhaps there was more to the art than it seemed.

"How often has Lamberti been here? Or sent letters?"

Clearly suspicious, the guard replied, "Often. Why do you ask?"

Lamberti, much to Artemisia's disgust, was as skilled as she. The foolish Medici had hired him, handed him their hair, and hoped he would use it to protect them. He had the knowledge to tie the Grand Duke and his wife to a pair of necrotic paintings. He did not need to kill them, only to make them pass the laws he wanted. The threat would have been enough. The paintings Artemisia had seen had been nearly complete. He must have told the Medici they could be unleashed at any moment.

Lamberti must have worked on the paintings day and night to complete them in recent months. Her Judith had drained Artemisia so much she had been forced to work slowly, even when she had been desperate to finish it. She refused to believe he might be more powerful than her. It must have been sheer luck he had not already died.

This explained why the Grand Duke had been acting so strangely, pouring his power into Caccini's hands. Madama Cristina had searched for some other logic, but there was nothing but coercion.

After all of Caccini's speeches about Artemisia and the Accademia, the biggest threat to the city was the painter he had commissioned for his own church's fresco. How ironic not only that Caccini had a painter using dark magics under his own roof, but that Lamberti was using them for Caccini's own benefit. The priest would have been horrified that even as he'd fought to 'cleanse' the Accademia, he was being helped along by a madman.

The new rules imposed on the Accademia and the streets of Florence, the expanded power to Lamberti's favorite preacher—how many of those changes had been due to Lamberti's influence? If he had guided all those laws, it meant he had been threatening the Grand Duke into following his whims for months.

If Artemisia could find a way to help the Medici against Lamberti, she might not only have the Grand Duke trust her, but perhaps he would even pardon her for her crimes. After all, her vengeance was against a convicted rapist and a corrupt preacher—compared to Lamberti's threats against the Grand Duke and his innocent wife, surely Artemisia's plans for revenge would seem tame. They would owe her their lives.

And having a hand in Lamberti's downfall would be sweet.

"Has the Grand Duke said anything about Lamberti?" Artemisia asked. "Has he been acting unusually?"

"You need to clear the premises," the guard ordered.

Artemisia wondered if she looked as manic as she felt. "It's important! Just answer me, damn it."

The guard's hand drifted to his sword. The hilt was decorative, emblazoned with the Medici crest, but his grip was steady. Despite the livery, he was not there for ornamentation. "Leave in peace." The alternative did not need to be said.

Artemisia glared at him. Her hand absently reached up toward her chest, but she had not had the time to create a new amulet after she had broken the last to steal Caccini's hair. Her priorities had lain elsewhere—and she had not expected a simple amulet could save her from the troubles she was creating. Her hard work was likely crushed to pieces in the mud by now.

What had the guard meant that the Medici were somewhere Artemisia was not invited? Half of Florence was barred to her these days. What was special about tonight?

She remembered then Caccini's gloat from last week. The priest had said he was hosting the leaders of Florence at Santa Maria Novella soon. There was no place in Florence less welcome to Artemisia than that church. It must have been happening tonight.

While Artemisia was floundering, her lover abandoning her and a blood drake circling overhead, Caccini continued to flourish. As hard as she had fought for a scrap of success, these horrible, grasping, close-minded men continued to rule, aided by the foolishness of those like Lamberti who thought instituting limitations would give them freedom.

Whatever her expression betrayed, it made the guard begin to withdraw his sword. She stepped back and held up her hands, and then swiftly left the shadow of the Medici palace.

If she was correct, this was the miracle she had been hoping for. She could have gone then to burn Lamberti's studio to ash, but without proof of what had been inside her enemies would call her a madwoman. She needed to speak to the Grand Duke first. If she saved him and his wife from Lamberti, suspicion would be lifted from her long enough for her to finish her mission. If anyone spotted her blood drake, she could claim it had been sent by Lamberti. No one truly understood the creatures.

Perhaps she could even hide her Judith after she completed it, blame the effects on Lamberti as well. It had been years since her trial in Rome. Maybe no one would make the connection between Tassi's and Caccini's deaths. She could emerge a hero, her victory intact with none the wiser.

Lamberti's downfall could be her salvation.

As she had expected, Santa Maria Novella was lit for an evening celebration hours after the final Mass should have ended. In the hot, still summer night, a group of finely dressed nobles mingled in the vast square in front of the open door of the church.

She scanned the crowd quickly, pulse fluttering in her chest. From the movement inside the church, the event would undoubtedly be starting soon, and the guards by the door would never allow Artemisia entrance.

She shoved aside a murmuring couple and strode through the crowd. It was disturbingly similar to the last time she had been at Santa Maria Novella. The memory of Caccini's words scalded her gut. He had called her a fraud, a whore, in front of dozens of witnesses. How could Francesco not understand her desire for revenge against him?

Finally, she found the Grand Duke and his wife surrounded

by a cluster of admirers. Did the Medici seem distracted and anxious, or was Artemisia only seeing what she wished to see?

This crowd was full of the most influential people in Florence. A delicate approach would be wisest.

Artemisia did not have the time.

"Your Grace," she exclaimed, pushing her way into the group.

He turned to her and his eyes widened. "Signorina Gentileschi." Beside him, the Archduchess pressed a hand to her bosom and looked between them. She was a delicate woman, slender as a flower stem.

"I need to speak with you," she told the Grand Duke, ignoring the muttering around her.

"Signorina," chided an older man. She vaguely recognized him from dinners at the Palazzo Pitti. "This is inappropriate."

"Just for a moment," she pressed.

The Grand Duke was looking around—did he have his own security in the crowd? He stepped back, and someone tried to pull Artemisia away.

She kept her eyes locked on Cosimo. "I can help you," she said. "I know. I know what he's doing." She held her breath. It was a gambit—if she was wrong, this moment would only cement her disgrace.

The Grand Duke held up his hand, and the grip on Artemisia's arm loosened.

The Archduchess stared at Artemisia as though she were the Virgin Mary come again.

A bell rang from inside the church, warning the crowd that the evening's event was about to start. The group began moving to the doors in a murmuring herd.

"Go ahead. I'll be one moment," Cosimo said, nodding to

his companions. "I can always spare a word for a citizen of Florence."

There were disgruntled protests from those around—perhaps they had heard the rumors against Artemisia, or simply wanted another moment with the Grand Duke's ear—but Cosimo stepped forward and pulled Artemisia away from the crowd.

Artemisia glanced toward the door, but the guards had not spotted her yet in the milling group.

"Speak," the Grand Duke said. "Quickly."

"It's true, isn't it?" Artemisia said. She had been right. She still had a chance to turn this entire situation around. Lamberti disgraced, Artemisia revered, and her revenge secured. "Lamberti has been threatening you into everything you've done."

Cosimo's expression did not shift. "How did you know?"

What could she say? As someone working on a necrotic painting, she could identify someone else doing the same? "An artist's instinct. I knew something was wrong, and had to come help you."

He glanced back toward the church. "Say what you wanted to say." He was not as relieved as she had expected.

"I can stop him," Artemisia told him. "He's been lying to you, whatever he's said. The paintings aren't a risk to you until they're finished. If you arrest him tonight, you'll stop him from completing them. He has no hold over you."

"The paintings are ready," the Grand Duke said. "He informed me it is only his will holding back the magics now. As soon as he decides they are finished, my wife and I die."

Could that be true? It was possible, though it required a discipline of mind Artemisia would have said was impossible. It was the artist's intent that released the magics inside a work, their will that gave art its power.

"You need to leave," the Grand Duke said. "This is ending tonight. He has promised to release us after this one final favor. I cannot have you risking my life, my wife's life, by making this public. Hold your tongue."

"Why tonight?" Artemisia asked.

He gestured to the church. "He's completing his fresco—and forcing every power in Florence to listen to his pet preacher while he does. He's sure Caccini will be able to sway us all if he only has the platform. He thinks he has me cowed. I'll sit through it, smile, and then he'll burn the paintings tonight. The power will be back in my hands." The Grand Duke's expression was icy. "He'll regret it."

"You wouldn't have sent your mother to the country if you were sure of that," Artemisia said.

"I have this under control. I certainly do not need *your* assistance."

Fury roiled in Artemisia, warming her cold bones. "You're a coward. How long will you let this go on?"

"I have a plan," the Grand Duke said. "You'll only interfere."

"You've given Lamberti the power to make this city miserable," Artemisia snapped. "He's terrorized the Accademia and implemented archaic laws on Caccini's behalf. You've handed over your power on a silver platter at a madman's whim."

"The Medici will outlast this," the Grand Duke said.

"Will Florence?"

A lord approached them, hailing the Grand Duke and waving him toward the doors. Either he was oblivious to their tense postures, or assumed there could be nothing of importance for Cosimo to discuss with an artist.

"Leave, signorina," the Grand Duke hissed before turning to the nobleman. The welcoming smile he gave the other man seemed so genuine Artemisia would never have believed he had just been threatening her. Politicians had to be talented actors.

The crowd filtered into the church. A guard in Santa Maria Novella's white livery checked names at the door against a list.

Artemisia seethed, watching the Grand Duke enter the cathedral without glancing back at her. Her hands trembled.

That fool.

Cosimo was permitting Lamberti's manipulation, too scared for his own family's safety to concern himself with the wellbeing of Florence. Certainly Lamberti would not burn the paintings as promised. Caccini's power was growing, but it was far from cemented. If the recent laws could be reversed, Florence could still return to normal. No, her enemy would keep the Grand Duke under his control for as long as he was able. She could not allow that to happen.

Tomorrow, the authorities would notice the blood drake on Artemisia's roof—if they had not already—and she would be arrested before she could complete her revenge. Yet again, she would be humiliated while her enemies walked free. Her righteous cause would become the gossip of Florence, and Lamberti would remain laughing in the shadows.

Artemisia kept walking until she could slip around the broad face of the church and approach from the side, cloaked in darkness away from the main entrance. A long stretch of garden pressed along the right edge of the church, the sculpted cypress trees peeking over the wall and casting narrow shadows down the street. A small wooden door at the transept was propped open, likely to allow for air circulation on the warm night. She slipped inside.

No. She would end this tonight. She would unmask Lamberti in front of everyone. No one could dismiss her then.

Artemisia came through the right arm of the cross that formed the building. On either side of the central aisle were a series of small, gated chapels, each designed by a different artist for a patron family. She emerged in line with the central pulpit, along the Filippo Strozzi Chapel. Though candles lit the center of the room, where the elite of Florence mingled while they waited for the evening sermon to begin, Artemisia's corner was dark and quiet.

The fresco behind the altar was a wash of soft clouds and lush, rich fabrics. Mary sat in the middle, dressed in vibrant pink and blue, surrounded by floating cherubs. At the bottom corner of the painting, a brush in hand, was an image of Bezalel, the first artist. Lamberti had used his own face.

All of Caccini's complaints about Artemisia's ego, and his own fresco was a monument to Lamberti. As ever, her sin of being a woman made her detractors blind to the corruption around them. Caccini was a close-minded fool, too proud of his own invented vendettas to realize the truth. When she unveiled Lamberti, she hoped that Caccini would be a laughingstock before she used her painting to destroy him.

Lamberti stood at the bottom of the scaffolding, preparing his palette. He was even more pallid than he had been when she had gone to his studio, waxen in the candlelight. He seemed not to hear the gathered crowd, focused entirely on the paints in his hands.

From her angle, she could just see the brushes set on the platform at the top, where Lamberti would be able to reach the top of the fresco that stretched over the entire back wall. The completion was perfunctory now. It would be a few final brushstrokes and then Lamberti's will that declared the painting complete, just as it would be tomorrow for Artemisia's Judith.

Just as he claimed it would be for the Medici portraits. Had he told the Grand Duke the truth? By confronting him publicly, did she risk him activating the necrotic magics and killing Florence's two leaders? Worse, if they survived, would anyone believe her if the Grand Duke still insisted on not cooperating with her?

Artemisia hesitated within the shadowed chapel, her thoughts whirling and writhing like the blood drake that lurked on her roof.

Her last attempt to defy someone in this church had ended in public humiliation.

She was being rash, letting her fear and anger propel her into a foolish confrontation. She could not afford to make the foolhardy mistakes of her enemies. They were more likely to laugh her out of the building than to believe her story. The chill in her stomach from her lost magics made her shaky and irrational, but she had to stay clever. If she did everything right, this week would be the culmination of her life's work.

Carefully, she slipped from the chapel and slunk back toward the door she had left open.

She knew the path to Lamberti's studio. She could find a way in, grab the cursed paintings, and be back with them before the event tonight ended. Once she proved Lamberti's plan, the Grand Duke would have no choice but to be publicly grateful for her help.

Then, Artemisia could complete her painting, pin the effects on Lamberti, and find a new status in Florence as the Medici's savior.

"Artemisia Gentileschi."

A hand closed on her shoulder. She lurched toward the door, an instinctive, terrified reaction to the unexpected touch, but another hand grabbed her around the waist and pulled her tight against a broad, warm body.

The man holding her turned them both around, and Artemisia found herself face-to-face with Tomasso Caccini. He was in his usual red robes, smug and arrogant as ever.

"Thank you, Marcello," he said to the man holding her. "I knew it was wise to have security here tonight, though I did not expect this snake to be so bold."

"I was just leaving," Artemisia said, twisting against the guard's grip.

"Of course you were," Caccini said, condescending. "Throw her out."

"You're a fool," Artemisia snarled. Caccini waved a hand for the guard to take her away. Artemisia sneered at him as she was pulled backward. "You're so concerned about what I'm doing. You've been dragging the Accademia's name through the mud. You think you're so wise, but you're blind to what's in front of you. You'll learn."

Caccini stilled, like the brief respite in wind just before a storm crested. "Marcello, I changed my mind. She's still a risk if she's outside, battering at the windows like a bird. Put her in my office."

"You can't—!" Artemisia's shouted protests were silenced by a heavy hand falling onto her mouth. Her pulse skipped and then raced forward like it had been tipped down a hill, rolling more and more quickly until she thought her heart might burst from her chest. Her attempts to squirm free were abandoned. She was stiff and still in the guard's arms, her mind locked inside an unmoving body.

She was the rabbit in a fox's jaws, her traitorous body sure that being still enough would save her from the disaster already happening around her.

32

Santa Maria Novella stretched far beyond the central cross of the main cathedral. Along its west side, two square cloisters were framed by red-roofed passageways. It was along one of those that Artemisia was dragged before she was shoved into a small room. It was cold and austere in design, a brutal contrast to the ornate interior of the cathedral. An open window along the wall looked out onto the serene cloisters.

Without giving her time to steady herself, the guard tied her wrists together in front of her body with a rough rope. He shoved her down onto a chair in the center of the office, facing Caccini's desk like a runaway dog brought to heel. She seethed at the indignity even as terror made her heart trip.

Caccini entered the room behind them. "Leave us, Marcello."

"Father, the gathering is supposed to begin—"

"I'll be there," Caccini said.

Marcello bowed and left, closing the door behind him.

"You can't keep me prisoner," Artemisia said, tugging at her restraints. The rope scratched against the vulnerable skin of her wrists. "The Grand Duke hasn't given you *that* power yet." And he never would, not if Artemisia could stop Lamberti.

"After tonight, I won't need his permission," Caccini said, sitting down behind his desk. It had been designed to present an impressive image. There was a painting—pastel colors, likely a few decades old from the style—of an angel on the wall behind him. When he sat, its golden halo framed his balding head.

"You're not the ruler of Florence, and you never will be," she said. Lord, she wanted to see him coughing blood. "You think you're some Savonarola returned? You're a fraud."

"Am I? Bold of *you* to say."

"The Grand Duke is not on your side. All the power you've been building is about to fall apart," Artemisia told him, grinning up at him. It felt feral in her teeth. "Paolo Lamberti has been using dark magics to *threaten* the Grand Duke and his wife into supporting you. As soon as he lets Cosimo slip free, he'll turn around and undo all the legislation he's passed in your favor. You put your faith in the wrong man, Caccini. You've been staring so hard at me and Galileo and the Accademia that you missed what was right in front of you. I'm excited to watch you lose everything, you pig."

"Lamberti is troubled," Caccini said, solemn, nearly bland, "but there are no dark magics in those portraits."

"There are," she said. "You'll see."

Caccini waved a hand. "He doesn't have that type of energy to spare."

"Have you not seen him these last few months? He's been pale, thin... Wait," she said, thoughts tripping over each other. "How did you know they were portraits?"

"Lamberti has lost his mind, clearly," Caccini said. "Using necrotic magics. Breaking one of the core values of the Accademia. It's a tragedy I didn't know earlier... before he used the fresco I commissioned in my own church to murder everyone gathered inside tonight."

Artemisia gaped at him. Surely he wasn't serious.

The sounds of unknowing conversation and laughter drifted through the window from Santa Maria Novella's cathedral.

"I was lucky that the Lord chose to spare me," Caccini continued, "but sadly, Lamberti and the entire current line of nobility were destroyed in one terrible moment. It's fortunate that the recent laws from the Grand Duke's office will allow the Church—led by me—to step forward to lead Florence."

"Lamberti isn't powerful enough to do that," Artemisia said, her lips numb. "A fresco that large, that necrotic—he'd already be dead."

"Lamberti has been resentful for a long time. It's been a slow, steady process. He's a determined man."

"Then you'll die too. God won't save you. Nothing can."

"Except my blood in the paint. Lamberti was eager to keep me safe."

"He might not feel that way when it's done. Finishing it might not kill him. When he's arrested, he'll tell them it was your idea. You think that man has loyalty to you? He only cares about himself, and what you can do for him."

"I know. There are ways to make it seem natural. I wouldn't let him ruin our plans."

"Natural. You'd murder him?" Despite everything, Artemisia was still stunned.

"I've done it before." Caccini spread his hands. "The Lord requires blood sacrifices at times."

"You're mad," Artemisia said, voice cracking. "You really would kill all these people."

"Florence is rotten from the inside," Caccini said, voice growing fierce and harsh. It was a more natural fit for the red-robed priest than his false casualness. This was the man who had stood at the pulpit and called for her destruction. This was the man planning a massacre in his own church. "Power has been stripped from the Church, and it started with our acceptance of art at the end of the Grave Age. Florence's star is fading while Rome's is rising. I'm turning that around."

"You're talking about murder. Mass murder," Artemisia said.

"Was it mass murder when the Lord sent the Flood to start afresh? Or when He destroyed Sodom and Gomorrah for their sins? Or when he killed the Egyptian firstborn to save his people?" Caccini shook his head. "It's not murder. It's a righteous cleansing."

"You can't do this," she said. "There are a hundred people in that room. And a curse like that with no specific target—it could spread out into the rest of the city. You could start a new plague."

"It had to be harsh enough that no one can ignore it, or pretend it didn't happen. Art should have stayed outlawed. After the first plague showed what it could do, art should never have become available again—especially not to the highest bidder, performed by any common man with a drop of magics in his veins. This will ensure that from now on, it will be cloistered off again like the poison it is. Art is not a miracle—it's a curse we have to control. Legitimizing Donatello was the worst mistake the Church has made in centuries."

"San Donatello saved this city."

"Donatello was a tool. If what he did *was* a miracle, then it was to save the Church. No one worshipped the ark that saved Noah. It was God's decision. God's gifts gave Donatello's statue its magics. Art must be controlled, or it must be suppressed."

Artemisia shook her head. "This is madness. No one believes more in art than Lamberti. How did you convince him to do this?"

"He's obsessed with proving himself—and ruining you. He thinks we'll use tonight to bring art into a new era of glory.

He thinks the world will see him as a hero for showing Florence's mistakes." He shrugged. "He's vainglorious. He deserves what will come to him."

"Hypocrite. You just want power. You're not noble. You can't stand knowing that people care more about artists than cardinals."

"Of course I can't stand it," he snarled, voice rising. "We're permitting the world to worship false idols. The plague shows what happens when art is free. They need a reminder, and blood is the only language they'll understand."

"Killing all these people will *devastate* the city."

"The corrupt leadership of Florence has gone on too long. It's time for the era of the Medici to end."

Artemisia shook her head. "You can't do this."

"It's already done. With a few more brushstrokes, the fresco will be complete. I need to watch it happen." He glanced at her tied wrists. "Don't go anywhere, signorina. If you listen closely, you'll hear the start of a new era. The screams will be loud."

"Why did you tell me this?" Artemisia demanded as he stood up. Her hands were shaking in their bindings. "Why not just throw me out—or lock me inside with the rest of them? I don't want to know this."

He dusted off the front of his robes and straightened his biretta. "People would ask questions if you die with the rest of them. You're not meant to be here. Don't worry—you're not leaving here alive. I'll deal with you once everything is settled," he told her. "Besides, you've been a part of this for months. When I got back from Rome, I knew I had to accelerate the plans. The Church made a mistake in letting Galileo roam free. I had to save Florence. But I needed the city to focus on someone else while we worked. You were the perfect choice. No one could have inspired Lamberti more. And your public cries for attention only helped my cause. It's time people saw artists for what they are. It's fitting you should be here at the end."

He swept from the office without looking back at her again, taking the single candle and closing the door behind him. There was a heavy thunk as a key turned in the lock.

Artemisia waited until his footsteps faded to push herself to her feet. The only light in the small office was from the full moon outside. She went to the open window by the door and reached through it. The warm night air enveloped her bound wrists, but the space was too narrow for her shoulders to fit through. The cloister was just beyond, and the cathedral, glowing with candlelight, loomed on the other side. She was so close, but it wasn't enough.

"Help!" she shouted, waving her fingers. "Somebody help!"

There was no response. Caccini had not even left his man Marcello behind to guard her. She was ignored, forgotten, trapped in a madman's office while he massacred the city's elite.

How long had they been planning this? Lamberti had been working on the fresco since last fall. When Artemisia started gaining a foothold in the Accademia, he had decided to burn it down around them. He had been cleverer than Artemisia, drawing out the necrotic process so long that there were no blood drakes swarming Santa Maria Novella despite the massive amount of dark magics needed to kill an entire cathedral. This was not a crime of passion. This was a calculated massacre.

How had she been so blind? Of course Caccini was pulling Lamberti's strings. The artist wouldn't have admitted it to the Grand Duke, not if Caccini was trying to hide his involvement, but Artemisia should have known. Lamberti thought he was using Caccini to take the Accademia back to its glory days, but

Caccini was draining him dry to undermine art forever more.

Artemisia clasped her bound hands against the handle and rattled it, but the lock was heavy and unmoving.

She wished fervently that she hadn't spent the last few weeks pouring her soul into her work. Her body and mind were weak now, drained and glass-brittle. If she were sharper, more awake, surely she could escape this dark, impromptu cell. This was an office, not a prison. There must be a way out.

She just couldn't see it.

She screamed, shrill and hoarse, but no help came. The guards were likely still posted at the front to stop uninvited guests from getting in—or Caccini's prey from getting out—but with the chatter inside the cathedral they must not have heard her. Were they in on the plot as well? Artemisia doubted it. Few people, no matter how well they were paid, could stomach the thought of necrotic magics.

Furious, she stumbled back to Caccini's desk and used her tied hands to sweep away everything stacked neatly on the surface. She would make him regret keeping her trapped. Loose paper scattered into the air, a goblet crashed into the wall, books thudded to the ground...and a sharp glint of metal flipped on its way down, catching the moon's glow.

Artemisia scrambled on the ground, patting around until she found the slender blade, half hidden by a fallen paper. She was gentle picking it up, but the breathless bubble of hope in her throat popped when she saw that it wasn't a forgotten dagger. It was just a letter opener, silver and ornately carved. She grasped it awkwardly, with barely room to close one fist while the other was so closely bound beside it. Leaning against the wall to balance herself, she levered the letter opener and tried to rub it against the thick rope around her wrists.

The angle was awkward, and the blade was dull. It rasped against the ropes but did not catch.

"Cazzo," Artemisia swore. She fumbled the blade down, testing the edges with her palms. Not even sharp enough to cut her skin. Frustrated, she jabbed the tip into her palm.

It sliced into her, sending a sharp shock of pain through the crease at the center of her hand. She swore again, pulling it back.

What good would a pointed tip do? She couldn't saw through her ropes with it, and it was too broad to be useful for picking the lock.

The blood was wet and warm against her skin.

Slowly, deliberately, she moved the letter opener and dug the tip into her palm again, harder this time. She gritted her teeth through the pain—she'd had worse, much worse—and dragged the sharp point down her hand.

Blood pulsed from the wound like mud, thick and slow after days of funneling her life energy into her painting. But it was there.

A drop slid down her hand and plopped to the ground, heavy. Dropping the letter opener into her pocket and cupping her hand to keep the blood in place, Artemisia stumbled to the window.

She dragged her palm across the rough stone of the windowsill. In the pale moonlight, her blood seemed black. Once the window was marked, she thrust her hands out again, letting them dangle in the open air.

With her head pressed against the wall so she could keep her hands as far out as she could reach, Artemisia stood quietly and felt the blood continuing to slip from the wound. There would be a puddle on the stone floor of the cloister, staining it until the next rainfall.

If Caccini and Lamberti finished their plans for the night, it wouldn't be the only blood staining the building.

She could hardly believe the recklessness of Lamberti's plan. Was he so desperate for attention that he would risk killing half the city?

Before Artemisia, he had stapled his identity to being an artist of the Accademia, and her presence had shattered his sense of self. In a way, he was fueled by the same terror as Artemisia. Artists were nothing but their reputation. But Artemisia's work had been smeared for months by bitter men. Lamberti's reputation had never been directly attacked; he felt threatened just by the possibility of being considered a woman's equal.

Lamberti's caustic energy would spread across the church, poisoning everyone inside. Depending on how vicious the fresco was, it could take them anywhere from ten minutes to a fortnight to die. If he had put even a drop more energy into the fresco than planned, the disease would spread beyond the walls.

The art world would never recover from a public attack like this. Not with Caccini's skilled rhetoric to fan the flames. The Grave Age would return to Europe.

And was she so different than them? Francesco had been right—she had been using magics she did not understand. There were unstable necrotic magics coating the painting of Judith and Holofernes, and an extra set of hair frantically woven in to confuse the target. If the painting went wrong, she could start her own plague.

Instead of planning for the future, she had been so terrified by the past and present that she had put her entire city at risk. She was not innovative or *brave* for planning a new form of murder. Every fool in history had tried to kill other people. She was no more special than her enemies.

Hot breath swirled around her exposed hands, and Artemisia straightened. Dry scales slid against her bloody palm, smoother than she had imagined. Carefully, she pulled her hands back and peered out of the narrow window.

As she'd hoped, the blood drake had smelled her and come to the scent of her bleeding hand—and the magics that pulsed through her veins. It watched her with bright yellow eyes, unreadable. It was massive in the small cloister, its sleek body twisted like a fallen scarf on the stone path beyond the office door.

She held up her palm again, and it stepped closer to her.

"Yes. Hello, beast. Stay right there," she murmured, reaching out and looping her bound hands over the blood drake's nearest horn. There was still a smear of dried blood on it from its fight with her griffon earlier that night. She prayed her companion was still alive out there, but she had to use any tool she could find.

The horn was as sharp as it looked, slicing through the ropes with only the slightest pressure. They fell to the ground, and she pulled her arms back through the window. Her wrists were red and sore.

"I don't suppose you know how to open doors?" she asked. The blood drake blinked at her, still watching her with fierce intensity.

With her hands free, she tried the door handle again, but the lock was firmly in place.

She went back to Caccini's desk, hoping against hope that she might find a spare key. Holding her bleeding palm close to her chest, she used her other hand to rifle through the fallen papers in case something else had fallen with them.

Then her eyes fell on the chair she'd sat in.

Gritting her teeth through the pain screeching through her bloody hand, she picked up the chair and swung it at the door handle. It clanged loudly, but the lock didn't give. "That man—" Artemisia growled, hitting the door again, "is not—" and again, "—beating me."

She brought down the chair once more, and with one final crash, the handle broke off. The heavy metal clattered to the floor, nearly landing on her slipper-clad foot.

The door swung open, and she pushed her way out into the cloister—directly in front of the blood drake. For a moment, she was still as they faced each other in the darkness. Its breath was so hot that the air steamed around the beast's snout as though it were winter rather than the middle of summer.

When painting blood drakes, the most popular motif was to show them locked in battle with a griffon. It was a metaphorical battle between good and evil, healing and illness, that Artemisia had seen in the flesh only hours earlier. Rarer were paintings where blood drakes were being ridden by humans or demons over vast battlefields, or in the fiery pits of hell. Was that only a symbol, part of the shared artist's imagery that had been repeated so often that it was accepted separate from reality?

Or could Artemisia hop astride that lithe, scaled back and escape Florence before the dawn came?

She would have to abandon her ill-planned revenge, but she would survive to fight another day. Perhaps Francesco would come to her when she found somewhere safe. She could leave behind Caccini and the memory of Tassi, and she and Francesco could get married somewhere far away and warm, like Naples.

Francesco might never forgive her for what she had nearly done, but she would not find out either way unless she escaped this massacre. She desperately wanted the chance to earn his trust again.

She placed a hand on the blood drake's horn. Riders were normally painted crouching on the blood drake's neck, though avoiding the spikes would be a challenge. It hissed, the sound vast and cavernous, but it did not protest.

Caccini's voice was bold as a trumpet from the cathedral as he began his speech. Dissatisfied with boasting to her, it seemed he was still going to give his sermon before he killed his guests. He was so confident that there was no one to stop his plans. He would ruin Florence, destroy art, all so he could grab more power.

What would she do in a world where Caccini succeeded and art was maligned once again? Her talents would be useless, and her fellow artists would be dodging mobs and state violence. Even if she could find happiness with Francesco, there would be no path forward for art.

And what would have happened if she had finished her curse against Tassi? How many future generations of women would have been locked out of the calling she loved so dearly?

Caccini was so sure Artemisia could not fight against him that he had left her unattended. He had chosen her as his target to satisfy Lamberti's petty bitterness, and had never once feared her.

If she remained in Florence rather than fleeing beyond the walls, she could reveal his plot to the world in the blood-drenched morning. She could make the world see who he truly was.

But no. That would be futile. Caccini would laugh at Artemisia's attempts to blame him for it all. With everyone else dead, it would be her word against his. He would point a finger at the blood drake on her roof, and no one would believe her. No one had *ever* believed her.

Caccini had not killed her yet because he was certain there was nothing she could do.

He had always underestimated her.

She would not let him win.

33

Artemisia ran for the church doors, fearing she was already too late.

She slid inside through the unguarded north transept. Caccini was standing in his marble pulpit, indulging in the sermon the gathered elite had been promised. On the scaffolding behind him, Lamberti worked to complete the cursed fresco.

"As Paolo Lamberti finishes the new crowning glory of Santa Maria Novella," Caccini was saying, "we are reminded that though the surface may change, the spirit of the Church is eternal. No matter the façade, no matter the art held inside that draws away attention, the Church is part of a single, great tree, and each individual cathedral is one of its many roots. That is why the Church is the only force that can hold this changing world together."

The Grand Duke and his wife stood in the front row, both impassive. There were other familiar faces in the crowd, men and women Artemisia had seen at Accademia events or at one of the Medici's parties. Some were as vile as Caccini, the type of men who gained their power by crushing those who couldn't fight back. Some were Artemisia's patrons, people she'd sold fragments of her life to over the years. Most had cancelled their commissions when Caccini tried to turn the world against her, but some were still watching his speech with contempt, muttering to their companions and frowning. They had not supported her in the face of controversy, but perhaps she could have earned their patronage again in the end. Men were often more cowardly than malicious.

If Caccini had his way, if Lamberti was allowed to finish that fresco, they would all die choking on blood and cursing art for ever existing.

Artemisia could shout to the assembled crowd and tell them to flee before Caccini's trap closed. Would anyone listen to her? The Grand Duke might take her side—or might try to hide the shame of his coercion. She and Caccini were infamous enemies. They would assume she was being vindictive. With Caccini's smooth rhetoric, he might convince them to ignore her while he found a way to silence her for good. Her voice meant nothing to these people.

Instead, Artemisia slunk through the shadows along the edge of the church, her heart pounding in her ears. Finally, she made her way to the edge of the church behind the altar, just under the wooden scaffolding. She craned her neck—Lamberti was focused on his work, sweat beading on his forehead as he completed the life-draining curse. He was in a painter's trance. Even if Artemisia shouted to distract him, he would likely stay enraptured until the fresco was complete.

Artemisia glanced around, and then hefted an iron candelabra. The candles on top flickered as the wound in her hand screamed in protest and she wobbled, but she gritted her teeth. She only had one chance.

Bending her knees for leverage, Artemisia swung the heavy candelabra into one of the posts of the scaffolding. A candle fell with the motion, rolling across the ground toward the closest table. The thin wooden beam she hit cracked on impact, and the entire structure tilted dangerously with a creaking groan.

There was a breathless moment where the scaffolding trembled. Artemisia skipped backward just as it crashed in a broken heap.

Lamberti hit the ground hard, and Artemisia leapt onto him without thinking, keeping him pinned flat on his back.

"It's the harlot Gentileschi!" Caccini roared. "She's trying to kill him!"

Underneath her, Lamberti's eyes were wide, the wind still knocked from his lungs. He had been injured in the fall—there was a thick, short gash across his cheek where he'd hit his face, and blood stained his sleeve from a cut on his wrist. She put her hands on his shoulders, shaking him slightly. "You would really kill all these people for him?" she demanded.

"You've never believed in anything," he said.

An acrid scent hit Artemisia's nose, making her look up. The fallen candle had set the nearest tablecloth on fire. The silk drape blazed, and the flames had already licked up to a framed painting on the wall above, curling the canvas and making the paint bubble as though it were alive.

The moment of distraction cost her.

Lamberti twisted beneath her, dislodging her unsteady grip. He was no longer a strong man, but her painting of Judith had sapped what strength she had. He lurched forward and sent her toppling backward, reversing their positions. Lamberti pinned her hands over her head, pushing her into the marble floor. She felt something heavy clang against the ground through her pocket— the letter opener. It was under his leg, though, and out of her reach.

Artemisia was gasping for air, though Lamberti had not injured her. Her lungs felt as though they had ceased to work as soon as Lamberti had climbed on top of her. The weight of his body was horrible and familiar, and she was helpless to fight it.

The gathered crowd noticed the spreading fire as well. "Everyone, out!" the familiar voice of the Grand Duke boomed. He was going to leave her there to make his escape.

Screams filled the room, and heels clattered on the tiles as people ran for the exit.

"You're ruining everything!" Lamberti snarled down at her.

She was so *weak*. She had poured her energy into her work, letting her body stay soft and complacent. Weak, just as she had always been. How had she thought she could fight them and win?

Lamberti and Caccini would make sure she died tonight for her interference. Art, the calling she had dedicated her life to, would be destroyed, and her enemies would succeed.

And she would never see Francesco again. That was the worst part of all. She would die, and the last memory Francesco would have of her was her rejecting his help. She would die with bare fingers, alone by her own design.

"Caccini is planning to kill you tonight," Artemisia blurted. Her hands shook as she tried to clench them into fists. She would fight back, even if she lost. She jerked against his hold, but though her muscles strained, she was held fast.

"He would never. This is the night of our great triumph," Lamberti said, as the flames danced behind him.

"It's murder, and Caccini won't let you live to tell anyone about what you've done here. He never wanted to help you. He wants to ruin us all."

"They'll remember me like San Donatello," Lamberti told her, eyes alight with the fire of fervor. "I'm changing Florence for the better. Putting the Church in charge again."

"You call yourself a saint? You're planning to kill a hundred people!"

"They have to die!" he shouted.

There was a gasp from the crowd. Some were still close enough to hear him.

"You don't understand," he continued. He glanced out at the crowd, then stared back down at her. He pressed down harder against her wrists, grinding them into the marble. The necrotic magics had left him gaunt, but he was unflinching. "I *will* be a saint. My soul won't be stained for this, not with the results. My fresco isn't a sin—it's just a weapon. You can't understand it."

"I do understand," Artemisia told him quietly. "I've been doing it too."

With a simple twist of her hand, she broke open the clotting wound in her palm, making it bleed sluggishly again. Then she reached up and grasped the wrist holding her hands in place, over his own injury. Their blood mingled, hot and slick.

"You've been spreading out your work, keeping your trail light," Artemisia snarled, lifting herself up to meet his alarmed gaze, "but there are far more dark magics in your veins than there are in mine. I met something tonight I believe will appreciate that."

Lamberti jerked away from her, eyes wide.

For a moment, she wondered if her idea had failed. No one knew much about the blood bonds, after all, and she was taking a leap in hoping at all.

But then there was a shriek from outside, and a stained-glass window burst into shards as the coiling mass of the blood drake flew inside. It bared long, yellow teeth as it roared. Unconcerned by the spreading fire, it twisted down toward them. Lit by the flicking flames, the blood drake looked like the Arno, dark and glinting.

A scream pierced the air from the fleeing crowd, crystalline in the smoky darkness.

Artemisia scrambled backward, freeing herself from Lamberti's loosened grip. Her hand throbbed, and her leather shoes had little traction on the tiles, but she was desperate to escape. Lamberti, on his knees, stared up at the blood drake in horror.

Without sparing a glance for Artemisia, the blood drake coiled around Lamberti. She'd been right—their blood bond had been new and weak, and the exposure to Lamberti's far more corrupted essence had shifted its fragile allegiance. Its grip on Lamberti was loose, protective, but Lamberti screamed as though he were being eaten alive.

"Enjoy what you've earned," she spat at him as she pushed herself to her feet. The smoke billowed toxic around them, making her cough. She needed to get out. Despite the church's marble frame, the fire was spreading at an alarming pace. At this rate, the building would be gutted within the hour.

She turned toward the door just in time to see Caccini lunging toward her. "You," he snarled.

Fingers fumbling, Artemisia grabbed the letter opener from her pocket and wielded it like a knife. Caccini pressed forward until she lashed out and stabbed his neck. The cut was shallow, but he stumbled back a step.

"Demon," he said, clutching the small wound on his neck.

"No," she said, panting. "Just a woman."

He examined the blood on his hand, dark in the firelight, but he was undeterred. He bore down upon her again, manic fury gleaming in his eyes, mouth slack in an undignified snarl. He moved like the wild boar on the mountain, feral and furious. He had lost his composure, his obsession with power and influence baring his most base self.

This madman had tried to destroy Galileo, destroy her, destroy the future of art. He was everything she hated about this world. If she had been quicker to finish her Judith, she could have killed him before tonight.

And she would have been just as broken as he was.

Caccini was a fool, the husk of a man so obsessed with winning a game of his own creation that he had gambled everything away. She loathed him, she pitied him, but she would not die for him—even in order to kill him.

"We need to get out of here before the building burns down around us," Artemisia said, tripping backward with the silver blade held in front of her. The smoke was thick in the air around them, suffocatingly hot.

He ignored her. "I was going to save this city!"

She felt the heat of the fire against her back as he pressed her deeper into the apse. The nearest door was in the transept she had first entered through, hidden by shadow and smoke, and they were getting further away from it. The flames had reached the necrotic fresco on the back wall, burning the paint and making the magics spill back into Lamberti before they could be unleashed on the world.

"Is this truly worth your life?" she asked, struggling for breath.

"I've *dedicated* my life to this," he shouted. "You won't take it from me."

There was a shrill cry as the blood drake unfurled from its place on the floor, carrying Lamberti in its talons straight up into the fire. The serpentine beast was wreathed in shadow above them. Then it slid through the broken stained glass, Lamberti tucked close to its scaled stomach.

As it left, its long tail dragged gently against the burning ceiling, like a lover with a farewell letter. Its dry scales cracked the fragile surface, raining a shower of burning plaster onto Artemisia and Caccini.

Artemisia lunged sideways, hampered by her gown, and ducked below the altar. An ember landed on her arm, scorching the fabric. She screamed and batted it with her other hand, burning her palm but extinguishing the flame. Plaster crashed onto the ground around the altar, narrowly missing her slipper.

Fire raged all around in an impenetrable cacophony. Hell surrounded her. This inferno was a nightmare made real.

When the worst of the avalanche stopped, she peered out through the smoke, coughing. Her eyes watered against the scalding heat and ash.

Where was Caccini? Her pulse pounded in her ears, terrified to find him grasping at her throat through the darkness.

A large piece of the plaster had crashed into the center of the apse. The rubble huddled on the floor like a crouching, smoldering beast.

A bright red robe was crushed beneath it, partially covering a pale hand.

Blood seeped into a black pool around the plaster. The hand did not move.

Caccini had been buried beneath the ruin of his own church.

Ducking her head, Artemisia half crawled, half ran through the burning building. The smoke clouded her vision, obscuring her way. She had only been in the church a few times, and in the chaos she did not know how to find safety. She might die here alongside Caccini, her life and legacy crushed in one ignoble moment. Another blazing chunk of plaster slammed into the ground in front of her, making her trip back. Her skin felt taut and scorched by the relentless, surrounding heat.

Finally, she found a solid wall. She shoved and pushed blindly, scraping her hands against the solid surface until she found a door.

Coughing, retching, she finally pushed out into the dark summer night.

34

After washing the soot from her skin and sleeping restlessly, Artemisia paced through her studio. Her nerves were still unsettled, and grew worse while she waited for a response to her early-morning messenger. The light was soft through her window, even as the summer heat began to grow with the sun's ascent. The knock came just as she was beginning to give up hope.

She lurched toward the door. After the chaos of the night before, she thought Francesco should look different, but it had only been twelve hours since he left her studio.

"I wasn't sure you would come," she said softly. Her throat was raw from the scorching smoke in the church.

"Neither was I," he said, but he was looking her over as though drinking in her appearance. "They're saying that you were in Santa Maria Novella when it burned last night."

"I was," she said.

"Were they really planning on killing those people?" he asked, and there was a glint of suspicion in his eyes that hit Artemisia like a knife. What did he believe her capable of? How far had she fallen that he thought she would—what, imagine the whole conspiracy? Create the necrotic fresco herself?

But was it so surprising, after his horror at her painting of

Judith the night before, that he might look at her the way she looked at Caccini?

"They were," she said. After Artemisia had fallen out into the street, she had been found by the officials responding to the fire. There had been mixed stories from the crowd inside—some echoed Caccini's claim that Artemisia had been trying to murder Lamberti, but others had overheard Lamberti's confession. Even more damning, many had seen the blood drake sweep inside and take Lamberti away. Though they had disappeared, their presence had convinced the authorities to believe Artemisia's side of the story. "Caccini told me himself," she told Francesco. "He was hoping to turn public opinion against art again, and take the power for himself."

She found herself crushed against his chest in a fierce hug. "Thank God you're all right," he said. "When I heard, I hoped it wasn't true. We could see the fire from my roof."

She hugged him back, desperately grateful.

"You still smell of smoke, Artemisia," he murmured into her hair.

"I'm all right," she assured him.

She melted into his hold, resting her head against his shoulder. When she finally pulled away, her eyes stung. "I'm sorry. I'm so sorry." She took a deep breath, pressing the edges of her fingers to her bottom lids, trying to force the tears to recede. "I asked you to come here to help me." She stepped back and pointed toward the cloth-covered painting standing the center of her studio. "I want to destroy it."

"You do?" Francesco's voice was careful, neutral. He may have been worried about her, but he did not trust her yet.

"Tassi destroyed my life in Rome. I don't have to give him—or anyone else—the power to do it here," Artemisia said. She stepped back and placed her hand on his face. He was warm and alive beneath her skin. "I can't shape my legacy if I'm dead. And I want to build a future with you."

"What about..." Francesco trailed off and pointed upward.

"Gone," Artemisia said. "I wasn't the most corrupt artist in that church last night. The blood drake found new loyalty. I expect Lamberti will be arrested soon, if he hasn't been already. I was lucky I was stopped in time, before the painting was finished and the blood drake was bound to me forever. I nearly destroyed everything I'd ever built." She searched his face. "Maybe I did destroy it. Have I lost you forever, vostra signoria?"

"Never," he said, and then his lips crashed down on hers. Compared to the cold that had hollowed her chest during her frantic painting over the last several weeks, the fire that blazed through her at his touch was a hearth in a long winter. "My love, my heart," he breathed into her ear, his hands hot on her hips. "You terrified me."

"I love you," she gasped, and let herself drown in him.

When they finally separated, they went to the covered painting with their hands intertwined. In the daylight, the red drape over the canvas seemed innocuous. If it hadn't been for the roiling dark magics staining the air around it, the painting might have seemed no different than anything else in her studio. Even unreleased, though, the necrotic energy was tangible.

Artemisia carefully removed the cloth, draping it over a nearby stool. The painting she had poured her soul into—every drop of her hatred and rage and grief—since she had come to Florence was stunning in the morning light. "This may be my best work," Artemisia said quietly, running a finger along the edge of the canvas.

"It may be," Francesco agreed, voice cautious. Perhaps he still did not trust her to follow through. "Is there a way to drain the magics without destroying it? It is…beautiful, despite it all."

She turned back to him and pressed a kiss to his lips. "No," she said, "but I appreciate the thought." She looked at the lush, bloody painting of Judith and Holofernes, the art she thought would be her path to revenge. "I have to burn it."

After seeing Santa Maria Novella gutted the night before, Artemisia was unwilling to bring any flame into her studio. Instead, she and Francesco climbed to the roof. With the caustic magics spilling out dangerously, Artemisia carried the canvas while Francesco followed her up the ladder. After the events of the last month, she was unsteady on her feet, but felt secure with Francesco at her back.

In the morning light, the blood spilled during the fight between her griffon and the blood drake was dark against the terracotta.

"Do you think it will come back?"

Which did he mean? Either way, Artemisia thought the answer was the same. "No," she said quietly. "I don't."

She held the painting stretched aloft as Francesco pulled the flint and steel from his pocket. Of the three figures in the painting, only Tassi's face looked out at her, fighting against the blade cutting his throat. In burning this effigy, she was ensuring that the man would never be brought to true justice.

Artemisia swallowed and looked out over the city. There was a still a haze of smoke in the air to the south. Tassi was not worth her life.

Francesco struck the flint once, twice, and then sparks sprayed onto the oil-soaked canvas. The fire caught and spread quickly, ravaging the paint. Once she was sure the flame was strong enough, she dropped the canvas onto the rooftop, where it curled and twisted until there was nothing left but ashes, flaking into the morning air.

Her spent magics rushed back to her, swirling through the air and into her body as soon as their bonds with the canvas were severed. Artemisia gasped, back bowing as she struggled to stand under the onslaught. She had never undone the magics of a painting so close to completion before. The power flooded back into her veins like the Arno in a storm, filling her veins to bursting.

The tang of the magics was acrid, but nowhere near as poisonous as they would have been if they had reached their intended targets. After a moment, as the power settled down inside of her, it blended with her life force once again, shedding its threads of malice. It was like stepping into the sunshine on the first day of spring, the warmth of her returned magics revitalizing her down to her bones.

Artemisia took a step back, and Francesco caught her arm to stabilize her before she could lose her balance on the steep tiles.

Had she truly been prepared to give so much energy to her enemies? It felt as though her entire life had been inside that painting, and she was only able to see how weak she had let herself become now that her energy had returned. Her body felt more grounded, as did her thoughts.

She had nearly lost everything, but it wasn't gone yet.

Perhaps she would never truly be free of the questing roots of her past, but she had to press forward.

Artemisia took a deep breath, letting the warmth of the summer morning fill her lungs. Smoke laced the air, both from her destroyed painting and the remains of Santa Maria Novella, but there was a fresh breeze coming from the west.

It smelled of the heat of sun-warmed tiles and the bright vitality of the city's orange groves.

*

"I leave you alone for two weeks, and you burn down Santa Maria Novella," Maurizio groused as soon as he came into her studio.

Artemisia laughed, shaking her head. "Perhaps you should stop leaving me alone," she suggested. It hadn't been Maurizio's fault, of course. In her drive to finish the painting of Judith and Holofernes, she had not reached out to anyone. She had been sure she would die, and now it was impossible to be weighed down by seriousness with her friend in front of her again.

He gave her an assessing look as they sat down at her table. "You look better than I expected. Better than last time, at least."

The magics returned from the destroyed painting had given Artemisia lasting energy. Her hands stayed steady, her skin blushed more easily, and her heart had slowed from its light, frenetic buzz. "You flatter me," she said, pouring them both cups of strong tea. "How is Gabriele?"

"He's fine. He'll be better when the Medici overturn the laws they passed for Caccini. Florence still needs putting back to rights," Maurizio said, distracted. He glanced around the studio, his eyes searching. "Have you done it?"

She stilled and set down the pot. "I nearly did," she said. "The hair you collected for me was all I needed to finish it."

"But?"

"It was killing me, Maurizio."

He picked up his ceramic cup and stared down at the dark tea. "Did you know? Did you know it might when you sent me to get his hair?"

Artemisia hesitated. She had, of course, though she'd hoped it wouldn't. The risk had seemed inconsequential when she'd been hunting her revenge. "Yes," she said finally.

"Damn it, Artemisia," Maurizio growled. "You didn't think I should know that before I helped you?" He ran his hand through his hair. "This is why Elisabetta was mad at me."

"Elisabetta?" Artemisia shook her head. "So, you'd help me commit murder, but not suicide? That's a flexible moral code."

"Is it so hard to understand? He deserves to die. You don't. You can't make me responsible for my friend's death. You don't get to do that to me." He shook his head. "We shouldn't make our enemies' lives easier by killing ourselves. That helps them win."

"I know," Artemisia huffed. "I did tell you that I stopped. I destroyed the painting yesterday morning. Agostino Tassi is safe from me. I hate it, but I have to accept it. The cost of killing him is too great."

"So, what now? You go back to draining out your soul with healing magics? The necrotic kind seem to work faster, but they're the same for the artist in the end." He slammed his cup down. "I'm tired of seeing you hurt yourself."

"Art is everything to me. It makes me special." Artemisia ran a hand through her hair. A bundle of strands came away at her touch like cobwebs. It would take time for it to heal fully after the intensive month of work on her Judith. "But you're right. I've been throwing my life into the hands of men like Silvestrini and Michelangelo for as long as I can remember, but they'll drop me as soon as it suits them. I give everything, but they're the ones with the power."

"You have the power to stop."

She scoffed. "I can't live a life without painting. What's the alternative? Find other work? Let Francesco pay me to fill his house with my canvases?"

"I don't know the answer, but you nearly *died* from this," he said. "I understand why you hate him, and I still don't think it was worth your life. How can you justify more of it? Is impressing

some stranger in France really as important to you as killing
Tassi? If Tassi isn't worth your life, why are your clients? Either
way, you're dying for someone else."

"I'm more careful with healing magics. I know how to siphon
off just enough," Artemisia protested. "Not all artists die young."

"Too many do," Maurizio said.

"Your job is not so safe either."

"After what you've just done, you don't get to point fingers
at anyone else for at least a year. Did you think about what your
death would have done to us? To me? To Elisabetta? She's already
lost so much. To Francesco? That man loves you. You nearly
threw that all away for your enemies."

She sighed. "This isn't the first time I've gotten this lecture."

"Francesco?" When she nodded, he scoffed. "That man
couldn't scold a kitten."

She waved a hand and settled back in her chair with her tea.
"Proceed, then."

Much changed in the week after the destruction of Santa Maria
Novella. Artemisia had gone from a pariah to the woman invited
to every gathering. The church had been filled with the city's
elite, making her the most talked-about person in Florence. She
declined most invitations. She was still shaken by everything—
her near fall into sin, Lamberti's dark fresco, Caccini's lunacy
—and did not need gossips haranguing her for details.

One of the many invitations had been from Michelangelo,
groveling for forgiveness. He had publicly taken the wrong side
in the fight, and hoped for her to help him regain his standing.
She had taken satisfaction in burning the letter.

She was becoming fond of the scent of smoke.

However, when Galileo sent an invitation for her to escape Florence for a day to visit him in the countryside, Artemisia gratefully accepted. Francesco let her borrow his private coach, kissing her fondly as she left.

Galileo's house sat at the top of a hill, providing an ideal view of the heavens. She could see from the window of the coach an array of telescopes on the roof. To someone who had only ever lived in a city, it seemed isolated, but after recent events she understood the appeal. Society was exhausting, and Galileo's mind needed space to sprawl.

They ate on his balcony. His cook made a simple meal of fluffy pastry stuffed with herbed quail. The early September air was slightly less oppressive in the countryside than in Florence. She directed the conversation toward his research—he was still looking at the sky, searching for moons an eternity away. He spoke of his discoveries with passion, but also weariness. "Every step I take forward is bringing me closer to the Inquisition again," he said. "They can force me to stop writing or teaching about heliocentrism explicitly, but I can't ignore the fabric of our universe. Everything in the heavens is tied together—I cannot look to Jupiter without considering the sun."

"I know better than to ask if you will ever stop studying the stars," Artemisia said.

He nodded. "No more than you would ever put down your paintbrush. I fear it is only a matter of time before they launch another attack against me. I hope that the recent exposure of one of my harshest critics will delay that moment."

Artemisia sighed, drumming her fingers on her plate. "I suppose you want to talk about Caccini?"

"We don't need to," he said. "Be assured I felt just as much grief about his passing as you did."

She laughed quietly. "It's still unbelievable."

"What happened at Santa Maria Novella will change more than people have realized yet. A member of the Church conspiring to use necrotic art to steal power? The implications for art are dramatic enough, but the implications for the Church? For Florence? The ripples may be felt for generations."

Artemisia could barely think of it. They had been lucky to escape without falling into another Grave Age. "They were only two men," she said.

"Two men who together represented an unreasonable amount of power," Galileo said. "It does not take more than that to change the world. I said once that you were a revolutionary. I hope you've seen how wide your impact could be. You are in a position to make changes."

"There are things that should be different, but I wouldn't know where to start," she said. "I barely know what to do with myself."

"You are young still," he said, and stared out over the rolling hills around them.

She tilted her head, considering him. "There's still something you want to discuss."

"You've known me a long time," he said.

"You think loudly," she countered, tipping her wine cup at him.

He laughed, but his expression grew quickly solemn. "I've just received a letter from my friend Cigoli in Rome. He's closely involved in both the worlds of art and mathematics. This news he's given me... it relates to you. I know you don't have many friends left in Rome, and may not have learned yet." He searched her face. "Do you know what I'm referring to?"

She shook her head, anxiety clutching at her stomach.

"Agostino Tassi is dead."

Artemisia's hands spasmed, and her cup clattered to the table.

Dead? Had something gone wrong with the destruction of her painting of Judith? She had thought she felt the power return to her, but she had never played with such magics before.

"They believe it was natural causes—drink, or perhaps a disease," he continued. "He died in his home."

She swallowed with difficulty. "When?"

"It took days for anyone to notice he had died. They found him when he did not appear for Mass. It would have been just before your troubles at Santa Maria Novella." He held up his hands. "I'm certain you are curious for more details, but that is all I know so far."

Before she had gone to Santa Maria Novella. Before she had destroyed the painting of Judith and Holofernes. Her necrotic magics had still been stuck inside her canvas.

It could not have been her fault, even accidentally.

It seemed impossible to believe that her enemy of all these years had perished in Rome without her knowledge—or involvement. It had always seemed as though their fates were tied, no matter how many kilometers separated them.

Emotions churned in her chest, but she felt mostly numb.

"Artemisia?" Galileo prompted quietly. "I wasn't sure I should tell you."

"No, no," she said. "Thank you."

She waited to feel something, anything, but her chest stayed hollow.

35

The doors of the Palazzo Pitti opened for her without a fuss. The guard on duty, the same one who had previously turned her away, bowed as she walked through. A servant led her down the familiar halls she thought she would never see again.

She had continued ignoring many of the invitations that had come her way. There were still too many people desperate for gossip or to use her fame for their own gain. After her visit with Galileo in the countryside, she had felt even less connected to the bustling of Florence. She was a tool they either overused or discarded based on their whims.

Galileo had only been the first to tell her of Tassi's death. Francesco had his own contacts in Rome, and had apparently long since asked for any news regarding Agostino Tassi. All reports confirmed Galileo's statement—Tassi had died before Artemisia had gotten close to finishing her painting. Life was beginning to feel like a strange dream. Artemisia wanted to lock herself away in her studio or Francesco's villa until surprises stopped coming.

Still, she could not refuse the Medici seal.

On display at the front of the central gallery stood a familiar painting on an easel. Artemis and her hounds looked out at Artemisia as she passed.

Madama Cristina was waiting in her office, standing behind her desk as Artemisia entered. "The woman of the hour," she said. "It's good to see you well."

"I'm glad you've returned," Artemisia said, kissing her hand and then sitting across from her. Though Madama Cristina had spent the last weeks in San Piero a Sieve, where the Grand Duke had sent her to keep her out of Lamberti's hands, she was paler than ever. Recent events had taken their toll.

"As am I. The countryside did not agree with me. I'd much rather be here. It's not time for me to retire yet," she said. "My son and his wife have told me all about what you did at Santa Maria Novella. They were lucky to have you there to protect them. You've always been loyal to this family."

Though they had not been loyal to her. "Of course, Madama."

"Unlike that Lamberti. Coercing my family with dark magics." She shook her head. "I should have known. I saw that my son was acting out of the normal, but I could not imagine something like this."

"What of the laws passed for Caccini's sake?" Artemisia asked.

"They're all being put back to rights. The Accademia will take full power of itself again, and the harsh restrictions on our citizens will be undone. We will all need time to recover from what Caccini and Lamberti did, but the city will be healed. Thanks to you."

"You flatter me."

"I was blind. I should have known my son would not truly support a man like Caccini. He's always been open-minded. Lamberti made him fear for his life, though, and he could not risk himself and his wife."

"Of course not," Artemisia said, her smile as wooden as a

marionette. How many people might have died for the Grand Duke? Not only in the massacre at Santa Maria Novella, but through Caccini's draconian laws. Caccini had told her the portraits Lamberti had used to threaten them had been fake. With all his magics pouring into the fresco at Santa Maria Novella, he could not have wasted a drop on an empty threat. If the Medici had been less concerned with their legacy, more willing to risk themselves or ask for help, the entire mess could have been avoided.

"They want to thank you themselves," Madama Cristina said.

The door to the office opened, and Cosimo II and his wife, Maria Maddalena, stepped inside. Artemisia stood up again to curtsy. "Your Graces."

"Artemisia Gentileschi," the Grand Duke said.

"The savior of Florence. You were so brave," Maria Maddalena said, putting a hand to her heart. "With the fire, and that horrible blood drake... It was all too much. When you showed up, I knew you'd save us."

Artemisia glanced at Cosimo. Had he told his wife that he had first rejected Artemisia's help in favor of protecting his reputation? "Of course, Your Grace."

"We must thank you, signorina," the Grand Duke said. "Without you, we'd have all been killed. Instead, Caccini is dead, and Lamberti will soon follow."

"The honor was mine." The niceties grated on Artemisia's tongue. It was all fake. He had left her to fend for herself. If Caccini's plot had not been revealed, would he have stepped in if Artemisia had been put on trial by the Church? To satisfy Lamberti and to distract the populace, Caccini could have had her sentenced to death. What did she matter to the grand legacy of the Medici?

"We would like to grant you an exciting new commission," the Grand Duke continued. "It's important for us to show that we're moving on past Lamberti and Caccini, and there is no artist in Florence who deserves immortalizing more than you right now. Your legacy is secured. Who knows—perhaps one day you will be Santa Artemisia!"

"I doubt that will happen," she said. "I haven't done any miracles."

"Still, you'll be one of the most famous artists of our age. The magics of our entrance hall have long-since faded, but our guests should be gifted with healing as they step into our palace. We want to have you do the new design. The whole entry hall, floor to ceiling." He smiled. "When people enter the Medici Palace, they will see Artemisia Gentileschi."

"Did the Medici apologize?" Francesco asked that night. They were at his villa, eating a fine dinner of fresh oysters and roasted pheasant in his private quarters. She had been spending less and less time in her flat since the night of Santa Maria Novella's destruction. The empty corner where her dark painting had once sat was only overshadowed by her empty rooftop. The absences were too loud.

"They did," Artemisia said. "Madama Cristina, the Grand Duke, *and* the Archduchess. They asked me to paint the new entry hall at the Palazzo Pitti."

He beamed and raised his cup in a toast. "Congratulations, my heart!"

"I turned them down."

Francesco blinked, clearly stunned. "What?" He shook his head. "I know you're angry with them, but this is everything you've worked for. Forget the Medici—think of every person who will walk through that palace and see your work. You'll be famous."

"I know, but I've been thinking a lot lately. All these years, I've been giving my life to everyone who asks, and even to those who haven't. There's not enough of me to hand around. The Medici don't *need* my soul to survive. The Grand Duke would never have looked twice at me if I hadn't been so public in saving them. And—I can't commit to another project so soon after nearly dying. I want to be here for a long time, Francesco. Here with you."

"I can't argue with that," he said, passing her another oyster from the platter on the table. "I have to admit I'm surprised they didn't throw you in a cell after. People like that don't like being told no."

"They weren't happy, but they can't afford to start another campaign against me so soon. The Grand Duke's reputation took a blow from having to announce that he was being bullied for so long. For once, they need *my* reputation, instead of the other way around. They want me to redeem their image after the disaster with Lamberti. Somehow, my name has more value than theirs right now. I don't want to use that for their benefit. This is a moment I can make a difference."

"So what will you do?"

"I asked them to fund a new chapel in Santa Croce," she said. "I've never done a fresco, but I can paint a powerful oil painting. Maurizio's neighborhood has been neglected too long. It's a better use of their money and my energy than a vanity piece in their front hall. Santa Maria Novella is going to set trust in artists back decades, but we can show the people that we can help them. I considered suggesting one in Oltrarno in Luco's memory, but

Elisabetta would have taken my head off. The Medici agreed to the idea, though I thought the Grand Duke's smile would fall off. They still want their name tied to mine, even if it's not how they planned."

"And after that's complete? Will you go back to searching for clients?"

"I don't know," she admitted. "Art is all I've ever done. I'm sure I'll have to start work again soon." The Accademia would certainly be eager for her to publicly represent them again, despite nearly abandoning her for Lamberti's sake. The Accademia leaned on her for glory, even as they kept their membership restrictively exclusive and hoarded art in their cellar. How could she balance her love for art with her despair at the politics?

"You don't *have* to."

"Francesco."

"Artemisia," he countered. "You know I have the money to support us both."

"All I've ever wanted was to paint," she said.

"You can still paint," he said. "I can afford the best canvases and pigments in the world. I've already been working on having a studio added to the villa, for when you move in. You could sit and paint all day long, and not have to spend a speck of magics you don't want to."

"I can't stop chasing my legacy because I'm tired. I don't want to be known only as the woman who stopped Caccini. I'm an artist. I want my work to stand on its own. I've worked too hard for anything else."

"Then take the commissions you want. You can pick and choose the projects that speak to you, and never work for men like Silvestrini again." He reached across the table to hold her hand. "I would have offered this before, if I'd thought you would listen. I know the drive that pushes you. But if there's a way I can ease your path, I want to do it. What else is my money for? I can help make sure you live a long life. That's all I want."

"It doesn't seem fair with other artists starving and bleeding for their work," she said. "They'll say I had it easier."

"You know they'll say whatever pleases them, no matter what you do," Francesco said. "There's no law that you have to suffer for your art."

"It seems too good to be true," she said. "You're a businessman—you know what they say about deals like that."

"It's not a deal. It's a gift."

Artemisia stroked his palm, tracing the broad width and following the curve up to his long fingers. "I'm not sure I could live with myself."

"Think about it. There's no rush." He lifted her hand to kiss her knuckles. His lips lingered on the gimmel ring.

The next night, Artemisia set a piece of paper on Francesco's desk. He looked up from his ledgers, blinking to refocus.

His study was a beautiful room in his private quarters filled with dark woods and the art he loved too much to place in the larger gallery. A self-portrait of Artemisia hung in a gilded frame behind his desk. In it, she was wearing a green dress, focused on an unseen canvas with a brush in her hand. The chain of her dangling amulet followed the swell of her breast.

She propped her hip against the edge of his desk. "I have no loyalty to the Accademia. They don't need me. I've struggled enough for a lifetime. I don't need to throw myself onto a pyre for their sake."

"Excellent," he said.

"But," she said, tapping a finger on the paper in front of him, "I can't stop thinking of the other women who will never have my chances. Elisabetta was right about me. I had to accept so much of their prejudices to shave myself into someone who would fit in with them. I thought I was different from other women, better than other healers. But my father was an artist. What if he hadn't had the knowledge and resources to train me? What if I had been forced into marrying that scum Tassi, or sent away to a convent?" She sighed. "Tassi is dead, but there are still too many women ruined by the demands of men. I can start fighting for the women who can't."

After Francesco confirmed Tassi's death, they had rarely spoken of it. Her feelings were complex, and her Judith was still heavy in the air between her and Francesco. She was grateful Tassi was dead. He had harmed too many people, and did not deserve to breathe. But she had long imagined that his demise would somehow erase the past.

His death had not brought her peace.

Francesco nodded and picked up the paper. "A noble cause. So, what is this?"

"I've done some calculations. I'll still take the commissions that excite me. I have my pick of them, after Santa Maria Novella, and I could no more put down my brush than cut off my arm. I'll stay a member of the Accademia, see what I can change from the inside. But I want to take time each week to teach at a convent outside of Florence. I thought I'd start with the one Galileo's daughters are at. Who knows—perhaps I'll find another female artist or two within its walls. Who knows what is hiding in women who were never given the chance to try?"

If she had succeeded in her revenge, she might have created

another generation too angry and scared to give women the chances they deserved. Now, she would leave a different legacy.

"I'll ask the convent if they can give me a stipend, but they may not have any funds. This," she said, nodding to the paper, "is how much money I believe I would still bring in from my art, even if the convent can't give me a single baiocco."

She waited while he reviewed the paper. He was silent for a long moment as he read it over.

"My commissions will fund their own supplies, but I'll need more paints and canvases to practice. Fewer than I used to, I suppose, without the griffon here." She paused, mourning its loss. There had still been no sign of it, more than two weeks after its fight with the blood drake. She had thought through every possibility, and all had gutted her. "But there will be a cost. You can say no. I am not marrying you for your money, my love."

"You truly believe I would say no to you?" he asked, putting down the paper.

"Most wives would help with your business or be an expert in managing a household. I will be busy with my own work. I'll be taking your money."

"Most wives are not successful artists. I love you because of your passion, not in spite of it," he said. He pulled her down for a kiss, rustling the books on his desk. "I thought I would lose you. To keep you safe, I would do far more than this."

"I love you," she whispered against his mouth.

Later that week, Artemisia sat with Elisabetta in the shade outside their usual bar by the Ponte di Rubaconte. There was a breeze sweeping through the street from the river. Fall was on its way.

"How was your trip?" Artemisia asked, accepting a goblet of

red wine from the waitress. Elisabetta had been out of town since she barged into Artemisia's apartment to yell at her. She had sent a note earlier in the week saying that she was back, but Artemisia had been pulled in all directions by those wanting her attention.

Elisabetta took a sip from her cup and leaned back in her chair. "Productive." She waved her goblet in the air, gesturing toward the west where the remains of Santa Maria Novella were being canvassed before its reconstruction. "I've heard that you've been, too. Your enemies are gone, your name is redeemed. Certainly a change since the last time we met." She looked over Artemisia as though cataloging her fuller cheeks and brighter eyes. Apparently satisfied, she drawled, "You're the biggest story of the century. Everyone is talking about you—and that artist, Lamberti. It seems every person I talk to saw him fly away on his blood drake, even when I know full well they were on the other side of the river."

"The blood drake will be resting on the top of the prisons until Lamberti is executed, now that they've found him," Artemisia said. The gory details of his coming punishment were being discussed by the city in delighted whispers. Lamberti had personally targeted nearly every person in power in Florence—there would be no escaping his sentence.

Though she'd imagined a hundred bloody demises for Lamberti, her narrow avoidance of the same fate soured her vindictive joy. With her amulet broken and her own necrotic painting burned, Artemisia prayed the blood drake would not attempt to find her after its bond with Lamberti was drawn and quartered along with the man.

"You have everything you wanted," Elisabetta said. "Are you already on to your next project?"

She shook her head. "I need time to heal myself before I pour out my soul again."

Elisabetta raised her eyebrows in surprise. "This is a new stance."

"Things have changed recently."

"Good for you," she said, raising her goblet. Her sharp eyes examined Artemisia's face. "So—why don't you look happy?"

"I am happy. It's only... We talked once about a man who had hurt me in my youth. I've relied on my hatred of him for a long time, even when I was determined to move past it. I always thought, in the end, it would come down to him and me again. I thought he'd haunt me forever, that I would be fighting against him the rest of my life. For a long time, I thought I might be the one to kill him. I thought his death would solve all my problems. I've just learned that he died."

"Oh, did he?" Elisabetta asked mildly, taking a sip from her goblet. "What a shame."

Artemisia stared at her friend, goblet slack in her hand. "Your trip," she said slowly. "Where did you say you went?"

What was it that Maurizio had said? That Elisabetta had known why he had gone to Rome, and had been angry with him?

"The last time we spoke, you seemed like you were about to do something stupid," Elisabetta said.

"I was," Artemisia admitted carefully.

"I know. You've spent too long handling everything on your own, Artemisia. You're a good girl. You didn't need Agostino Tassi's death on your conscience."

"Maurizio told you what I was planning?" Artemisia asked with a pang of betrayed hurt.

"No. I figured it out. I've known your story for a long time. When I saw you that day, I knew something was coming. I'm not a fool. I told you about the witch I once saw who had nearly killed herself with dark magics. You looked just like her," Elisabetta said. "I lost one person this year. I wasn't going to lose you to yourself."

"Elisabetta," Artemisia said, at a loss for words.

Elisabetta shrugged. "You were right, what you said before. There's no punishment for men like that. Until there is."

Artemisia leaned forward across the table. "Tell me you didn't go to Rome."

"I needed some new ingredients. Very rare."

"Elisabetta," she said, putting a hand to her chest. She was stunned, but moreso she was moved. In her darkest moment, when she had thought herself friendless, Elisabetta had been taking care of her.

"It needed to be finished, but you couldn't do it. It's like I said the first time we met," she said, taking a sip of her wine. "Art is not the best way to get things done, and I'm very good at what I do."

EPILOGUE

Few things tasted better than tart gelato on a warm Florentine evening.

Artemisia and Francesco strolled on the stone path along the Arno as they ate. Between them, their hands were linked. Artemisia could feel the ridge of the gimmel ring on his finger pressing into hers.

The Ponte Vecchio arched over the river in front of them, painted in pastels as soft as the gelato in their hands. The streets were busy with people taking advantage of the pleasant autumn evening, enjoying the final bit of light before the sun set. Someone bumped into Artemisia on the sidewalk, but she just shuffled sideways to walk more closely with Francesco.

"Galileo's daughters are as clever as their father," she said. "So many of the girls in the convent are bright as can be. I don't believe I was half as sharp at their age."

"I doubt that very much," Francesco said.

"We're still testing to find if any have magics—it's a long process, especially since they're all starting so late in life. I was finally able to convince Elisabetta to come teach her herbal healing arts." Perhaps one day she could convince Elisabetta to help her test her theory about the potential magics in her work as well. "She'll start next week. The girls will love her, and it will be good for her to leave the city for a bit." Artemisia had not told Francesco about Elisabetta's mission in Rome. It was a secret she would carry for Elisabetta to her grave.

"Those girls really will be sharp, with the two of you as teachers," Francesco laughed. "How are the new commission designs going?"

"I think these will be some of my best work. It'll take longer than it once would have, but I believe people will wait for an Artemisia Gentileschi painting," she said. The story of the fight at Santa Maria Novella was spreading internationally. With fewer projects in her queue and the return of the energy from her necrotic painting, her creativity was sharper than ever. She felt as though designs were flowing from her fingertips, tripping out of her onto her sketch pages.

"They'll be fighting to offer you the best ideas and positions," Francesco said. "I'm glad I got to you before you became in such high demand."

"I know how you hate to wait in line."

"You couldn't have bumped me to the top of the queue?"

Artemisia tilted her head. "No, I think you'd have to wait your turn."

Francesco gasped dramatically. "My own love," he said. He used their clasped hands to turn her toward the river. "You know, I saw the Grand Duke marry his wife right here, eight years ago now. They built a temporary island in the middle of the river so everyone could see, and put grandstands all along these paths. There was a play about Jason and the Golden Fleece. They had constructed blood drakes swimming through the river that spat out real fire."

Artemisia looked out over the sparkling river, imagining the scene, and then glanced back up at Francesco. "Is this a hint about what you want our wedding to look like?"

"Well, with a clever artist for a wife, surely we can come up with a story a bit more original than the Golden Fleece," Francesco said.

"I'm sure we can," she agreed, leaning up to kiss him.

The sun was just beginning to set, the light stretching out over the city like a benediction. The shadows grew longer, but the day would hold them off for a little while yet. The sunset glinted off the towering Duomo, painting its red roof golden.

Far overhead, a griffon with a scarred wing soared below the clouds.

AUTHOR'S NOTE

Despite the magical lens of this novel, the story of a young woman being attacked and violated, only to be retraumatized through a gruelling trial—both in a court and through public opinion—is not limited to history. Aly Raisman. Simone Biles. Chanel Miller. Dr. Christine Ford. For every name you know, there are countless you do not. The crimes never reported, or never tried, or never convicted.

This book is fiction. Not only did I give a historical figure the power to heal illness, I gave her a tool for revenge. Most women, like Artemisia, do not see true justice in the court of law. Despite that betrayal, despite their rage, their pain, and their fear, they do not often have the cinematic showdown we see in movies. Artemisia was not a warrior. According to her testimony, she threw a knife at Tassi's chest after the crime but could not kill him. Her revenge would not be by her own hand. But if she'd had an avenue with her art…?

It is a fantasy to imagine that painting, writing, or drawing could give us physical revenge as we express our pain. But I do believe there's power in art.

So many brave voices have spoken out eloquently and powerfully about sexual assault, violence, and rape culture. I recommend supporting organizations like RAINN and exploring books like *The Reckonings* by Lacy M. Johnson and *Know My Name* by Chanel Miller, among many others.

ACKNOWLEDGEMENTS

First, I owe so much to the centuries of scholars who have written about Artemisia Gentileschi and this time period. I am especially grateful for the book *Artemisia* by Letizia Treves, in conjunction with the exhibit at the National Gallery in London, which features closeups of Artemisia's paintings and scans of her letters to Francesco.

Thank you to my agent Michael Carr for believing in this story. Thank you to my editor Davi Lancett, my talented cover designer Julia Lloyd, and the entire team at Titan Books for working to get this book out into the world.

Since I started writing this book in 2018, my friends have continuously supported both me and the project, and I have endless thanks for them. Katherine, for being my rock for more than two decades. Anna, for bringing the light and energy of a star into my life. Shae, for grounding and encouraging me. Lu, for helping me navigate our parallel publishing tracks with humor. Thank you to the FYA ladies for all your love over the years.

And, always, thank you to Mom, Dad, Clint, Jenna, Paul, and Emily for being the most supportive family I could ask for.

ARTEMISIA GENTILESCHI:
THE HISTORY

In 2020, a terrible explosion rocked a port in Beirut, killing hundreds. In the rubble, a damaged painting which had been hung anonymously was assessed by an art restorer—and attributed to Artemisia Gentileschi. After her death, much of Artemisia's work was lost or misattributed, and her story was brushed aside for centuries. This discovery was particularly dramatic, but demonstrates that there are certainly still more paintings and history for scholars to uncover.

Though magics have changed the fabric of the world in *A Portrait in Shadow* and parts of the timeline are streamlined for the narrative, many of the events are deeply based on history. Artemisia was an incredible artist and woman, and her life continued on well past the fantastical events in this book.

Artemisia's youth was spent in Rome. She was born in 1593 to the painter Orazio Gentileschi and his wife Prudentia. Artemisia began working in her father's studio around age seven and was considered his equal in art by seventeen. In 1611, her father hired his friend Agostino Tassi to tutor her, but Tassi later raped Artemisia in her home. After a long, arduous trial, during which Artemisia was tortured with the sibille to confirm her honesty, Agostino Tassi was found guilty and sentenced to banishment. His sentence was never enforced.

Due to the ruinous damage to her reputation, Artemisia was

quickly married off to a middling painter named Pierantonio Stiattesi, and they moved to Florence in 1613. Their first child was born later that year. Only one of their children survived infancy—her daughter Prudentia.

In Florence, Artemisia's career blossomed. She befriended Galileo Galilei, secured the patronage of the Medici, and was commissioned for the new Casa Buonarroti by Michelangelo the Younger. (Her nude *Allegory of Inclination* really was covered with a modesty cloth, though not until 1684.) In 1616, Artemisia became the first female member of Florence's lauded Accademia delle Arti del Disegno.

Then, in 1618, Artemisia met the wealthy young merchant Francesco Maria Maringhi, and they began a passionate love affair. Letters from Artemisia to Francesco discovered in 2011, affectionately addressed to Vostra Signoria, reveal a blunt, fiery eroticism. Her husband was quite aware of the affair—the letters from Artemisia were often capped by footnotes from him asking Francesco for money.

Artemisia continued to paint for the rest of her life, spending time in Rome, Venice, London, and Naples. Her husband disappears from the historical record by 1623, and she continued to exchange love letters with Francesco until he moved to join her in Naples, where scholars believe they may have secretly married. Over the years, Artemisia worked for some of the most well-regarded patrons in Europe, leaving behind an oeuvre of powerful paintings which have stood the test of time.

Such lasting triumph was not to be found for her friend Galileo. As in this story, Tomasso Caccini delivered a controversial sermon against Galileo at Santa Maria Novella in 1614. The subsequent 1615 trial in Rome was not the last. In 1633, the Inquisition launched another investigation, and this time they forbade any of Galileo's works past or present from being published. He was sentenced to house arrest, where he remained until his death in 1642.

His death marks the beginning of the end of this story. Agostino Tassi died a few years later in 1644. Tomasso Caccini died in 1648 after using his public opposition against Galileo to gain professional success. Artemisia's death was unrecorded, though scholars believe she was the victim of a plague outbreak in the mid-1650s.

For centuries, Artemisia Gentileschi was underappreciated by historians and art critics, but she has found new fame in the past decades. The first exhibit dedicated entirely to Artemisia's work was hosted at Casa Buonarroti in 1991. Slowly, Artemisia is gaining the legacy for which she fought.

READING GROUP
DISCUSSION GUIDE

1. Artemisia Gentileschi was born in 1593. Why do you think she's left such an impact so many centuries later? Had you heard of her before reading *A Portrait in Shadow*?

2. Art is mostly reserved for the wealthy and influential—despite (or because of) its connection to the artists' healing magics. How does the hoarding of money, power, health, and beauty affect the characters and society in the book?

3. Jarvis filled the story with Artemisia's historical friends, colleagues, and enemies, but also added working class characters like Maurizio and Elisabetta. How do these characters change the story? How do they expand our understanding of Florence?

4. Galileo Galilei was one of Artemisia's most well-known historical friends. How does Galileo's fight for the truth impact Artemisia's path?

5. Healing from trauma is a long, nonlinear process, and we see Artemisia go through intense ups and downs. How is her recovery affected by her circumstances?

6. Artemisia is visited by a griffon on her roof. What does the griffon mean to Artemisia over the course of the novel?

7. We met several characters who suffer for their dedication to their work—gender discrimination, physical pain, persecution by the Church. How are the different characters compelled to work? What keeps them going?

8. Francesco Maria Maringhi is different from Artemisia in many ways. How do their similarities and differences impact their relationship?

ABOUT THE AUTHOR

Nicole Jarvis writes historical fantasy novels. A graduate of Emory University with degrees in English and Italian, she lives in Georgia. Her debut novel was *The Lights of Prague*. Nicole loves listening to musicals, learning strange histories and thinking about the inner lives of superheroes, and tweets @nicolejarvis.

For more fantastic fiction, author events,
exclusive excerpts, competitions, limited editions and more

VISIT OUR WEBSITE
titanbooks.com

LIKE US ON FACEBOOK
facebook.com/titanbooks

FOLLOW US ON TWITTER AND INSTAGRAM
@TitanBooks

EMAIL US
readerfeedback@titanemail.com